GUIGNOL'S BAND

By LOUIS-FERDINAND CELINE

DEATH ON THE INSTALLMENT PLAN

JOURNEY TO THE END OF THE NIGHT

GUIGNOL'S BAND

By LOUIS-FERDINAND CELINE

TRANSLATED FROM THE FRENCH

BY BERNARD FRECHTMAN AND JACK T. NILE

A NEW DIRECTIONS BOOK

Readers, friends, less than friends, enemies, Critics! Here I am at it again with Book I of Guignol! Don't judge me too soon! Wait awhile for what's to follow! Book II! Book III! it all clears up! develops, straightens out! As is, ¾ of it's missing! Is that a way to do things? It had to be printed fast because with things as they are you don't know who's living or dead! Denoël?[1] you? me?...I was off for 1,200 pages! Just imagine!

"Oh! it's good he's letting us know! We'll never buy the rest of it! What a crook! What a botched book! What a bore! What a guignol! What a slob! What a traitor!"

Everything.

I know, I know, I'm used to it...that's my music!

I give everyone a pain in the ass.

And what if they study it in school in two hundred years, and the Chinese too? What'll you say then?

"Take it easy! wise guy! What about the three dots? Ah! all over the place again! An outrage! He's butchering the French language! It's scandalous! Into jail! Give us back our dough! Nauseating! He's damaging our complements! The pig! Ah! things are bad!"

An awful session!

"Unreadable! Sex-maniac! Damned Loafer! ·Crook!"

---

[1] The author's publisher (Tr.).

1

For the time being.

Here comes Denoël, beside himself!...

"See here, I don't understand it at all! It's terrible! impossible! All I see in your book is brawling! It's not even a book! we're heading straight for disaster! Neither head nor tail!"

I could bring him King Lear *so he could see massacres.*

What does he see in existence?

And then it cools off...everyone gets used to it!...it all works out...Till the next time!

The same cackle every time. A lot of yelling and then it calms down. They never like what you give them. It hurts them! Oooooh! or it's too long!...it bores them!...always something!...It's never what they want! and then they suddenly go wild about it! Try to figure them out! Go get all hot and bothered! all a matter of whim! I expect it to take a good year to ripen...let everyone have his say, spit out his bile, shoot his mouth off, overflow...Then silence...and a hundred, two hundred thousand buy it...on the sly...and read it...and squabble...twenty thousand adore it, learn it by heart...it's the Panthéon.

The same scenario every time.

Death on the Installment Plan *was received, please remember, by a barrage of intensity, snarling and spleen, such as you seldom see! The whole works, the dregs of criticism, out-and-out swearing, churchgoers, masons, Jews, men and women, four-eyes, whisperers, athletes, ass-scratchers, the whole Legion, all standing up, wild-looking, foaming gibberish!*

The finishing shot!

And then it subsides and now, you see, Death on the Installment Plan *is more popular than* Journey. *He's even gobbling up all our paper! He's outrageous!*

So it goes....

"Oh! but there's the word 'shit'! Coarseness! That's what attracts your clientele!"

"Oh! I see you a mile off! It's easy to talk! Got to know when to say it! Just try! Not everyone can shit right! It would be too easy!"

I'm giving you some idea of how things stand. I'm taking you backstage so you won't get any illusions...I had some in the beginning...but not now...experience...

It's even funny, they jabber and get all worked up... arguing yes and no about the three dots...whether you're making damned fools of them...and now one thing and then another...what airs he puts on!...the affectation...etc... and so on...and the commas!...but no one asks me what I think!...and they make comparisons...I'm not jealous, please believe me!...I really don't give a damn! So much the better for other books!...But I just can't read them...I find them sketchy, not-written, stillborn, neither finished nor likely to be, lifeless...they're not much...or else they live on phrases, all hideous and black, ink-heavy, phrasish deaths, rhetorish deaths. Ah! It's pretty sad! Matter of taste.

To hell with the invalid! you'll say to yourself...I'll let you have my ailment, you won't be able to read a single sentence! And since we're on secrets, I'm going to let you in on another one...appalling, oh my, horrible!...really absolutely deadly...that I'd rather share right away!...and that warped my whole life...

Got to admit to you about my grandfather, named Auguste Destouches, he went in for rhetoric, was even professor of it at the lycée in Le Havre, and was brilliant at it, around 1855.

Which means I distrust it bad! May be an innate tendency!

I've got all of grandfather's writings, his bundles of them, his rough drafts, drawerfuls! Terrific! He used to write the

3

*prefect's speeches, I assure you, in one hell of a style! What a
hand with adjectives! How he stuck in the flowers! Never a*
faux pas! *Moss and vine leaves! Sons of the Gracchi! Maxims
and everything! In prose and verse alike! He won all the
medals of the French Academy.*

I keep them with strong emotion.

*That's my ancestor! So I know something about the lan-
guage, and not since yesterday like lots of others! I'm telling
you right away! down to the fine points!*

*I crapped out all my "effects," my "litotes," and my "perti-
nences" into my diapers...*

*I'm through with them! they'd be the death of me! My
grandfather Auguste agrees. He says to me from up above, he
calls down to me from the sky, "Child, no phrases."*

He knows what's needed to make it tick. I'm making it tick!

*Ah! I'm intransigent, something fierce! If I ever fell into
"periods" again...three dots! ten! twelve dots! help! Nothing
at all if necessary! That's how I am!*

*Jazz knocked out the waltz, impressionism killed "faux-
jour," you'll write in "telegraphic" or you won't write at all:*

> Excitement's everything in life!
> Got to know how to use it!
> Excitement's everything in life!
> When you're dead it's over!

*Up to you to understand! Get hot! "There's nothing but
brawls in all your chapters!" What an objection! What crap!
Watch out! Dopiness! By the yard! Fluttery twittering! Go
get God excited! Rub-a-dub-dub! Jump! Wiggle! Bust out of
your shell! Use your bean, you little hustlers! Break open!
Palpitate, damn it! That's where the fun is! All right! Something! Wake up! Come on, hello! You robot crap! Shit!
Transpose or it's death!*

4

I can't do any more for you.

Kiss any girl you please! If there's still time! Here's to you! If you live! The rest'll come all by itself! Happiness, health, grace and fun! Don't worry too much about me! set your little heart going!

It'll be whatever you put into it! storm or flute! as in Hell! as in Heaven!

Boom! Zoom!...It's the big smashup!...The whole street caving in at the water front!...It's Orléans crumbling and thunder in the Grand Café!...A table sails by and splits the air!...Marble bird!...spins round, shatters a window to splinters!...A houseful of furniture rocks, spirts from the casements, scatters in a rain of fire!...The proud bridge, twelve arches, staggers, topples smack into the mud. The slime of the river splatters!...mashes, splashes the mob yelling choking overflowing at the parapet!...It's pretty bad...

Our jalopy balks, shivers, squeezed diagonally on the sidewalk between three trucks, drifts, hiccups, it's dead! Fagged engine! Been warning us since Colombes that she can't hold out! with a hundred asthmatic wheezes...She was born for normal service...not for a hell-hunt!...The whole mob fuming at our heels because we're not moving...That we're a lousy calamity!...That's an idea!...The two hundred eighteen thousand trucks, tanks and handcarts massed and melted in the horror, straddling one another to get by first, ass over heels, the bridge crumbling, are tangled up, ripping each other, squashing wildly...Only a bicycle gets away and without the handle bar...

Things are bad!...The world's collapsing!...

"Stop blocking the way you lousy pigs! Go take a crap you slimy lice!"

6

Not everything's said! Or carried out! Still things to do!...
Pirouette!

The engineering officer's preparing something! Another
blast of thunder! Sets the fuse at the small end...It's a demon!
...But suddenly his gadget roars out and crackles right between his fingers!...the whole shebang blasts him, pours on
him, tears him apart, somersaults him wildly away...The
column gets going, the motors are all roaring and spitting in
an unhearable din!...Terrifying remarks and blasphemies!...
Everything! the carcasses! the junk! the tanks! piles upon
the crunching and rattling caterpiller-guns that smash all inter-
ference under the direction of a quartermaster! It's the saraband
of fright, the fair under the crawling-dislocating thunder! It's
the rubber man who wins! Ah! hooray for the cosmic scoundrel, the unscrupulous bachelor with the corkscrew bicycle,
the armored stinker!...

The Fritz is peppering away like mad, swooping down from
the skies! The louse! He's bzzbzzing us! he's sprinkling us
from the summits, he's enveloping us, he's whirring at us!...
It's the fury of murder, wild volleys and raging stabs! rico-
cheting all about! He's watering us, spilling us to death! And
then he starts us up again, he's getting a big kick out of our
dance! out of our stung and swaying rage! We're stuck all
right! A shell! Three enormous ones!...Fright! And much
too heavy! And one after the other!...The earth's dying upside down!...losing strength, shivering, groaning in the
distance, out of hearing...as far as the low and gentle hill-
sides! Bust, echo! Bust, bomb! No mistake! It's getting worse!
...We're going to die mashed up!...like bedbugs!...chok-
ing sulphurations! massed in the saltpeter, ravaging combus-
tions! The dunghill's raving! He's eager up there!...He's sore
about our trouble! The awful plane! He's sugaring us again!
And three loopings! And hail falls!...A frying in the atmos-

7

phere! The cobblestones full of bull's-eyes!...The lady who got one in the back hugs a sheep lying there, shuffles off with it under the axles, creeps and convulses...farther off... grimaces, collapses, knocked over, her arms stretched like a cross...groans...stops moving!...

The ambulance, our ship of grace, can't make the big cobblestones, skids, shimmies, wobbles, loses all its bolts, bumps into a flock of oxen, stallions, fowls, and then plops...a cart smacks it right in the ass...Bang!...The shock sends two tricycles flying, plus a nun and a policeman...it's the moment of absolution...all that on the bridge! Look at the poor auto lifted by the wind of the torpedoes twenty yards away! Horrible flight! And then two steps and two burps...There she is rolling down in the whirlwind of the slaughter...The mob catches up with us...squeezes us...The engine's racing to get the hell away...They're frisking us, they're hugging us fiercely! Our vehicle's getting damned sore...We're being hoisted in triumph!...scaling over heads!...roosting up there over the crowd...Bam!...Bang!...Three tough strikes! We flop! A "twelve-ton" truck full of railmen whacks us from the other side! Ah! made it!...Pushed around, torn from the tide! We're knocked apart right in the middle of the mess!...The ambulance loses its front wheels!...The surging scatters us to bits! ...It's the turn of a baby carriage being carried away over our heads!...A little soldier's lolling in it! His leg hanging out in shreds...pretty slick...Damned little soldier-boy! he's making obscene gestures...We're having fun with him! We're all together in the atmosphere!...All seething in the whirl! ...That devil up there's sore at us...He's coming back... strafing us like a tornado!...Tobogganing down on us, blazing away, spurting out all his lightning...The savage is cutting our heads off...the swine!... He's sweeping us into his belly! into his murderous din!...He's climbing back very

tiny into the clouds!...He turns about on the ceiling! a fly!...
Who's that dead in the gutter? They're stumbling over it,
it's soft!... There's a belly there! wide open and the foot and
leg twisted, folded in...One of Death's acrobats!...blasted
on the spot!
Zoom! Zoom! There's no time to think!...two enormous
thuds...It's the big river being hit downstream! The smooth
water's drinking two giant torpedoes!...That makes two wild
corollae for it!...Two astounding water-volcano flowers!...
It all falls back...cascades over the bridge...We're crushed
under the spout, soaked, rolled, flattened by the cyclone...
vomited back...the mob catches up with us, sticks to us...
and then they open fire again...It's cannon getting at us...
The parapet's full of flashes...It must be coming from the
little clouds over the church! must be a reconnaissance flight
...Other airmen trying to finish us up!...They don't give a
damn, men, cattle or things!...They're French or German!...
The situation's getting critical...My soaked clothes feel boiling...Confusion's at its height?...A mother in tears on the
parapet wants to throw herself into the abyss with her three
little children!...Seven workmen interfere and hold her back
...cool brave chaps...They first finish their ham and headcheese!...Just let them dare touch her! she shrieks! such a
terrifying shrill clamor that it blots out the other noises!...
You're forced to look at her!...A shell...Bam! hitting the
bridge!...The main arch blows up, splinters...Digs a hollow
in the middle...an enormous gaping...a crater that swallows
up everything!...The people melt and ram the crevices...
topple beneath the bitter smoke...into a hurricane of dust!
...You can see a colonel, of Zouaves I think, floundering in
the cataract...He succumbs beneath the weight of the corpses!
...topples down to the bottom!..."Vive la France!" he finally
cries...vanquished beneath the pile of bodies!...There're

others alive who grab on to the walls of the gulf, they're in rags because of the explosion, they make desperate efforts, fall down, they puke, they're through... They've been burned everywhere. A baby all naked surges up on the hood of a flaming truck. He's roasted, done to a turn... "Good God!... Good God!... Shit! It's not right!"... It's the father in a sweat ... Those are his very words... Then he looks for something to drink!... He yells at me if I've got anything... Canteen? Canteen?

The music's not over, another archangel's peppering us, swooping down from the sky at full speed... He tires us with his ravaging... We're so crammed that we stop moving... The bridge is rumbling... wobbling on its arches!... And then tic-tac! Rrooo! Rrooo!... It's the music of the big slaughter! the sky's rattling with rage against us!... The water from underneath... And then the abyss!... It all blows up!...

Everything I'm telling you's exact... There's a lot more besides!... But my memory's out of breath! Too many people have walked over it... like the bridge... over the memories... as over the days!... Too many people yelling battle!... And then the smoke again... And I dive under the car... I'm telling it the way I'm thinking... Going down toward the flood-gates, they were carousing something fantastic as far as the Orléans ramp!... They were dancing worse than on the other, a hundred thousand times worse than the one in Avignon!... In the forge of God's Thunder!... And boom! and zimm! and Saint Mary! and dead and dead! in the Hurricane Ball!... Look!... Look!... Unimportant!... Even the world there turned inside out, an old soft broken-down umbrella!... It drifted in the cyclones!... Too bad!... Rrpp!... and Bing!... Boom!... I saw it passing over the Grand Hotel! It was going fine! I saw it drifting... swaying up there... frolicking in the clouds!... The bumbershoot and the main span! they were

10

spinning around in the flurry...together!...among the massacring pussy planes, squirting gunfire...Rraap!...Whah!...Rraango!...Whah!...Rroong!...That's about the noise made by a real molten torpedo...the most enormous! In the heart of a black and green volcano!...What a burst of fire! ...Another bomb grazing us! goes exploding right into the current...The blast rocks us...Your guts all ripped out... Your heart popping into your mouth!...palpitating like a rabbit...What shame, shitting with fright...crawling... under the ammunition trucks with three...four...five legs all wound up...Arms everywhere all mixed up...smashed, melted into jitters! into a pulp of panic-mad slugs everyone for himself!...Sunk, wallowing, hiccuping, you come to, tossing in the air, ripped apart, shrunk, shot the hell away! head over heels! It's a motor about to catch fire!...We scale a mountain of wounded...Thick groans beneath our feet!... They puke...We're lucky! It's a favor!...We emerge! groggy, smiling...Another one attacking us! He's swooping down, a death drum! He smashes the clouds with bullets... His little tongues of fire shoot forth everywhere!...I see all his flames pointed at us...It's gray and black!...and cursed from head to tail!...He's looking for us...He catapults from the sky with a volley of rage!...He's bewitching us!...He's damning us!...We throw ourselves on our knees...We beg the Virgin Mary!...with big fervent signs of the cross!... God the Father...the North winds! the ass-hole!...Mercy upon us! which fails us in our gurgling drawers...It's the fall of the Spirits!...He keeps shooting away at us, volley after volley each one worse! hanging from the angels!...He flits about...bolts forward...wavers...He's closing in inside his cyclone...Ffrroo!...He's gliding again...A silky noise! ...We stop seeing him...He's enchanting us!...A sign of the cross!...three...four...five!...That doesn't stop the

11

horrors!...the murderous atrocities!...No conjuring him away!...He sugars us again from leeward! We're going to get the whole works!...He's at the height of his passion...He's hailing us...blasting us...on the wing!...It's the ricochets of the massacre!...The sheet metal's drumming away!...The suppliants swoon and collapse!...The mob's capsizing!...The convoy gives way!...the parapet splits!...the string of trucks starts kicking up...rioting...and pitches into the water!...Ah! I'm still being spared!...Got away from an awful upset! ...It's been that way for twenty-two years!...It can't last forever!...I take a stance with Lisette, a girl-friend who's not scared...between the wheels of the ambulance...you see the cavalcade from there!...all of it! all!...Capsizing in all directions...We also see Largot the barber, he hasn't left us since Bezons, he's been following us with his bike...He's been drunk since Juvisy, he wanted to kill a German, but he hasn't talked about it since Étampes...There he is against the parapet ...He's squeezing a grandmother in his arms...He kisses her at every explosion...In the throbbing of the motors...An old woman with white hair...in wisps, braids and curlpapers ...Her whole head's bleeding red...Largot's gentle with her ...He's drinking her blood...He's lost his sense of respect... but he's stubborn, greedy...

"Bah!...It's red wine!" he declares..."Bah! It's good, too!" ...He's joking besides!...But not her!...The grandmother closes her eyes...She's wagging her head...She's lulled by the thundering!...by the storms rocking us...Largot yells out to me again...

"It's red wine! Hey, ambulance! It's red wine! Say! Macadam!"

That's what he calls me. In spite of our being in a catastrophe I'm irritated by him...I don't like familiarity...All those drunken carcasses around sicken me...I feel some funny

12

ideas myself...I'm not drunk!...I never drink anything...
It's my reason tottering...under the shocks of the circum-
stances! just that! events that are just too much!...And
Zoom! it starts again worse!...

It's coming back bad, a horrible din!...A fantastic com-
bustion!...three torpedoes together, a bouquet! enough to
shatter sky and earth! you don't recognize the elements! enough
to blow the top of your head off!...and then your mind and
eyeballs! and it shoots horribly through your lungs!...stabbed
from front to back!...nailed to the shutter like an owl!...
and that backfire!...the thousand motors at it again...attack-
ing the ramp!...The mad racket's closing in!...the jerking!
...smashing mob!...and the howling of the trampled! of
those skinned by the wild column!...those crushed beneath
the transports!...and the caterpillar with the hundred-twenty
thousand grinding teeth!...to bite the echo...a rent calvary!
...under its three hundred thousand chains stuffed with dang-
ling steel...with guts of twirling hoops...cockeyed under
its crown...with its whole big cannon head to flatten you
from way off!...Sees you from way off, watches you! crazy
you, tearing up the road!...fleeing in a daze the Godawful
sight of that monstrous hodgepodge!...Ah! that tank, the
"Bite-Me-Awful"!...Tell me about it! Nostradamus Model!
...that there's really no surviving the hopeless racket!...
under the mechanical poxing, the oil-bearing tribulations!...
But the world-shakeup's musical...no stopping the dance!...
It's the "Damn-it-all Ball"!...And the string of the hundred
thousand dead, of the thousand squeaking birds flying around
cheeping, weaving their calls...

And then there's another garland with two accents and
heavy blunderbusses...It's coming from way back...from the
hills...Artillery's rolling in the echoes...You can't cut
capers you're so crushed by your body loaded with damned

frozen lead!...But the rhythm gets you again...the bottom of the bridge full of grenades is fidgeting for you...Got to prance the same way over the wreckage of people and animals...quartered by the dragging...then shriveled tight big as an egg depending on the bursts of panic...Ah! the case of rebellion crops up in those dazed whirls...There's Brigitte, the wife of Sacagne the District Attorney, she suddenly ups and gets out of her car, tears away from the anguished pleas, lifts her skirt up once and for all and jumps on the parapet, from there overlooking the mob, yelling insults through the torment!...

"Brigitte!...Brigitte!...I beg you! please come back to me!...your kind husband! Keep your head!...I beseech you! I summon you!"

"Shit! Shit! You don't exist!"

"Gentlemen, Ladies, my wife's crazy!...She's pregnant! It's the excitement! I'm District Attorney Sacagne of Montargis from the Côte-d'Or!"

"Shit! Hey, Chink, you're a pain in the ass! The hell with your bitch! The slob!"

That's what the crowd calls her...That's what made things bitter! He collapses on the world! Just then everything becomes fire, thunder and lightning again! a ripping from the sky inside and about...A blast crushes, pulverizes the wall...Ah! it was time!...scatters the whole panic, the people, arches, cars, the boiling river's steaming...Hell's right here!...The flames envelop us, we're whirled about in space!...I'm carried off with a cartload of plums, the little terrier that's stopped barking, a sewing machine and, I think, a cast-iron tank trap hooked with barbed wire! as far as I could see!...We split off in mid-air! The molten iron squirted toward the right, toward the locks, the whole works and the slugs! Me, the little terrier and the cart bore toward the left...in another volley of grenades

14

...toward the poplars...the Warehouse...at a good height and full of drive...I saw higher than the clouds...and bleeding drop by drop...a pale white hand and all about clouds of birds...all red...flitting about sprung from the wounds... the fingers all studded with stars...strewn on the margins of space...in long gentle veils...light and graceful...lulling the Worlds...and grazing you...and your pretty eyes... caressingly...everything carries you off...everything drifts dreamward...everything yields...to the fetes of the Palace of Nights...

Very well said!...Very well! You tell it well! **Told in vain!**
Done in vain! The obsession's there, gray, lingering, oppressive,
stumbles at every step with fresh doubt...Nothing stands out,
nothing shines...A big mass of horror and shadow!...

Is that all?

Lots of fuss! Going through hell just to get a little thirstier!

A somersault!

Like a drunken brute in early June

With madness in August wandering

Under a cannon

Emerges into delirium mid-September!

Right in a *bistrot.*

Murders a Fritz playing billiards.

Revenge of the Flemish!

Right away everything breaks out again.

The war's got to start all over.

You're here again all jittery.

Whinnying, eager for the whirl.

Under the flood of artifice.

Prancing at the challenges! and Tallyho!

In splendid health!

Torch in hand!

Death's hokum is waiting for you again.

You've drunk a charm!

16

You've been cooked and damned again!
Ah! that awful predicament!
Ah! the carrionish philter!
The stars are dunghills for the Century!
All the almanachs are for sale!
Not a single honest occultist left!

It's high time for me to get down to it! Damn it!
I have terrible doubts about Joan of Arc since the mass in
Orléans!...
It was a nasty chime...
There's an aftertaste in everything you touch...
I saw Saint Geneviève in Paris...
I was at mass in Reynaud...
The chapel was full of Jews...
And I never talk unless I know...
Are they going after the Freemasons?
Good! Nice to begin with...
But suppose they touch our cronies?
What if they lay hands on the manes of the Temple?
The joking'll be over!...
They're going to discover a powder in a diabolical pyrette!...

I predict it, and not without anxiety...
I'm warning! I'm warning! I'm blowing the siren!
Hell doesn't boil over in a day...
You need oil and knowledge.
Who knows?
You need collaboration...
You saw everything on the road...
The whole world in a rush!...
And what wild, furious, crucifying, fantastic gatherings!
Insatiable for martyrdom!

Did you see those vehicles!
The esoteric decoration?

Once you've been initiated you don't stand there dawdling over the abyss...To get yourself sublimated alive, to go up in smoke, fragile toys in the wind! By God! By God! The hell with the timid! Death to illusions! It's the moment for stout deeds! For sublime, bitter Trafalgars! The faith that saves! Anyone giving in is murdered on the spot! Hashed! Bled! all white with shame!

When the valiant come forward, the pure, the tough, the uncompromising, the lynx-hearted, then you can say it's getting hot! that there's a pungent sizzle in the fire! that everything's chucked in! except shreds of love, lily-of-the-valley, base doubts! As is! Torn away from the spell! No mercy! One after the other in the sulphurous regions to appear in line...That's the test!...the scowling and the sorry... into memory...The mumblers and cowards...terrible in their swathes of lies!...

I know all about it!

Proud brazen sneaks...arrogant or base or speechless...one after the other...all baleful and stinking whose throats should be slit under moon-gall torture and cursèd oaths! Poisons, dark messages...Martyred calves!...

Let everyone blame the demon! go for him, lock him away, slay him, revolt, find in his heart the song, withered...the gracious secret of the fairies...or else let him die a thousand deaths and then come to with a thousand pangs! With frightful choking, a thousand playful flayings and green contortions of wounds, boiling wax that sticks, torn apart, muscles in mince-meat, floundering around that way a whole day and three months, a week in the bottom of a greasy hot pot, hissing snakes mixed with swollen toads, with leprosy, juicy, yellow with venom, sucked by greedy salamanders, loathsome vam-

18

pires on the bodies of the damned, jiggers in your guts to stir your pain, shreds of sore flesh, munched with tongues of flame, and so from one millennium to another, slaking your thirst once in a while with a skinful of vinegar, of vitriol so hot that your tongue peels, puffs, bursts! and then to death from suffering howling from Hell all slashed up! day after day! and so on through eternal time...

You've got to see the thing is serious.

Y̶ou started in life with your parents' advice. Life was too much for them. You got into messes, one more horrible than the other. You got out of the awful catastrophes as best you could, more or less sideways, a slobbering crab, backwards, missing a couple of paws. You had some good times, got to be fair, even with all the crap, but always anxious, lest the dirty business start all over...And it always did...Let's bear that in mind! They talk about illusions, that they ruin youth. We lost it without illusions!...More trouble!...

As I say...It happened from the beginning. You were little, a born dope, with two strikes on you.

If you'd been born the son of a rich planter in Cuba, Havana for example, everything would've gone off smoothly, but you came from small fry, who lived where it was nasty and slummy, then had to suffer on account of caste and it's the injustice that crushes you, the sickness of the drooling worm that makes poor people go bragging after their blunders, their pettiness, their pussy blemishes, which makes you vomit listening, they're so vile and tenacious! Month after month, it's his nature, the poor slob expiates, on the Pro-Deo rack, his infamous birth, tied up tight with his service certificate, his voting card, his bloated face. Sometimes it's War! It's Peace! It's Re-war! It's Victory! It's the Big Disaster! At bottom, nothing's changed! In the end he's always a fall guy. He's the punching bag of the Universe...Wouldn't change places with anyone...He wiggles only for the hangmen...Always available for all the dunghills of the Planet! Everyone walks over his rags, gets worked up over his troubles, he's spoiled. I've seen all the tornadoes of the compass swoop down on our miseries, blowing in on our catastrophes, in on the kill, the Chinese, Moldors, Botriacs, Marsupians, the glacial Swiss, the Mascagats, the Big Berbers, the Vanutedians, the Inkspots, the Jews of Lourdes, all happy, having a great time, gleaming like lunatics! Doing us dirt and nothing to defend us. Cute François, imp of the liquor-bottle, stuffed dotard, mushy enough in speech to shake the Rights of Man, in the torrent of Oblivion, hide and soul driven crazy and disgusting with obedience, letting his patrimony be shaken, his sweet little savings, his darling, his dream flower, never any use for him to go pondering anything, more honest to become carrion and lazy enough to piss in bed, it's always even Stephen, he's always a sucker in any deal, he's not in the running, he's always doomed to be a washup. Besides, the world's got him so down that he's got surprise itself puzzled, the world's tired of pulling him apart, of destroying him even more, he's pushed around on all sides! the Stinker of the Universe! Hail! A little more injustice, he loathes himself, pukes out his lot...Awful protests.

Revolution in their hearts...Got to know a little about his disappointments. Everyone's made an easy punching bag out of him. The whole Universe has had a fine time with Dopey-François-huh-huh-jerk until he cracks up and comes apart at the foundation! Then he's the supreme infection, and the most eager run away...He stays there gaping on the counter... decomposing, green in shreds, can't look at him...He gives off such a smell that the most disgusting think it over, twist around to finish him off!

There're things you don't see! And yet which are essential!

Boy! Just wait! Hidden in the bottom of the rot itself! holes in the body! bowel philters! would you suspect? Only the initiated whisper to each other with their eyes closed...the Mass isn't over!...Still more to say!...Lots more!...as for the tainted, they're still around, they're not going to let us leisurely rot that way on the heap!...We're still full of pus and lots of flashy gangrenes, vested in elegant, bloody brocades! ...very slight scrapes...before brisking up for the dance, free, light diaphanous minuets! not weighing a thing in the waves, evaporated, a whirl of wings, most delightful, here, there, springish, voguish! all roguish and furtive and joys! secretly graceful to the world, everything magically reborn! a clip of flowers and moss!...Fluttering even lighter...amidst a wind of roses! All cares wreathed in music...scattered off to the sport of air! Zephyrs!

Naturally I'm not going to tell you everything. They were too vile with me. It would be doing them too much of a favor! I want them to taste a little more...It's not vengeance or soreness, it's just a feeling of prudence, an esoteric precaution. You don't play around with omens. It costs your life if you're indiscreet! I'm giving them just a small idea, that'll do! I'm making a bit of an effort, all right, I'm not exhausting my charm. I'm staying on good terms with the music, little animals, the harmony of dreams, the cat, its purring. That way it's perfect. A pleasure, no more, otherwise I fiddle around, sell myself, get worked up, I show off, I lose out boasting, it's over! To hell with the glamor! I get down to the pebbles, I stumble all over, I flop, I proclaim myself Emperor, the Prosecutor's after me, finds me, there I am like a dope, everyone's picking on me, cutting me to pieces, it's the third degree, Napoleon style.

And I'm not alluding to anyone! If the shoe fits, wear it! Wasn't born under a lucky star! "Quarantine's" my baptismal name, I know the oracles as I call them! I don't go far wrong in my dreams, but on the mystifying condition that I keep my ear right to the ground and my guts full of suspicion! All right then...

Let me wobble and break down to the depths! Ah! a sorry conviction!..."Don't let yourself be tempted!" Boy! have I seen witches!...On moors! meadows and shores! and a lot of

23

other places too!...on rocks! in abysses!...with their brooms and owl! The owl's what I understand best...He always says to me, "Watch out, pal! You're going to talk too much."... That's right, in a way. My good nature excites me and works me up, makes me talk without rhyme or reason. A sorry excuse! Here comes cop's meat...With an immediate come-back! Jeering, razzing, ferocities, demonic dirty deals, pouring out torrents of droppings for me to die haggard, swamped, beneath the disgrace, the repulsion of the righteous, of extortionists, legionnaires! Infamy! consummate cabal! I can't open my pen any more. Whether in court, under the blows of wild "evidence," or in the waiting-rooms of the big shots, I'm crushed on the spot, scraped, shriveled up slimy in the rank of stinking grubs, in spite of good intentions, loathed, beaten within an inch of my life, something absolutely unspeakable, squashed surreptitiously between saltpeter and hot ashes and the fact that proves it is that even the people on my side who are in a way in the same sort of boat are shy about my case, they've got scruples about discussing it, it chaps their faces a little, they'd rather keep quiet...It would be a pity for them to com-promise themselves because I'm a pain in the ass to them too ...So that way we've agreed...We understand each other without getting together...without the slightest consultation.

That's grace, discretion itself.

I knew a real archangel on the downgrade, though still rather frisky, even resplendent in a way. I never really knew his name. He had too many papers. They finally called him Borokrom because of his knowledge of chemistry, of the bombs he'd made, it seems, when he was young. It was hearsay, legend. He made me smile right away. I thought I knew the ropes at the time. Later on I realized the weight of the man, his value, beneath his unprepossessing exterior, of my own dumbness. He played the piano delightfully when he had nothing else to do. I'm talking about our odd jobs. He'd come to London twenty years earlier to take a job as chemist. He was supposed to work at Wickers, in the nitrate laboratory. He had all his diplomas from Sofia and Petersburg, but he didn't know what time it was. That played him a dirty trick. He couldn't be employed, and then he really drank too much, even for England. He didn't stay on long at Wickers National Steel Ltd., three months with board and lodging and then fired, probably also because of his ways which were really pretty doubtful, spotty in general, a sneaky look. He hung out with a low crowd, his friends looked like a bad lot...even worse than he...

He was always on the outs with his landladies at the end of the week. The police who knew him well left him pretty much alone. He was one of the tramps and that was that.

England's all right for that, they never really bother you, even if you're shabby-looking, even if you're a little shady, with the tacit understanding that you don't act like a jackass around noon in front of Drury Lane or at five around the Savoy. There's a certain etiquette, that's all. A conventional agreement. If Jackass you be, woe to you! There're times for the Strand and others for Trafalgar, and everywhere else at ease!...Got to know the English cops, they don't like force or scandal, they're just loafers like father and mother, just don't provoke them, don't bother them in broad daylight, in short, let them the hell alone...Even if they've got their pockets full of warrants with your photo, they won't hound you if you don't act like a wise guy, if you keep your distance, if you don't change suits too often to show off, or change lodgings, or hangouts. There's an etiquette, a way that's decent and proper for real tramps, that's the size of it! Mustn't upset Tradition! If you act temperamental, or aggressive, or changeable, first in one pub, then another, if you're not back at your game of pool at about your usual time, then don't be surprised, the cops come down on you hard, they suddenly get rough and crafty, you're complicating supervision, they get fed up with your ways, they get restless and keen to pin something on you. Any freakishness gets them wild, especially in clothes...
That was the trouble with Borokrom, who was in the habit of wearing plum derbies, never anything else on his big dome, always wearing his green plum, his uniform. He played the piano that way to earn his living between the Elephant and the Castle, the two limits of Mile End. Soon as he was kicked out of Wickers, he had to. All the pubs along Commercial, sometimes in one, sometimes the other...but always around the river. That's what they call the Thames. He was known, likable, gay with his fingers but serious-looking, proper as a pope. It paid well, especially Saturdays. He easily took in three

pounds between eight o'clock and midnight, plus the nourishing stout, so thick and creamy, absolutely all he wanted, thanks to the customers. And then the raucous song, the drinking canticle, as is the proud custom, with choruses by the drunks piled around the piano.

> *Yip-i-addy-i-ay-i-ay!*
> *Yip-i-addy-i-ay!*

Those were the first English words I knew by heart, *"i-addy-i-ay!"*...It sent terrific echoes out into the street, into the night outside where little children were waiting, shriveled up against the window, flattening their little beaks till their parents were finished sucking their beer, fun and joy of living, so drunk that the bulls would come in to kick them out so that they'd go puke somewhere else. We'd meet at La Vaillance, the pub of the swells of the lane, the busy street, the one with seven huge bars, with prows sculpted in ivory and twisted copper rails. A magnificent job. And a portrait of the Conqueror high as the ceiling, in a colossal gilt frame, adorned with sirens. That was where we were when the thing happened, when the fight started. It was Sergeant Matthew of the Yard who came in, at the sandwich counter in the swells' stall, he blew in whistling "Good day, Ladies"! He wasn't in uniform, in civvies like you and me, he was humming with the others, he was a bit loaded, and so he was in good humor ...Suddenly! what's eating him?...he stops dead, he stands there frozen...in front of Boro...in a top hat! ah! that gags him! the nerve!...busy there with his music, banging out his tunes, in a tart kind of rhythm, grinding out a cradle song, with the misty charm of tunes of that kind, they gather up your troubles, jig them away!...ding! dindin!...dong! dong! ...and whoops! presto! quick runs of trills and arpeggios! with his big dirty pudgy fingers...it was really magic the way

27

he had them spellbound with the fluttering imps springing out of the big piano. . .Grinding out any old refrain. . .all nipping away at the pain of laughter. . .The hesitancy of orange marmalade that's sweet and acidy at the same time. . .English tunes have the same kind of pitch. . .I remember well. . . Sergeant Matthew stood there dumfounded at his man's new hat. It knocked the wind out of him. . .it froze his smile. He couldn't believe his eyes!

He came closer. . .he wanted to get a better look. . .to appreciate it. He came up to the piano. . .and bang point-blank! rage! He started swearing at the performer. . .

"Where did he get the idea of wearing a topper in that dirty bar? Never saw the likes of it! He was really crazy! Where did he think he was? At the Derby? In the House of Lords? It was an insult, and swaggering for such a rotten foreigner. . .An immigrant of the worst kind! A cheap musician, failure, tramp! He had a hell of a nerve coming and mimicking a gentleman!. . .An unbelievable crime! He'd take him away on the spot if he didn't remove that thing at once. . ." And more jabber and fiery threats, he was wild with rage!. . .

Boro stuck to his topper. . .It was a gift from someone. . . The moment Sergeant Matthew started picking a quarrel he stopped weighing his words. . .To begin with, it was none of his business. . .Boro had a perfect right to put a sofa on his head, a kite, a baby scale, the more so a top hat. . .It was no one's business but Boro's. . .But the other one didn't see it that way, he was getting his dander up. A brisk spat. . .Things were getting worse. . .the racket!. . .the fever! it was steaming around the liquor. . .The crowd was swelling, closing in, bellowing, exciting and booing Matthew so that the whole works shook and floundered and wobbled!. . .Hemmed in close, Matthew got scared, I'm telling what happened, he took his

whistle from his small pocket...That set everything off!...
There was a rush!...He mustn't whistle...No re-enforce-
ments!...Down with the police! Knocked down and flattened,
Matthew covered with drunks, yelling, delighted, jumping on
him, a mountain of them high as the chandelier...Capering
with ease and victory! A round of beer mugs over his head...
Here's to Matthew!...*For he's a jolly good fellow!*...

He wasn't saying any more down below, he'd had his share
...I was waiting near the door for them to quit beating him!
...I'd have liked to be somewhere else...What if the cops
came and raided the place?...I was a goner with my fishy
papers!...my discharge, my phony stamps! Boy, oh boy!...
I was in a delicate situation with the Consulate people!...

"Beat it!" says Boro from below...right under the pile...
and motions toward the Hospital!...the other side of the
street!...

London Hospital, well known, Mile End Road...We always
made dates there, there were reasons why, the hustle was agreeable, a constant coming and going...impossible to supervise
...Especially around the entrance gate where the mob never
lets up...coming and going day and night...All the buses
pass Mile End. So I went and took up my post there opposite,
right under the blue gas lamp...Boro was corpulent, but very
nimble in a brawl...He had a knack for getting out of things
...Agile when he felt like it...frisky...Up and away!...he
wasn't long in joining me!...A big supple cat...He made his
way between the scrappers, he went through the storm, the terrible tornado of blows. The riot was awful all through La
Vaillance! a hurricane of lunatics! I realized it from the other
side!...Breaking things, hitting the walls, the window suddenly smashed! fell into splinters, spattered the street! What a
whirlwind! A vile din! enough to wake the Lord Mayor!...

29

The women were yelping loudest! and the little children in the dark! waiting for the head of the family..."Mummy!... Mummy!..." They already saw themselves orphans!

Boro came hobbling up, he'd been banged ow! ow! right on his left kneecap! he was bleeding...we looked at his knee in the light...What it is to go through a massacre!...He'd lost his hat, the topper of wrath!...It was worth the trouble! We said we'd never go back to La Vaillance, a damned dive! a shithouse! even with its mahogany, its famous bars! the railings! Boy, oh boy! a horror! just a flashy clip-joint! lousy, criminal! Where they beat up your friends! where cops behave like pigs!

Our serious opinion.

Let's say you're coming from Piccadilly...You get off at Wapping...I'll have to show you the way...You wouldn't find it...It's on the left when you get out of the "Tube"... between the Freezers...It's a kind of narrow street...brick walls, a string of little houses on both sides, all in a line...like weekdays...no end to it...there it starts again...a raft of them...an eternity of houses...not one bit of fantasy...two-family, every one of them...a narrow door to the pavement ...a brass knocker...and so on for streets and more streets... eastbound, northbound...Plymouth Street...Blossom Avenue ...Orchard Alley...Neptune Commons...scads of the same family...All of it nicely aligned, proper...Some people may say it's dreary...Depends on the day, time of year...With a little shot of sunshine it becomes sweety-weety, it dolls up... There's starvation...That's one thing...The window sills, the windows, are full of geraniums...keeps you happy...it's the bricks that're monotonous...greasy...sticky with smoke all around...stench of fog, of coal tar...The smell of damp sulphur, of moist tobacco over there towards the docks, gets under your hair, clothes you...Of honey, too...It's all things that just come to you, can't explain to you, can't explain talking about 'em...And the fairyland of children! That's what sticks in your memory!...

When you get to know the spots, at the first smile of the

sun, everything bursts out laughing and whirls around...A frolic! A saraband! It's the elves' ball from one end of Wapping to the other!...Tumbling from balcony to porch! on the run! on the sly!...Girls and boys!...loser wins!...try to beat that...A hundred mischievous and saucy games...The tots right in the middle...hand in hand...ring-a-ring-o'roses ...darling brats of the fog...so happy about a day with no rain...more playful merry divine and nimble than dream cherubs!...And all around dirty make-believe hoodlums pestering the girls...bullying the people going by...the squealing monsters!

Policeman! Policeman! don't touch me!
I have a wife and a family!

Other rascals up and charge! grab the girls by the pigtails!...

How many children have you got?
Five and twenty is my lot!

And then the ring starts hollering and shrieking again at the top of their voices...ferocious hoarse urchins...And then this rather bouncy one that's danced two by two...

Dancing Dolly had no sense!
She bought a fiddle for eighteen pence!

And so many other pretty and fresh and funny and dainty songs that dance in my memory...all on the wings of youth... And so for everything at the bottom of these alleys as soon as the weather isn't too bad...not quite so cold, not quite so bleak over the Wapping section between Poplar and Chinatown. Then sadness melts away in little gray piles in the sun... I've seen lots of them melting that way from sadness, the streets verily full of them, delighting in the water running down the gutter...

32

Pert brisk little girl with golden muscles!...Keener health!
...whimsical leap from one end of our troubles to the other!
At the very beginning of the world the fairies must have been
young enough to have ordained only extravagance...The
world at the time all whimsical marvels and peopled with
children, all games and trifles and whirls and gewgaws! A spray
of giggles!...Happy dances!...carried off in the ring!

I remember their pranks as if it were yesterday...their
impish farandolas along the streets of sorrow those days of
pain and hunger...

Glory be to their memory! Cute little monkey-faces! Imps
of the pale sun! Misery! You will always well up for me, in
gentle whirls, laughing angels in the gloom of the age, as in
your alleys in times gone-by, no sooner shall I close my eyes...
the cowardly moment when everything dims...Thus Death,
still, thanks to you, dancing a bit...expiring music of
the heart!...Lavender Street!...Daffodil Place!...Grumble
Avenue!...dank alleys of despair...The weather never really
very fine, the round and the farandola of the fog pits between
Poplar and Leeds Barking...Little elves of the sun, light shock-
headed band, fluttering from shadow to shadow!...crystal
facets of your laughter...sparkling all around, and your cheeky
teasing...from one danger to another!...Startled faces right
in front of the huge drays!...Champing dray horses grinding
the echo!...Enormous hairy pasterns...belong to Guinness
and Co., one fright to another!...Little dream girls!...lively as
larks on the wing!...soar!...flutter o'er the lanes!...in the
mist...in the sticky black gum!...Warwick Commons! Cari-
bon Way where the frightened hobo roams...sniffling along
the gutters...clad in fear!...and the minstrel, the fake soot-
smeared darky, harlequin rags...prowling around here, there,
everywhere...banjo in his fist...t.b. voice...from one fog
...from one mist to another...jigging a sore foot for a penny,

for tuppence!...the back-somersault!...three coughs one after another!...spits reddish and goes off a way toward the gray of the clouds...far as the streets can see...and then again another stretch of hovels...Hollyborn Street...Falmouth Cottage...Hollander Place...Bread Avenue!...All of a sudden rings out the alarm, way off over there!...from the end of the rooftops...the moan of the ship!...At the far other end of things!...Watch out, bums on the lookout!...Watch out, peeping Toms and snoopers!...Vermin, cockeyes, wretches of bad luck!...ship rats! pepper-red mugs! toothless stumpy riffraff! Flabby-armed good-for-nothings!...Whore lice! Load of stinkers! the Spirit of Water summons you!...Don't you hear its exquisite voice?...Shake a leg, carrion, and get going!... All pouring from the gangplank!...All ages!...origins!... foul races! the scum of the four Universes! black, white, yellow and chocolate! Rogues of all kinds! No question about it! All cankers! All vices! Politely with a curtsy!...Please do!... Flinching and funking and shying at the moment...Curse it! dodging to trammel the maneuver! religiously, skullcapfuls... On with the punishment! with the flogging!...souse that he be!...Truce to vehemence!...To your stations, men!... Swarm of cables! traps shut, bolted, dumfounded, transposed, agog with excitement!...prostrated at the prodigious spectacle of the fragilities of landing, of the subtle miracle!...the big bundle of packing falls right on the dot! on the dock! ropes taut! groans stop! grind crush, between port and dock...Let us pray! O what a moment! A tiny click! a thread too much! a bellyful of boat busts!...O Ship!...anyone not left breathless...just looking at it...is a dirty slut of a dungy cow's ass! dead and done for! to drown without a gulp! pronto! not in the waves he blasphemes, but under immensities of crap, a hundred thousand truckloads of dull piss! That's it! Song without words!

34

"Shame upon him! Shame upon his accursed ill-begotten henchmen!...May the Door close forever upon that vomit! Scandal in the Seamen's Palace! A mess to the mutts!"

You said it! This way! I'll go first...

Let's make it snappy!...Shake a leg! Two more blind alleys, a completely deserted market...and then the rubble of a fire ...and then a tiny little square, a lamppost right in the middle, three putrid houses, ought to be torn right down, another that still holds its own, it's the North Pole Shop where Tom Tackett would take my pennies, he used to hold them for me day after day, weeks when I used to do little odd jobs here and there... on the Docks, easy chores because of my arm, my leg...At the sideshows with Boro in order to pick up a few cents for necessities...a couple of shirts, pair of new soles, a wool sweater. Tom Tackett, foresight itself, he had everything in his shop, he'd hold my dough for me, I wouldn't have kept anything by myself, I'd draw a little at the end of the month. "Ship Chandlers," that was his game, everything for the sailor, everything the crew needs, and the captain. Jackknives, all sorts of boots, and lanterns, flares of all colors, and then gamy smoked meat and pickling brine that sticks in the memory, that I haven't digested yet.

I'm doddering around like an old bumblebee, I'm all tangled up in the air, Ah sees it, I ain't tellin' things in the right order, what about it! You'll excuse me somewhat, kidding about my memories, digressing from rhyme to reason, jabbering away about my friends instead of showing you around!...Let's go! and let's keep going!...Let me show you around nicely... straying neither right nor left!...Let's bear northwest right off!...We'll follow the walls of the Temple..."The Disciples and the Anabaptist," the Temple all yellow inside its railings, the bells chime only Sundays and no great shakes! just three-four strokes!...Here around the big lot all green and black...

A puddly stretch of white and pink jerseys...where it's the color that's pretty...Some of them all blue or all purple... the Poplar team for instance...gets them excited easy...The wad-chewing fans boo the enemy team, bad going and they get sore! And then come bloody brawls all because of a little lost ball!...Like I tell ya!....It ends in a slaughter for a contested place kick...There's dirty playing, sorehead sport, specially the Italians, who're cocks o' the walk in all the pubs from Limehouse to Poplar...a clan playing on the team, tribefuls of them sweating away on West Docks...A population that's carried away...It served another purpose too, the slimy Ana-baptist lot. We buried our tubes of opium in its mounds, in the ratholes, the cane boxes, the dope from the river, the fine con-traband, that the Chinese flutters back and forth at the porthole, day or night...Fffftt!....It's gone!....The boat slips gently off...almost to a stop...veers at the lock...the pilot fools around with his dial..."Ding! Dang! Derang! Dong!..." A second!....A breath!....Box hits the water! Plunk!...Spray! Dope overboard!....Get it back!....At first I didn't feel a damned thing! Came close to missing it a lot of times!... Blind as a bat!....Yessirree! Boro's the one who wised me up! ...He showed me the fine points of the game...Have to heave off right on the dot...The porthole spits out...Zzpp! ...shoots out!....Plop! in the water!....Courier of the Waves! ...the accomplice!....the dinghy darts off!....let 'er go... and snap it up!....c'mon, scull 'er!....I got it!....Keep to the side! Fish out the bundle...Watch it!....go look!....Scram! ...beat it...to the wharves...stick in the shadow....duck the bulls...lay low...head for the mist!....

I'm telling you all these details because subdued in memory they lie lightly on the years...they gently enchant you to death, that's their advantage. There's sorcery for you, really

there, tangible, lined by the water!...I'm warning you!...
A lot of good it'll do you!...Let's forget it!...

After the strings of houses, after the unvarying streets
through which I gently accompany you, the walls rise up...
the warehouses, all-brick giant ramparts...Treasure cliffs!...
monster shops...phantasmagoric storehouses, citadels of mer-
chandise, mountains of tanned goatskins enough to stink all
the way to Kamchatka! Forest of mahogany in thousands of
piles, tied up like asparagus, in pyramids, miles of materials!
...rugs enough to cover the Moon, the whole world...all the
floors in the Universe!...Enough sponges to dry up the
Thames! What quantities!...Enough wool to smother Europe
beneath heaps of cuddly warmth...Herrings to fill the seas!
Himalayas of powdered sugar...Matches to fry the poles!...
Enormous avalanches of pepper, enough to make the Seven
Floods sneeze!...A thousand boatloads of onions, enough to
cry through five hundred wars...Three thousand six hundred
trains of beans drying in covered hangars more colossal than
the Charing Cross, North and Saint Lazare stations put together
...Coffee for the whole planet!...enough to give a lift during
their forced marches to the four hundred thousand avenging
conflicts of the fightingest armies in the world...never again
sitting, snoring, exempt from sleep and eating, hypertense,
storming, exalted, dying in the charge, hearts unfolded, borne
off to superdeath by the hyperpalpitating superglory of powdered coffee!...The dream of the three hundred fifteen em-
perors!...

Still more buildings, more enormous, for the loads of cheap
meat, preserved carcasses in dry freezers, in mustard sauce, in
prodigious venison, myriads of sausages with chopped rind as
high as the Alps!...Corned-beef fat, giant masses that would
cover Parliament and Leicester and Waterloo so that you

wouldn't see them stuck underneath, they'd be swamped so fast! two mammoths all stuffed with truffles just transported from the River Love, preserved, intact in ice, refrigerated for twelve thousand years!...

I'm now talking about jam, really colossal sweetness, forums of jars of mirabelle plums, surging oceans of oranges, rising up on all sides, overflowing the roofs, fleetloads from Afghanistan, sweet golden loukoums from Istanbul, pure sugar, all in acacia leaves...Myrtles from Smyrna and Karachi...sloes from Finland...Chaos, vales of precious fruits stored behind triple-doors, incredible choice of flavors, exquisite sugared Arabian Nights' magic in amphora jars, eternal joys for childhood promised from the depths of the Scriptures, so dense, so eager that sometimes they crack the wall, they're squeezed in so thick, burst the sheet metal, roll into the street, cascade right into the gutter! in pleasant torrents and delights!...Then the mounted police come charging in, clear the area, the view, lash the looters with blackjacks...It's the end of a dream!...

Immediately on the other side of these docks there's the big violent sweep of air whirling in from the green heights of the valley in Greenwich...the big bend in the river...the gusts from the sea...from the pale-dawn estuaries below...after Barking...lying just below the clouds...where the tiny cargoes come up...where the waves break against the jetties, splash, fall back, swoon into the mud...The ebbing tide. It all depends on the kind of thing you like!...I say it in all simplicity!...The sky...the gray water...the purplish shores... it's all so soothing...No control of one or the other...gently drawn round...in slow circles and eddies, you're always charmed further off toward other dreams...all to expire in lovely secrets, toward other worlds getting ready in veils and mists with big pale and fuzzy designs among the whispering mosses...Are you following me?

Farther off in the current toward Kindall, you see the worrying barges, cutters and sloops ready to tack, loaded to list...
All the morning's vegetables, the whole cargo of "perishables," carrots, potatoes, cauliflowers, high as the yard, doubling in the wind, struggling broadside toward the city, Housewives' Cape!...Not much traffic at the moment, except the citrus fruits, bargefuls, tide downstream around seven o'clock!... water up to the arches, far as the channel of Major Bridge when the weighbridge loosens up, lifts, grinds, breaks in two! ...the Australian Mail sweeps in with high, slow majesty, strutting to the river, its black bow cutting clean through the spray, its frilly train of a thousand waves, rippling off, lapping the pebbles...

A few more steps toward the pier, please!...and then a detour outside the tide gate and here we are again at the towing ...the sticky passway, all slimy, seaweed, watch out!...A bit lower down, on the pebbles, we inch forward on eggs!... feeling our way!...here and there...Now we're in front of a tunnel...Better say a kind of sewer, we go down into it, we're swallowed up! we climb the dozen steps...and we come out right into a pub...Not much, but still and all roomy! a pub that can hold, all the shutters closed, around forty or fifty people...You've got to know how to get there...Better arrive at low tide, that way no one sees or knows, or at night from a boat, high tide, and easy does it now!...It's picturesque!

The Dingby Cruise, the pub I'm telling about, the name on its license, between Colonial Docks and Trom.

Not much of it's left, I can tell you right now, it ended in a disaster, you'll hear about it as you keep reading.

Besides, now with the bombs probably nothing's left at all, even the ashes must have blown away...It's too bad! I've got to remember about everything! I'd have gone back to take a look!

Really a pretty orderly pub and well known around the three piers, and not bad, nor criminal, there were much worse kinds! . . . Mostly dockers, regular customers, workers, with a handful of smugglers, naturally, you always find some. A small school of hoodlums.

The boss wasn't talkative. Agreeable, obliging, but reserved. He didn't get confidential. . . You'd start the talking. . . His gestures which always amazed me, a knack of catching glasses, sometimes four or five at a time, in the air, like flies, juggling them! never breaking a saucer, trapeze artist. . . Must have been a performer at one time, rope dancer, not allowed now on the public stage, a fine métier lost. . . Besides his pub, did some pawnbroking on the side for the drunks, handled dope a little, too. I can't deny that. He took commissions, deals that had to be handled just right and never the slightest slipup! discreet with the cops! never a word out of him! That's rare in the underworld.

We hung out regularly in the joint, at least in the early days. The place was practical for us, right near the Wapping buses and yet in the center of the docks. . . It was a rare location. You could get away by the bank when the dicks from the Yard came around, when you heard their graceful steps. . . their shoes squeaking. . . all over the cobblestones. . . As for the others, the River Police, when they were snooping around the pylons with their motor boats, ptup! ptup! . . . sly motor. . . velvet fart. . . slip through faultlessly. . . makes you want to crap. . . would last more than an hour, the time for their job, to go up to the locks and then back. . . Always that to the good! What rats, I see them, mangy rats between river and bank, I never could stand them. . . the supreme scum, earth and waves! . . . Real water garbage! . . . The River Police! . . . Beyond the bounds of treachery! . . . And I'm not telling everything! . . . I boil with rage thinking about them! . . . I get steamed up! . . . I go haywire just talking about them! . . . at the memory! . . . It's not

40

polite!...Shame, shame!...Sorry!...No way to act I realize!
...not very artistic...or reasonable...I bring you back to the
table...I welcome you!...I offer you something! inside with
everyone...I'm not going upstairs...I'm setting you up on
the main floor...It's a long room, that's all...with partitions
for the pub...dark, sticky, but warm around the stove...you
appreciate it during the season...the boss handles the orders
himself...Prosper can manage it...He doesn't need bouncers
like the Mile End saloons...at La Vaillance for example...

You cough slightly when you come in because of the thick
smoke...also because it's the custom...it's opaque all the way
to the back of the room...and as far as the bay window on
the Thames...the little wide panes...Got to get right against
them to see clear...Prospero Jim's at the bar...He's squint-
eyed but he sees his people all right...He's a flash size-up
artist...He's not too keen on me...He must be a little
jealous...

"The rope, you understand?" he reminds me..."That tells
everything...Right, my boy? The rope! That's the whole
story!..."

Talking about his old job perks him right up...dancer in
the Bordington Company, the big world-wide circus, a month
in every city, record sellouts, always the same triumph, flowers,
cigars, and girls galore...He had just about one joke, always
the same, about the sun. When it was pouring outside he never
let up with it...

"Lovely weather, my Lord! Lovely smile! London sun! Don't
you think so?"

He'd shoot it from the bar at everyone who came in, that was
his Italian's revenge, they called him Ravioli, he came down
hard on the z's.

"Here, you zee, it only rains twize a year!...But zix monthz
at a time!"

He knew all about the river, the people, the ways, the

41

trafficking, just as he did about his pub and his customers. He was always suspicious of newcomers...he was afraid of anything that prowls...He wasn't a bad sort, but soured because of the climate...he made dough, that was all...He wanted to go back to the sun...Home to Calabria, and well-heeled! That was his program...It didn't happen by itself...There were hard deals!...

"Big? Fat?" he'd ask me.

That was how he felt me out. I could see what he was insinuating. If I'd got something from the boat. If I'd answered right off, I'd have done myself harm...Had to grunt at him just so, "Ooh!...Oh!..." anxious, not slobbering...a good impression...our way of talking, French style, did us a lot of harm...Answered "Hm! hm!" He's got a good opinion of me...We're going to sit down in the daylight at the long table against the window...time passes...the customers doze a bit...Some of them even snore...It's the fatigue, and then the smoke and the stout dulls you...A pint in each fist...It's a sort of maneuver...They're waiting for the whistle to blow again at the Poplar wharves, for the noise to start up again, shrieking, for the trucks to unload...then a dash to the storerooms! tearing away everywhere! disappearing into the works, the big uproar starts again, they're sweating away inside, grunting with effort, knocking themselves silly, groaning, working punch-drunk at full steam! Chnooff!...Chnooff!!...Chnooff!! ...the crane winds up, swings, carries off the slops!...it goes up! down! it dusts! a whirl of junk! Still got time to see how things're shaping up! the tide starts floundering out around eight o'clock...The clients don't gab much!...they're sort of dozing with fatigue...they're waiting...Just have to be on the lookout from time to time, to keep an eye on things, on the flats beyond...toward the trees...the break around the bend ...toward Greenwich after Gallions Rock where the ships come up with the pilots on the ebbing tide...Nor'west-nor'-west...little ones first right at the head...the measly plunderers, the caravan...the big ones afterward, the mastodons, the steamers, the sober buzzing with triple-echoed sirens...the hoarse one...the bassoon, the ailing...the Indias...The P. and O.'s...they blast out!....majesty!...What Lords! the mail boat! the clients tear out of the joint! A rush to the moorings!

The ship's pulling in!...The pub empties in a second!... all the clients on the rungs!...to the sculls! and I know you! ...at the stem! at the rails!

The Mate's looking out from up above.

"Fifty going up!"

The Mate bawls out to the echo...

"Two extra!..."

Go to it, riffraff! jump windward!...Getting crushed! killing themselves on the ropes!...

The dockers climb up.

The big propeller's churning at their asses!...Prroof!!... Prroof!!...Prroof!!...grinding through the mush! bulging bubbles!...

Telegraphing...from the bridge: Ding! Ding! Ding!...

"All astern!"

Easy does it! big tremble!...Nearing the dock!...groans at the side!...slowly pulls in...Tucks in there, tiny-enormous ...docks!...It's ready!...Oof! It's over!...A big bellyfull of sigh...Oof! Oof! Over! Over! big little-boat!...Sad, the end of the music...Sorrow comes down on it!...Back to port!...All tied up everywhere by a thousand ropes...Pain covers everything over...blots it out...Stop!

Cascade was at home and in such a boil that no one dared open his mouth. After all he liked his crew and the gals in particular. There were nine of them around him, some nice, some big, some skinny, and two who were pretty awful to look at, Martine and La Loupe, I got to know them well later on, they always had the best takes, his charm-champs, what scarecrows. Men's tastes are a hash, they stick their noses anywhere, they bring back cockeyes, hags, they think they're cream puffs, that's their affair, it's not yours, they'll never know, so let 'em screw.

They twaddled away, a regular birdhouse, jabbering, squealing, enough to make you dizzy, on edge for a fight, you couldn't hear yourself. Cascade wanted it to stop, he had a speech ripe, important things. He was dashing around in shirt sleeves, he was yelling for it to stop, for them to shut up. A pearl-gray form-fitting vest, tight pants, a spitcurl flat against his forehead nicely twisted down to his eyebrows, he still looked pretty good, he stood his ground all right, he'd stopped trying to be a lady-killer, just a little with his mustache, his handle bars, he must've been quite slick in the old days! But he was getting gray, he'd changed, especially since the big worries, the beginning of the war, he couldn't stand screeching, especially the girls' yapping, he'd fly right off the handle.

There were decisions had to be made. . .

44

"After all, I can't pimp for all of you!...God damn it!"

They were laughing at his troubles.

"I've got four of my own! That's enough! That's my load! Am I the Chabanais? I don't want any more, Angèle! you hear me? I don't want another single one!"

He was refusing women.

Angèle must have smiled. Her man looked comical yelling away. A serious woman Angèle, his real one, who ran his stable, she had a tough time.

"I'm not crazy, Angèle! I'm not Pelican! Where's it going to end? Where'm I going to hide them all if this goes on? What do I look like? What's got to be has got to be! All right! but what the hell! let it stay as is! The Sharp wasn't beating his brains out...he cleared out just two days ago...he'd been looking for me, the fairy...starts bending my ear...He tries to reason with me: 'Take mine, Cascade! you're a pal! the only one I've got confidence in! I'm a-off to war!' he tells me. 'I'm a-off to fight!'...Well go!

'You're a pal! I know you! It's a break!' No sooner said than done!...Satchel! The gentleman beats it, doesn't even turn around! A job lot, a gal on my hands! Poor Cascade! One better! No time to grunt! I'm all swelled up! 'I'm a-off to war!' that's all there's to it! Cool as a cucumber! 'I'm in it all right,' he tells me, 'the Sappers! 42nd Engineers!' All is forgiven! The gentleman gives another encore! The gentleman looks like a young man! The gentleman's getting rid of his worries! Woman trouble for me, and how!...I say to myself 'The Sharp saw me! He's taking advantage of the circumstance! He's appointing me goodhearted manager!' I didn't like that kind of trick! Let me tell you I was pretty sore! I left and went toward the Regent...I said to myself 'I'm going to wake up the bookie, got an idea...Four o'clock! that's the time for the Royal! Pay-off time! I'm going to drop in and get my money from him! A wad! Stuttering Phil owes me a pile! He's not in much of a hurry! I'm going to scare the hell out of him!' Who do I bump into at the door but Jojo!...He goes at me right away...in some state!...What heat! I say to myself he's drunk!...Not at all!...He'd just enlisted! Another one! He was shooting his mouth off...'Cascade,' he says, 'take my Pauline!'...Begs me just like that!...He grabs hold of me! ...'You'll be doing me a favor!...and also Josette and Clémence!'...Ah! that was the limit, I started gagging! 'Wh-wh-what?' I said...He didn't let me finish...'I'm leaving tonight! I'm joining the 22nd in Saint Lô!'...Like that! Bang! No time to say ouch!...He grabbed me...strangled me!...In the stomach!...I couldn't refuse him!...

'You'll send me my share! You'll keep your little fifty!' That's the way he talked to me!...'But keep an eye on Pauline,' he comes back and says...'She goes to sleep on blonds! ...Break her ribs, you'll be doing me a favor!...She's not lazy, but you've got to reason with her a little!...Well, I'm going, pal!...Say hello to the boys...The train leaves at midnight!'...'Don't get killed!' I answered...And that makes two!...I had a mean look on my face!...The situation was getting worse...I sat down...I ordered a vermouth...Sluts! ...They don't let me breathe! along comes Poigne who sits down at the next table...I act a little deaf at first, she shakes me, calls me...Poigne, you know, from Piccadilly! the one who does the bar with her daughter, she starts plaguing me ...'Cascade, I'm counting on you!'...Another one!...She wasn't listening to my opinion...'Take care of my kid and her cousin! neither of them has a passport!...I'm going to meet my guy in Fécamp, he's been away for three weeks, he's setting up a house in Brittany, I don't know where yet, but it's nice!' That's how she begins...'It's for the Americans! You're not leaving! Do me the favor!...' 'Of course, of course!' I

46

answered! Yours truly a sucker again!...I couldn't refuse her
either...Poigne's a remarkable woman, not many like her, few
like her in the world! A real model for pimps!...regular and
simple and sociable, no sleeping around! Straight as a die,
obliging and everything! I've known her twenty-two years!...
I said, 'All right, bring your slaves around!...but watch out
for the mixtures!...I don't want them spoiling my babes! I've
got enough trouble holding 'em...Vice is the death of work!
...a little dykish, all right!...but too much is too much!'...
that's how I talked.

'I agree, Cascade,' she answers. 'Beat 'em up! Don't be shy!
It's all right! I know your principles!'...I said to myself,
Good! War profits!...Now are they going to let me the hell
alone?...Still and all they all ought to be gone by now, joined
their ferocious outfits! Drums, trumpets and God damn!...
In Berlin right this very minute! Musn't have any women
dragging along!...Phony fighters! Don't be silly Nénette!...
Along comes La Taupe!...Who does she talk to me about?
Guess! Little-Arm Pierrot! He was just nabbed! Three years
in the clink! Another bang on the head! And the lash, too!
Good news! Little-Arm Pierrot! An angel! In the jug in Dart-
moor! Could be! Since Friday! Damn it, they come whining to
me again, that there's not a guy around, that I've got to act
as lawyer!...They're counting on me!...his savior!...his
friend!...his brother!...And so on and so on!...Another
twenty-five pounds for yours truly! and I inherit again!...Two
girls and cute! La Taupe and Raymonde!...Two hard workers!...My lucky star!...Promise made, promise kept! Bring
the dames along! It's Pierrot's first slipup! Tough luck, I say!
Things not getting better! His first muff! I can sniff trouble!
No mistake about Pierrot's women, with their vices and what-
not, if they make three pounds a day it's the end of the world!
...He's passing 'em on to me cheap! I was the one who sold

'em to him. I know something about 'em!...They weren't broken in yet!...I wasn't going to say anything! a man in need...Of course!...Still they cost three hundred quid all raw and I'm not talking about linen! Before I'd get my money back from the bitches, Pierrot'd be wearing a wig, he'd have made a pile of slippers over there on the moor! Beg your pardon! His women won't have any more customers...I could fatten 'em up for twenty-five years! I know 'em, nothing'll help 'em! You'd think they ate fog!...Dried-out string beans!... Well, there's got to be some like that!...It's a pain in the ass to have 'em back! They're just the servant-girl type! And what about Quenotte? Another fine yegg, the one who put 'em on my hands!...Boy do I remember that bird!...Came from Bordeaux! With that accent, and the way he hit the bottle!... Quenotte! boy! what a crook!...His women were no better than he was!...That's a type I don't like!...women pick-pockets!...Business is business!...Mustn't mix one line with another! But watch out, I'm getting mixed up!...I'm getting lost, can't help it!...Then along comes Max...He jumps at my neck...I was in the middle of thinking...

'I'll take the saucers,' he shouts. 'Listen to me, Cascade! Listen to me! I'm leaving tonight!'...Another one, I think. 'Where for?' I ask...I'd stopped being surprised...'I'm join-ing up in Pau!'...

'In Pau?' I laugh...Everyone at the table busts out laughing ...'Naked!'[1] His mug tight.

He jumps up sore! He starts raving...'Dopes! Dopes!' he yells...'You gang of fairies! You got nothing in your pants! Rejected!...Aren't you? Rejected!'

You'd think he was talking to me...Ah! that's the limit!

---

[1] An untranslatable pun explains the outburst. "I'm joining up in Pau"— *je rejoins à Pau*—might readily be twisted to "I'm joining up naked." (Tr.)

...But I wasn't keeping him from leaving! Why'd he insult me?...Another one for Alsace-Lorraine! It gives me a belly-ache! Good-by! A bang on the bean!...I didn't want to hear the rest!...I cleared out...I jumped up from my seat! I tore out! right in front of me!...Like all sixty!...I thought I was saved!...Keep quiet! I went into Berlemont's...Bob was at the bar with Bise...I didn't want them to talk to me, I dashed through the alley with the tailor shops, came out on the other side, Soho...Who do I run into? You tell me! The one chance in a thousand!...Into Picpus and Berthe, his gal!...The one from Douai!...I know her all right! she's a ball and chain! A gift! I don't want any! I say to myself he's going to stick me with her! It's my day, it's the style!...Bang! Doesn't fail! ...He takes me in hand...'Ah, you loafer, you wouldn't do that to me!'...He wants to kid me along!...He begs me!... 'You're the only one left and the Wops...they're going to take the bread out of our mouths!...You're our last hope! Cascade! they're going to take away all our breadwinners!...If you drop your friends, they'll be the only ones left and the Corsicans! We'll be done for!...It'll be awful!...It'll be death!... Doesn't that get you?...Where's your heart?'...It was sure as shootin'!...he was strangling me!...'What about you, you rats?' I shoot back...'Why're you running away?...panic?' ...'You, you've got varicose veins and albumin!' he answers ...'You can talk calmly!...'

I'd told him once.

'You, you're all drunk!' I snapped, 'and sick and dead, crazy drunk! You've been eating bugle!'

I wasn't satisfied in the end.

He wanted to reason with me anyway.

'Don't you understand the blues?...That we're in the dumps?...Don't you realize anything?...The blues? Want me to make a drawing for you? We're mopey! Don't you get

mopey?...Take a look at the guys around you!' He mentioned Le Bubu, La Croquette, Grenade, Tartouille, Jean Maison
and The Sharp...They left in order to get there!...That's
proof!...

'And my brother who's on leave got the military medal...
He's in the Cahors Regiment!'...

'So what? What does that prove? That it's the one who gets
most wacked up!...you'll all croak and feet first! That's where
your brains are! Not up there! Down there! I'm telling you!
...And with shit on your kisser!'

'All right,' he says, 'go on, work yourself up, Cascade! it
does you good! I won't get sore!...But take Berthe! I swear
that's all I'm asking!...But then it's definite, you know her!
I'm putting her in your hands!...It's hell getting her to take
care of herself but God knows she needs it!...'

It's true she was dragging around a bad dose of syph, the
kind you don't see often...I knew all about it...that she
couldn't get rid of it! The doctors, boy! they'd lap up her case!
Sores all over 'er!...Berthe had cost her weight in gold just
for injections, buboes...But that was his affair, wasn't it!...
Sometimes three months easily in the hospital for a bubo...
Times when she was rotting away everywhere, chancres even
in her ears...Berthe and Picpus, they're a whole world!...
Got to see how he handles her when there's really an argument...He once broke three of her ribs!...Always because
she's stubborn and won't go to the doctor...Women who don't
take care of themselves are repulsive!...'I don't want to go
for my blood test!'...What bellyaching!...Wah!...Wah!
...All blah!...What crap!...Me, I go to the doc all right!
...And not since yesterday!...for fifteen years! regular! I
haven't skipped a single time!...Health first!...Why the hell
should the women get out of it? Because they just don't feel
like it? You listening? 'Ah! so I don't wash my ass!...I'm

50

pretty, people like me!'. . . What you get for picking up kitchenmaids! They're plain filthy! They drag around!. . . get full of
muck! never in a hurry! never put their ass in water!. . . I'm
keeping the lot and that's that! Syph and the rest!. . . never see
a bidet if their men weren't always after 'em, rough with 'em.
They'd rot from head to foot! Ah! the customers don't realize
the trouble a woman means!. . . The way they're so anxious to
be sick and disgusting! Nice and veiled, all primped up, always
natty! But when it comes to the squoosh! the hell with that!
. . . they don't give a good God damn!. . . Berthe's worse than
the others!. . . Really got to have class, and more!. . . It's not
every pimp! hmph! when it comes down to knowing his goods!
. . . I'm telling you!. . . Picpus insists right off. . . 'Take my
Berthe!' He hands me a line. . . He's dead set on it!. . . 'Take
her on trial!. . . She makes whatever she wants at the Empire
. . . You won't have trouble! Fifty-fifty!' Still and all it hurts
bad to see a pal leave that way when no one asked him for
anything. . .

I argue with him all the same.

'What are you running away for, you poor dope? You want
to leave your place to the others? There's a real boom on now!
You can rake in all you want!. . . It's lousy with dough!. . .
Never had so much work in London! Ask Red!. . . Been with
us thirty years! Never saw the likes! You make a pile in a
single day! furloughs all over the place! The girls come back
loaded with dough!. . . You'll have your house in Nogent!
You'll be able to leave in six months. . . Just a little patience!
. . . You've got your chance!. . . Now you beat it! It's a gold
mine! You're getting dumb! dopey! You're hurting me, Picpus!
Go on, get your equipment! You disgust me! That's what! You
make me sick!'

What else could I say? That's how I talked!. . . He wasn't
even listening!. . . He starts all over about his girl!. . . Both of

51

them were there, Berthe and Picpus, on the sidewalk...They
sure looked like dopes!...'Go on!' I said. 'Get away! That'll
do! you're crazy! It's over!...Let me have your punk! I don't
want to take advantage of your weakness!...But be careful!
No finagling and no monkey-business! If she doublecrosses me
while you're away, I'll hand her over to Luigi!...He asked me
for some!'

I knew she couldn't stand him.

Luigi the Florentine! he knows how to train them!...He
sure can handle his women!...Picpus is velvet compared to
him...You've just got to see Luigi's bunch! Both hands, all
his fingers broken!...Smack!...that's it! At the edge of the
sidewalk at the first slipup!...Streetwalker! Smack! she gets
it!...Penance!...Not a murmur!...You've just got to see his
breadwinners...I assure you they watch their step! they're on
their toes...They don't take their gloves off!...They do Tottenham. I assure you they don't feel like laughing! Berthe!
that burp! soon as you talk about Luigi...He almost pimped
for her once! You can imagine!...'No! No! No! Cascade!
I'll be all right!...I swear! I'll never bother you!'

'All right! All right, Berthe! We'll see!'...That's how I
talked...I wasn't very encouraging...

'Beat it, you! It's agreed!...Only you're just a worm! And
don't forget it! that's all I'm saying!'

'I don't give a damn as long as you give her back to me!
I'm crazy about her!'

It's like dope, I tell you!

'When I get back it'll be cushy!' He was slobbering and
raving. He talked to me like the Salvation Army!...'What we
need is real Victory! Alsace-Lorraine, my boy! I want to see
Berlin, you old sourpuss!...'

That's how he talked!...

'Balls! that's what you'll see!...You'll spit your little guts out...France has been getting along without you! There're already seven or eight million over there getting smashed up! Ten thousand a day kicking the bucket, big dopes like you! A little pimp like you isn't going to change things! Remember what I'm telling you!...You'll be just a crap in the hay... You won't even be seen any more!...Your lousy war's either lost or won...You're just a blank!...Glamor!...Do you have to die for that? Anybody asking your advice?'

'You're talking crap, Cascade, you don't know a thing!... You going to keep her for me? Yes or no? My Berthe? My love?'

We'd have kept on arguing.

'Go on!' I said. 'You're raving! You've got it coming to you! Let the damned Fritzes knock hell out of you!'

Another stripe on my arm!...I get all the luck! I'm running a garage! Got all the chickens! I've got a head, etcetera!... Where'm I going to put 'em?...It worries me!"

Big Angèle was listening to it all, she could take his temper ...she saw her man getting worked up...there were pros and cons...She could have put a word in...because after all she had a right to...being his woman and not since yesterday... since always, practically...The others?...Just little understudies to the big-shot gals...She'd come back from America just two weeks before with a nice roll of dollars and a cute little number she'd picked up in Vigo, just like that, at the port, a kid, a little flower girl, prettyish, but still shy, not used to it yet, she'd been pushed into it right away, the city, the mob, the cars, it was all too dark for her, the sky and the pavement, there wasn't enough sun! It was hell and high water getting her out on the street...Another complication... The Portuguese was in the dumps. Cascade didn't even look at her, just to see what she was like!...He even wanted to ship her back!..."I don't want any wet blankets around!...I'm

53

unlucky enough myself!"...And he blew up again!...He got sore at everyone again! at the war that screwed up everything! at the way things were done! at the cops! at people! at the little Portuguese! Big Angèle, who hadn't said anything, suddenly spoke up.

"You're too good-natured, Cascade!...You're too good-natured!"

What was that she said?...Boy! did that half-ass remark set him off! What a sock he took at her! Smack! Enough to stagger a donkey!...She sat down in a daze!...

"I do what I can, Cascade! I do what I can!"

More wailing.

That made him scream at her! He was stamping with rage!

And since we were standing there and watching, we irritated him too. He yelled at us.

"There!" he says, "there're my henchmen!...Indeed, gentlemen, indeed! I'm very kind...The gentlemen certainly think so, too!...They've got good reason for running after me... The Queen!...Tootsy-wootsy Cascade! That's how I am! Wait my little rascals! There's some for you, too! You'll get a look at the police! You'll get a look at Matthew!...He's coming back in a little while!...It's a promise!...It's agreed!...The Inspector from the Yard...Sergeant Matthew! Indeed! Indeed! That's pretty! That's fine! A scandal! The gentlemen make a scene right in Mile End! Ah! there's going to be shit to pay in five minutes! Inspector Matthew hasn't digested the hat!...I might as well tell you...Sergeant Matthew doesn't like wise guys! Matthew the Bull, Sergeant Matthew of the Yard, Inspector Matthew, who does he come to see?...Me, of course! ...Damned sure!...That was all I needed!...We met at the Haymarket...He gets in front of me at the ticket window... He puts a pound on Chattèrton...And it wasn't the favorite!

54

...It surprised me a little about him...I didn't make any remark!...He was the one who buttonholed me...I let him start talking...

'Say, Cascade!...Don't you know anything? There's a war on, my dear fellow!...There's a war on!...'

A dumb remark.

'Again?' I said...That gets him! It's a peculiarity of his! Always the same gag since he saw my certificate!...discharged, class of '87...that I did my time...my seven years! that I'm not going to start all over!...I'm not bugs! like the others!... that kind of gab, nuts to that!...they know me at the Consulate...at the Yard too!...Besides I've got my albumin... with a checkup and everything...just let 'em try and kick me out!...that Matthew won't get my hide, he'd sure like to see me yanked in!...For me to clear out! Ha! Small-timer!... he'd treat me to a drink in Waterloo!...after that...he can have the cuties!...Big-shot dealer and everything! The police don't worry them!...hypocrites!...All the gals in bunches for the Corsicans!...for the Belgians!...for anyone!...Ah! that matter! Business fine!...I know what that fox's got in the back of his mind! I haven't been on the Strand since yesterday! Beg your pardon!...No fog!...He says to himself...he'll be drunk like the others...They're all wacked up at the moment ...they're all bitten by the war!...I'm going to make him ashamed!...He'll beat it!...Zim! Boom! Patriotic, those frogs! Beg your pardon!...A bone!...Just wait!

'Your papers!' he asks...he's getting sore...my papers? Papers are in order I'll have you know!...Mr. Cascade!... Papers!...Papers!...

'Here, Inspector.'

'All real Frenchmen enlist!' he starts off, looking at me.

'I agree!...I agree!...I grant you, Inspector!...I'm not

contradicting. . . They leave their places to the clients. . . Seems to be the fashion! . . . But that's pure nuts, isn't it? Stark madness! in my opinion! . . . Don't you think so Inspector?'

'I don't think so, Cascade! . . . I don't think so! . . .'

'The pretty war'll go on without me, Inspector! . . . I feel comfortable with you, Inspector! . . . No reason for me to leave you!' And I just keep jabbering away at him! . . .

Ah! he says to himself. . . It's the death of the horse! . . .

He stands there dreaming! . . . He starts hearing spirits! . . . Just stands there sniffling! . . . Ah! the phony! . . . I act childish . . . I know the Yard all right! . . . dopes, but doublecrossers and stubborn! . . .

We talk for a while. . . He puts it another way. . .

'Yes! It's a terrible war!'

That makes him sigh.

'Those Boches are real savages! . . . Did you see the *Mirror* this morning? Those photos? That atrocity? The way they cut off children's hands?'

'Ah! It's true, Inspector. . . All too true!'

'Got to kill those brutes, Cascade!'

'That's right, Inspector!'

'I'd go myself if I were free! . . . Ah! how I wish I were free! . . . like you! . . . If I hadn't my job! . . . Ah! if I were free!'

And then a shitload of sighs. . . the louse!

'I'm sick, Inspector! Haven't you seen my certificate? Not strong! Delicate! Sensitive legs!'

'Sick!' he says, 'but turbulent!'

Ah! I feel it coming. . . I see it's getting fishy. . . I've annoyed him!

'Me turbulent, Inspector? . . . Ah! I wouldn't like to be that! Oh no! . . .'

Ah! I protest.

'Quite well behaved I suppose?'

He's skeptical.

'Absolutely, Inspector!'

What's coming next?

'No violence? No breach of the law?'

'Oh, not at all, Inspector!'

'And what about your gang, Mr. Cascade?'

Ah! here it comes!

'My gang? my gang?...' I'm startled...The first news! What's he insinuating?...

'Oh! it's going to get you into trouble! What an outfit! What riffraff, Mr. Cascade!...What a gang you've got!...What reckless people! Oh! I just don't understand you...With such roughnecks!...Ah! I'm warning you, my dear Cascade, in all sympathy!'

I didn't see what he was driving at.

Then he starts telling me things...in detail...the low-down tricks...the business of the hat...La Vaillance...your fight and everything...some stinker that cop!...Oh! Sister! what hot air!...I don't say anything...I listen to him...I see what's coming...He's looking for trouble!...He's been given orders, the rat!...They want to pin anarchism on me!...That way they can deport me!...Not a word of truth!...But that's enough!...They invent, that's all!...Anything goes when the cops are after you!...Just keep your mouth shut!...I stop dead!...I play dumb!...I plead guilty, not proud...If I make a wrong move, I'm a goner!...he'll pull me in! I'm sure he's got a warrant for me!...He's warning me and means business!

'I don't want to see them at La Vaillance! Your friends!'

'Very well, very well, Inspector!...They're hoodlums! You're right!...Mustn't let 'em get away with anything!'

I agree with him.

'Neither one of them!'

'Of course not!'

'Who's the young one? with the arm like that?'

'He's one of the war casualties, Inspector! A boy who's suffered a lot...A victim of the present horrors!'

'Is Boro a victim of the present horrors too?'

He's getting sarcastic.

'That's his tenth offense!...And I'm sure it's not over! He still has bombs!...I'm sure he's still making them!...You know something about it, don't you, Mr. Cascade? You associate with awful people! Gallows birds!...An abuser of freedom!...I'm ashamed for your sake, Mr. Cascade!'

'Oh! Inspector, if I may say so! the quietest man in the Borough!...where there're still some pretty bad eggs! Just between us, Inspector! let's admit, without any hard feelings!'

That's a stone for his garden.

'I don't want to see them in the pubs any more!...Neither of them!...You get me?'

He doesn't look as if he understands...

He's obstinate!...A swine!...

All the same, God damn it, I protest!...

'Still and all, they're not anarchists!'

'Damn you, Cascade! What do you need?'

'The young one's not an anarchist!...He doesn't know what it is!'

He disgusts me! What a stupid accusation!

'We'll see about that, Mr. Cascade! We'll see!'

Stubborn, the louse! He was getting nasty!...better not insist!...Soon as you cross him he gets vicious...All his whiskey goes to his nose!...Couldn't touch him then with kid gloves!...And yet he's got dough!...I know what he's been costing me for fourteen years!...He was able to build himself a house, I'm telling you, and a nice one! with my handouts!...It's a hell of a long time I've been greasing him!...In exchange he's nabbed me only twice!...And for two jail terms where I was perfectly innocent!...Just plain unjust! A clean alibi! A shame! It was Tatave's women who'd given the guy a shakedown!...Not mine! Ah! Not at all! He knew all about it, the louse! Only I owed him for a dozen matters! That squared him!...He'd never been able to pin anything on me! ...Had to get me!...For honor's sake!...I think he'd have lost his job!...They all kidded him at the Yard! That was in Pretty-Eye's time! Ah! there were out-of-town jobs in those days!...Boys, things were moving then!...They did a cottage a week!...in cahoots with the maids!...They'd bring back three or four hundred pounds!...That was youth for you!... They'd jump from one town to another!...Those maids were the death of their bosses!...Pretty-Eye, some good-looking kid!...Only the swellest homes!...Practically invited guests! ...You realize?...Matthew was boiling in his pants!...all pissed up!...I had to take the rap for Tatave!...It couldn't last forever!...He even warned me!...Got to get you, Cascade! Got to get you! Put in eleven months for Tatave!... seven and four...That was my share!...I saved Matthew's honor for him! I lost thirty-five pounds!...So I know the guy a little!...We'll settle accounts later on...There's nothing lost I'm telling you! For the time being I was nice! Didn't want to sour things!...I shifted the conversation!...I said to him, 'Inspector, I see you're putting something on Chatterton ...It's a good horse!...I'm not denying it!...but...after all!...'

'Have you got something better, Mr. Cascade?'

'I sure have!...It seems to me!'...never come straight out with it in England...they think you're scatterbrained!...'If I may say so, I'd put something on Micky instead, Inspector! After all, there's a better jockey up, isn't there?...I'm not giving you any advice, Inspector!...bear that in mind!...I wouldn't allow myself!...Look, I'm putting six down for you! ...But on Micky to win! All or nothing!...'

He looks as if he doesn't understand me!...I lay down my six pounds!...Bim! Bam! he sweeps up all the tokens! Like that, no gabbling! and bye-bye!...I see that he catches on without a word! Total loss six pounds!...because of you, you big fatheads!...you! for your damned extravagances! Otherwise he'd have taken me away!...Just an act! hot air! Just a song and dance in his pocket! Blackmail pure and simple!... That's the crap I've got to take! And you're the cause of it!... I can tell it to you straight to your face! Isn't it a damned pity? Isn't it a perfect shame that at my age I'm still knocking around for ass-holes like you?...My gang?...My gang?... So it seems! Ah! hello, my gang!...Pianists who raise hell in Mile End at four in the afternoon!...Swell! my gang!... Yours!...God damn it! In a jam for stinkers like that! Ah! it's awful! I'm telling you!...Justice is dead! I saw the cop in a stew!...He was saying to himself, 'I'm waiting for you, Cascade! If you don't cough up, you'll get it in the neck!... I'll yank you in and whoops!...love!...' He was picking on me!"

"You're too good-natured, Cascade!...You're too good-natured!"...Angèle was at it again!...a downpour...big sobs!...hearing such stories, all the troubles of her poor man! ...She can't resist!...She leaps to his neck again! She hugs and kisses him wildly!...She gets another smack. She plops down on the couch again...

"I lose out every time!...That's my affair!...I always get it in the neck!...But I want you to stop giving me a pain in the ass!"

That's Cascade for you!...He lets it out! and now right away it's poetry!...

> For don't you see that every day
> I love you more and more?
> Today more than yesterday
> And less than tomorrow!

He reels it straight off.

"I learned it, you know, in Rio!"...and oops! he flies off the handle again.

"I've been getting the dirty end of it, guys! I don't dare stick my nose outside! Things are bad, boys!...Things are bad!... Cascade here!...Cascade there!...They want me!...They're looking for me!...Maybe I stink?...All the dicks sniffing at me!...And her, always yowling!...In manilla I lose like all sixty!...At the races my nags dash backwards...Only girls keep coming in!...There I've got all I want!...I've got to admit!..."

Berthe and Mimi were enjoying it, sprawled in the cushions choking with laughter...Berthe, the skinny green-looking one, and Peg-leg Mimi were beneath the lamp splitting with giggles...

"Either they're yowling or nagging, they can't keep quiet!" They were getting on his nerves.

"Go get the Calva! You hear me, Mimi?"

He was sending Mimi downstairs...The two of them bounce down...Angèle was sobbing with her head in her hands from the clout she'd just got, she made the whole table shake... Cascade didn't want to look at her...He turned his back on her on purpose, sitting astride his chair, that's the way he grouses...He was rocking. He was burning up inside...

At bottom, he's proud, no doubt about it, that Matthew let him have it as if he were a big shot...it puts him up there with the real moguls!...Even so, for his six pounds!...He doesn't give much of a damn about the six pounds!...doesn't come to much these days! Us, his gang! and some gang!... Gives him real class!...Not just an ordinary guy!...Arranging things was a little weakness of his...He'd have gladly forked over a hundred pounds to take on that kind of weight! ...With his stable?...A hundred pounds more or less!... And ten and twelve and a hundred fifty? What the hell was

that?...Matthew had taken him!...Especially with the rein-
forcements!...We sure were living in style!...Open house!
...fat of the land at the Leicester...piles and piles of food!
...Phonies, spongers and tramps!...A real perpetual parade!
...A real boarding school...You didn't know who or why
...Someone always dropping in!...bringing others along...
pals traveling through...girls arriving...no more chalking it
up in twenty-five pubs!...always just because he was a big-
timer...he didn't know from where or how...he always settled right off!...Man's reputation! And then the races and
the Derby where he bet damned high...and poker with the
sky the limit and the cost of medicines...That came to something! Beauty care, hairdressers, settings, all the little whatnots
for women who didn't deny themselves a thing, fancy-priced
massages, Houbigant perfume! and heavier expenses, hush
money for the cops who were snotty and blackmailers and
devoured his money, one after the other, six, seven pounds at
a clip! weekly! monthly! just in so-called small fines! In the
theatres up to a dozen pounds! Week-end dough for the big
jobs! And it was never enough! In short, a whale of an outlay!
...It kept dribbling the hell out in all directions! Especially
since the year 1914-1915 when it had become a real massacre,
a gold rush, a parade of profits, since the suckers were just
handing it out all over the place! Cascade was positive...
Dough had to keep rolling in or he'd fold!

"The war! the war!...It's driving 'em wild! Just take a look
at 'em!...They don't know what they're crapping about!...
They want all the dough!...Then they don't want anything!
They all want to leave! They can't see straight! Their pants
are on fire! Their dough's on fire! Just take a look at my
pimps! They did the damnedest things, committed crimes to
bring their girls to London...If you'd said to them a year ago,
'Pal, got to beat it! Be heroic! Go back to the Bastille! Business

is dead! London's finished!'...they'd've called you King of the Loonies!...Today trumpets and tata!...You tell 'em, 'Get going, soldier-boy! Bullets a penny a dozen! Up and at 'em!' Off they fly! They're all raving bughouse! They can't stop running! Just tearing off like mad! Does it make sense?... You tell me!...They leave their women and kids behind!... They won't have 'em for all the money in the world! Completely nuts!...Making dough hand over fist!...and a couple of sure-fire rackets, besides!...Gold galore right now! It's being spoiled that's killing 'em!...Pity the poor pimp! He can't stand being stuffed with dough!...Take my word for it! ...I'm not scratching!...'Tatave, you make me sick! your woman's bringing in twelve pounds a day!...It's a crime to kill the golden goose!'

'You!' he says. 'Look who's talking!...You got it easy!... You got your albumin!...'

'Albumin or not! You're just plain dumb!' It drives me haywire listening to 'em!...I can't take any more of it!...It's not Verdun, it's the Somme! and so on and so on!...and citations, look, like him!...You'd think they were kids!...In school! That they'd swallowed cannon!...and they claim to be smart Frenchmen! Ah! damn my balls! I'm going to explain to you!...They read the papers too much!...Oh, I eat up all the articles! and quack quack! and parrots!...Do I read them? shitzoff! the magazines and their crap!...That's what sends 'em off their nut! the jabber! the jabber!...Do you read the sheets, you, huh?...Admit, Boro! admit, you dirty yegg!... In the first place, I've seen you!...You start drooling!... Here's my penny! The *Mirror*!...the *Sketch*!...the *Star*! please!...What crap...Look, you can look around here, you'll never see a single one of 'em around!...Even in the toilet I won't have 'em!...I tell the girls, 'Just let me see one of 'em here and I'll clout you!'...You can look all around! You've

63

got a mug like a client! I want you to be less idiotic! All the same it gets you! no stopping you...War here!...War there! ...Keeps eating you!...Indeed, Madame!...Victory here! ...Victory there!...Offensives!...Cannon fodder!...They need it!...Send back the bones! the goo! the mug! all for nothing!...What's there to write about?...I see just one thing in war!...It means raising hell and making dough! Just have to lie down to get it!...It's women's work!...I'm not victory!...I'm not defeat! I don't disembark!...I'm no offensive!...I'm no retreat!...I have a good time, that's all!... What's the difference! Not just a laughing matter!...They pay for being dumb!...The proof is that they run away! the faster the better!...They get scared, in my opinion!...Just that!...Blind fear, that's all!...You half-wit! I'm not scared, damn it!...I don't need a travel permit! I get along by myself!...The hell with Matthew! and the rest of them!...and Marshal Haig! and the Czar! and Poincaré! and the Lord Mayor, too! All in the same bag! I want to cash in, me too! Ah! timid! They're having a good time! Let's us too! All right with me!...They're bloodsuckers! All right! I've always said so! I'm known! I've got my card! You go look me up in the records! I'm just a poor fish! Not a general!...I don't want to bother anyone! Here's mud in your eye!...I could cash in more! My girls are enough for me. I could make munitions! I got an offer!...Bigger dopes than me are rolling in dough! ...or drafty condoms!...or fake cardboard shoes!..."Victory Pumps!" It's not hard...but me, my business is tail! All right, good! I'm staying in it!...Yes, Majesty!...So what're they handing me?...I had three girls, all I needed...plus Angèle of course...now they slap a dozen on me!...What kind of business is that?...Will you tell me?...I don't read the papers! I'm not bats!...Even Little-Arm Pierrot realizes!... Now he's in jail!...He knows I talk straight!...no beating

64

about the bush!...It's straight stuff or they get your hide! I'll let him have his Clémence back!...But it sure gives me a pain in the ass! I didn't ask for anything!...It's not an ordinary traffic!...I've got a dozen on my neck!...I've got to arrange for a house like Pépé the Hump! Where should I go?...Tell me, you grafters!...You all read the papers!...And I see you like cognac!...I'm so glad!...So I see!...And you smoke my cigars, don't you! Cuban tobacco, bear in mind!...Ah, you're not letting yourselves get depressed!...Ah! that's delightful...Everything to keep up the morale, gentlemen!... It's a mug's game! Quite right! you'll get out of it!...So!... Boom! Morale's everything!...My old man, who was in the war of 1870, who was a cabinetmaker in Bezons, always used to say to me, 'Sonny, watch out for the omnibuses'...He was the one who got run over by one!...You see what use it is to be careful!...Catastrophe!...The poor world's full of syph! Luckily there're some free men!"

We'd had three drinks, we were beginning to feel pretty warm.

"Mimi!...Mimi!...Bring up the Burgundy! I don't want these gentlemen to leave on an empty stomach!...And the sausage!...and the headcheese!...I want the gentlemen to have a bite!...I can't ever do enough for them!...Kidders! ...Wise guys!...Real characters!...Matthew kept telling me that!...They're genuine artists! And he knows about those things!...The kind of men you don't meet often!...

" 'Artists! Mr. Cascade!' Boro! Boro! sing me my song!....So I can really see if you're an artist!...Or I won't talk to you any more!...for ten years!...That's how I am!...Come on, the Dark Waltz...and all the girls in the chorus!...To the victory of the little guys and the bathhouse boys!...Ah! Ah! need some imagination! Wilhelm's listening to us."

There was a small Gaveau in the corner, with some notes

65

missing...Boro obliges...he starts off!...They get going in chorus! they're ripping along!...*The Knight of the Moo...oo...oon*! They're so off-key that we're all splitting!...The yowling doubles!...makes the windows creak!...and what feeling!...Big Angèle's bellowing the loudest...There's pain in her voice...She's sobbing, she's so unhappy!...Because she's upset that her man's so nervous...

He shouts to Mimi again!

"Burgundy, Mimi!...Burgundy, sweetie!"

The drinking's not over! he yells down the stairs again...

Mimi was downstairs in the basement kitchen goosing around with the others...You could hear them all clucking away...They were having a great time!

"She doesn't give a damn what I say, that trollop...just doesn't give a damn!...Mimi! Mimi! you hear me?...Tell Joconde to come up!...Boys, she's got to read the cards for you! You'll see something!...You're going to have a belly laugh! Joconde's a real circus! Boy, she's something!...Cards! ...Cards!...Hands!...You'll split!...My wench used to believe in cards! She used to say to me, 'Darling...' In any case, I don't believe in it!...Not a bit of superstition in me!...But I get a kick out of watching Joconde! She's right once in a thousand! it's the real thing with her!...She even knows the Tarots! Since the cradle...All kinds of cards! Life! Past... Future!...A hell of a character! You'll get a look at her face! ...She's not from Seville for nothing!...They've got it in their blood!...I brought her back in 1902 from the Castilian Exposition!...Her name was Carmen...I call her Joconde! And, well, she's still around! Leaves today! Comes back tomorrow! In the kitchen!...She takes a little outing...she comes back!...She says to me, 'Good-by, Cascade!...You'll never see me again!'...It doesn't worry me!...Three days later my beauty's back! Faithfulness in person!...The same song and

66

dance for twenty years!...Gypsy to the core!...steals, cheats, lies, everything!...She drinks only water! It's not from booze that she's batty! It's something worse...Got to see her castanets too!...Some workout!...Hailstones!...You'd think it was hailing!...You don't see her fingers!...I never ask her for anything...She brings me a pound...two pounds!...Sometimes a fiver!...No discussion!...I take it all!...so does she!...A gypsy!"

"Joconde's busy!" someone answers from downstairs..."She's preparing the rabbit for this evening!"

Mimi yelling from the bottom of the stairs.

"Damn it! tell her to get going! We're waiting! Are we going to wait all day?"

"Coming, darling!...My sweet Precious!"

What a cooing! coo-coo-coo!...

It's Joconde cooing like that...from downstairs...all the way in the back...

"And all the cards! Don't forget anything, Precious!... And not the junk! You hear me?...The real stuff!...Luck, Baby!"

He tells us about it..."It's a passion of hers! She'd cheat with Deibler." We bust out laughing!

There she comes, scaling up, Carmen has annunciated!... she sniffles...she spits...wheezes...

"Sacro mio!...Sacro mio!... Quouelle casa!...craouha!"

The two...three...four flights!...Finally she emerges! Ah! what a vision in laces!...He didn't lie!...She clutches the rail, gasping...she's all in!...A short-winded doll!...a plaster cast!...black eyes!...embers!...Chantilly lace... furbelows!...velvet flounces!...a whole train!...and her skirts full of medals!...in tiers...they jingle! little bells!... they chime soon as she moves! More lacework...narrow waist!...all of it with spots!...more spots! grease! dust!

67

sauces!...In her ears barbaric pendants that almost drop to
her shoulders...She's choking after the rail...Suddenly she
perks up!...Here she is! She's giving us the once-over! She
plants herself!...she grumbles!...

"Greatness av my life!"

She's defying us!...crap like us! It's an outrage! She's flar-
ing up, puckered, twitching, lips twisted, violet, black...from
looking at us with anger...towering rage...

"You wanta me, Cascade?...You wanta me, pimpa?"

That's what she calls him.

"Get the cards, baby-doll!"

That's an order.

"In front those roughnecks?"

"Yes! And shut up, slut!"

That gags her...her innards are tied up in knots...she
starts coughing!...and coughing!...

Angèle stands there not saying a thing.

Carmen sees her.

"And that bitch?"

Angèle lets out a shriek.

"Cascade, throw that pig out! Back to the doghouse, you
hag!...back to the doghouse! If she stays another minute!...
I'm going to clear out!...I didn't come from Rio to be made
a fool of!...I already find seven floozies on the bed! Do I
have to stand that lunatic besides? The idea! Good-by!...I'm
no angel...Goo-oo-ood night!"

They're off!...The doll starts choking...she shakes the
whole place...She'd better rest...better sit down there on a
step...she's going to faint!...

"Dumb bitch!" she chokes..."Dumb bitch!...and you
haven't seen everything! Just wait for the thirteenth! You'll
have thirteen in your bed!"

She's having a high time, a little cracked!...dizzy!...she

68

suddenly lies down...she can't sit up!...she's squirming and convulsing on her belly!...What a time the other kids are having, in seventh heaven!...The way they giggle!...They're all over the place!...On the cushions! the rugs!...cackling ...kicking up! They're twisted into one another with delight! ...the old ones, the young ones, big necking!...It's like a movie!...life in a castle!...and pretty loose! They hand around glasses, bottles, first the Calva and then the sausages ...There's no crapping around!...Everything goes!...The old-timers yell at each other!

Boro goes back to the piano...The chorus starts up again...

"The Knights of Misfor-or-or-tune!" The girls tuck up their dresses...they unhook themselves to breathe easier...They slap their thighs...wild laughing!...cheeks all red...Some are thin and some chubby!...

Cascade starts getting sore, he's riled, they tickle him, pull his hair...Not a bit of respect left!...

"What! My women! And you too, you tramps? Trying to get in my hair?...Well I'll be damned!...If that's not the limit!...Where'll it all end? Bughouse!...The grandmothers worse than the brats!...The world's cracking up!...It's the sidewalk of vice!"

Suddenly the fun's over...They're all in!...Everyone's crying...He stands up, indignant, sits down again astride...he mops his forehead...

"So it's only a joke? Gentlemen! Just wait a minute! Peace! ...health!...Now Mimi the *foie gras!* the rillettes, the olives! ...I see the gentlemen are still hungry!...Boro!...Boro!... Play "The Golden Wheat," Boro! You hear me?" But the girls preferred "The Poet"..."*A poet told me!*" All right, "The Poet"! *"That there was a sta-a-a-ar!"*...But they got no further ...Everybody started squabbling again!...about Angèle!...

Some were for!...Some against!...about the airs she put on
...etc....etc....If she had a right to make faces!...that she
wasn't very polite!...The whole coop was clucking away!...
It made a wild racket...jabbering so you couldn't hear yourself!...The two of us would have liked to talk some more
with Cascade!...About our brawl with the cops!...to explain
what happened...After all, it was serious!...about the rioting
and violence...I didn't want things to get nasty...If the cops
were getting shitty with me...it meant someone must have
done me dirt...tipped off the Special Brigade...It was teeming against the windowpanes in sheets, cats and dogs, it was
pouring buckets, winter wasn't far off...I'd been in London
four months...four months already! It wasn't always comfortable because of the nosybodies! Still it was better than
across the Channel!...much better than taking a beating with
the 16th Cavalry...croaking wet every day from Artois to
Quercy...counting if you still had all your limbs in every
foxhole...barbed wire everywhere, waiting for you!...Good-
by!...I'd had three years of it!...my youth knocked around
in the army!...it had ended pretty badly with the Viviani
business! Hail Déroulède!...I brought back my bones and the
mortgage! holes everywhere!...my arm twisted! Just a hunk
of flesh left...maybe enough for them to yank me in again!
The little game wasn't over!...War hooks on!...You've got
to watch out!...Wars keep going...My ear got a lousy
screwing too...A buzzing inside!...whistling!...Like that,
a bullet...In a way it's alarming...the whistling's hell on
sleep...My leg dragging along...Not much to joke about...
The little pimps made me smile...They'd eaten up the hokum!
...it turned their little heads!...I didn't say anything!...
That's experience!...I knew!...No need to boast!...They
were children in a way!..."emancipated," my ass!...They'd
learn somersaults over there in the sectors!...Everything that

wasn't in the papers!...It wasn't enough to talk out of the corner of your mouth and chew the fat!...They'd see the rest of it!...I was all right at Cascade's!...I was staying put!... It looked magical to me after what I'd been through!...The others would see! the guys who were steamed up would get over it!...they could all argue as much as they liked, life at the Leicester was all the same a real treat...Too happy, that was all!...Leave that?...Youth is crazy!...Go looking for slaughter, crazy contraptions, poor sucker! eat gunfire!...You rot in the water...trench mud...your dome full of gases... Here's to your health, Meatballs!...I love you!...Wacky with duty!...And taratata!...Shit! I wasn't going to wise them up!...Never wise up a dope! There's the bugle, men!... They'd have argued with me!...Aah!...Information's no use!...They want a change!...Bon voyage!...They'll be dead before I do it again!...When it was full of customers outside...Just think!...Right near...full of traffic!...And they were throwing away all their chances!...The streets jammed! full of dough!...The girls never stopped...It was a real circus of customers, couldn't pick a pin up!...a merry-go-round, a crowd of lovers! Shaftesbury, full! Tottenham! full!...the kind of thing they never dreamed of!...Right side by side, in a hurry, continuous! easygoing! happy-go-lucky, Tommies, Sammies, Boys, my balls! sweating whiskey and little presents!...Sidewalks made of gold, that's a fact!... Just had to lie down to pick it up...Cascade wasn't exaggerating a thing!...Those were the palmy years, the end of 1914, '16, '17!...The take had never been so good...The pimps had it wonderful! and there they were evaporating!... They were slipping away!...Nitwits!...Their bunions were burning 'em!...Whooping cough and panic! They were getting their knapsacks ready!...They were storming the consulates!...Bedford Square was full of 'em!...Rarin' to go!...

Stung all at once!...Bamboozled by the newspapers!...
Cascade stuck to his guns!...They'd gone off their nuts!...
In the frenzy!...the wind of glory!...The girls all up in the
air!...in distress!...That was the result of it!...The hurricane had left him a queer heritage!...He was still complaining!...Twelve pieces...Twelve items! all at once! Everything
for Cascade! Ah! some joke!...Maybe it wasn't over yet!...
Now how to handle it?...Ship the whole lot of them to the
Leicester?...With Angèle in charge?...that was the most
practical thing...Whoring right at the corner...right nearby!
...not a hundred yards away!...You couldn't want any better!
...fine location for a boardinghouse. The six floors all continuous!...Leicester Street...Leicester Square, W.1...You
could see the people on the sixth floor going up from the door
...big spacious premises!...for treating friends right!...
hygiene on every floor...French bidets...gallantry everywhere! toil and honor!...the motto! The whole basement all
a well-stocked kitchen, a dream! Nothing petty at Cascade's...
Open and generous house! hot dishes at all hours...day and
night! No woman can deny it! London's the proving ground
for hustling...the delicate ones are always coughing! Murderous sidewalk in winter!...Tuberculous fog!...Have to eat
things that stick to your ribs...Not titbits and noodles...Boy,
oh boy! everything! solid stuff! choice quality!...When it
came to grub, Cascade wouldn't trust anyone! He did the
marketing himself three times a week. He'd bring back the
tastiest things he could find, the plumpest poultry, turkeys just
right! perfect fowls! the kind of leg of lamb you don't see any
more!...So that the platters'd sizzle in the oven! superfine
mutton...when he found woodcocks we'd have a dozen!...
Baskets so loaded that the maids dragged along the stores...
and special butter!...and in blocks!...Never a question of
economy...The Table first!...That was the boss's other

72

motto!...nothing cheap on the table!...Fine fruit!...The best peaches in all seasons! That accounted for his success!... The Leicester Boardinghouse had lots of other advantages... Centrally located for appointments, near the Regent, two minutes from the Royal, the Exchange of the business, the pimps' favorite spot, but no fakes, no small stuff!...Get it straight! the ones who know how to handle things! Class! the laws of the trade! The real established procurers who go back ten, fifteen, twenty years! The big shots of the profession!...

Shame on the small-timers!...on the little guys!...they'd get the cockiness knocked out of them fast! eliminated one two three! ...Should've seen them when the gambling started, the big poker games!...the stiff betting!...laid out at the first call!...washed up!...wrung out!...curtains!...You never saw them again!...Where things were treated seriously at the Royal from 4 to 6...Buying, selling, discussing, all the refunds...In the promenade of the Empire, which was the gold mine of the trade, a woman cost three pounds, just for the doorman's percentage...and the same amount for the cops... That gives you an idea right away...Cascade had five working for him alone, often more, Léa, Ursule, Ginette, Mireille and little Toinon who went out only with her mother...They were all just resting when we arrived...They were waiting for the theatre hour to start the grind...the 8:30 standees...And we dropped in just at the right time! in the midst of the teasing and cuddling!...Especially around the gossip being peddled ...those who'd just lost their husbands...who'd been widows since morning...the nervous guys who'd joined up!...They were planning little kitchy-kitchy teams...They were consoling themselves as best they could...The cognac was helping things along fine!...they were all hitting it off together!...It put new heart into Cascade to see them all getting along...

He was looking forward to some quiet...Cascade adapted himself quickly, not Angèle! naturally! She was tight-lipped and suspicious! and not keen about vagabonds. Cascade was offhand, impromptu...even on the afterbeat...he'd suddenly get playful, just like that. That's why he'd quickly forget about raw deals...you could disarm him by laughing...women as well as pimps...Some bitches, of course, as everywhere, told awful stories about him and his girls! and about his woman! ...A number of these vicious slanders dragged at his ass, but they weren't his headaches!... He'd box their ears for them every now and then...Jealousies, treachery, but didn't dare grumble about it when he was around. From the Royal to Soho, from the Elephant to Charing Cross, he claimed respect. He'd get into a jam from time to time, the cops would come down on him for form's sake, like that fairy Matthew, but just to show that it was normal, that the Law was for everyone, that every big shot had to take it and that even Cascade took his turn. It was a sacrifice, that was all!...They weren't tough with him. They seldom pestered his girls, at the Yard they thought he was regular, they knew that he was a square shooter, handling his affairs right, his women going home at reasonable hours, never abusing their patience, never strutting around the clubs, never using bad language. The English cop is mainly a loafer, down on everything, as I've said, war or no war... Mustn't complicate his life...Otherwise you're in for one hell of a time. Cascade really had an experience of things English that was rather special! Knew all the angles! Never away a single day in his twenty-five years in London, since his leave in fact, his three years in Africa, in Blida, except for his two trips to Rio, always on the job...actually a sedentary man... and just a little broken English...maybe twenty or thirty words...at most...no facility of speech...He admitted it himself...

All the ass-work at Cascade's came from France, except the Portuguese!...and Jeanne Jambe, the blonde, who was born in Luxembourg...

As for his health, he was graying around the temples, he had his albumin, but he was still pope at the table and the bottle and elsewhere, too! he wasn't much of a shot any more at the rifle ranges, but he was always a man with real class! in everything and for everything! He'd still pick up girls, and slick ones, show girls!...real cookies! He hung around stage doors... Just so, for the hell of it! Innocent-looking!...and more than his share. And no worrying about conversation...just wild laughing and pantomime!...giddy and gallant!...He used to waltz like a prince in Angèle's heyday!...He didn't dance any more because of his varicose veins!...But all the same, two or three dances while he was on the make!...It's true he liked skirts, his little weakness, his venial sin. Couldn't stand drips, the grocer-pinochle type...though they were pretty frisky when it came to tail.

And I'd like you to know he was always ticklish about respect, not familiar, even when he was high, even at the "Whoremarket" with the men...a pretty low dive where they gulped down vitriol by the pitcherful and tableful...Ah! better not lack any with him!...The young ones would snicker a little...they'd make little digs...They'd learn what's what right away!...He didn't tolerate impropriety, he was a chief and that was that!...Cordial, pleasant, but touchy...A smudge on his honor!...Never women's gossip...His word was all!...And never aggressive! even drunk!...even staggering!...never held grudges!...only, and get it straight, if there was any impudence, a tiger! lightning!...let it be the Strong Man of the Market, the Cannon Man of the Ternes, the Terror of the Corsican Heath, the Swallower of Flaming Pythons, the big Dinosaur in a cap, he let him have it straight in the kisser, and clean, and then and there!...and in front of everybody! and no arguing, no nonsense!...let them see what law and order mean! good manners, politeness! It often started when they made cracks about his rings, about his "Brazilian six-carat" and his "knight's sapphire," two magnificent stones. They made some people jealous. The little hoodlums thought they were too showy, they asked him whether they were heavy? Whether they didn't twist his wrists? He didn't tolerate wisecracks, when they repeated it two or three times, the smacks started flying...As for his lock of hair, that was something else...then he was the one who was aggressive...he'd start things...he wanted exclusive rights...He didn't want to see another like it, a spit curl smooth as himself, in any pub in the neighborhood. He'd fly right off the handle, had to get his competitor out, he'd have ripped up the joint and the spit curl with it!

But there was no real harm in all that. I remember that he was respected, even by his enemies, even by the worst bulls of the Yard, who were nevertheless low cheap bellyachers, greedy and jealous. I've said that he was well thought of, the man was certainly imposing, but there were also the presents, that was his generous side, he scattered gold right and left...Matthew would turn up from time to time with his District Constable, a matter of not being forgotten...to see whether things were going properly...whether the Boardinghouse was in order... whether the "license" was in the frame...whether everyone was "registered," with photos, fingerprints and everything!... that it was wartime! Be careful!...He knew the rigmarole!... it was always reeled off the same way!...They'd arrive as serious as can be, like that, right after lunch...looking as if they had a lot on their minds! as if they were after something! a nasty trick! as if they were some phenomenal pot of roses! ...and then bumpitty-bump-bump!...It was only a tin can

76

and eyewash!...Just that the squeeze was late, and so the sudden concern...The thing was arranged as usual with the little present...They'd leave happy and spoiled, except for the two or three rough times...That's how life went...But now ...no more of that!...the tune was different!...Cascade felt it all, that it wasn't all easy sailing now that the guys were leaving...Not by a long shot! Take it easy! He wasn't having any pipe dreams!...He didn't find it much fun inheriting eleven girls all at once!...It didn't thrill him at all!...even if there'd been ten times as many, it wouldn't have turned his head!...Don't get any wrong ideas! For the women it wasn't the same thing! It's the moment that counts with them!...All they had to do was drink and smoke! And yowl! And guzzle! And not a damned thing more! there was no more discipline...they were cuddling together all over the beds as consolation for their sorrows, and their endless sobbing! the widows were managing fine together, there was nothing terrible after all, it wasn't as killing as all that, the work went on, you just had to see the bright side of things...and then write often to the men and send them their packages...arrangements were made...They'd write once a week.

"We're widows, Cascade! We're widows!"

They came sitting on his lap, announcing the fact, nibbling at his mustachios...also wetting him with tears!...so that he'd share their sorrows...And then another swig! Calva and little cakes!...Cascade didn't want them to smoke...no end of arguing! he thought it was plain awful, damned whorish...

"You'll have teeth like horses! yellow and repulsive! Your customers'll never get a hard-on! I'd never screw you if you smoked!" And then he asked for the cards again...He was getting back to Joconde...

"Well, you going to work on them, sweetheart?"

He was getting impatient.

"God damn it! You going to start?"

"Why don't you kizz me any more? Because your zlut is looking at you?"

She let that one fly! right in Angèle's mug! and in front of all the women! Did they laugh! Angèle couldn't let that go by! It was too much of an insult in front of everyone!

"What was that? What was that? You old bitch! You come up here to insult me? You old shit! you old punk! you old rag!...Scram before I throw you out! I won't take any of your crap! You scum! Back to the sewer!"

That was Angèle, red hot! she was wild!...Some of the girls were for, some against! what yelling in both camps!

"She's got a right!" some were saying...

Hearing that made Carmen jump!

"A right! a right! a right shit! I'll show you her right!"

Steaming away at the nostrils...

"I'm going to turn her inside out!"

The crying stopped dead!...Angèle was a fury! She set herself against the buffet and was going to jump on the old hag! to tear her hair out then and there!

"Just a little, a little!" the girls were saying...They were working them up. Always standing up for rights!

"A little!...A little!...A little what? I'll show her the rights of my ass! Come on, you witch!"

That was provocation!

Cascade jumped between them...That got Joconde real excited! she got wilder!

"I want him to kizz me or I won't do them!"

That's how she was talking about the cards...she was showing them!...spread fanwise! she was fanning herself with them! swaggering!...Cascade didn't know where to stand!...or what to do, or say!...He'd lost all patience! Then the explosion!

"Gentlemen, this has been going on for twenty years!... And I've been putting up with this kind of nonsense!"

He was calling us to witness...Jealousy and pigheadedness!

"I've had enough! Bah! I'm getting the hell out!"

His mind was made up.

Then the big hysteria broke loose!...Angèle threw a fit, she was foaming, and with a nervous laugh!...Boy, she started snorting! and twitching!...she couldn't stop...She was ripping her clothes, shrieking, tearing at herself, kicking in tears, on the floor! at her cruel man's feet!...What a Trafalgar!... Her bun came off, and flew apart...He was walking in her hair, tangled in it!...What screams! He didn't know where to stand!...She yelled worse!

"My jewel! my darling! my love! Don't do that! Don't go away, Cascade!...Don't go away!...I'll be nice! Stay with your girl! I beg you, Cascade! I beg you! I won't pester you! It's her!...Listen, pet!...Kiss them all! But not her! Not that hag, you hear! Not that hag! She'll give you the jinx! I know! I know! Take all the girls!...Lay them! I want you to! I'm giving them to you! Wah! Wah! Wah! But not that hag! Oh! not the hag! Oh! dear heart, that! my angel! I couldn't! I'll kill her! I'll find girls for you! Say I'm jealous! Wah! Wah! Since you enjoy it! I'll bring you one every day! I'll pimp for you if you want!...But not that bitch, you hear! not her!... I'll get you some from outside! I won't deny you any pleasure! ...but not the bitch! not her! You're driving me to the limit! You're breaking my heart! But don't go away, my darling!"

"You, my jewel, you're a pest! There! You hear me?... There!...you slut!"

She bucked right up and awful and let him have it!

"Just look at that broken-down wreck! That grandfather with one foot in the grave trying to cheat on me! He's a fine one! Who took him out of the gutter? Who'd have rotted away in jail? Who's he putting on an act with now?...with a dead mutt! Yes, Madame! you old slob! exactly! if that's not enough to make you puke! Just look at her!"

She points to Joconde...

Immediate laughter on her side...Cascade doesn't look too good!...

"Monsieur wants her to read the cards! That old low-down punk! Monsieur isn't satisfied now with his vices! now he wants futures!...He's after minors!...Monsieur Fresh-Meat!...I'll read the cards for you!...It'll be something!...Let me tell you!"

"Shut your mouth! Come here, Carmen! Here, my little baby! Whoops, darling, in my lap!"

The old one doesn't wait to be begged!...She dashes forward!...there she is!...some sight!...The two of them necking! Hoop la! Hoop! dada! Perfect love! Fade-out!

What an effect! What a trance! The girls laughed till it hurt!...they were choking! they roared!...they were peeing in their panties! They were splitting so that they couldn't hold themselves in!

They were yelling at the top of their lungs..."Encore!... Encore!" and then the lyric:

> *Your big gentle eyes*
> *Have enchanted my heart!*
> *For the rest of my li-i-i-ife!*

Li-i-i-ife!...that sets it off! Got to get high all together! They're off-key! floundering! miaowing! roaring away! enough to crack the windows!...The voices get together again, they start over! Boro gives them the key...he's an angel when it comes to the piano! never an impatient oath!...First it's for Victory!...They scream it a half-dozen times! Toasts with real cognac! not cheap rotgut! No! sealed, signed six stars from the cellar of the lords at the Savoy...genuine stuff! got it straight from the wine-waiter! They call him Monsieur Gustave, Dry Gustave! A tall, pale chap who comes every Thursday or Friday to be whipped by Mireille...No whipping unless he brings cognac! That's the condition, sometimes she sulks at him for a whole month when he's stingy! Dry Gustave would turn thief for his whipping! Mireille can sting! Ought to see the whip she carries around!...It's something different from English brandy, that paintshop mixture!...The bottle goes right around, the lords' brandy perfumes your whole character! heart, guts, everything!...Life smoothes off!... enterprising decisions...Everyone trying to be most gallant! ...Even Boro, who was rather orderly when it came to girls and screwing, who was rather for music, took his broad in his lap and was giving her a workout! he was playing with one hand! looking jaunty! Cascade with the good cognac in his belly wanted everything patched up...no more sulking!... no pigheadedness!...He wanted Angèle to dry her tears, to joke and sing with spirit!...They'd read the cards together!...

"Come on, Chick! Come on, Chick! Come!"

She wouldn't have it!...Didn't want anything! Didn't want to laugh! She was all tied up inside and that was all!...She was yelling any old thing at him!..."You cuckold! You decrepit old prickhead!" She wanted a fight...

"You boloney! Men like you! A pound a dozen!" That's what she said. "Give me the red wine, Véronique, red wine!"

Véronique was clubfooted, squint-eyed and redheaded, she did the stations...A very nice girl, rather discreet, obedient. Véronique gave her the bottle...Cascade jumped up, he wouldn't have it!...Ah! he suspected what was up! He knew about her and bottles! She was going to let her have it in the mouth! He grabbed hold of her on the run!...She resisted... She clung, she scratched! A kick in the schnozzle! she toppled over, sprawled out, and yowled...Joconde sees her chance, her rival on the floor! throws herself on top with all her weight! she wants to rip her face apart!...She's a man-eater! Got to bleed! Cascade's forced to jump in!...Joconde's yowling louder!...

"You filth! I don't have a wig! Do your damnedest, you bitch!"

More challenges!

She's mounted on Angèle and screaming in her ear, "I don't have a wig, you filth!...Pull on it! You skunk!

"Wait with the wig! Wait, you tramp!"

Joconde's choking!...Hooked up together like that!... But Angèle's stronger, she twists the old one's arm, she flattens her on her back!...Now she's on top...Biting her cheeks with her fangs, like that...grr! and grr!

The old gal's waving her arms, squirming...Angèle grabs her again full of blood!...She's going to turn her upside down ...bang her head...

Cascade still wants to separate them! he dashes forward to save the bottles! he trips! upsets the table! all the glassware! Crrash!

The old one gets away, tucks up her skirt, capering about, dashing between the tables...the girls run after her!...she gets away, jiggling, fluttering, it's wonderful to watch! stumbles, stops! She stands there, planted...she winks...she takes out her castanets...Ah, it's a big challenge!...And stamps her heel!...she's a fury!...it's a dance!...a trance!...her fingers all nerves!...her hands quivering all over!...crackling, spluttering!...small...small...tiny...still smaller... grains...grains...mill...even still smaller...trr!...trr!...

grainy...grainy...rrr!...that's all!...silence!...and...
tzix!...she's off again!...The devil's tail!...the tail's caught!
...trr!...rebounds!...hup!...her whole train!...and
roundabouts! and twirls! bounding like a panther! at the end
of the room! her train running after her!...over there!...
hop it!...she's here!...a kick at her furbelow!...hup! sweeping off! Angèle's foaming...That's the limit! She can't take
any more!

"You won't do it, you punk! You won't do it!" she screams!
...And she stands there motionless, staring popeyed...Just
hypnotized!...And then, hup! Without time to say oof! She's
up in the air! she sprang up! a knife in her fist! I see the blade!
...Plop!...she launches out!...plunges it sideways!...Plup
into the old one! right in the ass!...in the old one's ass! What
a shriek!...It cuts through everything! tears everything!...the
walls!...the blinds!...the street! They must have heard it
from the square...They fall over one another!...I look at
the door there wide open!...I take another squint!...Mat-
thew's standing there!...in the doorway!...No one saw him
come!...He saw a real show!...Joconde sure bounded!...
with the knife in her ass! She's jumping all around screaming
...she's running all around us!...she's yelling "Help!" She's
squeezing her ass in her two hands...flying all around!...all
around the table!...Ow! wow! wow!...all around us!...
She's miaowing!...We're nice and quiet!...We look all
right!...Not a peep out of Matthew!...Cascade bolts like
lightning!...He runs after Joconde!...

"Where'd she stick you, tell me! The bitch!...Where'd she
stick you, tell me, Mimine?"

"There! sweet darling!...there!...Ow! wow! ouch!"

And she starts sobbing and sobbing away!...

She stops running all the same!...She lifts up her skirt...
She shows him her ass...all bleeding!...How it's flowing

from the wound!...how it's trickling!...All the girls lean over to see better...What it looks like? two lips like a mouth! right in the buttocks...and how it's bleeding!...

They start discussing it again....

"Don't cry!"...Cascade's consoling her...He kisses her... coddles her...rocks her...Right away she starts yelling as loud as she can! Angèle's standing there flabbergasted...she's sniffling...sobbing...doesn't know what it's all about! she drops her knife...plock!...the sound it makes...

They've got to decide now!...Got to take her to the hospital! Cascade's giving orders...Ah! it starts all over!...at the word hospital!...

"I want to die here!" she roars.

"You won't die here, you slut!"

She doesn't insist.

"I'll die wherever you want, darling! But kizz your unhappy little girl!"

Has to kiss her again...She's bleeding all over the floor.

Her wound keeps trickling...We take a look at it...

"You've got a pretty ass, you know, you little rascal?"

He's the one who thought that one up...He tries to make her laugh...so she'll let herself be convinced quietly...so she'll leave without a fuss...so she won't bellow in the street while they're taking her....

"Look! look!" says Cascade..."Look! You're not the only one with a nice ass!"

He's unbuttoning himself!...Some idea!...He lets down his pants so we can see!...He shows us his can!...that it's tattooed on both buttocks!...a rose on the right...a wolf's face on the left!...A face with long teeth, just like that!... and over it..."I bite everywhere!"...tattooed in green. You can't say it's not funny!...It's some show for Matthew standing there in the doorway...still saying nothing...Cascade

hasn't noticed him...he's too busy on the floor on all fours!...
wiggling his can, jigging...with his little polka...

Matthew didn't budge...He had a good view...I didn't
dare move either...The old gal finally burst out laughing...
He managed her!...Ah! he's a scream!...

> *The Queen of England*
> *Fell on her fanny*
> *Dancing the polka*
> *At the Opera Ball!*

He was singing at the same time!

Good humor was restored!...The old gal was still whimpering a little...But between smiles...and she was ready to
leave...

"Boro!" he says..."and you, Foxy!...You'll both take
her!"

He's buttoning his pants.

"You'll ask for Clodovitz! London Hospital! Dr. Clodovitz!
...Will you remember? You'll say I sent you! Mireille, go
get a taxi! You hear me, Mireille! And you two guys! Snap it
up! Clodovitz knows me! He knows me! He knows what I
need!...And don't screw things up! That I'm around!...And
I'll be there!...I'll drop by! in a couple of days! Get going!
He'll understand me!...Clodovitz is a friend!...Clovis!...
Go on, baby-doll! we love you!...Go on, get a move on!"

He was shipping her off!...

She was still holding her behind, she was squeezing it in her
two hands!...She was groaning again!...

"Good God! It'z not zat!...God damn it!"

Now she didn't want to leave any more! Boy! some shitty
mess!

The blood was dripping all over again...the floor!...the
rugs, all soaked!...

Oop! Cascade spots the inspector! Ah! all the same!...He saw him!...What a gasp!...He starts jabbering right off...

"Oh! I beg your pardon, Inspector! Excuse me! I didn't see you! Wouldn't you think there'd been a crime?...What would people imagine? Oh! Inspector! Oh! Just look at that!...Oh! I'm very upset!"

All of it, of course, jokingly...But Matthew wasn't laughing...he was standing there planted in the doorway...not a word out of him yet...not even "Well Well!" as usual... Absolutely nothing...a wooden pole!

"Angèle go get some towels! And the cotton!...There's some downstairs in my drawer!"

Angèle stood there dreaming...Whack!...she's swept away! A slap!...lifted out of her chair...she falls back!... Badaboom!...the whole stairway!...she tumbles down three flights!...That wakes the girls right up!...they'd been watching fascinated like dopes! They wrap up the old gal in the tablecloth like a sausage...turned over...laced up...and the towels...the pads...all the same it's bleeding!...Angèle brings some oilcloth...they lay the old gal on her belly... They swathe her like a baby...It's still a good joke...

Matthew's frozen, he watches it all...a pope!...

He doesn't move...

"The cab's here!" Mireille announces.

We've got to go down now...Boro and me...Cascade slips us a pack of bills, a fistful, just like that...It's to arrange things...The old hag's still bawling too loud...She demands her little remedy!...Otherwise, she won't go! Blackmail! Mireille dashes off again to get some!...It's a whim, got to give in!...needs her remedy!...Cascade hardly knows what to say to fix matters up...so that the guy'll say something after all...Mr. Conscience! who's been there an hour, who hasn't said anything...A log!

"Believe me, if you like, Inspector! But I was insisting that someone read the cards for me! Well, I got it!...I've got the question...the answer!...Look! catastrophe!"

A little joking, to loosen him up...

"Ah! Inspector, you've witnessed a nasty family scene!... You walked in! as if by chance!...What do you run into?... Lunatics? Positively!...Lunatics! I'm very sorry, Inspector!... Really!...Please excuse me!"

Not a word...Wooden...He lets him talk...

"The cards! the cards! of course!... But Angèle's a terror! ...Did you see, Inspector? By yourself!....What a character! ...I don't have the last word in my own home!...It's really no life!...I'm not exaggerating a thing!...And all these girls besides!...All these kids they shove on to me like that!... Bang! My arms loaded!...And me so peaceful!...quiet!... Is that a life?...You know me, Inspector...I get pushed into complications! What kind of business is that? I ask you?"

The Inspector still speechless.

"We'll see later on! We'll see! Who's at fault, responsible ...They say it's Wilhelm! I wish it were!...In any case, it's never me!...You know that, Inspector!...Everybody's mind is topsy-turvy!... It's awful the way people're going batty!... I'm not going to look for the whys and wherefores!...I'd go off my nut too, just hearing them!...You too, Inspector!... I'm convinced!...I'm sure it worries you!...With all due respect!...Look, Inspector, I'm not making any comparison...Let's get that straight!...It's obvious...But I'm sure that in your family, Inspector, you've got trouble, too!...Ah! I'd bet!...The events affect everybody!...With all due respect!...It's obvious! Of course!...But the circumstances affect everybody, don't they?...everyone gets it according to his station...and the toughest situations! the worries, the ups and downs aren't only for poor people!...Ah! that's a fact!...

it's a real fact! So it is! Just look at the men!...Ah! I won't say any more...That's war, Inspector!...That's war!...It's a subject that makes me terribly sad! There you've got the sadness of Life!...And how unhappy everyone is!...And how that kind of thing ages you!...If only they noticed it...An hour's like a year!...The things we've got to go through!...Ah! it's no exaggeration!...You're reasonable too, Inspector! ...It's really bad luck!...You won't deny it!...I'm not making any comparison...Of course! It's obvious!"

While he was jabbering away like that, occupying his attention, we fixed the old gal up, she could just about stand... supported under the arms...with the oilcloth in her ass, the towels, all tied up tight...outfitted for the trip!..."Forward, Madame!"...We walked in front of Matthew...he moved aside a bit...Not a peep out of him...He was listening to Cascade clacking away...

On the stairs...more shrieks!...our chippy wasn't feeling well! she screamed at every movement!...We stopped and started a dozen times...Downstairs, another session!...We had to lift her...get her into the cab...people gathered around...get her among the cushions...so she'd be all set... Damn it!...there was already a crowd around...We started at a snail's pace...we'd asked the chauffeur to drive "in low"! forward!...Tottenham...the Strand...and the East streets ...That wasn't where the hospital was!...At the other side of Mile End!...A real journey! Luckily it was already dark... She'd stopped yelling except at the bumps...The air outside did her good...she almost kept quiet...We'd propped her up pretty well..."It won't be anything," I said to myself..."It won't be anything...It's not much of a wound."...I knew about wounds...We could have taken her to the Charing Cross nearby, the other hospital much closer! The most practical thing to do...But Cascade wouldn't hear of it...He'd

88

forbidden us!...to him Charing Cross Hospital was just a cop's hangout. He stuck to the London...All right, the London!...Giddy-ap, horsie!...It was some haul!...It was at least a two hours' ride at the rate we were going!...London's big...It's fifteen or twenty towns laid end to end! the same road as for the docks...Fleet Street, the Bank, Seven Sisters... then the Elephant, and the Port East...Cascade trusted the London...London Hospital!...He had confidence only in the London...It was all right with me...with Joconde too! It seems it was very serious...that you could count on the pal, the Clodo medico...the Dr. Clodovitz in question...that they'd known each other since their army days...Never a slip-up...the injured went through like clockwork!...nothing indiscreet...no gabbing..,In the hands of Dr. Clodo...London Hospital...They must have hit it off perfectly...Had to remember the guy...Clovis like old King Clovis and the Vase of Soissons...Maybe it wouldn't work out so easily...Maybe Cascade was kidding himself a little!...He was often optimistic...We'd see!...The streets...the little lamps!...There aren't any before the Elephant...you start imagining things just looking at them...things dance!...thousands...thousands...the way they unwind...dangling that way...in a daze...The ride reminded me of the 16th...the patrols... the platoons...tup! tup!...tup! tup!...the rhythm...the irons...I knew something about that...the night tup! tup! ...but mustn't forget the guy!...Ah! Clovis...Clodo! Clodovitz!...Clovis like the Vase of Soissons!...Boro'd already forgotten!...Good thing I've got a memory...

When Clodovitz saw us coming, he made a kind of sour face...got to admit it...The nurse went to let him know that someone was asking for him very specially...He was in the back of the hospital treating an emergency case...according to her...I rather think he'd been sleeping...He arrived drowsy, he looked bleary, he was rubbing his eyes...All the same he was pleasant, we could see he was explaining matters so that the old gal would be taken before the others...Two men put her on a stretcher...We waited outside...in the vestibule, that is...We weren't alone...Even at ten at night it was full of families and people...whispering together...

They put our maniac to sleep, they sewed up her buttock, it didn't take long...They put her into a common ward. We still hung around...Eleven o'clock, then midnight...We could see her in her cot, with her face all purple...drooling all over the place...

As soon as she came to, she started raising a row, demanding her Cascade...They gave her another injection, she went to sleep again, it was one in the morning. Clodovitz wasn't the boss, not even the important doctor, he was just a second-stringer at the London Freeborn Hospital, almost without pay, there were several like that who drudged away at all the thankless jobs, especially at night, on duty, Clodovitz almost every other night! Especially the foreign doctors who were interns at

90

the London, that helped them get a start before they set themselves up.

I got to know Clodo well later on. It's true that he was obliging, eager, you might even say zealous, only he'd falter for a moment, he was vague with words, had to tell him right away what you wanted, to put it on the line. . .had to know how to handle him. . .

The London, in the East End, wasn't a swanky hospital at the time! They were waiting for donors who had to be begged! . . .It was written on all the doors that they were waiting for them, and pretty badly. . .in pleading terms! The philanthropists took their time. On the other hand, the corridors were full and so were the vestibules, every hour of the day and night, crowds, mobs, of all ages and origins. . .whispering horrible things, how they all felt on their last legs, and that they'd rather croak there, sitting on the tiles, then be sent home to suffer again. . .They wanted a bed or to die! That was the kind of thing you heard. Not to speak of a hundred little children outscreaming each other all over the place. . .after their bottles and toys. . .the vestibules full of their whooping. . .the chairs full of their muck everywhere. . .It wasn't at all big enough for the patients squeezed against the doors, there were always some waiting outside, filling the sidewalks, the streets . . .Still, it was an enormous place, a big lengthwise joint, wards and wards, with God knows how many windows, as far as Burdget, almost the other avenue. . .The donations weren't rolling in, only poverty kept coming. What a crowd! even in winter, in the rain, for admission!. . .Lined up hours on end! . . .They caught the rest of what finished them off spitting out complaints and catarrhs! I always saw crowds being refused. It was very warm inside, naturally, from October on, a furnace. The undernourished are always cold. Coal's not expensive there, they use it for everything. . .

They cried to be admitted, they cried again when they left ...they didn't want to go away...they were comfortable inside, they even were delighted with the ordinary food, red cabbage with mashed peas...

It was a dense crowded area, all Poplar, Lime and Stepney, all the surrounding neighborhoods, and Greenwich opposite, naturally, for medicine and surgery. In short, the whole East End, I'm talking of those days, from Highgate to the Docks, look at that mob, the jamming! It was so full when we came that if we hadn't known Clodo, we'd never have been taken in with our Mamma! Even in the dark night, cuddling together shivering, they'd noticed our getup, and right away insults! Ah! a furious line! We came parading, bluffing them all! An enormous mob, take it from me! People who'd been there since morning trying to get in, one fellow even came to let us know, bellowing right in our faces, just like that, damned sore, that he had a double hernia! that he'd been waiting there for three days, while we with our cab and our dressed-up doll and her behind, we gave him a swift pain in the ass! it was no use explaining to him...It was a general chorus, a frightful agony! ...They didn't want to let us in! In order to get out we had to get a lantern and show them the blood, the towels, the dressing on her ass, which was dripping all over, that they were real clots!...They moved aside a little, but they were grumbling, rough, ready to bite, we walked past the insults, we came to the ticket window, we immediately asked for Clodo... Luckily!...Dr. Clodovitz! Boro was the Soissons business all over again! We barely escaped getting tossed out.

Later on, over the years, I often passed by there, in front of the London Hospital...It still has pretty much the same walls, the same raspberry and yellow color, the same soot everywhere, the same enormous window cage from Commercial Road to East Port, only the people have changed a lot. The crowd, the mugs, the gait all surprise me, I no longer recognize them...They're not the same noisy squabblers, bullying tramps...still a few bedraggled women...not many youngsters...No longer the same bums...they now discuss things soberly, they've taken on vocabulary...They still gabble away in the fog about their varicose veins and their aches and pains ...but not so peevishly...They've stopped smacking each other in the puss if someone gets ahead of them...they hardly swear any more...the very neighborhood's been changed... I mean just before the war...the one of 1939 until doomsday...

It's the population moving, if you think about it...There're almost no sailing vessels, that's what brought the real savages, they were the unmanageable ones, the real horrors...yellow skins...blacks...chocolates!...hell-raisers!...They often came about their injuries, they had them on all their fingers... one dressing, another...on their feet, too, and their bodies... they'd start a riot over a trifle, at the door of the hospital, they'd bleed at the slighest provocation, rip each other's guts out the way you'd say hello, especially from the Islands and from America! real wild men, from the tropics, from the Sunda Isles, from the equator colonies, and from the North too, have to be fair...At bottom, they were all man-eaters... all that on the "entrants" line. That made a mixture of yelling, terrific gales of laughter...with the cockney housewives and the drunken bullies of the neighborhood, the peg-legs, the whisky cirrhoses, the fistulas, the broken heads, the dyspeptics, the lumbagoes cut in two who squalled about everything, the albuminous, their little bottles, the finical bellyachers, the anti-everythings, the death-dodgers, the people with little pensions, the choking asthmatics, all of them corralled, roped in, pushing one another, squeezed against the door...Often there was entertainment...an interlude...a minstrel...with his clappers, his

93

mouth noises, the whoah-whoah blackface! and a mandolin!...
the popular tunes!...He'd pick up a couple of pennies...he'd
beat it...I did that later on...a button-up tailcoat, all kinds
of colors, a real carapace!...I think performers of that kind
are still around...Whitechapel likes hoofers, they drew a crowd
quickly, but they cluttered up the street, stopped the trolleys,
then the cops would swoop down, everyone would be pushed
against the walls, women, legless cripples, one-armed men,
spitters...It would break up fast!

The days when there was too much fog, when the frost
spread out the crowd, the line wound round La Vaillance...
there was a permanent session in the pub...One man would
keep two others' places...They'd go to warm up a bit around
the liquor...They'd have a sniff of cherry punch...The ones
who still had a penny would treat themselves to a small glass
of beer together, the others pretended to be having something,
it created a constant coming and going between the bar and
the street when the weather was stinging cold...

Naturally there was always a slightly carbolic smell at La
Vaillance...inside the pub...

They're not the same men today, the same clientele, as I've
said, there's decorum...the neighborhood's making progress
...Poverty's going in for furniture...They were already looking for white wood, they'll soon be fixing up cozy-corners, one
fine day they'll be having their nails done...Unless it's all
smashed at the time I'm writing, gone up in smoke beneath
the bombs, the peccadilloes and the whims! Naturally I'm no
longer up-to-date, we're separated by the events, in ten years I
won't recognize the place! The streets, the walls were gloomy
in those days, I mean the buildings. The house-fronts were
coated with soot, the goo trickled...should've seen the way it
came down from the port, the docks, the factories...the
clouds kept bringing in smears, coal tar...gusts, tornadoes of

94

it in winter, and sticky mists, a real affliction. It was sticky inside the hospital, too, and dark, the walls, even the beds, the drab almost yellow linen. The odors stuck in my nose, the urine, the ether, the coal tar, and the honeyed tobacco. I still get a whiff of them. Once you're used to it, it has a charm... Only the operating room was nickel-plated, whitewashed, gleaming, even blinding, coming from outside.

As soon as there was a bit of mist you couldn't see the big hospital, yet it was a building that had bulk and breadth...It melted into the surroundings, you had to go near it, almost touch it...It was painted like fog with some yellow and raspberry added. It's a slimy depressing mess from October on, gets into everything, mixes up everything, your head, things, makes you gently dizzy so you don't know what time it is and that time is passing and night falling...It rises up from the river, sweeps in from the end of the neighborhood, takes in all the landings, docks, people and trams...makes everything hazy and stumpy...

Days when it really streams in you can't see the hospital from La Vaillance, the pub opposite...when it comes steaming out, in enormous torrents...You just catch little gleams ...it blinks a little in the windows...and the big yellow lantern at the door...It's almost blotted out already...It's not a bad thing for your worries...they drift away...it leaves you quiet...I can't help saying that when I die I'd like to be left on the sidewalk as is, just like that, all alone in front of the London...let everyone go away...you wouldn't see anything happening...I think I'd be carried off gently...That's my notion...faith in the gloom...It hasn't any basis, of course ...Ah! good thing I'm aware of it...I'm joking, it's just an impression...brief futility...an idle thought...Boy!

Once her ass was sewn up, Joconde was impossible! there was no holding her!...All the way to the end of the common ward you could hear her roaring out awful curses against Angèle, that snake in the grass, whom she wanted to finish off right away, to go home and pound her to a jelly once and for all. Good thing she couldn't do anything! she lay stiff in bed, wrapped up from her neck to her heels...in bandages, cotton ...wasn't allowed to move...

She stank of iodoform, she sickened the whole ward more with her stink than her screaming! Never a second's silence. The nurses, who weren't prudish, snapped right back at her, hung on till they got the last word...That caused some awful sessions...Always thinking about Angèle, that ghastly hag, she boiled in the sheets..."That fart! that fart!" that's what she called her, brooding away. "Murdering an arteezt!...The jealousy of that bitch!...Zlut!...Oh! woe eez me!"

The suffering patients protested right and left...that they were fed up with the noise...

There were all kinds of patients around...but mostly women of the neighborhood, housewives and maids, some waitresses from the bars, and some Chinese, too...and also two or three Negresses, women under treatment...most of them for the belly...breasts, and also for the skin...running sores, ulcers, chronic cases...Joconde wasn't in for long, but

96

all the same at least twenty-five days like that on her back, that was Clodovitz' opinion, absolutely motionless. He came by at least three or four times a day to examine and check. He came to look at her drain, whether it was running...He was as attentive as could be...Recommended by Cascade, that wasn't to be sneezed at!...Clodovitz wasn't old, yet he already looked rheumatic, sickly, shriveled up, and his joints full of arthritis ...He even made the patients laugh at his aches, he made dry, ropy, creaky noises at will...

"Ah! if you had my knees," he'd answer when they complained. "You'd see something! And my shoulders! And my back! Boy! What would you say then?...And I've got to go running around! I don't lie in bed!"

Rushing through the wards, up and down the five flights, three times a day, he'd ask on the run how things were going. And that nose of his! unbelievable! out of Punch and Judy! it dragged him along! He'd lean forward everywhere, over everything, nearsighted as a dozen moles, his big popping eyes rolling under his glasses. As soon as he'd start spouting, it would all shake rhythmically in time with the words, nervous by nature, his ears would wiggle too, sticking out, wide-open, wings keeping his head up, but gray, like a bat's. He was really pretty homely. He scared certain patients...but a kindly smile, ah! no denying it! a kind of girl's smile, never brusque, never impatient, always ready to be pleasant, to make himself agreeable, to put in the right word, in the teeth of destiny and fatigue!... a word of comfort, a compliment, to the worst wallowing pissy flattened-out bellyacher, all delicacy with the worst down-and-outers! with the most snarling tiresome sluts...rotting and peevish, the dregs of the "chronic" wards, where the others, the "staff" doctors, practically never set foot...there were some pretty queer customers, hard to imagine such perfect wrecks, who nevertheless were pests for months and months...some for years it seems. . .who fell away piecemeal, bit by bit, one day an eye, the nose, a ball, then some spleen, a pinky, it was a kind of battle with the big bite, the horror inside gnawing away, without a gun or saber or cannon, that rips a guy's whole works apart, that drills away at him piece by piece, that comes from nowhere, from no sky, and one fine day he no longer exists, skinned alive, cut up nibbled with ulcers, just like that, with little squeals, red hiccups, groanings and prayers and awful pleading. Ave Maria! Sweet Jesu! Jesus! as the tenderhearted English sob, the elite of sensibility.

And what an assortment, a choice, a whole world, a calamity bazaar, departments for everything, for the stomach, heart, kidneys, bowels, the eight and fifty common wards of the London Freeborn Hospital! Especially during the winter months when there was coughing!. . .terrific coughing! at least ninety-three wards! with catarrhs all over, besides the street accidents which came up in series. . .often ten or fifteen at a time. . .mornings when the fog was too thick. . .

In the wards themselves it was dark from late September on, except for two or three hours in the morning, and then very close to the window, the high guillotines, it came from the river in big dense waves, it penetrated the whole building, it choked the gaslights, the lamps in the corridors. it brought in a smell of coal tar, the coal smoke from the port, and then the echo of the ships, the movements on the docks, the cries. . .

Clovis fortified himself for the checkup with an enormous oil lantern, a "mail coach," when someone called him as he passed, he could hardly see, but heard well, he'd come very close to the bed, he'd light up their faces, it made a white circle all around, the face of the suffering chap stood out in the darkness, he'd lean over against him, he'd speak to him in a hushed voice. . ."Sh! Sh!" he'd say. . ."Sh! old boy! Don't wake any-

one...I'll be right back! I'll give you your little injection!...
Soon be over!...Soon be over!"

The same words to each sufferer...and from one ward to
another...on all floors..."Soon be over!"...It was a kind
of quirk of his.

He did lots of injections in the course of a night, lots and
lots!...among the women and the men...He was so nearsighted that I'd hold his lantern for him up against it...right
against the buttock...so he'd dig the needle straight in...not
sideways or crossways...

After about two weeks when I'd been coming to see Joconde,
we became such pals that I did the injections for him, with
camphor, morphine, ether, the usual things, and he'd hold the
lantern for me. "Soon be over!...Soon be over!"...the refrain.

With my trick paw I got the knack of the injections right
away, a trick paw's automatic, the patient feels nothing...a
puff...

That's how I got a start, a little on the sly like that, at the
London Freeborn Hospital with Dr. Clodovitz, in my profes-
sional career. I learned to say, just like him, immediately,
everywhere, "Soon be over!" It became a kind of habit, a sort
of quirk...All kinds of awful things have happened since the
Freeborn Hospital! here, there, good, bad, horrible, too, you
can be sure of that. You'll judge for yourself. Without any
definite idea...Simply in the course of things...it's fine already!...Soon be over!...

We spaced each other by two minutes. We were on the lookout along the streets...Orchard Street, Weberley Commons,
Perigham Row...First Boro and then René, the little deserter
who had impossible papers, his photo in all the newssheets,
and then Elise, the "crazy peddler" who'd jumped bail, with a
gang of plain-clothes men after her, since for years she'd been
handling harmless little opium pellets all through Maida Vale
and the West End, without getting into trouble, and then she
suddenly went in for hashish without telling anyone, because
of the war. That's what the Yard didn't excuse, variations of
habit!...

It was bound to end in trouble. They were watching us,
unluckily. Even at the hospital with Clodo, where after all I
was very quiet, where I was useful as a kind of nurse lending a
hand when there were too many people, it started smelling
fishy...Joconde had done us harm...She'd been telling things
about her personal worries and her troubles at the Leicester
that were just plain crazy...Since she spoke a bit of English
and the place was lousy with blabbering chambermaids, it took
on real proportions...loafers who hadn't a damned thing to
do but screw things up even more...it became risky and dan-
gerous...They spoke of kicking us out, pure and simple, and
Clodovitz first of all...a foreign doctor, an extra, just good
enough for the night shift...The Management had their eye

100

on him...He was in bad odor but since they didn't pay him much, even for the backbreaking work, awakened ten, fifteen times a night, they weren't at all sure of finding another intern so utterly devoted, neither troublesome nor a drinker, just a little queer in his ways...The management hesitated about giving him his week's notice...Just about hesitated...Fired would have been a catastrophe...He had such queer papers, such suspicious stamps on them that they weren't fit to be shown...Diplomas that were even more weird!...but the way the fellow had got there, happened to be in London, was still the biggest mystery!...Ah! a dead duck if they bounced him...He'd be washed up! For some time they'd been picking up "aliens," as they called them, every day, who were less doubtful than he...

Clodovitz knew all about it...he'd mention it to me occasionally, he didn't think it was funny...

Cascade had promised to come soon to see what was happening...After three or four days, not a sign...Suddenly someone phoned...that he was on his way!...tell him to shake a leg...we had a thing or two to tell him...

The date was for six o'clock at the Dingby Cruise, the old lunchbar in the middle of the docks, a little to the west of the hospital, right on the edge of the river...You could get there by the bank or the maze of alleys all around that led to it from Commercial Road, from between the "Stores," the high warehouses. That was really the prudent way of coming and going...

So there we were...We were waiting for him...The boss of La Vaillance had also come to see us...But he didn't talk much, he was wary, he kept his distance, a scalded cat...

"I want to speak to Cascade!"...He wanted to talk only to Cascade! Stubborn, disagreeable...Cascade hadn't arrived. It was a rush hour, the tables were filling up, the change of shifts, the bunch from the cranes, from the holds, naturally they made a lot of noise, mainly because of their brogans, the place was all made of wood, all crosspieces and daub, it resounded. The slot machine and the dice added to the din. . .in short, a general racket all around. . .

Ah! chug! chug! there's a car! It's Monsieur, after all!. . .

"Hello, men!". . .he calls out.

"Hello Monsyoor!". . .they answer.

It wasn't any too soon.

"How's it going, Brainstorm?"

He's talking to me.

"Does it still hurt?"

He points to my head.

"Still does! Still does! Monsieur Cascade!"

It bothers him that I'm having trouble with my head, he talks to me about it every time.

Anyway, Clodo starts explaining to him, that we've made him come, etc. . . .etc. . . .to tell him about Joconde!. . .that she's not behaving herself at the hospital. . .that she's shooting her mouth off. . .

"And how's her ass coming along?"

"That part's all right!"

"When the ass is all right, everything's all right!". . .he answers.

That's the only effect it has on him. . .

"And what about Angèle?" we ask.

"She went up to Edinburgh! She's on business, boys! Placing Biglot's two girls!"

"Biglot's?"

"Yes! Biglot's! That's right!"

We can't get over it. . .

"A man who'll be forty soon! He's beating it, too! The sap! yeah! yeah! He's off for the infantry, Ladies and Gentlemen,

102

the infantry! Yessiree! Ah! I don't want to think about it any more! But what about Joconde? Some class, huh? I didn't lie to you, did I? Estocadero! And Pfft! What a spurt! Youd've thought she was a quarterback! Whtt! What zip! Lightning! Eh?...Lightning!"

"Don't you want to go and see her?" we suggested gently.

"Ah! Hell no! She can croak!"

That's how he answered...He'd had enough! Fed up!... He didn't want to get mixed up in that again!

A bit selfish!

"Listen, boys, I know what I'm going to do!"

He was off again on his pet subject.

"I'm going to buy me a trombone! I'm going to get into the parade, too! I'll drop in to see you around noon!...You'll see me, pals! You'll see me! I'll play my music all by myself! For those who don't want to leave! I'll be the anti-recruiting guy! Get that! I'm going to start a society! The 'I-ain't-having-any-Boys'! If this continues, guys, I'm going to learn English!... I want to find out what they're batting about, the hokum they're filling 'em with! since it's driving 'em all crazy!...it must be terrific! I'd like to listen to their line! Men are just plain morons, eh?...I know 'em all right!"

Ah! he sat there gaga!

It was really pretty amazing!

Over his glass, deep in thought...thick stout...

Prospero Jim, the boss of the Dingby, comes up, he talks ...he sees things Cascade's way...the crime of the news-papers!...always the papers!...He never reads them either! ...and the movies!...

"Say, did you see the newsreels? Trenches in one place! Boches in another! Look at my helmet! Oh boy, am I brave! Am I dead! It's a joke! Me telling you! Mmph! Bah! For their mugs! Bull-shit!"

It made them both mad just to think about that crap!
They were getting upset just talking about it!

"I love you! I love you!" Cascade said, in imitation!...
"You're right! They're infants!...yokels spoiled by good
cream! stuffed with butter! Too much yum-yum!"

I listened to them jabber...It still wasn't any of my business...I could have stuck my word in! I was keeping my
mouth shut!...When it comes to experience, every man for
himself! I'd been to school! I had a bellyful of dearly acquired
knowledge!...and especially in my ear! A tiny bit of hardware left! but it added up in whistling!...so that I couldn't
sleep!...and enough migraines to make me bark, the way
they tore at me like pincers, revulsed my eyes by force...so
that I'd squint for hours...In short, real terrors...Ah! no! I
had mine!...I thought of my father and mother peaceful in
their shop, in the Passage du Vérododat, having a good time
being pitied by all the neighbors because their son had been
so badly wounded, whimpering...I thought of all I'd seen
from one hospital to the other...Dunkerque...Le Val...
Villemomble...Drancy...and also me, myself...How they
get the injured on the operating table...whisk 'em up again!
...perk 'em up again! They stitch up the main business and
off you go!...Hop to it, Humpty-Dumpty! Three cheers!...
You'll be in the next whirl!...In the nick of time, straight as
a bullet! On the spot for the big offensive! You can have the
joys of the Charred Woods! You won't be cold this winter, my
merry hero!...There'll be sport around there!...I guarantee
it!...Not a minute wasted!...Try to be quick soldier-boys!
...You won't look much at the pieces! It's not a nice thing
for a man to do!...

I was thinking about all that...I didn't say anything! Cascade was still talking. He was glad someone was listening to
him...He was producing his effect.

104

"The sergeant, the one with the ribbons, comes up to me! He stops me, he hands me a line! Boy, what a sour grouch!"

The thing that happened to him.

"Me! I'm telling you, boys!...Can you imagine that! What did he take me for? He wanted me to follow his parade! to go with him to the Recruiting Station! Just get that!...'French!' I said to him...'French are you?' he'd pulled a boner! What a face he made! Nose to nose! Started sucking his stick! Did he look dumb! Boy, everyone was splitting! You should've seen the crowd! Smack! A sock! Shot right in! Ah! angry! 'French rascal! rascal!' he calls me. The crowd's against me... I wasn't sticking around! Just think! A thousand against one! ...Good-by!...Off like a shot! I wish you'd seen the Recruiting Sergeant's mug! What a slick getup on the guy! Boy, some swanky tunic! What a nifty can to go to war with! The Jerries'll have a good laugh! Boy, you see everything! Twirling his stick and woo-woo!"

Cascade was having a great time!...So were the customers all around him...What a brilliant talker!...and even the boss of La Vaillance was forgetting his troubles...

"That's a sergeant for you! you realize? All right, I'll shut up, Prosper! I'm driving myself crazy! Just thinking about it! ...Hand me the poison! Their bedbug juice!"

He poured himself a big whisky-fizz...He treated everybody, generous, absolutely...

"It's for everyone! You hear me? I didn't come for nothing! They talk to me about sickness! About God knows what!... about croaking! God damn it! I want to laugh! That reminds me of Little-Mouth Jeanne!...I picked her up, you know, in Santos!...I took her for a ride! I put on a real show! I was out with her all afternoon in a high-class landau! I wanted her to enjoy herself, have a good time...What heat, pals! like that!...A plaster furnace, boys!...I wanted to go one better

105

...I made the driver stop at a bar, the finest saloon in the town! It was called L'Origone, a swell club! I wanted to put the finishing touches on!...Along came a *torero*, with his guitar, you know! Whango! He cops my gal! Just like that! Bango! Just time enough to look at her! He sized her up! She fell all over him! That's what it cost me to be a sucker! He just blotted me out! He took her off on his arm! I blew up! Boy, I'm telling you! I jumped on the grease-ball! I smothered him! ...I broke two of his molars for him! He runs to the cops! ...My first breadwinner!...Santos is all railings! The prison's right in the open air! Both of them came to see me! On Sundays, just to get a laugh! to make a damned fool of me! arm in arm!...You get what lousy punks they were?...Me on the other side of the bars!...I put in six months! Ah! youth! ...I was twenty, that explains everything! That cured me of taking rides, I'm telling you!...The only thing to do is break their ribs...You're nice? You get it in the neck!...Down the drain!...I love you!...I didn't want to show my strength! She was the boss! She sent me back to the kitchen! Get that, my boy!...You with the fruit salad! You toy-soldier! You listening? You don't know everything! You don't read that kind of thing in the papers!"

Prospero was in full agreement.

The customers around, those with tattoos, the men from the pier, the fellows with big arms, they nodded, they didn't understand a thing...Prospero translated some of these practical remarks into English...It made them guffaw with liquor... Their glasses, their lips, their mustaches were full of it...They were clinking and cackling...shaking all the glassware with noisy jokes to the health of their crony, so generous, such a philosopher!...They were so dazed with the malt gin and the stout and the thick clouds of tobacco and the cut-plug besides and the fatigue of loading that it was a waste of effort explaining to them what it was all about...They didn't understand anything...But they wanted, after all, to toast the gay dog who did things so handsomely! who treated the whole crowd ...who gave you a shot in the arm with a one-two-three and whisky-fizz! and "sailor's vitriol" which was one of Prospero's secrets that turned your mouth inside out as soon as you were hit by the first drop that would have melted all the fogs from Barbeley Docks to Greenwich just breathing at them, with that horrible breath! across thirty-six Thameses. But you had to hold on to the bar! It knocked you clean off your feet.

"For he's a jolly good fellow"...the whole crowd took up the famous chorus, sent it booming against the windowpanes! the menagerie was roaring! The smoke was getting so thick you could have cut it with a knife...made everyone teary, close his eyes, stinging and blinking, red, burning with sooty pepper...and lots of other smokes besides, more pungent ones, filtering in from all over the river, sulphur, coal, saltpeter, getting everything sticky, blotting everything out, even the gas, the lamps, giving you queer looks, funny faces, molasses heads, pasty-looking through the blur. The pubful of bellowers all dim-looking...the whole mob of howling phantoms...

For he's a jolly good fellow!...

It was starting again...the whole bacchanal...and then a big pull for the war, the popular refrain, the song of the day that was all the rage at the Empire...

Hide your trouble! Hide your bag!
And sing! sing! sing!...

Even Cascade barked out *"Sing! Sing! Sing!"* to beat the band! At just that moment along came Boro who'd been in the back, playing cards. He came up to us.

"Where are you coming from, Fatso, eh?" Cascade shoots at him.

"I'm coming from bed, boss! Here's to your health! At your

service! I'm not coming from jail like a lot of other guys," he adds...discreet allusion.

"But you've been there, let's be honest, Monsieur Boro!"

"And no less than fourteen times for my honor! Monsieur Cascade!...Forrr my ideas!...I'd like you to know! And I'm prrroud of it! I expect to again if necessary!"

A terrible accent and thundering rrr!

"Go on! Go on! Don't boast!"

"Never do, Monsieur Cascade! I never do! You hear me! for peempping!"

Telling him off!

"No one's asking for your opinions, Monsieur Borokrrrom! Since you're so distinguished, it's your papers we'd like to see!"

"Why here they are, Monsieur Cascade!"

He rummages around deep down in his pockets, he digs out a whole litter, booklets, wallets, bits of passports, all patched up, full of grease-spots...

Cascade examines them, returns them.

"Oh! Oh! you're not difficult, my fine bandit! All that record's yours? Pretty bad, Boro! Pretty bad!...And what about yours, Monsieur Jinx?"

He's talking to me.

"Let me have a look at your sweet little papers! May I?"

I take mine out...He unfolds them, hands them back to me ...He frowns...

"But you're not in velvet either, Monsieur Jinx! They came looking for you, too!...All right...Let me explain!...They want you at the Consulate!...Sure! Sure!...You can see why!"

"Have you seen the posters?...You who read all the *Mirrors*...That's all they're talking about at Berlemont's...All men in the class of 1912...They're all being called back!... rejected or not!...And what about you, my dear Clodovitz? Dear doctor! dear scientist!"

He spots him.

"Let me have a look at your rags!...Ah! I've already seen them, of course! Ah! but so long ago that's all!...I miss them! I miss them!...They were so funny two years ago!...Do you still have them with you? Fine! You're hatching them, so to speak!...They've made little ones! Clodovitz!"

Clodovitz dives down, his linings were full of them, some a bit genuine...some all fake!...Erasures everywhere...his passports were a scream! flim-flams! jokes! He himself admitted it!

"They're too scratched up, that's all!"

He explained the reason...

"Well, fatheads! You're getting along all right! You're going to be taught another tune! Artists! that's a fact! But as for the fake papers!...Ah! Mother of God! my ass could do better!...Some people think that's going some! Proof? Clients! amateurs and serious ones!...Take Matthew, he wants you! There's the amateur! He's been asking for you everywhere!...He's all worked up about your fake papers! He came back to see me day before yesterday!...on purpose!... just for that! I welcomed him in! 'Inspector!' I said to him just like that...I'm not shy...'You look preoccupied!' I took the liberty of saying...I know he's as phony as a rat...and when he comes in good humor it's even worse!...It's a trap! ...I go straight to the point...I take out the Calva...He sips it...he sits down...That's all!...Still not a word...I want him to warm up!...I take out the cognac...and then the big glasses!...It's coming along!...I see his head!...He says 'Myum! Myum!' He sucks his tongue!...Hell, I'm in a hurry!...I look as if I'm trying to find the corkscrew!...the little one in my pocket...I rummage around!...I search in my pockets!...all just an act!...I take out a handful of pound notes...bang! like that! on the table!...I get up... I start going...'I'm going to take a leak!' I say...I come back...they're not there!...The conversation gets easier right away!...It loosens up!...There's confidence...A lot more ease!...Ah! I'd done the right thing! He had a thing or two to tell me!...I might have thought he wanted to bluff me!... But he shows me his warrants...It was a serious matter...It concerns you, and in detail!...Better get a load of what I say! ...You, Jinx, he wants to see you again...The Consulate's asking for your certificate...right away!...and fast!...it's getting hot!...And you, Clodo, it's the Home Service, they're fed up with your mug...And that makes two!...you've got to go back to Folkestone!...to the Polack quarantine!... that's where you belong and not elsewhere!...And you, Monsieur du Boro, who are so delicate! It's the 'Scots' who want you...and the Yard besides and right away!...They're disgusted the way you act up!...That's the way they talk! You've got to get your junk and beat it within five days!...They don't want to see you again!...If not, you'll get it in the balls... and overalls with a number on them!...maybe a touch of the cat too!...That's the news!"

I hoped that Cascade was stringing us along, that he was handing us a line like that just to throw a scare into us...just to give us an idea of his connections, all the same it wasn't just talk!...There must have been some danger...no doubt the cops were nervous, and greedy and shrewd...Ah! but we mustn't let ourselves be taken in!...Both of us started getting excited too!...We squawked about violating our rights!... unheard-of injustice!...that you could see the streets of London full of worse-looking bums than us...much more suspicious and dirty! hoodlums!...terrors!...out and out apaches! ...that there was no name for such downright unjust dishonesty!

And then we had to stomach the fact that probably he was the one who was squealing to the cops...that he was getting

rid of us treacherously!...We weren't feeling so hilarious!...
It's true that he looked pleased, as if he were wiping his hands
of us!...Ah! it was fishy!

"You're jealous, that's all! Admit it!"

That's what we said...and then his whole pack of nonsense!
that he seemed to be getting a kick out of the jam we were in!
That he seemed to be damned cynical! That he didn't have
much honor!

Oh! my, oh my! the way he shot back!

"Me! you fags! me listen to that?"

He was choking.

"They'd have been whipped to death! Croaked in jail! sausage meat! if I hadn't greased Matthew only yesterday! They
keep ruining me!...And I keep saving their lives!...They're
meat for the police and in cahoots! That's the way they treat
me!"

More indignation, he takes out a package of pounds, sterling
and tens...only big bills, a whole fortune! He crumples them
in his fist...wipes the whole table with them! on purpose in
disgust!...just to show us! He sponges up everything! the
liquor spots!

"There! you rats!...Is that what you want?"

He throws them at us like a dishmop...like a red rag...

"Are you satisfied?"

He's humiliating us.

"No, Cascade...No!...Look...Just think about it!"

"It's all thought about, God damn it! Your papers are toilet-
paper! They're recruiting you, they're locking you up! It's only
natural! It's all thought out! And they damned well mean it!
...There's a war on!...Ought to hear the way they talk!...
I'm not the only one, you know, who gets 'em sore...Every-
thing's getting their goat!...Even dough!...You can shove
it down their throats! just like that!...They're back again.

111

They show their teeth again!...It's crazy, there're no more limits!...'There's a war on!' all they can blurt out!...The war!...A fat lot of good it does you! Just a lot of crap! Cop or not!...Pimp or jerk!...God-damned crazyness! Those who can stay out of it don't stay out! You get rough with them? they're not satisfied! They don't know what they want!...Shit! ...No more good manners! Lousiness by the yard!"

Ah! all the same he was just kidding!...You could see he was teasing...that he was stringing us along...A bogeyman! A natural-born rascal!

In spite of everything, I wasn't sure...I only had a half hard-on!...Boro was grinning green around the gills...Clodo couldn't find his eyes the way he was goggling behind his glasses! he was so jittery that his glass kept jumping out of his hands!...all because of the terror of being kicked out of London! Damn it all! It wasn't a dream!...We all had good reasons for staying in London! serious and personal ones!... It made Boro stammer!

"You?...You?...think so, Cascade?"

"I don't think so...It's as if I were there!"

It was a horrible kind of joke...

Around us the customers weren't a bit worried...They were taking advantage of the windfall, they were having a free drink! Cascade was treating!...They didn't understand the reasons, why we were getting so excited!...Why we were so worked up about the posters! about cops' gossip!...why we were on pins and needles!...You couldn't explain it to them ...we kept repeating that there was a war on. The war, that didn't bother them! They'd never have signed up...They were only good for the docks! The rest of it was none of their business...

Load...unload!...that was all! Period! and that's that!...

Dockers! Dockers! That was all!...Commercial or war goods ...No other job! That was what their destiny was like!... They wouldn't have changed it for anything in the world!... They seemed like vagrants, pigs, drunks, pitiful, dazed, in rags, yet we were the real bums after all! The real outcasts of circumstance! Suckers and cannon fodder! Nobody was asking the English guys for anything...The army? out of the question!...All they had to do was continue sordid and comfortable, lugging their load! and that was all! Gentlemen, to the hold! No one asked them for anything. Us, that was a horse of a different color! We were on the "French-frog" lists marked riff-raff everywhere! Men of original sin! born for battle! numbered clowns the whole carcass! Donkeys, scrap iron! Pretty bad! Bad I say!...A fellow's only five liters of blood! ...You realize that much too late!...You don't get the difference at first glance! The earth's just a roulette wheel!... good...bad numbers!...Everything's out of joint!...those born cooked!...those born lucky! At first it's all the same!... All the lice in the same bunch! but go fuck yourself! And not at all!...Day and night!...In the worst classes of poverty a world's spinning round! The best and the worst!...It's like mountains seen from the clouds, from way up, from an airplane, it's all sinister, dark and evil, but from close up, below, ring-a-ring-o'-roses! It's all full of charming spots, of rich shade, of pretty chalets!...Got to go through it to know... you don't learn that in school.

That makes the lucky numbers nice and optimistic!...Let the others rush to the slaughter!...The guys in clover sing well together in chorus!...It's music to your ears especially when there's lots of trimmings!...jaunty pals like Cascade!...

Another round!...And another!...The Maharajah on a spree!...The whole pack of banknotes on the table!...He didn't want them any more!...Let 'em go!...All down the hatch!...They were cheering him to the rafters! *For he's a jolly good fellow!*

They were roaring out in chorus, so loud that it resounded all through the joint, it made the walls shake!...The gas chandelier was rocking, waltzing over our heads...The whole works was swaying, the whole room, the whole pier...Prospero started the refrain again...I think he was yelling loudest of all! *For he's a jolly good fellow!*

Waang! the door booming! A package comes in from the street!...In a heap! Waang! in the middle of the pub! She threw herself in!...She didn't see...There were three steps! ...She trips!...Tumbles! sprawls! It's Joconde! in a package! ...in her cotton...her bandages!...she gets up, she screams, she's awful!...starts blaming right away!...there it goes... she hoists herself up, clings to the bar!...A fury! She's choking with effort...she's suffocating...she ran through the whole neighborhood...looking for us! she's green beneath the chandelier...a panic!...She looks all around! She shrieks ...Isn't he there?

"Where are you, Loulou? Where are you? my precious peegy!"

"Here m'love! Here you pain in the ass!"

Cascade answers her right off.

"Come on, catastrophe! Come on!"

What an effect!...The tables! Boy how the guys howled! Some family scene! Right in the nick of time!...He's sure sore!...Ah! it's the doctor who's going to get it!...

"Look at that!...Just take a look at that!...Dr. Clodovitz! I entrust an injured person to you! I put her into your hands! ...Thinking she's going to keep quiet!...I pay for the hospital! I pay for everything! I load you with dough, my fine doctor! And that's the thanks I get! Say, tell me something!...

114

They can leave your place whenever they like! They go out for a stroll, they run around, they raise hell! What do I look like? I'm asking you! Your joint's a plain cathouse! Your London Hospital! Monsieur Clodovitz!...It's worse than the Charing from what I can see! It's a regular circus! Like your papers, Doctor! just plain garbage! Incapable of watching your lunatics! The bed-wetter! Take a look at the bitch!"

She was standing there doing nothing. She was pulling at her dressings, she was chucking them all around, all over the floor, cotton, bandages, shreds...Boy, what laughing in the joint!...some ovation! Clodovitz didn't know what was what! ...he was circling around the trollop...He wanted to arrange her bandages! she didn't want him to! she was defending herself!....They were each pulling at an end!....The whole crowd was roaring so that the floors shook! the walls! the windows!

"Go back Joconde!"...Clodo was pleading, begging on his knees..."Go back! It's not a wise thing to do! Your wound'll open again!"

Her whole bandage in clots, she was tearing it off! Loosening it from her skin! the blood was pissing out again...it was dripping all over the floor!...ah! she wouldn't obey!...

"Keep quiet you bum! You murderer!"

She was the one raising the riot...all foulmouthed...

Then they started yelling, in the pub. The dockers didn't know what it was all about...their minds were fuzzy...they thought we were being mean to the gal!...They suddenly got sore at us...A sudden tempest, just like that...Taking her side, the poor little thing! Now they were rooting for her! ...At least a dozen giants who wanted to rip Cascade's guts out!...Then and there!...Terrible arms! There'd be hell to pay!...tattoos...muscles like a gorilla's...

Ah! when she sees danger threatening...that they're going to jump on her darling, she's the one who protects him!...

with her whole body! She rushes up in front of him!...she covers him up!...She rages at the peril! the lioness roars!... All her dressings unwind...she gets caught in them, she's all tangled up...she yells louder than the whole mob..."Grrr! Grrr!"

"Darling prrrreciouz! Make a little zmile for your baby!"

But the big guys are boiling!...Got to beat up Cascade! Now in a raging fury!...There they go grabbing bottles, siphons, chairs! and whang! it starts ringing! squirting! bouncing all over! Bang! A-bing! A-boom! over the mirrors!...the door!...An awful riot!...Cascade wiggles out!...jumps back!...the battle's at its height!...tables upside-down!... Barricades and zoom!...they dive for shelter! He and Prospero!...The cash register, the cupboard, the coat-rack...And zoom! everything goes flying!...whirling!...Down comes a bombardment of chairs!...crashes, rocks!...The dockers, all red, come tearing down! they buck into the pile...Assault! Massacre! Yelling on all sides!...Zoom! Zing! Boom! It's the mechanical organ, the big one in the back, suddenly starting to play!...It started going! Taraza! Zoom! the monster with the trumpets! flutes! drums! Should have heard it pounding! whacking out its waltz! Boro who started the machine going! God-damned instrument! It's a storm! I see him fiddling around in the back...He sees me!...He signals to me..."Get the hell out!"...broad gesture! I don't get him, like a dope! He's yelling to me! He's screaming!...

"What's the matter?" I mumble...

No time! Wrraang!...thunder! The joint's exploding! Boy that was something! and the flames!...Damn it! I saw! Damn it! It's him!...In the flames there...In the leaping fire! He threw the gadget! Sure was something!...TNT!... It burst!...there under the table!...Wang! Bang!...Another one! Right there!...He threw the contraption!...A grenade, I know them! Ah! the skunk!...the gorilla!...A spray of sparks!...A hail!...The blockhead!...He's pulling us!...Oh! panic! The way they're beating it!...Three guys laid out flat! I jump over them! The ceiling's collapsing!... Everything's caving in behind us...falling to pieces!...the plasterwork!...the tiles!...An avalanche!...Cascade's safe! ...He's running ahead!...So's Prospero and Joconde! It's curtains!...She's running behind!...she's chugging away, she's yowling...She wants them to wait for her!...it's hurting her!...And what insults! She's calling us cowards! Boro's on his way, too!...any old thing!...not at all shy!...He's running after us! His paunch doesn't keep him from running! ...All shaken up, he's chugging along! and pretty pleased!... No shame!...He's laughing! His hands are bleeding! He stumbles! he picks himself up! The hell with the old gal behind him who's running after us...her with her gimpy leg!...wah! wah!...She's squealing that we're killing her! ...But she's tearing along, anyway!...We don't go back through the same alleys...We dash through Lambeth Highway...and slow up at Grave Lane...Ruysdale...then zigzags ...we're covering our tracks!...threading our way...Cascade's in the lead!...The Doll hooks on to Boro...She's holding him by the sleeve...Cascade won't bother with her! ...Doesn't ever want to see her again!...

Every time she get to a sidewalk she howls!...it hurts her wound...she jumps up screaming!...Good thing the streets are all empty!...The whole gang's racing along!...It'd be a fine sight in broad daylight!...Prospero galloping too...I can't see his mug!...I hear him snuffling...He's in front of me. Nothing the matter with him!...His joint had been pretty flimsy! Shit! A flame!...Wood! mud! Jerry-built! That's the truth...All the same, Boro's cracked...He's running with Joconde...He's dragging her along...she's yelling at him!

. . ."Not so fast! My God! Not so fast!". . .Another spurt!. . .
Moorgate Street! from end to end! Ass on fire, that's the word
for it!. . .

Right after the Square come the docks. . .I think we've lost
Clodovitz. . .I yell after him. . .while running. . .no answer
. . .His hospital's there. . .right near. . .Aren't we going to
leave the old gal there?. . .We pass right by it. . .I ask. . .I
call out on the run! We're tearing along! We keep going!. . .
. . .One! two!. . .One!. . .two!. . .obliquely left!. . .Maryle-
bone. . .straight ahead!. . .then Mint Place. . .So's we're going
to Tackett's?. . .I didn't know. . .No one had said!. . .Here
we are!. . .Stop!

And zip! We dash through the door! We all come tearing
in!. . .The whole cavalcade!. . .Ah! surprise! He was in the
midst of tidying up! Poof!. . .All his junk! ropes! scrap iron!
his shed full of gewgaws! He throws himself against the door,
he closes it. He's pretty choked up!. . ."Where are you all
coming from?" he asks. . .No one answers. . .Everyone's snorting, gasping. . .wheezing. . .the whole mob's sneezing wet!
collapses on the heap! Boy! some fun!

Cascade's the first to start talking. . .got his wind back. . .
He points to Boro. . .

"Tackett, you want to see a murderer?"

And then he tells exactly what happened. . .he saw the grenade, too!. . .

"You don't have another in your pants?"

Then we all rush for Boro! Ah! the big half-wit!. . .the
louse!. . .the drunk. . .everyone jumps on his paunch!. . .
rummages through him, searches him all over!. . .maybe he's
still got another one?

"You big butcher! You big lunatic!"

They bawl him out something awful!

He takes it well...That doesn't worry him!...He's laughing!...he giggles because they're tickling him!

"Do you have another one?"

They rough-and-tumble him again, they're really after him ...Tackett wants to kick him out...He's worried about his premises!...his goods!...his wood!...Prospero was so down in the dumps he didn't say a single word. He must have been worrying about his pub, his customers, mainly about his lease ...He was always talking about his lease...78 years more to run!...He was proud of it!...Shit, Matthew was right! ...Boro was just a dirty grease-ball! a wild sneaky firebug!... Ah! You could see that right off! I'd never have believed it!... And the way he sent it flying! No doubt about it. I'm telling you!...A wrecker!...and insolent besides!...not bothered a bit!...Now he was thirsty again!...He wanted everyone to have a drink! "Always a thirst on!" he announces! Someone open a bottle for him! not in an hour! then and there! it was bad enough waiting around with his hand injured!

It's true he was still bleeding, so was Joconde...The two of them were comparing...It was a real ambulance...I didn't feel thirsty, but somewhat cold...

Joconde, now that she was back in the bosom of her family, was getting snotty again...They did up her bandages, patched up the whole works, her towels, her cotton...Everything was hanging between her legs...They laid her down on some bags ...Cascade stretched out beside her...so she'd stay a bit quiet ...so she'd finally shut her mouth...

There's Clodovitz coming...He knocks...He bangs at the door...He barks out his name...How did he find us?...that rheumy-eyed chicken! He comes in...He blinks...He starts talking...Doesn't know what he's saying...He thinks it didn't explode!...He's jabbering away!...He doesn't remember a thing! He's had a shock, he got knocked on the head, some skin's been torn away...he's bleeding pretty bad, too... and from his mouth also. Got to heat up some coffee for him ...He's going to be sick...He'd been running at full speed ...That gives him palpitations...We take advantage of bringing him around to get ourselves a grog too, two salad bowls! ...Tackett hasn't finished!...His guests are greedy!...We all huddle together...We roll in the bags! the piles!... There's not a bed in the house...Sheds and that's all...

Boro's beginning to feel better, he decides he's going to leave...He announces:

"I'm leeeaving!...I'm leeeaving!"

It must be around two o'clock...

"Get the hell out!...We've seen enough of you!"

That's everyone's opinion.

Prospero hasn't let out a peep...He's sitting on the bags ...he hasn't even lain down...Just there with his head in his hands...

"You get the hell out too! You hear me?"

That was Cascade who went and shook him, he didn't want him staying around...Still he hadn't said anything! hadn't opened his mouth! not a word out of him...

"Go on! get going!"

Brutal!

I think he suspected that Prospero and Boro were going to fight it out at night, to settle about the grenade, that they were just waiting for us to sleep!

"Go murder yourselves!"

He kicked them out just like that!...There was no comeback...Tackett was with him...Tackett was some brute! he used a crowbar for his arguments...His favorite weapon... He'd let you have it in the legs.

So Prospero got thrown out and Boro with him.

120

The shed was ours now!...We'd be able to sleep...Boro had a place to sleep! I wasn't worrying about him! I wasn't anxious. He'd go to his pal, The Horror...he always went there...It was opposite, on the other side...after Cubitt Docks...

But now they were yelling from the street..."You cocksuckers!" they were calling us...it rang out in the darkness... "Peegs!...Peegs!"...When the other one joined him he started cursing us too..."Cocksawkers!...Cocksawkers!... They were both swearing at us.

We heard them far off...We heard their steps...For a long time...till the end. We fell asleep.

The moment the shadows come up, when soon we'll have to be going, we remember something of the frivolities of the stay...Jokes, courteous chats, witty banter, kindly acts...and all that no longer is, after so many trials and horrors, seems but heavy and freakish funeral trumpery...Drapings with leaden folds, wasted effort! the huge mantle of the rigors, arias, sermons, mournful virtues, the dead all crushed...spruced up under pinewood, in empty crypt. Ah! how dazzling it would be if, at that very moment, as we were being nailed up, there should escape, gush from the coffin, the miraculous trill of a flute! so brisk, delightfully gay! What a surprise! what pride! Sighs in the dwelling place of the dead! Ah, what a lesson for families!...Joyous crony of a corpse, phantom larker! Minstrel for all precipices, enchanted places, accursed paths! The first Mr. Kick-the-Bucket not having lived in vain, having finally surprised, understood, all the graces of springtime! the renewal of the fledgling! of the finch in the coppice, bearing everything off! Revolutionary of the Shades! Troubadour in the Sepulchers! Buffoon yodeling in the Caverns of the World!...I'd like to be that fellow! What an ambition! My only one! By Gosh! Blast it! A thousand graces the shrewd fellow!...Better the Eternal's rigadoon than the human calamitous Empire, the mammoth scheming molehill...A heap of crumbling mirages! ...Hail to the monarchs! Liven up the subjects! make them

122

jig all in time! What a scramble!...Crazy to give yourself to
the Ephemeral!...A thousand times better to perish nicely
carrying off the flute!...But still you need the moment of
high ecstasy! Not all who want to can go off to music! The
chosen moment!...You have to last while waiting...That's
what I always say! Pros and cons! Jump here!...Bounce
there!...get hold of the daily bread...A flea's life!...They
spy on you!...What torture!...I gave you a violent picture
of the kind at Tackett's...Running off with the flute is another
matter! You'll see. No time for a jerk-off!...

Since the blowup at the Dingby what a scramble! What ex-
ercise! From waiting-rooms to shady hotels, from basements to
attics, from rats to rats, what drops! what climbs! from Salvation Army joints to tuppenny landladies at night, what a runaround! Cascade had scared me stiff with his stories about the
Consulate's being after me...My nerves weren't too steady any
more...I went off my nut easily...I'd dash from one neighborhood to another...Never twice in the same room because
of the suspicious questions...I was being sensible...I hadn't
seen any of the others!...followed to a T the careful advice
...I avoided Leicester and Bedford, the beat, the sidewalks
with the women, where I might have learned something...Still
I was on pins and needles!...And there was a good reason!...
Not a line in the papers. Cascade must have forked over!...
We weren't to see one another until he got in touch with me!
...I'd kept my word...The critical stage had passed!...the
cops were sniffing elsewhere...after other riffraff...Only I
was getting low in cash!...Before the blowup I'd borrowed
about ten pounds from Cascade. I hadn't been extravagant,
all the same the end was in sight...I couldn't sleep on the
bare ground, it gave me howling cramps on account of my
arm!...I was forced to take a bed...That's always expensive
...even in the most modest places. I spent my time at the

123

movies...I still remember the programs...They were mostly Pearl White in *The Mysteries of New York*...In spite of the hours I spent there, I still had a lot of time on my hands... I'd take the little streets in Soho, the bustling busy ones... where the people kept going...where it's a perpetual little fair...they swarm around the shops from Shaftesbury to Wigmore Street, the windows full, in the doorways, all teeming with crowds, it covers you up, reassures you, at the same time it's lively, it distracts you...still and all after ten or twelve days like that, of coming and going in the streets, it began to be enough. I'd had my bellyful of penance! After all, hell! I hadn't done anything!...I didn't quite dare look up Cascade but I wanted to see Boro again!...One Sunday morning I made up my mind...I said to myself, "My boy, let's go!" I was around Barbeley Dock, the Ferry was waiting, the little boat was inviting, it took ten minutes along the river...As soon as I see water, I'm tempted...Ready to go at the drop of a hat!...I'd sail around the pond in the Tuileries at the slightest pretext! in a watchglass if I were a tiny little fly...Anything just to sail! I walk across bridges for no reason at all... I wish all roads were rivers...It's the spell...the bewitchment ...it's the movement of the water...Just so, without wanting to, an idea in my head, right at the lapping of the Thames... I stood there having visions...The charm was too much for me, especially with the big ships...everything gliding around... twisting in and out, foaming...the dinghies...the south landing of the docks...cutters and brigantines tacking...coming in...drifting...skimming the bank...Floating lazily!...It's magical!...no denying it!...A ballet!...It's hallucinating! ...It's hard to drag yourself away!...You got into the swing of things a bit with the little ferry, the *Dolphin*...two little trips...from shore to shore...I've done it five or six times! like a holiday!...round trip!...Barbeley-Greenwich...almost touching the big cargoes...the colossal potbellies going upstream, the propellers buzzing away like mad...drifting in the eddies...roaring, grunting in alarm...scared of the landings...What beauty!...gulls flying! glide to heaven! enough dreaming! down to earth, boy! Not a penny left in my pocket! Get going! Greenwich...it's sad! Let's go now! enough dawdling! mooning!...I've got to find that son-of-a-bitch! It was understood, definite! at The Horror's place.

He'd told me...Greenwich Alley...Greenwich Park... Van Claben Junior, his real moniker...he'd explained it carefully...not far from the south wharf...What would they say when they saw me?...They'd surely spot me from outside ...Maybe they wouldn't open the door?...Ah! my mind was made up! But no undue confidence! I was going and that was all...

I look around a bit...to see if I don't smell cops...The name of the place?...."Titus Van Claben"...If there're any suspicious characters around...It's all quiet...all reassuring ...Three or four people on the steps just chatting...probably clients...they were waiting their turn...In the park kids running around, dashing all over, racing through the lanes... In short, everything pretty normal...Besides the weather's fine ...bright sun, almost warm...That's rare in London in early May...From the open windows on the first floor I hear Boro pounding it out...same as usual...that's fine...It's his touch all right, his music, I don't think I'm wrong...He's there, the tramp!...I say to myself, "I'm in luck!...He's at the piano ...he might have been in jail!"...I was beginning to get dopey walking from one neighborhood to another...day and night! A nasty kind of fatigue!...Still, not completely shot! ...but almost...well, just about pooped...and besides, a pain in my arm from sleeping any old place...from snoring on bumpy beds!...and besides, buzzings in my ears so shrill and painful they'd make me close my eyes...A cripple's life is lousy...and it's bad to be broke...it gives you nasty, vicious ideas...But anything was better than the army! What if they ever made me go back? It was God-damned possible according to that windbag!...What if they were looking for me at the Consulate?...Suppose they were scraping the bottom of the

126

barrel...It was a chance I was taking, all the same, still and all...It was that much to the good as a matter of fact...One chance in a thousand being there in London...I'll tell you how...Downright luck!...A real treat!...A reversal of fate! ...What a break!...And Cascade, no denying it, what a windfall!...All of it through Raoul...There was a poor guy for you! What tough luck!...I'll tell about that, too!...Mustn't sulk about destiny!...I was lucky, and how!...All the others like me were cooked! They were digging their foxholes in the Artois...or elsewhere!...in the 16th Heavy!...in the armored division...Some of them had switched...to the hungry infantry...splattered, piled up in the lime...shelled ten, twelve hours at a time! Here's to their health! It was better here! Got to realize!...Roses! Even in delicate moments!... Ah! no getting soft!...Grab everything!...Always on the lookout! I pulled myself together! I held on! My pals weren't too respectable, of course, I agree, but a wonderful family for me, knew all the ropes...Since I was well recommended, coming from poor Raoul, a fine welcome right off!...Till then... just a couple of little slips!...and then the blowup at the Dingby!...They'd dropped me a little...It was inevitable! ...Now had to make a comeback...I'd find them all right through Boro!...So there I was in front of the door, "Van Claben Titus"...It was the moment for decision...I ring... I knock...Nobody answers...I bang again...I insist...

"Boro!...It's me!" I yell out right from the park.

Finally Monsieur is so good as to appear...He leans out the window...There he is!...He's amazed to see me...He motions to me...

"Take it easy! Take it easy!...Come back a little later!"

I show him my belt...that I've had to tighten it!

"Sh! Sh!" he starts again...He shows me the lane of trees away off, I've got to go away!...

Hell no! it's not possible! Enough walking!...

The clients, the people around coming and going, waiting on the steps, don't give a damn about our gesturing...Just then the door opens!...There's Titus!...Titus Van Claben! known as The Horror!...That's his nickname!...I recognize him right away from the stories...He simply appears in the doorway in a big pasha's costume, that's the way he runs his business...all got up in yellow and purple silk with an enormous turban and also a cane full of precious stones and a big jeweler's magnifying glass. That's exactly the way he is in the shop. He carries on his business in oriental fancy dress...He wants to chase me away immediately...his first instinct...He doesn't know me...What's the difference...I don't bat an eyelash! He looks me up and down...

"Ah! so it's you making all that racket!"

He talks French, but with a thick accent, he comes down on it hard, like the one upstairs...They're both greasers...

"You can go to hell!" I answer...

Right off, Boro starts giggling! He's above us, he busts out laughing! He contemplates us...from the front boxes...

The caliph blinks...He chorts...He wants to bluff me!...He's attacking me, he's in a rage, he's flapping around...he jumps up and down in his pants, his enormous baggy silks...Ah! the big nasty stinker!..."You going to get out of here, you little bandit? Go beat it! Go on!"

He starts waving his stick at me.

I stay put...

"Go beat it! Go on!" He's starting again...He's in such a stew his turban's wobbling on his head...

"Get out of here! Don't let me see you again!...You want to debauch him again?...That what you've come for?...You don't think he's depraved enough?"

He points to Boro up above laughing out loud, splitting so

that he's hanging limp on the window sill...What a couple!

I thought he was funny at first, the potbellied stinker, now he starts running at me.

"I'll give it to you, you wretch!"

I don't like threats...It's happening in public...it's grotesque...

"Go 'way, you scoundrel!" he repeats. Me! A war cripple! ...Hell no!

"I'll have both of you arrested!"

He points to both of us.

My, my, another jealous guy!

Now the other one starts talking, he's delivering an address from the window, right to the public, he's speechifying...

"Greetings! everybody!...Greetings, gents!...Greetings, mopey!...Greetings, pal!"...

He's brandishing a big bottle, a whiskey gallon, he takes a swig, right down his throat from the bottle...He's making a spectacle of himself...The people are laughing themselves sick!...They're roaring! They're waiting for what comes next!

The pasha's stamping, sputtering, he's wild with rage...

"Get inside! you damned dog!...Get inside!" he yells... "Aren't you drunk enough? And you, you little wretch, do you know what's in store for you?"

Ah! it's a threat, a direct one!...

Ah! no! I don't know a thing about it...Ah! It's a fact!... He still sickens me, that's sure! It's true I've got only one arm! ...but he's going too far!...I'm going to let him have it!...I go through the spectators...that'll do!..."Wait, Caliph of my heart!"...I rush up to him...Seeing him right in front of my face flabbergasts me, he's unbelievable!...Right in broad daylight! All made up!...A mug like a plaster mask!...Some job!...even worse than Joconde! and jowls, Madame! and rolls of fat with cream! and powder!...even lipstick!...The effect upon me is fantastic, a terrific illusion, a mirage...he fascinates me. He's looking straight at me too...Looks me up and down...he's blinking...He starts scrutinizing me with his big magnifying glass...

"Oh! Oh!" he suddenly screams..."Oh my! young man! But young man! You're not at all well!"

Ah! I brush him off!...

"But you look very ill to me!...Come in!...Come in!... Rest yourself!"

He's inviting me...He's suddenly changed his tone...obsequious now, sympathetic...oily...

"You must be very tired! Come in!...Lie down!"

He's just too polite!

I come out of my daze, I dash through the door, I find the stairway...I bound up the steps, two at a time...

A room...what a shambles!...I stumble over everything! ...Boro's sprawled out...oof! shapeless on the sofa...He sees me...he gets up...

"Ah! there you are! Oh! my boy!...Oh! my boy!...Oh! what a mess! Have you run into Matthew?"

His first words: Matthew!...That's all that's worrying him...

"Where's Matthew?"

He just keeps mumbling "Matthew!"...He doesn't even ask what's been happening to me!...

"No!" I answer..."I don't know where Matthew is!... You big drunk!...But I think he'll be along soon!...from the way you raise hell!...the way you collect a crowd!"

I was giving him my opinion.

"Me raise hell?"...Ah! he's bristling...Right away violence!...He's brandishing his bottle at me! He wants to throw it in my face...

He stumbles...He moves forward!...He falls all over him-

130

self!...Ba-da-da-boom!...The old guy downstairs starts howling!...by repercussion!...he's yelping at me...a shrill whining voice...a crazy bitch!

"Will you stop it, you riffraff! You'll break everything! Boro play me the Merry Widow Waltz!"

There's also a piano in the corner...The pasha wants music! ...quite exacting! a wish of his!...he's screaming with desire!

"The Merry Widow Waltz...You hear me? The Merry Widow!"

Immediately he throws a tantrum...He flutters around! jumps about...a real madwoman!

He sets the whole shop bouncing, shakes the floor! What a racket! He keeps time by knocking on the ceiling!...with the cane!...he's raging for the Merry Widow Waltz!

"Shit!" the other one answers..."Shit! you dumb hussy!"

That was Boro from his sofa...He shot that one down the stairs...

"You're already drunk, Borokrom!" the old guy answers... "You've been drinking like a hole!"

They're at one another now...

"Like a hole?"...Ah! that's the limit!..."Tell me, what kind of hole? What kind of hole? Ass-hole, is that it?"

It's too outrageous!...Boro gets up! He wants to hear that to his face...what the old guy's insinuating! he's going downstairs...shit! He stumbles...he staggers...He gets to the stairs...His shirt hanging out like a smock, his belly sagging ...He's reeling again...Boom!...he tumbles, upsets...rolls down...crashes into the shop...A mess...Right into the whole works...Right into the crockery...The pyramid of fruit dishes...plates! Thunder!...A cataract!...The old boy's choking with fury...The client in front of the counter yelps ...she's bleating with horror...She wants to run away...she can't!...Everything falls all over her!...The old guy tries to help her, to pull her out! he yanks at her, by her shoes...he takes a firm stand...ho! hip! hup!...the whole works tumbles down again!...

"You, you tramp? You just standing there?"...He's talking to me. I go downstairs...He wants me!...I dash forward...I grab her by the feet...I get her out of the chaos...back into the light...The two fatsoes immediately start brawling again. Insults, threats, right over the lady's belly...With her underneath screaming to death!...

Boro grabs the old guy by the hair...Ah! now he's going to bash him!...The turban wobbles!...He's squeezing his Adam's apple...He's strangling him, by God!...He calls the customer to witness...how he's going to strangle the old guy...

"And he wanted to murder me!...I'm telling you, Madame, a pirate!"

And then, so she won't misunderstand, they both fall on her, they come crashing down on her...they roll over her, body to body...she was just a slender thing...She'd come to borrow on her "bond," her Mexican stock...She's still holding it in her hand...Ah! She won't let go!...She's clutching it...She was too scared of robbers!...and she keeps on yelping...

"Help! Help! The door please!...the door!"...But Boro didn't want her to slip away...He was holding on to her skirt! ...while squeezing Claben by the collar...He was afraid she'd yell outside...but there's the caliph escaping!...flattening himself, making himself flabby-wabby under the grip...he sort of melted himself from enormous to all-shriveled-up under the force...his whole big ass, his big belly...he's slipping... dissolving...he gets away...just look at him! Pop!...he's up again! All balloon! He springs up from the combat! He rushes to a big knife there on the table...Luckily I move fast, I grab him by his skirts...his baggy pants...I tear at his

132

silks, head over heels!...Pa-ta-ta-boom!...His ass in the air!
...Ah! good thing I came!...Boro lets right go of the client
...he grabs a rifle from the umbrella stand, a big-game Winchester, an awful bludgeon...and he runs after The Horror!
The fight goes on! He's going to whack him with the butt!
He's brandishing his blunderbuss in the air! There's a scramble
in the back of the room!...It's all closed in...muffled...I
can hardly see...just the light of a water-lamp...an odd-
looking gadget on the table, there near the customer...a big
globe...a drip glass for oil underneath...

I can just about see the hysteria!...the way they're both
whacking away at each other!...I want the lady at least to
be saved!...my presence of mind!...I grab hold of her again
in the pile of crockery...I pull her out again by her skirt...I
yank! Oh! whiss! I get all of her out! I stand her up straight!
vertical! she's wobbly!...she can't stand up! she sits down...
she's breathing hard...

In the back...in the darkness...the two keep at it like
mad! a struggle! terrific hmphs!...The old guy's moneybag
turns inside out!...It'd been slung across his back...clink!...
clink!...clink! It all spills!...rolls out...pours...scatters
...clinking everywhere! A whole wave of gold!...coins!...
coins!...They go on strangling each other...they roll over
together...right in the gold!...horrible grips...They come
up against the customer...They knock her off her chair again!
...She rolls under them again...she's caught under the wres-
tlers again!...she's being crushed!...

"Mister! Mister!" she begs..."The door please!...the
door!"...she's starting it again...

I can't pull her out from under the lunatics this time, that's
the end of it now! they're planted squarely on top of her...
she's all flattened out!...I crawl toward the door...I give up!
...air!...I'm all in!...I'm croaking too!...A puff!...A

breath! Have pity! I've made it!...Oof! I push! The door!
The cool wind! Ah! the old man's choking! Ooh! awful!...
Right in the breadbasket, on top of the other, in the back, in
the dark, arms locked!...The air got him! choking outright!
...It was too cool! "Asthma! Asthma!" he gasps at me! he's
suffocating!...puking!...Ah! he's going to drop dead sure
thing...his eyes are rolling! And it all collapses! caftan, silks,
puffed pants, the guy himself...He's there on the floor...he's
drooling...groaning...We unhook his jacket, he's having
convulsions, foaming, a mess!...he's going to pass out!...his
eyes are rolling like crazy!...The customer spins round with
fear...she flies out through the door!...she leaves everything
there!...her things, her bag!...her stocks!...

She just about gets out when another dame breezes in...
This one was even worse!...Starts screaming right away...
clamoring! a fit of barking! she's hardly seen the thing, the
pasha like that on his back...a horrible scene right away...
Boro knows her.

"Delphine! Delphine!" he calls...

It's the maid...He tells me it's the maid!...

Where's she coming from?...She immediately throws herself on her boss...She covers him with tears, with kisses!...
She's very fond of her Mr. Titus...She wants him to come
right to his senses...to open his eyes!...Boro's busy with
him, too!...He also wants him to come around!...He's doing
all he can...He's squatting in contortions...He's breathing
into him everywhere...in his ears...in his mouth...Ah! the
battle's over!...Now it's everything to save the man!...He
stretches out his arms in the form of a cross...He lifts him up
...lowers him...artificial respiration...That does him good
immediately...He starts breathing a little...they sit him down
...with his back to the wall...they prop him up with cushions...he breaks down again...slumps again...he falls to

134

the right...then to the left!...He wants to inhale smelling salts...he mumbles...groans...he *wants!*...The salts are in the closet! on the first floor! quick! quick! quick!...Boro can't go up! He has to work on him...So I jump up!...I find them right away...The bottle's empty! Woe upon woe!...

It makes Delphine roar!...What an ordeal!

"Mr. Titus!...Please! Wake up!...Be yourself!"

Awful clamors! she grabs him...shakes him!...He's got to come to! got to revive! All means! use everything! She's an extraordinary maid! blazing with affection and zeal!...You can't deny it! she's a fine person! Her boss isn't a pretty sight! Her hippo's not dainty! He's lying there in his silks full of his filth...his vomit...he's still gurgling!...his eyes are swiveling...they get rigid...revulse...Ah! it's horrible to watch! ...and then poof!...He turns crimson!...So livid just a second ago!...He's swelling up with big gobs...his mouth's full ...he makes an effort...Relief comes!...She holds his head ...she helps him...

"Good! Mr. Claben! Good!"

She's quite pleased...She's down on her knees, holding him up...she's encouraging him...at every gasp a nice word... Finally he pukes it all out!...she's quite happy!...He's still disgorging his bile...and more green stuff...all around... even over Boro at his side...who's looking on...it splashes around...I get a big gulp of it too...He's feeling much better! He wants to be put back on his bed...There behind the screen...in the shop itself...on the enormous four-poster... I take a look...I see it...full of furs, piles of them, mattresses ...in big soft heaps...We hoist him up on it, whew!...He's heavy! We arrange his pillows...Have to put his jacket on him, his yellow and purple silks, his turban, he insists on it! He's getting kittenish again! Ah! that means he's feeling better!...Got to let him have all his trinkets, all his pasha

135

junk, his bells and moire ribbons! and now his moneybag! and his blunderbuss!...top to toe! Fine! He wants all of it right there on his bed!...all beside him!...Right away! He's quite demanding...He's got no more confidence...and his jeweler's glass!...and his carved cane!...Got to have it all right there!...He's had his head punched in...he's got a shiner!...blue and red and bleeding!...and his left eyebrow's split open!...Delphine's kissing him...she grabs him around the waist, hugs him...cajoles him, adores him!...She's an ardent servant!...Ah! she came in the nick of time!...She's not too young a woman...I can't get a good look at her in that damned dive...all windows closed...just that dirty disgusting lamp that gives light like a turd...They haven't opened a blind! He refuses to, won't hear of it!...He starts groaning a little...still a bit weak...She throws herself on him with caresses!...He doesn't want anyone to send for a doctor...He absolutely refuses...Delphine's soothing him... fondling him...He demands music...All his ideas are coming back...

"Boro! Boro!" he mutters, whining, unhappy..."Boro! Boro! ...The Merry Widow Waltz!"...Still wants it!...He insists on it...

Boro's sprawled out there collapsed, in a pile of furs at Claben's side...He's fallen asleep on the pile...The battle royal's done him good...His nerves were wound up...He's snoring now with his belly in the air...We shake him...He's got to obey!...It's the sick man's will...

"Get up! Get up! Get to the piano! You big loafer!"

Delphine doesn't give a damn that he's sleeping! Everything for her boy!

"Get up!"...He's got to get up, the louse! and right away! "Go on! Go on! Merry Widow Waltz! pianist! damn it!"... That's the way they handle him!...

The piano's upstairs...he's got to climb up again! He yawns...stretches...All the same he goes...Good God, get going!...He grabs hold...staggers to the rail...Delphine hustles him along...She has authority over him...Old Potbelly's still groaning...he wants his music, he's wailing!... He's starting to choke again...

Finally, there it goes!...It starts!...There's his waltz!... the notes! at last! the runs!...prelude!...He's made up his mind!...After all!...A shower!...two trills!...we're off! pedal!...cascades! triple-time!...spinning round!...it's delightful!...the waltz whisks you up!...the shading...the arpeggio!...and then largo, rich chords!...

Once started...all you wanted...never tired...forward! ...evenings...nights...if you wanted!...it sort of excited him too, in a way.. his big can on the stool, he just kept bouncing around...jigging away in rhythm...it kept him pretty busy.

I have been telling it all like a stick...First I've got to organize myself...give you something of an idea, something of a picture of what it was like...the place, the setting...It's the excitement that throws me off, flusters me, spoils the effect. I've got to react!...got to describe the whole setup to you... the Van Claben warehouse, his pawnshop...

It had a wonderful location, just outside Greenwich, right on the park and overlooking the Thames a way off, the whole panorama of the river...a magical kind of spectacle...From his first-story windows you could see the riggings, the whole India Dock, the first sails, the tackle, the April clippers, the Australian ocean liners...Farther off, beyond Poplar, the ocher chimneys, the wharves of the Peninsulars, the steamboats from the Straits, dazzling white, with high decks...

Ah! it was an ideal spot, no denying it, for looking out, the view and everything, for anyone who's got a turn for voyages, navigation, playing truant...

A wonderfully situated house, a whole theatre in front of his windows, an amazing setting of greenery on the greatest port in the world...In the good season it turned straight into a dreamland...Should've seen the display of flower beds!...all kinds, yellow, red, purple, dazzling, all varieties, enough to get you all worked up, restore all your confidence, pleasant giddiness...

Only a sullen mope would contradict me!...Especially after the winter of 1915-16, so harsh and merciless...It was a terrific springtime!...Nature's maddening sweetness, a blossoming of the grove, enough to bust open the cemeteries! to make the tapers dance a jig!...I saw it! I can talk!...

When spring started cutting up that way it always had a bad effect on The Horror, whose story I'm telling...it made him jumpy! out of sorts...He didn't want to hear about blithe blossoming...He'd shrivel up in a bad temper at the back of his shop, closed in, shifty-looking, he was suspicious of the radiant season, he kept all his windows and blinds shut...He couldn't tolerate the whiffs of spring. He'd lock up his shop at six in the evening. He was afraid of clematis, of daisy magic, he tolerated only the customers...All he wanted to see was business, customers, not little birds, no, nor roses. He could take care of himself! He spat on crazy nature!...There was only one thing, for example, that made him woozy, moony, tender, soft, that was music...Greedy enough to gobble up his hands, a disgusting pig, a damned first-class usurer, you could moisten him only with melody, and not a little either! ...Totally!...Didn't give a damn about tail, tobacco or pretty faces, dead set against whisky, not a homo either, nothing at all, he was really frigid, except to little piano tunes, to melodious fantasy. And he never went out...you had to go and get him. He didn't go out because of his asthma that the fogs from the river would bring on at the first whiff...I've given you an idea of an attack...Boro knew his boss, he'd take advantage of the magic spell!...When he was down to nothing, beaten by the cops or the races, he'd come in from London unexpected, he'd fall on The Horror, attack him by the digestion, and put him to sleep melodiously...If you could have seen the job, the style!...The old guy would never have admitted that it gave him such pleasure. It was almost his damnation, especially after lunch. Must have been something exceptional, all the circumstances of life, that they'd known each other formerly, in the past, a way off in their youth, for him to let himself be bewitched that way by such a crafty scoundrel, even worse perhaps than himself...I learned all about it little by little...in the course of things...piecemeal. Boro didn't complicate things, he'd go straight through the shop, without shilly-shallying, not a word, he'd climb upstairs, impolite, attack the ivories...The old guy would curse and swear as he passed, he'd yell out insults, he'd go nuts for a while, he'd call him a hyena, a blackmailer, a stinking disgusting fat pimp...Boro, who wasn't tongue-tied, would let him have it right back, there'd be a nice show of fireworks!... and then it would subside, pretty quickly...They were just being a little kittenish...They were quite pleased with one another...

On the first floor under the beams was the big stock of instruments, especially the strings, mandolins, pledged harps, and cellos, a closetful of violins, bits of guitars and zithers, an awful hodgepodge...a whole cartload of clarinets, oboes, cornets, flutes, piccolos, an entire trunk full of ocarinas, all kinds of trick gadgets for the wind...and exotic instruments, two Madagascan drums, a tom-tom, three Japanese balalaikas, enough to make all London dance, to accompany a continent, to stock a couple of dozen orchestras in The Horror's garret alone...merely with the securities of musicians who'd evaporated...the unredeemed pledges, the junk hanging around. The old guy was supposed to clear it out, to get rid of it all in Petticoat, the headquarters for secondhand stuff, their flea market, so as to give himself room! But he kept putting it off from day to day...It was too painful, he couldn't make up his mind...He was too fond of his instruments...He even bought up others...especially pianos...The latest one a

Pleyel, a perfect baby grand at retail price, a smart-looking model from Maxon's, a dream...Shows you how bad he was bitten!...How music got him...Not that he played personally, he couldn't have hit out a note, but his place was full of it and it gave him such a kick that he couldn't find a reason for putting it on sale...He accumulated piles of harps and trombones, it was such a jammed chaos under the rafters that it just wasn't possible...you couldn't push the door, it blocked all the skylights...He could have made dough, he who was so damned tight, whence his nickname, old sordid, a monster who'd eat rat, a miser who'd skin a penny, he'd have sold fishbone if there'd been a taker anywhere, but when it came to music he took such a stand that he forgot all about his natural bent...

In order to make room Boro would knock everything right and left...with big kicks...he'd pick at something in the pile, a saxophone, a piccolo, a mandolin...he'd fool around with the gadget for a while...just so...a bit of a prelude...a fantasy...nothing at all...he'd drop it...just a whim!...then he'd yank out his piano, ferociously...clear away all the junk ...whatever was in his way...the whole museum!...Baraboom!...finally installed, stool, all ready!...on with the waltz! Arpeggios, trills, gingerbread...you know...plugging it, street stuff...with the best possible variations for charm...plaintive, tinsel, sob-stuff, it could go on forever... it was irresistible...It would make a crocodile start daydreaming...But you've got to have the knack...It's the magic know-how...to turn on the charm anywhere, jolly place, dull occasion, smart salon, cuckold ball, gloomy lofts, sinister squares, hopeless streets, communions, country inns, All Saints' Day, low dives, July 14ths!...a zim! bang! ding! and it starts ...never meets resistance!...I know what I'm talking about ...Later on, after lots of ups and downs I sold some of that

market-place stuff with Boro, that nice strummed jigging...
Should've heard our "three-handed" numbers...I did the "one-armed" bass, my octave run, I had time to think about how the charm works...later on, as the days went by...it has to keep going! that's the big secret...never slow up never stop! it's got to keep popping away like seconds, each with its little tick, its little dancing hurrying soul, but, by God, kept on the move by the next one!...perks you up with a trill...nicks you!...tinkles right into your worries...plays tricks with time, tickles your trouble, teases, pleases and tinkles your worries, and tum! tum! whirls you round!...carries you off...constant gallop! notes and notes!...and then the arpeggio!... another trill! the English air sweeps along cool and saucy!... a high jig!...pedal thunders! never backs out!...or sighs... rests!...that's what's sad when you think about it!...all that wild sweetness, always shooting ahead, note after note... Should've seen Boro at it! some performer! when it came to the ivories...flashiness...but flighty rhythms!...and what a repertoire!...some memory!...variations ad infinitum...He, rather uncouth by nature and really just a brute and pretty impossible with his mania for explosives, would get all fluttery, all showery, all elfin!...His mind was in his fingers...Pixy hands!...butterflies on the ivories...He'd spin about the harmonies!...snatch them on the wing!...dreams and fancies! ...garlands...twists and turns...nimble pranks...Possessed! ...that's the word for it!...by twenty little devils in his fingers!...Never out of sorts or tired! for hours and hours I've seen him like that capering from thirds to fourths and dotted rests...a run...gingerbread...never just musing, or sighing ...never a single word..."That's enough!"...always brisk ...gay hypnotic nodding with his big dome, five, three fingers, crash!...back to the keynote!...A big chord! sharp! He made it!...The charm follows through! It's the old refrain

142

dignified and tricky...Never coming...never ending!...all hearts!...and so much for that!...and no nonsense!...and let's drop the music! and good night for the pedal!...and it's just sob-stuff!...just a plugging!...sleight of hand!... crossing fingers!...beat it, cheapjack!...and go on, go on! ...break down the F!...the A!...the B!...the C! C! skid ...at it again!...beat it to the end of the sharps!...There it goes again!...never dies out!...What a break!...Rum-ti-ti-tum!...Everyone's puffing! swooning...giving up!...kidding the ivories!...low-down style...rough and winning!...brutal and stinging! with ping! pang!...loosens the notes!...wizard with his hands! conquers and strikes!...dum-ti-ti-tum!... sweeps all before him!...everyone's sailing!...everything's spellbound, dissolved, blinking! blinking at the waves! ding! ding! dong!...Don't buckle!...Hold on to the B! sharp! sharp! sharp!...tum!...

The thing's been all the rage since, done a thousand times, chewed up, puked out by all the tin pans in the world, by all the jazz bands of the continents!...by jukeboxes, practically everywhere...botched-up tinsel...But at the time I'm talking about, it was still new...a hash no one had ever heard...the tough sentimental kind of thing, the kidding throb, message of the low-down times that were on their way! roguish tinkling at the corners of squares...at the doors of pubs, the tart nervous music...soft-pedal and oop-la staccato!...the poker-faced screw, by far the best!...the cream and pepper!...no one wanted anything else! cynical, basic and hurried!...notes stripped!...heart stripped!...tum!...tam!...tum!...frol-icking, four, five, three-fingered crack! on with the whirligig and with arpeggios and you know what!...hold pedal!...and it's up in the air!...and not tired on the left...the accom-paniment full of little dreams...naughty as possible!...I can't tear myself away from it!...No use talking...it sounds deli-

143

cious!...It's spellbinding, it's free and easy! It's a treat rolled off by a pianist who knows zum! pim! wham! the heart of things!...who knows how to get at it, merciless! to take command, cruelly, right from the start...to pack the theme in!...to carry way...and yoop! and zoom!...zim! Keep moving, trills! and chords!...Shake it, scales sharps galore! Waves all screwball!...It's tough!...It's masterful!...puffy!...the spell of technique!...

Titus understood it...You wouldn't have thought so at first from his face, by looking at him, a potbellied sneaky-looking hippo, stuck away in his filth and semidarkness, and yet he was sensitive, influenced, in seventh heaven as soon as it got going ...hypnotized, frozen, swooning, especially when it went on and on and on...He'd sit there all washed out, prostrated, aching with the charm. He didn't dare move at all...It was just too much...he'd close his eyes...he'd shrivel up in his pillows, deep in his easy chair, he'd let the customers float by, he'd stop answering questions...He'd even put them out... impolite...with their pledges, their saucers, their secondhand junk...he wanted to be let the hell alone!...

He became indifferent to everything as long as the music kept coming...still kept falling from upstairs!...the waves of harmony!...the pretty tunes, the playthings, the little ripplings, the string of variations!...reeled off this way, that way ...everything that came from that big hulk's fingers... sorcery...

Ah! but he mustn't stop! Ah! by God!...mustn't slacken a single minute!...not a second!...He'd suddenly get awful! he'd yell, swear something fierce!...He'd grab anything... He'd lose all control!...Banging on the ceiling, enough to scatter everything!...to bring the house down!...in a fury! ...fit to be tied!...Keep playing!...Get started, by God! Death!...

144

Boro upstairs knew all about it...he knew the act!...the charm or death! shit!...shit!...shit!...He'd claw out the little torture...He'd announce, yell out his price...his tax!...

"Hand me the money!...One bob, Mister! One bob!... right away or I won't ever play again!" One shilling! One shilling! or nothing! The categorical condition...take it... leave it!...

The musician stuck to his guns!...his shilling right away!

"Have it you dirty dog! Have it you rascal!"

The old guy thrashed about...insults!...but he had to fork over!

"Here, take it! you pig! you bandit!"

He'd get them...force his hand!...about two or three shillings an hour...two or three pauses!...Boro had character when it came to that!...He wouldn't have played again! never!...The old guy had to bring up the two shillings himself!...with difficulty...he'd struggle up the stairs...Boro wouldn't budge from the piano...he'd never have gone down ...and then he'd make him wait a little while...work him up...susceptible as all that!...after all, he was fed up!... let the old boy rave downstairs...let him get jumpy, let him beg again...Then he'd start, very low, muting it all, with a sly turn on the pedal, with a plaintive refrain...dreamy... doing the whole bass in arpeggios...the melody, B-minor beaded, and always ragging the tonic! Ah! watch it! Bringing back everything to the quick tremolo rigadoon rhythm. That's the trick!...the magic!...the lost plaintive sweetness!...flim! and ding! bim! dead little things dancing to the tune...three fingers...five fingers...and then the rest of it...and then the chord and everything rushes off!...goblins!...and it's won spruce and shrill!...all the little live ones dash in! dawdling from a scale played in thirds, weaving motifs, and spattering! all the fingers spattering!...the brisk rondo!...the

refrain! and everything topples!...and it all zips up again!...
giddily!...Zim! Zang! Ping!...

And so on until dinner, sometimes three or four hours at a
stretch!...wilting, galloping! octaves in D!...ding! dim!
bim! twitteringly!...hearts and flowers! five! three! four!
Zim!...a shower of sharps! from sad to gay! and rigadoon!...

In his three or four hours of banging away Boro easily
wangled his quid!...from pub to pub, always his style, "Sugar,
please!"...a dead stop...and off again...It was flashy stuff,
hard work, but not so tough as his number outside. He didn't
like being indoors, he much preferred the street, life in the open
air! the piano on wheels to play outside standing up...Still
the street's no joke, you can realize, much worse than the pubs
when it comes to cops...You're in their paws, that tells everything!...Always there crabbing and bullying, that you're
bottling up their gutters!...treated like mutts!...And then
the street...the competition! the minstrels! the blackfaces!
...Ought to see the type! what yappers! coal-heads! they
banged out the bamboola! the thing they were doing at the
time!...the day's jazz...screaming it out a little like Joconde!
...their yowling!

The people ate it up!...Those bums came up from the
beaches, they were allowed since the war. They'd finish a sidewalk in three yelps. They'd take in enough for a week! For
that, it was less dumb doing the pubs, Boro was forced to
admit...

Circumstances forced us to work in the open too, pushing
around our instrument on rollers!

Naturally it turned out badly...I'll tell about it later on...

The mountains of junk around Titus were an amazing sight. Everything was just itching to fall down...Things would topple over for no reason at all. It would collapse in avalanches, in valleys, in rushes of hardware, over baby carriages, women's bicycles, crockery and knickknacks, curios, it would thunder down, down on the mattresses pillows blankets enough to cover the fourteen docks, loads of bottle baskets, fiendish slaughters, pyramids of top hats, fans for a thousand tropics, enough to uncurl the cutting blasts, to brush off all the north winds, such a wall of quilts that if they came down on you it meant sure death by soft swooning, a coma under feathers!... Titus felt quite comfortable in the midst of this enormous mass!...in the heart of trading...right in the chaotic crater, that's where he felt in top form, with a reason for living, right in the sanctuary, behind his globe, his water-lamp...Had to see him in action, there was no one like him for breaking down a customer, for brushing away all his shrewdness...just by undoing the package, his way of feeling the weight of the thing under the lamp shade...the lace...the tea service, the delicate knickknack, the cherished bauble, the way he depreciated the article, just by breathing on it...so that it wasn't worth a thing...it was just cheap junk, a rabbit fart...it was amazing enough that he, Titus in person, so difficult and delicate, let himself be interested in such cheap, shoddy stuff, such paltry filthy slop, it wasn't worth the string it was tied in!...He'd start just by putting it on the scale...the way he'd tap the pan ...it didn't weigh anything...really nothing!...a piffle!... He'd listen to the sound of the poor thing...the bright red coffeepot...really it was worthless!...He'd question the person with a frown...How much did he want? very skeptical... He'd reset his turban...He'd scratch his head...He wouldn't hear the answers...The remarks were blotted out because of his hearing device...He'd take it out just at that moment from under the table...at the end of the discussion, at the final veto...his ear trumpet of great deafness...He'd blink... squint...whistle...He couldn't believe his big eyes...the naive person was exaggerating so...the nerve!...He'd put in his trumpet again...He wanted to hear it again!...the terrifying figure!...Ah! shocked!...couldn't be possible! He didn't believe his ear! He'd raise his eyelids to pronounce judgment ...his offer? a tenth!...if that! And maybe!...first a fiver and then! and then that was all! Take it...leave it!...he'd bring the drama to a quick end...Ah! not another word! not another sigh!...It wasn't worth insisting...He'd settle down in his easy chair...He'd pull his big coat over him...lower his turban over his eyes...He stopped seeing anything!...You wouldn't see him!...

It was dingy in his place, almost dark, except for the globe lamp on the table which gave out a kind of gleam, an aquarium green...The blinds were never opened except for a moment before dinner when Delphine was cleaning, when the governess came, his "governess"! she wouldn't have any other name.

"Call me Delphine or governess! but not your maid! I'm not your maid! I'm not your maid!"

As soon as you arrived she let you know then and there what her rank in the house was, so you wouldn't look down on her, as soon as you said hello, that she wasn't a maid,

"Governess"!...and in a tone which you couldn't answer!...
It'd been going on for twenty years!

She didn't overwork keeping house, it was impossible at
Claben's, she'd sweep the centers of the rooms, she'd pile up
the heaps, she'd arrange the valleys, so you could worm your
way, get to the door...

Claben didn't talk much, I mean with his customers, he
stuck to his kind of mystery, he'd say things to himself in a
sort of Yiddish, had to catch a word here and there...he'd
bluff from the start with his pasha's jacket, his enormous
purple and yellow puffs, his jowled pierrot's head, his three-
layered turban...he'd bewilder them...he'd shock the timid
ones...he'd let them do the talking...whereas Delphine was
the opposite, constant clamoring...endless monologues...
about nothing at all...her troubles shopping, in the street, in
the stores with arrogant people...that people had stepped on
her feet, here, there, practically anywhere, in the trolleys, in
the buses...Touchiness itself!...She'd go to do her shopping
in the center...as far as Soho...at the same time she bought
her tickets...she needed her theatre at least three times a
week...Which means that she followed what was going on!
Ah! not like a maid at all!...like a real lady, like a governess!
...Sometimes...not very often...there'd be spells of absence
...she'd stay out a week...she'd come back streaked, swollen,
her face all mottled, she'd got into a brawl with riffraff...
her dress in rags...and she'd drunk all her dough...her whole
ex-teacher's pension, all her wages from Claben, plus a tiny
bit of cash that came to her from an aunt...she had to resign
from teaching three times, we learned how, little by little...
because of violent rows she raised with her pupils over trifles,
terrible changes of character!...much later she realized what
she was really cut out for...her true vocation...her tragedy!
...she knew how to tell about it...to anyone who'd listen...

149

and even those who weren't interested...she'd let them see how educated she was! and what feeling she had!...what emotiveness! what soul! ah! it was something out of the ordinary!...

She'd interefere in the business, too, at the drop of a hat... she took all kinds of liberties!...in the midst of a discussion about a pledge she'd put her word in...these unheard-of interruptions would drive Claben crazy, but he kept his temper and didn't bawl her out, she would have been sore, might never come back...And he couldn't do without her...not that she was very honest, she stole lots of little things from him... but someone else would have been worse!...It was far too tempting in his shop...too much of a bazaar, the whole enormous place...He preferred to keep Delphine and spy on her to death...They didn't argue very often except over the word "governess"...but about that every day. He hated the word "governess"...

"After all, Delphine, I'm not weak in the head!"

"I'm not your maid either!"

That was the answer...Always the same argument...Still if she'd done housework elsewhere she'd have been called a "maid"! She wouldn't have got away with it!...

Later on in all confidence she told me about it...she confessed everything...

"You understand? Between you and me...I've acted, I have!"

Big secret...hush-hush...

"I've acted, haven't I? In the theatre! Ah!"...She enjoyed your surprise...Were you by chance interested in it? Delphine? Delphine?...Didn't that name mean anything to you?

Besides, always dressed up, hat, gloves and everything, all rigged out, except when she'd come back from her big drunks ...in awful states...her swinish sprees...

She'd stand in line for hours for the pit, the English nigger-heaven, all dolled up, feathers all over, silk evening dress...

At Claben's she had a fancy choice, wardrobes galore! a whole floor of evening gowns, she was spoiled, all colors and materials, she'd borrow them, bring them back, she could bluff all Greenwich with her outfits, and even the streets in the center of London, and the lounges of the big theatres!...And she did!...She didn't miss a single *première!* nor the slightest artistic "event"...She'd walk there and back...she didn't go unnoticed, she'd be seen in all kinds of outfits...she'd strut about between the acts, first and last one in the lounge... She'd take from Claben's wardrobes all the styles, winter and summer, of the past hundred years...Naturally people noticed her, they'd take little digs at her, it sometimes caused incidents ...but altogether things went off all right...Dignity!...But once at the Old Vic, carried away with enthusiasm, she'd disturbed the performance...

They were playing *Romeo and Juliet.* She'd screamed from the balcony...screaming congratulations at Miss "Juliet" Gleamor...The cops had thrown her out...She'd been wounded to the quick...She'd postpone it to the intermission ...Not tamed by any means!...let the two thousand spectators see what real theatre was!..soul!...fire!...ringing text!...She herself had played the text from the very top of the balcony...jammed with people!...the big "Duo" scene!

What a triumph! Endless applause! Romeo Juliet! Of course, they'd thrown her out again! The police!...But how the spectators ate it up!...All standing and yelling enthusiastically! ...She'd done the same thing all over again elsewhere... from one theatre to the next...always impromptu!...always from the balcony!...the whole theatre would turn to her... acclaim her! and always after the second act...

The performers would get to know her, she'd go to see them

in their dressing-rooms...She was often disappointed by the personal contact..."Excitable...but no soul!"...That was her verdict! She didn't want any actors' photos, even personally initialed, she'd refuse outright, even the great Barrymore's...

"Poor mortal soul!"

That's what she called him.

She took pity on all of them, however famous they might be, she thought them pygmy, piddling, lost in the presence of the masterpieces...crushed by the text...Glad that she didn't get angry!...She didn't miss a thing during the season! Punctual at all the classics...first in line for the pit...often two and three times a week...of course it cost something!...But she was independent, she pointed out, her little income, her pension, but still a little close for all her "spirituous" needs besides and her worldly life!...She wouldn't have been able to dress up...But being "governess" at Titus' made ends meet ...the evening gowns and the pubs, and in addition all her freakish ideas, theatre, big musical galas, charity evenings... She'd be everywhere...More so since the war with parties for the wounded, recitals of the great virtuosos...

She was ready out of kindness to do some errands...to do little things for Titus...But only as a personal favor she let him know...not at all as a servant!...Ah! not a servant! She never took off her hat or her veil or her gloves, she did her housework as she was, harnessed from head to foot! with her feathers, her lorgnette, corset, high shoes, handbag...

"Just let some hoodlum touch me!"...She'd flare up thinking about the impertinent scoundrel...Brandishing her hatpin right away!...A dagger!...

With all her grand manners still and all she'd swipe things ...not much!...just odds and ends...that she'd sell in Petticoat Lane for her little incidental expenses...not very much, just little trinkets, leftovers...Titus wanted to catch her...

152

He suspected, of course!...It was a sort of comedy...He'd been mistrusting her for twenty years...The mistrust was mutual...From the moment she arrived he didn't take his eyes off her...until she left! In order that not a single movement, the slightest gesture, might escape him, he'd observe her with a spyglass from the other end of the room, his navigator's "Zeiss." He wanted the windows wide open while she moved the furniture around, it was the only time of the day he wanted to see clearly...so she wouldn't run away with some treasure, an item in his great collection. He'd climb up the stairs, to the very top, he'd put on three or four overcoats because of the drafts...on top of his pasha brocades. He'd pull down his turban, squatting on the stairs, his blunderbuss on his knees, he wouldn't let Delphine out of his sight...with the spyglass ...It might last for hours...

"Delphine! Delphine! Hurry up!"

She'd whip up a sirocco on purpose, whirlwinds, hurricanes of dust...They'd be completely enveloped. He'd cough, spit, choke, he'd stick to his guns...He'd stay perched up there yelling away at her...

In order to make a little room, she'd poke at the piles, setting off torrents of junk, it would all come tumbling down!... when it crashed on her, that was another matter! she'd be buried!...Had to be pulled out from under...the way I'd done for the customer...They'd have to stop yelling at each other, they'd be choking in the dust...When it came to weight, the worst was the bunch of old armor, the whole wall on the left, and the dentist chairs stuck into one another... When all of that upset!...Woe!...In a second the wild session would be over...they'd had enough choking and yelling and raving!...

"Stop! Delphine! Stop! I'm all in!"

He was the one who'd ask for an armistice!...Then she'd

open the other window, the one on the dead end, the draft would rush through...All the wobbling junk would come thundering down again!...And it was over for the week!...Delphine would be triumphant on the heap!...
The whole effort for nothing!

> *My name is sweet Jenny!*
> *My father 'e's deafy!*
> *Now I am the Queen!*

The refrain! Quite satisfied! So much for Titus!...She'd won!...The customers waiting outside would start getting restless...grumble, frowning.

Claben would start snarling too.

"Come on! Hurry up, Delphine! You see I'm catching cold!"

She still had to do the bed, the enormous heap of furs... the back of the den...He never left his premises, never got undressed, he kept all his clothes on, his cloaks and his turban, he buried himself as is beneath the pile of sables, sealskins, minks...he slept with one eye, always worried about robbers ...Protected against drafts by the huge tapestried portiere, I still see the gigantic thing that cut the whole place in two, the "Prodigal Son"...

He'd cough, sniffle, wheeze...he was really going to catch cold...He was sore at Delphine...It was just about over... The two or three big valleys of junk just about under control ...shakily stacked against the walls...Delphine would shut the blinds, Titus would light his globe, his water-lamp...poke at the Greco-Byzantine incense burner...swinging from the ceiling...when it sizzled, smoked hard, he'd take a deep sniff ...he was ready for business!...The customer would sit down facing him...the discussion would get started...but interrupted immediately..."Ooh!...Roch!"...another coughing fit! Asthma! His asthma! from having sat there like that in

154

the cold! in the dust!...."Ah! now! by God!"....He tried
everything for his asthma, all possible medicines, everything
in the advertisements...and for emphysema...everything that
Delphine brought back from her conversations with the asthmatic housewives in the neighborhood...Clodovitz' remedies,
unguents, powders, bottles, all shapes and sizes...Each new
specialty...Delphine would drop in at the hospital, would
never return without a few drops, two or three phials, the day's
wonderful new product!...He tried everything!...All the
weird smells, all the worst quack powders...he'd sniffed them
all...the headiest aromas, the most awful fetid scents...abso-
lutely everything for asthma...wheeziness from the fogs...
When that got him! what a panic!....Should've seen his eyes
then!....the horror that seized him! All kinds of plants in a
plate that were burned at the critical moment...Once it was
Senegalese herbs with a bitter stink that'd knock you over and
then little ground shells that he took before going to sleep...
It could also be smoked in a pipe...The customers, in order
to win him over, so that he'd be a little less of a louse when
it came to renewals, were very anxious about his condition,
they'd talk to him about his illness, they'd ask how he was,
they were very concerned, they'd bring him candy, eucalyptus
tablets to be inhaled over sugar as they were being burned...
You can't imagine what a stinking horror that was! He tried
all their stuff, he tried whatever they wanted, but he wasn't
much better...In fact it was even getting worse...his nose
was rasping more and more...especially since the big bomb
explosion, since the night of the Zeppelin, when it fell on Mill
Wall, less than a mile away!....it had shaken everything, his
house had got a jolt, been hurt...he'd thought it was the end!
he'd sprung from his furs, squirted into the air, fallen on his
belly with his full weight! Och! What a shake! a catapult-
shock! He reacted two days later by throwing a fit, so intense

155

and acute that he lay gasping at the bottom of the staircase!...
his tongue drooping to the mat...trying to catch his breath!
...for at least forty-eight hours unable to go up or down or
even move, or call for help, his tongue completely tied, unable
to answer anyone. The clients, after waiting, had alerted the
neighborhood, sent for the firemen, the neighbors, the park
guards, they'd forced the locks, they'd thought he was dead.
That gives you an idea of the character.

They didn't complain about him at Cascade's, they didn't
think he was too much of a snarling haggler, considering the
kind of louse he was, taking advantage of poverty, a bloodsucker, and so on. Naturally he'd handle things that came to
him from Cascade's, but never large quantities, just knickknacks, odds and ends that the girls wangled from the customers, small stuff...more or less as a joke...more or less
gifts...Cascade didn't encourage them...He didn't like thieves
...but it was hard stopping them...they were stubborn about
it, they had to rummage around in pockets!...gold pencils!
...cigarette holders!...and even watches and chains!...Cas-
cade didn't want the stuff around!...he'd fly right off the handle! Had to get rid of it! then and there!...Titus for that, the
sleight-of-hand artist, never a question!...right to the melting
pot!...And that was the end of it!...And he'd forget about
it at once...Never a slipup...mum's the word!...And he'd
stop remembering even more quickly!...neither the objects
nor the women!...He'd forget everything, lightning! He'd
even kid us!...He didn't even remember our faces!...That
was his charm! the lightning way he forgot!...Lots of people
came to his pawnshop...what a stream from five to six! people of all conditions...the modest and arrogant!...hell-raisers
and ass-lickers...Bad luck strikes everywhere...but his real
business, his regular clients, were the ordinary people, the little
crowd from the neighborhoods opposite...jobbers, workmen,

small business...Mainly from the other side of the Thames
...Eastwall...Wapping...Beckleton...also a lot of little
retired shopkeepers, waitresses, fishwives, artisans, a little of
everything...But the number of self-respecting people who
didn't want to be seen carrying their gewgaw "to be hocked"
...And he had competition! He wasn't the only one in the
East!...Mile End was jammed with pawnbrokers, hock shops
in every building, but on top of one another, shops side by
side, it got them pretty upset to be seen like that waiting
around there. Whereas at Claben's it was after all much more
discreet!...there weren't windows all around, just the clear
view of the park...And then it was a trip, had to take the
penny boat...And besides, right next to the park...if you
met anyone...if you were a little low at the moment...it was
easy to be taking the air...you were just out walking...you
could carry it off...

I've said that Claben didn't talk much with the customers...
but he'd give the article a long going-over...he'd examine it
in detail...he'd squint at the trade-mark...he'd come closer
with his big glass...it would squeeze against his jowls, he'd
press so hard on it that his cheeks would touch his ears...so
passionately...He'd forget his asthma...He'd take another
glass...a still bigger one!...an enormous one...so as to see
the thing better...he'd be so nervous examining it that in his
excitement he'd jolt everything, the table, the water-lamp, the
armchair...he'd snuffle and flounder around so that he couldn't
talk...He didn't have many teeth left, he'd splutter over his
stumps, it kept him from swallowing...Delphine had to chop
up everything fine, especially meat, his big beefsteaks at two
and six! The customers liked him as he was, that's a fact,
maybe because of his hocus-pocus, his oriental jacket, his Ali
Baba style, his incense, his hangings, everything...The English
like it when foreigners remain quaint...and don't start playing

157

the gentleman, and stay as is, humbugs...a sort of monkey ...I never saw Claben bawled out for his performance, his extortions, yet he was a louse, the worst vile stingy hyena when it came to usury and dishonesty! A skunk when it came to "lend and lease"! Never a day's, a penny's grace...the worst tyrant about extensions...he'd fleece them to zero!...he'd finish off even the most decrepit woebegone wrecks...he'd suck them beyond the bone!...and he'd insult them besides into the bargain! Called them lower than worms for being the tiniest bit late! Should've heard his jabbering! The way he shook down poverty! It didn't do him any harm...on the contrary!...When he had one of his big attacks, almost dead, there'd be a rush, a crowd from all parts of the city asking about him, bringing him consolation, good wishes, flowers and fruit...he had some small customers who'd been skinned to the quick, from whom he'd taken everything, their tables, watches, door mats and who still came back to see him...just so, without any hard feelings, who even brought him other customers, acquaintances from here and there, people who were also hard up...He didn't even say thanks...Often they came from far away to pay him a quick visit, leaving their work when it was cold, freezing, rainy, hailing, just for the satisfaction of seeing their Horror at the back of his den gasping, sniffling, groaning, just to see that he wasn't dead...That was the wonder of his charm. All he spoke to them about was hard cash, hardly ever a decent word...That's how it was and that's all there's to it...The worst cutthroats of the poor enjoy prestige...often fawned upon, soft-soaped, while the nice ones are massacred...pulverize some poor guy and no crapping around!...take advantage of utter misery so they puke blood, that's the very essence of magic, real spellbinding, the height of beauty!

Let's talk about it some more.

158

Here's how the man and the shop presented themselves...
Titus Van Claben and partner...The sign over the zinc
emblem *The Three Globes...Pawnbroker. On Securities and
Personal Word*...right on the balcony in yellow and gold...
I never saw the partner...Probably didn't exist...The per-
sonal word surely didn't exist!

Titus wasn't in a hurry to open his shop, he'd start around
four o'clock...sometimes later...The customers who got impatient could take a walk in the park while waiting...could
look at the landscape...cross the lawns till they reached the
trees, the big poplars a way off...I mean when the weather
was nice.

It was full of games, merry-go-rounds, flocks of children!...
If the kids got in their hair the waiting customers could take
refuge behind the kiosks, it was quiet there...they'd feel their
linings again...Whether they'd lost anything...their locket,
their gadget...Often it was more important, a household
article...the coffee mill...the teapot...they'd redo the package...the newspaper...As soon as Titus opened they'd all
rush up...

"Don't shove! One by one! Close the door!"

Fine, very well, so the other one's playing, the old guy's keeping more or less quiet. . . That is, he's wheezing less. . . We hear Big Ben ring out eleven o'clock. . . Boom! Boom! . . . The strokes roll off into the clouds. . .

Briefly that's the setting. . .

It's not much of a risk now. . . I can tell you everything. . . the whole comedy. . . It's been ages and ages! Boy, and how! That's all done with! . . . It's a dream. . . just images left. . . imagination! . . . and then there's been the war of 1939. . . and then what you know about. . . It's like another world now. . . Too bad. . . Really too bad. . . I'll probably never see the real places again. . . They won't let me go back there. . . still, let me tell you, it would be my last wish. They'll hang me first . . . It's too bad. . . it's a pity. . . I'm forced to imagine. . . I'm going to create a little artistic effect. . . You'll excuse me. . . I wouldn't have liked being reduced to melodrama. . . All the same isn't that my case?. . . Just put yourself in my place. . . I wouldn't like someone to be telling you things the wrong way . . . later on. . . when there won't be a single witness left. . . no one living. . . when it'll be just loose talk. . . old wives' tales . . . scraps of cheap smears. . . Ah! They'll get a good kick out of my suffering, tossing dirt at me right and left! . . . If I don't take full precautions I'll be blackened in advance, if I don't tell all the details starting today, starting now! not in an hour!

160

everything very scrupulous, exact, meticulous!...So I'll go on with my whole story, at Big Ben's Boom! Boom!...the strokes rolling off into the clouds...rumbling in the echo...that's exactly how it was...I'm not trying to play on your feelings ...I'm not straining for effect...The foghorn...the boat going upstream...You hear its big puffing close by...It's true, it's passing right alongside you...The power it breathes, the way it inhales, its propellers grinding away like all sixty ...right near the bank...the water whispering...just enormous..."Choo! Choo!"...It's passed by...

Upstairs Boro's fallen asleep playing the Merry Widow Waltz. He's slumped on the keyboard, his head on his elbows ...That's how he's sleeping, very uncomfortable...

Downstairs in the shop the two of us and Delphine are dozing. We've finally fallen asleep...But the old guy's starting to choke...He's asking someone to go get his salts!...He's acting up again...Delphine's all in...she's also choking a bit ...muzzled up...the atmosphere's awful...thick with fumigations, all the muck for asthma...Ah! I'm getting fed up!... getting tired of all the guy's quirks!...

"Hello, Mr. Claben! Hello! Please now, try a little air!"

She pleads with him to let her...let her open the door a bit...it's true that we're dying in the joint, it's so thick and close, but he's hostile, he won't have it!...

"Open it?...Open it?" he gasps...

He stays like that with his mouth open...

"Mr. Claben! Mr. Claben!" Delphine groans.

But he absolutely won't even let her touch the latch.

The stubborn louse!...

I go to get the brandy, we wet his lips with it...

I can't find the salts...The brandy's strong, he writhes and squirms...Then Delphine and I have a drink...I'm not a drinker but there're times you need it...need it or not, Del-

161

phine's always boozing...I leave her the bottle, she helps herself...two...three...four stiff ones, one after the other ...then she gets an idea...

"I'm going," she says..."Don't hold me back! Neither of you! I'm going to get the doctor!"

There's decision for you! She rearranges her gear, her skirts...

"Dr. Clodovitz! naturally!...The perfect man! the perfect man!"

A pronouncement!...It wasn't a bad idea...I'd even say it was a fine one...but the hospital wasn't around the corner ...Boy, what a stretch!...First she had to go to the Tunnel ...then cross under the river...and then all along Wapping, on foot, in the dark, and all alone.

It was foolhardy...pretty unhealthy alleys...and not lit up at all...well, almost not...They were expecting attacks, maybe some more Zeppelins and they were saying even airplanes which were supposed to fly all over Wapping because of the factories and loaded with terrific bombs...The streets weren't at all safe...Not only because of the Zeppelins!...There were also prowlers taking advantage of the darkness...But she insisted, she wanted to save her Claben!...At once!... absolutely!...It's true he was having a pretty bad time...He wasn't red now, as he'd been awhile before but pale pallid almost gray...He was fully conscious...He was groaning quietly between gasps...We finished the bottle and a second one, too, discussing whether she'd go for Dr. Clodovitz or not ...The second bottle was cognac...We got so excited that we woke up Boro...He was grunting upstairs...

He comes down. He starts wanting to drink everything!... So does the old guy!..."Myum! Myum!" he mutters...with his whole mouth...he can't budge, still and all he winks at us so we'll understand...We soak his lips with booze but he can't

162

swallow anything...Seeing him so sick Boro starts petting him, smiling at him...he kisses him...soothes him...That starts Delphine wheedling him...what a big tender moment! ...You can see she's jealous...she wants all the kisses for herself...Finally they huddle together...they fiddle about and cuddle, they get all tangled up right in the poor patient's bed...I hardly knew what to say or do with all that going on, but I was comfortable, that was all I asked for, I'd fixed up a kind of litter with the oriental rugs, the woolens and the coverlets, stuck in between the wall and the wardrobe...It was pretty good!...I wasn't asking for anything else...It reminded me of when I used to be on stable watch, but I wasn't in the manure now! in brocades and plush! "All right!" I said to myself..."Let them enjoy themselves! let them enjoy themselves! youth doesn't last! That's all right with me...But I'm going to take a serious nap! afterward I'll go to the kitchen ...I'll find a bite to eat...But after the workout I've had, hit the hay first!...Ah! a good snooze!...hunger can wait!"... Go fuck yourself! Just at that moment Delphine starts yelling! Bawls us out!

We're murderers and ought to be ashamed! we're not letting her get the doctor! Our behavior is frightful!...She's raving!...

"Mr. Claben! Mr. Claben!" she yelps..."You need a doctor! ...You need a doctor!"

The old man's in a state of collapse but he's still wary, damn it!...He's not staying alone with us!...He doesn't have confidence! He grabs on to her lace!...

"Be a lady!...Be a lady!" he whines..."Don't go out at night!"

"But I am a lady, sir!...I am!"

She a lady?...Ah! What a question! a lady and how! quite a lady!...and of the very finest quality!...He mustn't doubt that! She immediately takes offense! She shows him!...She grabs her gloves, she straightens her hair, her hat, her flowers, her plume, a pin for her veil! and there she is all dressed up! ...absolutely ready!...Mind all made up!

Hail Delphine! Hail you beauty! O hail! Nobody'll prevent her! So have a drink!...and courage!...hurrah for her determination!...Madame Daredevil!...Even Claben's singing, gasping hoarsely! The dashing verses! the galloping send-off! The parting shot!...So all together!...Glory to valor! She's not scared of anything!...of the darkness! of hoodlums! of ruffians! no more of Zeppelins than of butter! Let 'er bring back Clodovitz!

> *Delphine! oh! Delphine! oh!*
> *For she's a jolly good fellow!*

En route!

She's gone! at a quarter to two in the morning, dressed to the nines, in fine array!

It was dark in the streets, as I've said, just a small camouflaged street-light here and there around the crossings.

We go back to sleep again, good-by!...We'd opened the window to let out the smells, we stopped bothering about the old guy, he was choking comfortably!...Time passed!... Sleep, it's easy to say...First my ear wakes me up...buzzings, jets of steam...I go back to sleep...the nightmare gets me again...I'm awakened four or five times in a row!

Ah! it's bad!...I toss! I turn!...twist around...two hours pass like that...finally just about...a racket at the door... it's Delphine...she's calling...There she is again!...back again!...Ah! the old hag!...All I needed!...I wanted to go back to sleep...She was in a stew!...I'm telling the truth... Half-nuts!...terrified!...shivering!...out of breath!...wild-looking!

164

"Ah! Gentlemen!...Gentlemen!"

She couldn't get it out!

She was panting!

"If you'd seen that face!"

"What face?" we ask her.

"The man's face!"

"Whose face?" we insist.

"The one who gave them to me."

"Gave what?"

"The cigarettes!"

She opens her hand...cigarettes stuck together, gummy... in green paper, pasty...

She starts puffing again, then she explains...she finally gets it out...Here's the story...Right at the exit of the tunnel, at the Embankment...after Wapping, a man had fallen on her, just like that!...Plunk!...from above!...A dark little man! ...He'd sort of tumbled down on her from the very top of the lamppost! right on her hat!...They'd rolled over one another in the tunnel! Luckily he wasn't heavy! not at all heavy! She hadn't been hurt at all! Fortunately! What luck!...The little man was light...Like a kind of bag of bones!...light!... light!...A real bag of bones!...He was even rattling all over while she was tussling and struggling with him!...When they'd both got to their feet the tussle continued...The little man's arms were like sticks...She'd noticed that right away... and she'd yelled! but it hadn't done any good! There'd been no one around! Wapping Alley! just imagine!

And that wasn't all!...The man had spoken to her!...That terrible bony ruffian! She remembered his words! not as crazy as that!...She even imitated him!...In a nasal voice, like that...in a queer kind of English besides...She thought it was rather Scotch...He certainly wasn't from London...

"Don't be frightened, pretty Delphine!" that was what he

165

said..."I shall be the angel of your big love!"...his very words..."I wish you all the luck in the world!...I want to save your dear Claben!...My gentle dove, won't you make him smoke these magic leaves?...Here you see them rolled up preciously ready for use in these lovely water-colored petals! ...Let him inhale the three elements!...Fire!...wind!... smoke!...How intoxicating to smell them!...Run! Run!... Run, gentle Delphine!...Go back to his bedside quickly!... Don't go any farther!...I am the Sky Physician!...The Magus of souls!...I can give breath to the dying!...Don't go getting lost in the city! Don't let yourself be lead astray by the spells of the Cloven Hoof!...The devil is a sprite to mad maidens! Be careful, Delphine! Be careful!...The charm of the air!"

Smoke!...Smoke!...hardly had he uttered these words than he shriveled up, curled on the sidewalk...there beneath her eyes!...a piece of rag right under the lamppost!...and then nothing at all!...it hadn't lasted long!...She'd dashed straight ahead!...double-quick time!...He kept shriveling as he spoke...she was still telling about it...he was curling up ...finally just a tiny ball!...there under the light!...a little heap of rags!...then nothing at all!...Ah! she hadn't shilly-shallied! she'd dashed straight off! her skirts under her arms! her belly absolutely to the ground! gone back under the Thames! taken the tunnel of the depths!...She arrived home spluttering, all pooped, knocked out by the running! He was a little man all dressed in black!...That was all she knew about him...He was full of bones, supposedly...pointy everywhere...

Some hell of a story! The way he'd thrown himself on her! Plop! from the lamppost!...swooped down on her!...right at the Tunnel exit!...with all his weight!...not heavy! just bones!...sure of that! positive!...

166

All the same he was strong in spite of his being so light! struggle as she did, he'd kept her in his arms!...in his bony embrace!...covered her with kisses at the same time! and then right away the cigarettes!..."Here, Delphine!"...his hand full of them...There were the cigarettes!...no denying it!... sticky, gummy, green...She lifted her veil to get a good look at them...there on the table...and it wasn't an illusion!... She couldn't get over it!...There was even a bit of bone with the butts!...a tiny yellow piece! A bonelet!...Ah! it was beyond dispute!...and then the words he had uttered..."Oh, Delphine! I'm your friend! Your friend! The Sky Physician!" She kept repeating it to us..."Your friend!...The Sky Physician!"...His very words!...

We tried to figure it out...who could it have been? all three of us...maybe it was a vampire?...maybe a priest?... maybe it was a German disguised as an eccentric?...a funambulist? a ghost?...some practical joker?...But we really knew nothing!...We sniffed at the cigarettes...They had a queer smell!...not at all the smell of tobacco...rather like honey and sulphur...a mixture...really not a tempting aroma... But it got the old guy at once...Naturally! his taste!...He wanted to sniff at them over and over!...Kept sticking his nose into them without a stop!...pushing his whole face into them...stuffing them up his nostrils!...a real infatuation on the spot...Then he wanted to chew them...that seemed to do him good...I must say it might have worked...Both of us tried...with a drop of cognac! but smoking them was another matter!...The dark man had told her! Ah! he'd warned her and kept repeating! that it cured the sick but would kill a healthy man outright!...Ah! no mistake! any healthy man! That left us a little puzzled...All the same chewing made us awfully thirsty...There was some gin in the cupboard...more gin! it's refreshing with water...We tossed off a whole bottle!

167

and then a whole bottle of cider with it at the same time! first-class cider!...with kirsch in it!...there goes the old boy drinking!...That does him even more good!...Ah, now we're getting all nervous...We start arguing again! We've got to make up our minds!...whether we smoke these phenomenal butts or not?...the sky weeds, God damn it!...That's the word for it!...We stood there in a muddle...

Boro starts tearing one open!...he stuffs it into his pipe... lights up...it was burning all right...It smelled all right as smoke...I wanted to try, too...it might be good for The Horror...We were always thinking about his good...it resembled eucalyptus in a way...he always smoked a lot of eucalyptus...the poor guy...Immediately we all take a puff ...then two...then three...The old guy's inhaling the smoke all the way down...he swallows it...ours too...he's inhaling everything...it seems to be working...he's breathing better ...it eases him!

"Feeling grand, boys! Feeling grand!"

He's feeling high...and letting us know...Suddenly I'm happy with him...

"It's going to my head!...I'm woozy!...I feel just delightful!"

Those were my words after about ten minutes...I remember exactly!...And then I felt like vomiting...not much, just an idea...I held it in...Plain nausea...It sure went to your head...It came out of your eyes...like sniveling...Boro said he wasn't seeing straight either...

"You're double!" he says to me..."You're double, fathead!"

The Horror was getting high!...He was inhaling more than we were...he was jumping around in his furs...He was more comfortable, too...He was lying down...it was getting him real hot...He was jumping on the bed...He was getting all passionate...even while choking away...He grabs hold of

168

Delphine...He squeezes her with all his might...he throws her down on his couch! still out of breath...He puts his tongue into her mouth...all the way in...he's declaring his love...while coughing and smoking away...It was quite an act!...the smell was revolutionizing him!...Ah! I thought he was going to croak the way he was tossing around coughing... Delphine, that was another matter...She was cluck-clucking away!...she escaped!...came back!...

"Oh! cluck! Oh! cluck!...please Mr. Claben!"...while twisting around on the bed swooning...most happy...cluck! cluck!...

They were both urging me to take a cigarette!...

"Smoke, my boy!...Smoke!"

It was making me sick...Everything was going round...I was seeing stars...but mine was just starting!...It couldn't've been tobacco...It was far more brutal!...It was wooziness with a wallop...the real thing!...no laughing matter...It immediately made Boro queer...maybe in a quarter of an hour ...maybe just two or three cigarettes...completely off!...He wants to go up the stairs...I see him trying...holding tight to the rail...Oh! Whiss!...Step by step!...When he gets to the landing...he turns around...he rolls about-face!... Zoom!...He topples straight into space!...It's fantastic!... He's not scared!...not at all!...through the air!...Boom! ...He falls right in!...into the junk...He disappears into the crater!...into the porcelains! the crockery! He emerges delighted!...He brushes himself off...shakes himself! He's going up again! He hasn't dropped his pipe...it's still lit!... His hands are bleeding a little...He wants to start all over ...He's going up!...to the top of the stairs...Whiss!... hop! a tumble!...He's off again!...higher and higher!... He's torn a whole ear off!...Now he's full of blood!...It gives Titus a big laugh!...sitting there in his bed...he ap-

plauds! he applauds! and then the chortling starts him choking!. . .The fun's strangling him!. . .Our patient can't take any
more! He rolls and convulses over Delphine!. . .ah! we're
having a great time!. . .the little loonies!. . .He loses his turban!. . .They put it back on. . .Boro's laughing hard, too. . .
all smudged red. . .ah! we're plastered to the limit! Those
weeds must be poison. . .that's what I'm thinking, the way I
see it!. . .even with all my nausea!. . .My idea!. . .Just have
to see those poor wretches. . .the way they're yowling!. . .
squirming!. . .

"Poison! Poison!" I yell to Delphine in English!. . .

She doesn't give a damn about poison! she hasn't taken off
her hat, or her veil, or her gloves, she's simply tucked up her
skirts. . .she's on top of Claben again! she's frolicking on him!
astride! Giddy-ap! she's singing. . .she's roaring with laughter. . .

> *Hep! Youp! horsey!*
> *See me that horse!*
> *Trot! Hi! gallop!*
> *To Burberry Cross!*

The charge of the children!. . .

Ah! some fun!. . .The old guy's drooling in the furs. . .The
smoke's so thick I can barely see them. . .we'll pass out in that
atmosphere. . ."I'm going to run all around!" I say to myself
. . .A sudden idea. . .it'll do me good!. . .around the big heap
of furs. . .I was squatting. Then Boro grabs hold of me. . .He's
colossal. . .He lifts me up, he carries me in his arms. . .I kick,
I rear, I bite at his wrists. . .He carries me off, anyway!. . .He's
as strong as a bear. . .He rocks me on the bed next to the two
pigs. . .He lies on top of me too. . .He's crushing me. . .belch-
ing at me. . .jabbering at me. . .

"I love you!. . .I love you!". . .He's fondling me. . ."Ferdinand my baby-face!" he calls me. . .

170

And now the other two, The Horror and his maid, go for my pants!...they want to take them off!...they're dead set on it...they want to go down on me!...They say it right out! ...they yell it at me!...they clutch me, pull at me, roll on me...they're drooling on my head...but Boro won't let go of me!...he grips me, chokes me!...He's much too strong... All three of us are rolling...we fall down! plop! plunk! from the bed! Whack!...on the floor!...we go sprawling...I tear myself from his grip!...I get out of it!...I stand up...I'm seeing red...I'm going to kill Boro!...I see the yataghan hanging there in the middle of the room!...in the air...very sharp...right in the darkness...just at my height!...Ah! it's going to be a cinch! I grab the saber!...It eludes me!... What a dope!...Am I boiling!...

"Shit!" I say..."Just my luck!...It's an illusion!...."

The rest of them were in stitches watching me carry on that way, their little zany!...they're laughing at me! They're in seventh heaven!...The old guy's stopped choking!...He's cured, sure thing!...They're necking away hard...giving each other love taps...They adore each other...and big gooey kisses...right in the midst of the hodgepodge!...

"Come and see!"...he calls to me. "Come and see! my little bunny!...My little onion!"

It's The Horror urging me!...I don't want to go near... Immediately he leans over his table, he shows me his globe, his water-lamp...with the light in it...

"Look!" he says..."Look!"

We all bend over it...We look hard...to the bottom... We don't see anything at first...

"Don't you see the man?...Don't you see the man?" he insists in my ear...

I squint harder...I press my beak...I'm sort of hypnotized ...maybe I see something in the crystal...sort of jigging in the ball...but I'm not sure...I lean farther over...I get all

171

the way down...And Boro goes for me again...He takes advantage of my leaning over...he wants to spank me in public...I give him a stiff clout in the eye...a real hard sock ...he goes staggering backwards!...He goes smashing into the sofa! He stays there collapsed! then I go for him! I climb on him! on his big body! I stamp on him! I kick him! I let him have it!...I go right at him!

We're all pretty tight, no denying it!...Worse than that! ...We're boiling!...We're thundering!...It can't be what we drank that's affecting us like that!...There's no such liquor! ...After all, I've still got my common sense...It's the poison cigarettes! That's it! it's the cigarettes! I said it as soon as I saw them...I'm going to cut their throats, all of them!... right now! and no one's going to stop me! No doubt about it! ...I feel it!...to make them spit out their lies!...all their lies!...all over the place!...I'm going to save them in spite of themselves!...I see a big battle scene!...It's a vision!...a movie!...Ah! it's going to be something out of the ordinary! ...in the darkness above the tragedy!...There's a dragon munching them all!...tearing their behinds out...their guts ...their livers...I see it all!...Ah! the poor carcasses!...it's all dripping bleeding! it squirts in my eye! rip their buttocks out! Ah! there!...that's a juicy piece...That dragon's got hooks like sabers!...the louse!...He digs into the meat again ...It goes "Rrrpp"...each time!...The blood squirts all over ...spatters!...I'm going to pep myself up, too!...I'm going to smoke up all their tobacco!...That's it! That's it! That's the big miracle! I swipe some from Delphine's bag...one, two, three, four cigarettes!...the sticky ones...just wait!...They'll see how I smoke them!...No monkey business!...another one and then two!...then twelve!...I smoke nine of them together!...all at the same time!...My mouth full...all together!...The spoiled brat!...I light up nine of them at the

172

lamp!...I take a good squint!...I immediately see the things!
...the queer things inside! At the very bottom of the ball!
...Ah! he sure was right!...damned old Horror! I'm fascinated!...It's my head moving!...And Boro, his head beckon-
ing...He's after me, the louse! He's coming from the back of
the shop, feeling his way...blindly, from one thing to another
...

"I see you!" he screams..."I see you clearly!...I see you,
you wet blanket...It's some job, huh? you big dope! Come
here, pretty boy! Come, I'll tell you something!"

He takes me by the ear...He whispers to me...He's got an
idea! Ah! but I've got the saber in my hand! I'm armed, fear-
fully! That's why he's joining up with me now!...Something
bad's going to happen!...I'm holding the saber in my left
hand!...my strong and powerful left hand!...Invincible! I'm
going to slit the skunk's nostrils!...I don't like homos!...
What if I cut off his organs?...ah, that'd be something! I'm
thinking about it!...I'm thinking about it!...but suppose he
went around telling?...Ah! that scares me!...I'm palpitating!...ah! the gab! the yellow doubt!...Boro's really a stool
pigeon! A big dirty double-crosser!...He's in the police, that's
it!...Ah! a rotten hunch! I see him as a policeman! I see
him double!...I see ten of him!...with his ten helmets at the
same time! Ah! still and all it's funny! I've stopped killing
him! I give up the idea!...The old guy's clamoring again!...
He's bellowing! He wants the piano!...He's dreaming a con-
cert!...He's having a sweet dream about the piano! The fe-
male, too!...They insist! They're both crying!...But Boro,
that's another matter!...The pound they owe him!...They
squabble...It's his dough he wants!...Titus gives in!...He's
ready for great sacrifices! He doesn't have the strength!...Any-
thing so long as he plays!...plays the pretty piano! magic!
charm!...One pound!...two, three pounds!...ten!...for

173

the Merry Widow Waltz!...It's a craze for chords!...In short, he's in good humor...He's under Delphine at the moment, just swooning, she's lapping him, kissing him voraciously...straddling him...Suddenly he brutally tears away ...he wants to grab me...he wants to play with me!...But Boro rushes in between us...He doesn't want it to go on... He wants his dough and right away!...He wants his twenty pounds!...Twenty pounds, he demands!...He swears!...He curses!...He's in a rage!

"You big pig! Twenty pounds! You hear me!...Twenty pounds or I'll croak you!"

That doesn't trouble the old guy...on the contrary!... you'd think it delighted him...he immediately grabs his moneybag...he who's usually so shrewd...who'd skin a flea ...he lays the bag on his belly, his big game pouch...He opens it wide!...He plunges into it...It's the charm acting! ...and no mistake!...it's miraculous!...We stand there pop-eyed looking at him!...He's being as nice as can be...It doesn't matter that he's coughing and snorting, he smiles anyhow! he drools, clears his throat, spits out his asthma! with enormous effort! Another big whoop...an awful one!...And then he turns his whole bag inside out...there, plop! on the bed!...clink! clink! clink!...a wave of gold pouring out!... all over the furs...the bedspread!...the rugs!...How it flows!...sparkles!...clinks!...I plunge Boro's hand right into it, right in the cool glittering flood...and then all the coins suddenly go flying off! right in front of our eyes!...all the money!...they whirl around! spangle! scatter!...the whole magic flutter! across the room!...I see a hundred, I see a thousand louis! little ones, big ones, sovereigns!...I've never seen so much dough!...The way it twinkles in the atmosphere! nice and dainty! frisky! flighty!...it lights up the whole shop!...with gold and glints...it tinkles!...I stand there

174

popeyed!...The others are getting a hell of a kick out of me!
...They're laughing...howling at me...the way I stand there
like a dope!...The old guy opens his bag again...leaves it
yawning in the air and all the coins flutter in! come home to
the dark hole!...rushing in like little birds into a cage!...
And then he spills it all out again! It tumbles over the table!
...the whole heap shining!...It's time to wash our hands!...

All three of us plunge into the pile, Boro, me, Delphine...

We give our hands a good washing in the treasure!...boy,
it's pretty extraordinary...It's a real hallucination!...Sud-
denly we feel like smoking again!...And Delphine's the one
egging us on...Ah! mustn't weaken! in spite of the nausea!
...since that's what prodigies are like! Strength, by the God
of the Treasure!...happiness in the air!...you can see it!...
we're not scared!...the nausea's getting worse! We'll puke it
all out!...We're down to the last cigarettes!...They're really
intoxicating weeds!...The old guy keeps jeering!...He's
shaking the whole shop with his snickering...Especially since
he's choking too...

"Stop it, you hyena! Stop it!" Boro yells at him.

The bawling-out steps him up! What joy! he writhes! he
chortles!...He keeps guffawing like mad!...We start laughing too! and big cluck-cluckings...We're making big gurgling
belly music! it echoes all through the joint...That's the noise
we're making now...It was Delphine who started it...Cigar-
ettes like that make you awfully thirsty! so hot and bitter!...
There's nothing left to drink!...It's awful!...We start counting all the gold again!...We're so god-damned hilarious that
we're practically fainting with laughter!...

No one'd ever seen The Horror displaying all his gold on
the table! his entire treasure!...all the money!...and he's
busting with exaltation! I was helping him hold down the
little rascals!...Take it easy!...None of that!...they're

beating it! running out the door!...Oh God!...wide-open there!...Whizzing off!...at top speed!...We all pile on them!...We crush them!...We squash everything!...right on top of them!...Right on the bed!...flat on our bellies! ...All three of us!...in the big fur!...like nice pleasant friends!...you'd think they were delighted rummaging around in the fortune...rolling in it on the bed...wallowing in the big heap of gold. It was Boro who got rough...he started it! ...Ah! that's a fact! He wanted to eat one of the coins!... just swallow it down!...all raw!...a half-guinea! 10 shillings! 6 pence! and then ten!...and then fifteen at a time! ...whole mouthfuls...The old man says something to him ...Right off Boro gets red and green with anger!...

Ah! right off, immediately!

"Claben! listen!" he barks at him..."Go on! you're eating them, too! You big slob! You louse! You big pansy!"

That's what he calls him!...

"Open your mug!"

The old guy was giggling so that he couldn't defend himself! ...Fell flat on his back with his mouth open...Then Boro starts cramming him...he stuffs him...he rams it down!... coins by the fistful...like that, by force!...The old guy swallows it all! He puffs for a second!...and poof he rams in another!...another fistful!

"Go on papa! go on! have some salt with it!"

That's how he talks to him.

No pity!

Delphine was holding up her big darling's head while Boro was stuffing him...She was giving him big kisses...smack! smack! smack! on his big cheeks...on his big jowls...The old guy's appetite was enormous! In spite of his choking he kept wanting more! still more!...he wanted to wolf it all down...another little one!...another one!...all the coins!

176

...all the little coins there on the table!...The whole pile!
...he was still hungry!...He chewed everything! he gobbled
it all!...the greedy pig!

"Another one!...Another!" he kept calling...His throat
was full...shaking with wild laughter!...his belly was full,
making noises...it jingled in his pants!...the more it jingled,
the more he laughed!...his whole paunch making golden
noise!

"Another one!...Another one!...My love!"

Delphine kept encouraging him that way...to swallow two,
three more!...There were none left on the table, since he'd
gobbled them up...or on the bed either...They turned his
bag inside out...they slapped the bottom...Nothing left!...
Nothing at all! He'd guzzled them all!...all the gold!...Ah!
the big fat dirty glutton!...And he was exulting, delighted!
...through his coughing fits!...He couldn't stop laughing,
the freak!...His whole guts jingling!...All the gold in it!
hardware!...Jangling! Jingling!...Ah! he was feeling much
better!...He sits up...He wants to smarten up, put on makeup!...a little lipstick!...do his eyelashes!...his eyebrows...
Kittenish! Kittenish!

"I want to love you, you little rascal! you little savage!"...
he's teasing me...He's steaming, drooling, bubbling, grunting
...I can't move any more...I'm not like him...I feel like
lead!...My head! legs! everything!...I'm groggy!...I force
myself...uh! uh!...I'm rolling...I tumble off the bed...He
grabs hold of me...he hoists me up...he puts me down near
them...

Then Delphine starts acting nuts!...she grabs me, she sucks
at me!...She's a vampire!...I'm revolted, tear away!...A
mighty leap!...Into the air!...I get away...I'm saved!...I
fall down on the rifle!...the big Winchester!...his hunting
gun!...I grab it...I don't let go!...it melts in my hands!

...that's a fact!...I'm telling the truth! it melts away on me!
...The butt stretches like putty, it trickles through my fingers
...Marshmallow!...everything I touch melts!...and everything starts turning around the globe! like a merry-go-round
...the water-lamp...I'm seeing things inside it! I see gar-
lands...I see flowers!...I see daffodils!...I see birdies!...I
realize it's not so...I tell Boro!...He belches at me!...He's
between Delphine and the old guy!...They're still at their
dirty game!...there in the big bed!...They're making me
sicker!...The guy who guzzled all his dough!...he doesn't
feel sick!...all the money in his bag!...he's satisfied...he's
hilarious!...he's jumping around on his big can...he's squealing with joy!...

Boro's getting annoyed, he's getting sore...He demands
twenty-five pounds and right away...Twenty-five pounds then
and there...twenty-five! A big stink, right away!...no kidding
around!...He's getting hot under the collar!...He starts
boiling!...He's acting like my father!...his eyes are rolling,
goggling, popping out of his head!...that's the way he is.

"My pound!" he screams..."No my twenty-five!...No
thirty!...Shit!" He's always wanting more!...

He grabs him by his overcoat...by his scarf...he's throt-
tling him!...

"You going to puke it out, you skunk?"

Delphine's lying there with her head thrown back, grunting,
dazed...She's wailing, puking...The old guy feels like throwing up too...He's making horrible efforts...he's barking!...
He's beating the air!...waving his arms around...All you
can see is the white of his eyes!...He wants to vomit but he
can't!...not a single little goldpiece!...he's convulsing, even
disgorging! but only drool!...only gurgles...not a single
coin!...Oooach!...Oooaach!...No go.

"Slit open his belly!...Slit it!" Boro yells to me...wild,

dishonest..."Slit it! I want mine right now!...Stop thief!...
empty him!"

He's talking to me.

That's an idea!...It's superb!...Ah! I get enthusiastic
pronto!

Ah! but what'll Delphine say?...Ah! I've got to wake her
up right away!...Got to see the face she'll make! We're going
to open her guy up!...Come on! I'm shaking you, baby-doll!
...I grab her by the hair, I jolt her!...I yank her!...Nothing
doing! She grunts but doesn't wake up! Then Boro gets on the
old guy, mounts on his belly!

He's crushing him with all his weight!...squeezing his
Adam's apple meanwhile...and harder and harder!...The
Horror turns all yellow right away...his tongue's hanging
clean out...He's not breathing any more, that's sure!...He's
just a big enormous yellow piece of wax!...It's awful to look
at! I can't take any more!..."I don't want to see it!" I tell
him right out!...

"Come here!" says Boro...he's ordering me besides!...
"Come on, mopey!...Got to give the poor guy some relief!
...You'll see! We're going to do him lots of good!"

Ah! it's about time!...what a fine idea!...I'm all for it!
...right away!

So we grab him by the shoes...we lift up the whole damned
bulk another little bit!...Wow! He's heavy!...He's heavy!
...Good and heavy!...head hanging down!...heavy as an
ox! Whiss! lift! Ah! It's tough work!...I'm sweating!...
streams of it!...makes me close my eyes!...Whiss! Another
big tug!...Whiss!...and poof!...let go!...plop!!! his hard
skull on the stone floor!...it jolts the whole shop!...The
whole place jumps with the shock!...the turban comes off...
rolls away!...and we start all over!...Whiss!...once! twice!
mustn't give in!...Up in the air...and bangg!!...all his

179

weight!...he's going to puke up his nest egg!...No go! No go!...Doesn't puke! Nothing!...Doesn't throw up a single coin!...It's dumbfounding! It dumbfounds both of us!...It gets us damned sore again!...It's not high enough from the bed!...Got to lift him way higher! an enormous height!

Ah! that's the idea!...hoist him up again by his capes, head down!...Up the stairway!...all the way up!...Oooh! whiss! all the steps!...the whole flight! Oooh! whiss! and up! let 'er go! boy, it's hard work!...keep at it! Ah! that does it! here he is! Let 'er go! Whang! What a crash! whang! his big head! ...the whole floor shakes with the shock!...not a peep out of him!...not the least sigh!...not an oof!...He crashed. That's all!...We can't leave him like that!...We jump on his belly...We bounce up and down on it!...to see if he's going to puke!...Go fuck yourself!...Doesn't say oof!...not the slightest hiccup...We bend down to look at his face...we put the globe lamp right against it...his head's split! Wow! ...a hole right between the eyes...A crack!...a noseful of snot dripping...Hasn't said oof! Just like that, ringing his head!...Boro stares popeyed...It's all white...all gooey... all the same it's a surprise...He didn't say oof!...hasn't puked up a coin!...not one little sovereign!...Ah! the mule! He's stubborn!...

"Hey!" Boro exclaims..."Hey, you!...Can you imagine such a louse? Didn't even burp!"

I look at him...I don't get it...And then I sit down, God damn it!...That was some job!...He sure was heavy!... We had a tough time!...I wouldn't've believed it!...It made me dizzy!...Even Boro was knocked out!...And yet he's a real husky!...We both sit down...We just sit there like dopes. We're resting on the furs...On the bugger's couch! let's hit the hay, brother!...we sure accomplished something! ...That's what I said to Boro...

180

Delphine doesn't give a damn! she's sleeping! She's snoring again! She's sprawled out against the old guy...I close my eyes to see if I'm not sleeping...I feel myself...If it's not a dream...Hell no!...no it's not a dream!...it's true enough all right!

"Listen!" I say to Boro..."I can't get over what happened!"

He can't get over it either...

"We've been acting drunk!"

I'm talking about the incident...

He doesn't answer...he pukes...He's the first one sick.

"It's the booze, all right!"...I point out..."Maybe the cigarettes, too."

Ah! that's my idea...I stick to it...The cigarettes!...I always said so!...That's Delphine's fault, too!...that old faker!...But what about the guy there on the floor?...the skull there!...the hole!...Ah! take it easy!...

I try reasoning a little...

"Say, you drunk! Didn't you see his dome?"

"It's you, you bastard!" he answers right back at me..."It's your affair and that's all there's to it!"

He's accusing me!

Ah! That's a new one!...He's waking up! He stops vomiting...Now for the complaints!...

"Ah!" I say..."Aren't you ashamed, you big louse? I suppose it wasn't you who banged him?...It wasn't you who jumped up and down on him like that on the floor?"

I point to him...

"It was you!...It was you!" he insists..."All you had to do was hold him up...You were the one holding him!"

Listen to that!...some gag!...I can't get over the phoniness of it! such dishonesty!...ah! the pig!

"It was you!...It was you!" he insists...

"Oh!" I exclaim..."disgusting!...I suppose it wasn't you

181

who split it open?...I suppose you haven't seen his poor head?"

"His poor head!...His poor head!...Ah! listen to him!... his poor head!...Talking to me like that! to me!"

He's outraged by my insolence!...He sits down on the edge of the bed, he can't stand my guts, he's choking with fury!... he's gagging and snorting with such rage that he can't even say a word!...he's rocking...jumps up...Delphine wakes up, she's crying...she doesn't know what she's bawling about...

She looks at us...she's all shaken with sobs...I go at him again, the matter's not settled!...It's still on my mind!...

"But it was you, Boro!...You were the one!"

I want him to realize...to stop shooting his mouth off!

"Me?...Me?"...he repeats...in a real daze...

"Me what?...Me what?"

He doesn't understand a thing.

Outside it's getting a little light...it's starting...you can see it through the blinds...sort of vague...greenish...then gray...It's not ordinary daylight...it has an effect on me... it's different from the usual daylight...

"You got to be careful you know, you dog!"...I'm warning him...eye to eye!...."Got to watch out for drafts!...you see the old guy there?...He died on account of them"...That's how I talk to him. To me it's funny!...Jigging! there! writhing around!...let him laugh too, the dirty gorilla!

"What about the gal?...Is she moving?"

She's stretched out...she's crying again!...I give her a kick in the ribs...so she'll straighten up!...She lets out a yell...She's reacting and furioso!...Her eyes are all stuck together...she rubs them...she gets the moths out...bango, a riot!...She spits at me...she insults me...She calls me a garbage pail!...Who'd've thought it!...She, usually so lady-

182

like!...she forgets all about her politeness!...just a little kick!

"You little pirate!" she yells..."you little hyena!...you cholera!"

Ah!...some nerve!...I answer back!...

"You pig!" I say to her..."You bitch!...Look at your guy!"

She hasn't even seen him!...The fathead hasn't seen a thing ...I grab her by the back of the neck, I force her, I make her bend down so she can look! Right up against him!...With her nose on top of him!...

"What do you say about that?...There!...Take a look! ...now say something!"

But it's too dark in the room...she doesn't see a thing...I bring over the lamp, right against him...the water globe... That does it!...She sees him all right! She sees it all...she wobbles her head...she stands there gaga, without moving...

"Ah!" she says, "ah! oh!"...she can't believe it...just petrified...and then wow!

"Oooh!...Oooh!"...she starts howling, and what screams! She plunges forward...throws herself on the body...she grabs it...hugs it...she kisses it all over...mouth!...eyes! she lies on top of it!...She kisses the head, the blood...she slobbers all over it!...and then she goes for us!

"You murderers! murderers!" she calls us, and she points at us!...she's counting us..."One!...Two!...One! two murderers!"

"Go take a shit, you whore!"

It's getting on Boro's nerves..."Sh! sh!" he whispers...she doesn't give a damn!...she's high! she's in a trance, that's all! ...Now she's at us!

"Why, you murderers! don't you know me? you don't know who I am? Finish your job!"

She's offering herself up like that as a victim...her, too!...
the martyr! the volunteer! Right off! immediately!...she's
egging us on!...She's challenging us!...

"One more to kill! here! here!"...She shows us her skinny
chest...she bares herself...

"Finish your job!"

All exalted...panting!...

"I'm Mary Stuart! Yes! I've just arrived from France!"

She's proclaiming it!...Then she dashes to the body again
...she kneels over Claben in prayer...all shuddering...she
lifts her veil high up, over the feathers...her hat...she un-
covers her neck...she's offering it to us!...to cut it off...her
slender neck...

"Cut it off!...Cut it off!" she wants us to behead her...It's
her last breath..."Cut it off!...Cut it off!"

She's ordering it...she starts all over...

"I'm Mary Stuart, from France!"

Same refrain!...damn it! that's enough...Boro's enjoying
it, the big ape! Ah! I've had more than enough!...He doesn't
see it's getting light outside! almost day...I point to it.

"Look!" I say to him..."Look!"

I sit down again...I'm too tired...and the other idiot's still
yelling her head off! I can't kill them all!...Ah! it's getting
too light...The yataghan's back!...It's on the table...I see it
there!...I'm going to take it now!...I'm going to grab it!
...No!...Not worth the trouble!...Everything's been said
...First of all, it's getting cold!...dawn's breaking...the
cold...No denying it...Cold and anxious...Boy, but it's
cold!...I'm shivering...the questions going through my mind!
...loads of 'em, real ones...not drunken nonsense!...real
questions with the cold!...You can't just go on raising hell,
it's got to come to an end...and then you've got to get out
of it! Doesn't work out all by itself!...You finally come to

184

realize it!...I throw up a bit...gives me some relief...it was the right moment!...Boro's puking, too...We sit down in a reasonable state of mind!...Enough foolishness!...We try to think!...It's cold now!...It's almost daytime!...Delphine interrupts us!...Ah! that old fart!...she's yelling again... whining louder and louder!...Mary Stuart's over...She's got a headache now...Like pincers twisting her head around!...

"What a headache! What pain!"...She turns to me..."Do you hear me, Froggy?"

She's insulting me as a Frenchman!...Then she starts putting on her act again...she plunges into prayer...kneeling over the body...with tears streaming!...she starts begging us to cut off her head!...her headache's too bad!...That's how she is!

"Go on, you rascals!...Go on, you brutes!" she begs us... "Here's Mary Stuart for you! Here's Mary Stuart! The poor little queen!"...She gives us a pain in the ass!...All the same, we're going to have to get out! arrange things in the place! at least try to!...I was used to it, I'd already seen bodies and bloodier ones than this!...much more messed up!...I'd seen much worse!...especially in Artois!...under the mortars... really chopped up!...I was quiet, in a way, it was Boro who was worried...

"You think it's really him?" he asks me again.

Some idea.

It's a funny question to ask me...he touches him again, he's in doubt! he messes around!...He leans on his belly!...

"Say!" he calls to him..."Say!"

He'd even like to make him talk!...He picks up the turban ...He puts it back on the head...It's hard for him to realize ...It doesn't seem possible to him...Still he's sobered up... he sees straight...But he still doesn't realize...

He doesn't yield to reason...

185

"You think it's really him?"

Ah! the idiot!

"Of course!" I answer, "of course!...and you're the one who split his head open!"

"Me? Me?"

He stares at me flabbergasted.

"Of course!...Sure!...and how!"

I want him to get it into his head! So I insist, damn it, I've got to!

"Say! Delphine! Listen! Listen to him!"

He's calling Delphine to witness, he's acting phony again! ...But Delphine's not listening...she's leaning her head forward...her neck bent over her body...she's offering herself up...that's all she wants...she wants to be beheaded...she's dead set on it!

Boro's wild with anger, with rage at me!...He's acting flabbergasted, out of his mind!...

"But God damn it!...But it's a shame!"

Ah! the skunk, he's trying to bluff me!...He flies off the handle!...

"Who fell on his head this time?" he asks me...the nerve of him!

"The old guy!" I answer..."The old guy!...He fell from his stepladder all by himself! Now are you satisfied?...Is that enough for you?...He threw himself down...Does that explain it?"

I bust out laughing...Boy, that's a hot one, the stepladder!

Clears up everything, doesn't it?

Ah! I'm proud of myself!...

I stand up...I want to take a look outside! I want to breathe the air! I feel dizzy again...I sit down...I want to get it straight, still and all...But I've got an awful headache!... my ear's buzzing bad...my arm's throbbing...the orgy! the drunk! the cigarettes!...I try to figure out what might happen

...I can't think straight!...The old guy, that's a fact!...
There he is!...His head's split all right!...No mistake about
that!...He's in a heap in front of us!...In all his embroider-
ies!...the turban, the overcoats...It's all there!...

"Well, got to get him out!"...the idea occurs to me..."Got
to send for the police!"

There's a brilliant idea!...

"Shut up!...Leave him there...We'll go get Cascade."

That's the way he answers. It's certainly more reasonable!
...I immediately agree...I even congratulate him!...I
wouldn't have thought of that by myself!...And then I throw
up again!...It's some relief! but not much...I invite Delphine to come outside...She's nauseated too...but she won't
go out at all...doesn't want to get any air.

She never wants to leave the body again!...That's Delphine for you!

"Come on! this way, little birdie!"

Boro grabs her by her bun and ouch! she's got to get up!...
We're all pretty seedy...We don't look so good!...I'm staggering...It wasn't an ordinary drunk!...Ah! now I'm quite
sure of it! We finally get to the door...We open it...The
light comes rolling in. It blasts me!...absolutely right in the
eyes! like a punch! I grab hold!...I don't know what it is!
...I open again!...It's the park!...Right in front!...Right
there!...the steps...I grab the railing...it's clearing up!...
The veils are lifting...it's gray...purple...in front of my
eyes...it's dawn...What time is it?...No bells are ringing!
...Maybe five o'clock, six?...in my opinion!...Delphine's
whimpering...that it still hurts...that she'll never be able to
move again!...She forces herself, anyway...She gets to her
feet...Now she's simpering.

"Gentlemen!" she calls out..."Gentlemen! it's all a mistake!...It's the fumes of drunkenness!"

She straightens her hat, her feathers, her gloves...She puts on a smile...she's enjoying herself..."What a mistake!"...a lady of fashion...just bantering...just a joke...She's amused at the sight of us...woebegone, crestfallen...she finds us funny, childish...She treats us like little rascals...

"Boys! Boys!" she calls us..."You drank too much!... You're sick!"

She plants herself there in front of us!...She's going to whip the little devils!...going to restore us to reason!...

Ah! then Boro grabs her...he lifts her up!...carries her to the back!...throws her down on her knees so she can get a good look! so she'll stop being a pain in the ass! so she can get a good look at the stiff! so she'll stop dreaming!...

"Look!...Look!" he tells her..."That's not him, eh?... That's not him?"

She hangs back...she grumbles...she doesn't understand a thing...then suddenly she starts screaming again!...

"That's the man!...Yes that's the man!" she screams..."It's he...It's the devil! Gentlemen, we are all damned!"

There goes another riot...

She rushes toward the steps...She yells it across the park ...to the trees!...to the open air!...to the echoes!...Boro grabs her again...He brings her back in...She throws herself on the stiff...she starts kissing it again!...

"Darling! Darling!" right on the mouth!...above his wound...all around...she sucks the opening...she gets all spattered with blood!...

Boro yanks her away again...

"Go wash!" he says..."Go wash!...Shit!"

He pushes her under the faucet...he takes her completely in hand...he gives her a good rinsing.

"Come on! you mope! Let's go!"

He holds on to her...he keeps her head under the running water!...She howls...she protests...

188

"But I'm Lady Macbeth! Never! Never! Never shall I be clean again! Never more!"

She thrashes about. . .but he doesn't let go!

Now we've got to make up our minds!. . .Do we go?. . . Or don't we?. . .Ah! I'm trying to think!. . .I want to put my word in, too! I don't say anything!. . .It's sleepiness, my eyes hurt too much. . .sleep first. . .I couldn't have told left from right!. . .Ah! it's pretty bad, all the same!. . .I force myself . . .I take a look outside. . .there on the steps. . .I see the trees climbing in the park. . .I see them growing visibly. . .there in front!. . .right in front of my eyes. . .branches and branches! . . .the way they're going up and up!. . .to dizzying heights! . . .and then they get tiny. . .tiny little trees, tiny little branches, they all shrivel up small. . .they get into my pocket! whole trees!. . .I don't believe it! No. . .I don't believe! Ah! can't fool me! It's just dizziness! a mirage! But I see them moving! Ah! no denying it! it's a fact! they're rising up!. . .It's still the smoke I see! as far as the Observatory up there! it's in full blossom. . .All those moving treetops give me a pain in the ass!

Ah! but Boro's in charge. . .he's doing the talking. . ."Let's go!"

So we're out in the chilly air. . .Boro's dragging us along. . . We don't go far. . .Just to the bench. . .We squat in front of the lawn. . .in front of the bed of heliotrope. . .I remember clearly. . .I still see it!. . .on the other side is the water! the bank!. . .and farther on Poplar. . .the gray house-fronts. . .the anchored barges.

The three of us are sitting there. . .on the bench. . .We're wondering. . .got to know!. . .Delphine's between us. . .she's afraid we'll run away. . .

"What do you say?. . .Talk, wise guy!"

I wasn't saying anything.

"Listen!" I exclaim. . ."Listen!"

189

It was striking six o'clock over London...ah! it was true...
exactly six o'clock!...I was right! Boom! Boom!...Real loud
above the wharves!...from way off in the distance!...

"Say!...Say listen!"

That was all I had to say!...

"Don't you know anything, you dumb dope?...Don't you
know anything?"

He insists on my knowing!...But God damn it I don't
know anything!...What I like is the Booms!...it makes me
fluttery...hazy...the sound of the chimes...especially as I'm
already bleary, already off center...I get lit up! that's it! lit up!
I'm sensitive! I vibrate!...He can't understand, the big lug!
...Dirty filthy dope!

"They're drifting!" I say to him..."They're drifting!...The
chimes are drifting, don't you hear them?...Listen, you slob!
...You blockhead! you murderer!"

Pop! just like that! whack, right in the teeth! It simply
came to my mouth!...

The hell with him!

"What?" he gasps..."Wh-what, you louse? I'll show you!"

He's about to leap at my throat...He thinks it over...He
sits still...

"Shit!" he mumbles..."Shit!"...he's grousing...

"You don't give a damn, you stinker!"

I do give a damn! But I'm cold...that's the size of it!...
I'm shivering!...So's Delphine...Is he warm?...Delphine
and I are shaking the bench...We're trembling so much that
we're going to knock it over...People are passing by...the
early-risers...men from the dock opposite...They stare at us
...They wonder what's up...why we're yelling at each other
like that...what the hell we're doing there...We shouldn't
be talking so loud...But he's the one shouting, not me!...

He's ill-bred!...his voice booms through the park!...his Bulgarian accent...

"So, you mug! you don't give a damn?"...That's how he talks to me!..."You're leaving it all to me?"

"No! that's not so!"

"Maybe it wasn't you?"

There it goes! he's at it again!...He's starting!...he's stubborn! God damn it!

"It wasn't you who tossed him around!....I suppose it wasn't you? Maybe I was the one who was drunk?"

The gall! He's pulling a fast one! He still dares!

"A dream!....A dream!" I answer.

Ah! he can't control himself...He's foaming!...Some act! ...He gets off the bench to yell at me...for better effect! Ah! he's on the wrong tack! He makes us laugh!...he's trying hard!...he's working himself up!...he's gesticulating, the lunkhead!...standing there right in front of us...He absolutely wants me to confess! He bounces around, jumps on the grass!...with fury! with hot air!...

"And the hell with you, you big dope! A dream! A dream!" I shriek...I'm not at all excited!...I want to see how far he'll jump!

"You're warming us up, lunkhead!...But a cup of coffee would be even better!"

I let him have it!

Ah! I'm not at all excited!...It calms me to see him in such a stew!...

Can you imagine! Can you imagine! What screams! The lunatic! hysterical!...worse than Delphine almost! She starts having fun too!...she makes a spectacle of herself...yowling! ...laughing!...kicking up!...I swear, at it again!...now they're both at it! she clucking away like that and he crazy with rage! that I'm just sitting there indifferent!...taking it easy and not giving a damn!

He can croak there raving!...I won't budge except for coffee!...good and hot! and a nip! Won't budge, Delphine neither!...Our mind's made up!...we huddle together!... we're shivering...and we're laughing!...He starts insulting us again!...People are walking around us...

"Come on!" I decide..."Let's go!"

It's getting idiotic.

"Let's go where?" he asks.

"Why, to see Cascade! you don't remember?...it was your idea!"

It really was his idea...

"And what about the old guy? You're leaving him like that? ...You don't care?...with the door open?"

He thought of everything.

It's true that we hadn't closed up!...that we'd left everything as is!...That was bad! what a binge!...You could see the door open from our bench, you could see it from there... Had to go back and close the door!...The least of our troubles!...

"All right! Then what're you going to do?"

I saw he had a scheme...

"We'll take him down!"

"Down where?"

"To the cellar!"

"And then what?"

"We'll come back tonight with the men."

"Good!" I said..."You're smart!"

It's true that it wasn't a dumb idea...in the cellar, that was a little better...

"You want me to help you?"

"I sure do!"

192

Good! I make an effort...I stand up...I shouldn't have...
feel like vomiting again...sleeping too...I feel the torpor
getting me again...
"Let's go! Get a move on!"
He's hustling me.
I'm on my feet again...I take Delphine's arm...we're in
front of the house...the door wide open...that's a fact...the
shop as is...We go in...nothing has moved...Still and all
it was queer...We weren't drunk...We walk through the
shop...there was the body on the floor...there on its belly...
in the overcoats...the silks...the soaked rug, a pool, the turban in the puddle...
"Come on!"...he shakes me..."Let's go! take him by the
cape...Delphine, you the legs!...Let's go! Lift!"
You can't imagine how heavy he was! Even heavier than on
the stairway!...He weighed around two hundred-fifty pounds!
It was like lead, only soft...He was rolling all over...You
couldn't get a grip on him...all flabby, enormous padding...
The three of us got him down...the cellar staircase...the trap
door open, luckily...the two of us eased him down...the wide
staircase...the cellar passage full of sand...We laid him
there...he sure was heavy!...We just laid him right down...
in the middle of the cellar, on the sand...and it was all dark!
just the water-lamp for the whole maneuver!...
It was quite a big cellar...a vast vault...but what a junk
heap! much worse than the shop! what a chaos!...All the
secondhand odds and ends! tons, piles of rubbish!...cartloads
of everything!
"We'll leave him here! Hell, that'll do!"
I sit down, I'm puffing, it knocked me out...on one of the
steps...in the darkness...I'm resting. Delphine, right on the
sand.
"Ah! we made it!" I remark..."It's done!"

We were about to go up again...I'm telling everything exactly as it was.

"Hey!" Boro suddenly calls out, he grabs my arm as if he's heard a noise...something upstairs in the shop. I listen, I don't hear anything...

"Sh!" he orders..."Don't move, I'm going to see what's up ...There're people!"

He scoots up, he leaves us all alone just like that...It wasn't funny...with the corpse!!!...He does what he says...He goes up...And he shuts the big trap door on us! right in the dark...Ah! that was laying it on!...I didn't understand! Ah! he's shutting us in!

"Hey! hey!" I call..."Shit! What the hell!" He doesn't answer...Not a word!...I hear him walking, moving furniture, putting things over our heads, right on the trap door... Ah! then I start roaring!...

"Boro! Boro! What the hell are you doing?"

He continues, he's making a lot of noise...he's throwing things down...a raft of stuff on the trap door...Ah! he's shutting us in!...I don't hear anyone with him...he's all alone in the shop!...Ah! that does it!...suspicion!...hell! I'm sure!...Ah! that does it! he's shutting us in!...He's locking us up!...

I clutch the steps!...I bang the door!...

"Boro!" I scream..."open up!"

Go fuck yourself!...I try to do something...I set my back against the wall...It's stuck! Shit! What did he put there?... the lousy traitor!...Everything in the shop!...I heave again! ...I'm forcing...Oooooh! whshhh!...the rat!...it's giving! ...just a crack...I see the shop...a ray of light!...I take a better stance...I've got a strong back...Oooh! whshhh! oh whshhh...there it goes!...it's coming! I've pushed it back!

...I've got an opening!...Just then plop!...right in the mush!...I get smacked!...right in the mug!...wham!!... I get groggy!...I tumble over!...backwards!...from the crack! I let go!...the trap door crashes!...falls back! clack! It's that bandit! Boom!!!...Thunder bursting in the darkness! ...right in the cellar!...at the same time!...amidst all the junk!...Ah! it's magical!...right in the mug!...The rubbish comes down on me...He's the one who threw the gadget! Dirty dog!...a terrific explosion!...Him again!...That's it! ...like at the Dingby...I suspected it!...I should have suspected!...I'm whirling around in the plaster!...in the dark! ...I'm pulled in! rolled over! flattened out! all the junk and timber fall on my mug!...I call Delphine..."Delphine!"... She answers!...She's stuck in the sand...she's screaming... she's not dead yet...everything fell on her head!...under a heap of chunks of wood...I feel my way...I don't see anything...I catch hold of her...I clutch her!...by the shoes... I disentangle her...I yank at her!...She screams...but it's nothing...she's in a kind of sand tank...under a heap of broken cases...I tug at the whole shebang...pull it all along! ...all that in pitch darkness...

"It's a bomb!" I explain..."It's Boro!"

She doesn't understand...she's choking...it's full of bitter smoke...the whole cellar...but not cigarette smoke...the real thing! It's coming from the back, I sniff, it's burning! It's a fire!...I see sparks...in the smoke...Delphine really starts screaming...as if I were killing her!...

"All right, Delphine! There's nothing the matter with you! ...Help me!" I shout...so she can push the trap door with me!...

"I'm blind!" she answers...

"You're not! It's the smoke!...the cellar!"

She's panicky...she wants to get away! to run to the back! into the fire! I get hold of her again...I pull her to the steps!...

"Come on, you bitch!...together!"

I want to raise the door again...A last effort!...

"Push, darling!...push!"

It rose a tiny bit...things were toppling down! wobbling ...Boom!! it was furniture piled up...all the junk!...We weren't getting anywhere! They were cabinets!...dead sure! ...buffets that weighed a ton!...

"Push!" I repeated...

"But I am!"

She was protesting. Smoke was coming from the shop... more smoke!...it was rushing in through the opening!... smoke from everywhere!...into the hole!...into our cellar! from our pit! from the shop!...We were caught in the spirals ...it came rushing up!...choking everything!...Now the vixen was giving all she had! with all her might! Come on, no more groaning! whiss! against the door!...She forgot about wanting to die...no more Mary Stuart!...no more whining! ...But it wasn't giving, damn it! Whiss! it dropped again... catastrophe! the door Ba-ta-boom!...it was too heavy!... Needed something else!...I didn't lose my head!...in spite of my sniffling, gasping and choking....I'm not flustered... keep cool!...I look for something hard...there...an iron! ...something...I feel around among the junk...in the dark ...I grab an iron in the rubbish, a crowbar!...I ram it into the trapdoor, groping...my eyes hurt like mad...from the smoke...I ram it into the door and oop!...Oooh whiss! both of us! we press down! press down!...we get it up!...ah it's coming!...Oooh whiss! that's it! it gives! tumbles down! everything! the whole works!...topples over! cases! ward- robes!...the whole shebang...everything he'd piled on us!

196

...The door loosens, opens! That does it!...made it!...but it's murder! The shop's burning! what smoke!...the whole place! the whole floor! The fire's roaring!...all over the house ...the flames are licking, racing, snarling...Wow! Lady!... There're sheets of flame...We're sneezing...sniffling...suffocating...It's too much!...It's worse than in the hole!...

"Do something!" Delphine yells...She grabs my hands!... She clutches at me!

"No!...No!...come on with me!"

We've got to push the door some more...so we can get out...out in the open...make a dash for it!...and oop! outside! out through the flames! right through everything! knock the stuff over!...Come on! Let's go! No monkey-business!... I see the door at the other end...the daylight...the white frame...into the smoke...we've got to tear through!... ah! ...right in the bull's-eye!

"Let's go Delphine! careful!...together! now! one! two! three!...right through it!...Come on!"...We dash forward ...I hadn't noticed!

Plop! I stumble! I topple over! I'm lifted up! carried away! two hands! ten hands clutch me! grab me!...rush me off!... the works!...Ah! the smoke!...I couldn't see a thing!...But outside! in the open! The firemen!...the people!...They're all over!...We're outside! we're saved!...What a crowd... Ah! the firemen!...Ah! what acrobats! with their helmets! brass! ladders! the streams of water...shooting, spattering! squirting all over! They grab us...water us!...drench us!... I'm not burned!...Neither is Delphine!...That doesn't matter!...They douse us anyway!...they soak us, plunge us into the enormous tub!...They fish us out, shake us, rub us down, roll us up in blankets...It's the excitement!...A rescue!... And then questions, words...bowing and scraping! they congratulate us! Shake hands!...Hurrah for our courage!..hugs!

197

"Hello! Hello!"...They saw us cut through the flames!...
It was magnificent!...Ah! a rousing rescue! Marvelous! Superb! Attaboy! What a jump! Atta good girl!...They're all talking together; And the questions! They're screaming! Claben!...the crowd's yelling for him...

They want to know where Claben is! Old Claben!...What's happened to him? His customers are very unhappy!...Ah! they're worried!...They get close to the flames...They come back!...The whole house is on fire now!

"Inside!" I point, I'm breathless...dying from the effort ..."He's in there!...in there!"...I point to the flames...the giant fire...The furnace that's roaring, growling...

"Oh!" they all exclaim..."Oh!"

It's too horrible.

"Yes, he was sleeping in the shop!"

I keep repeating it, mumbling...I'm fully convinced... it's got to be sure...absolutely!...naturally...

"Did you see him?"

"Yes, yes!"

Not the slightest doubt. That way there won't be any mistake...It's a sure thing!

The house was crackling horribly...from top to bottom!... the firemen couldn't get at it any more...not even approach it from a hundred yards!...it was just a torch...a wild enormous torch...the flames were shooting from all the windows...The crowd was getting bigger and bigger...they must have come from all neighborhoods...a terrible jabbering in addition to the crackling of the flames...all around the burning mass...they must have seen it from far off...from farther off than the devil...They'd come rushing up in crowds! ...a storm of jabberers!...The rescuers of the Order of Saint John with their soft little hats took good care of us...Delphine and me!...quite specially...their heroic survivors!...They

cheered us up...crammed us, coddled us...biscuits...brandy
...hot coffee!...ah! at last...

"Coffee!" I said to Delphine...

She straightened her hat, coquettish immediately!...Her
silk dress was scorched...That shows what a close shave we
had...she'd lost her gloves...We watched the house flaming
...the House of Claben...I wasn't thinking of anything else!

Nothing's so fascinating as flames, especially flying around
like that, shooting, dancing in the sky...It just makes you
stare ...spellbound...the shapes they take...just dazed,
dopey, gaping...sitting on the grass...Delphine, too, beside
me...

Someone takes hold of me...shakes me, damn it! grabs me,
hugs me to his body!...What's going on?

"My child!...My child!"

I thought it was the firemen again!...that they were going
to dunk us again! that they were going to rescue us again!
Oh! what a horror! I scream! I yell! but it wasn't the firemen!
I look! it was Boro! the louse himself! suddenly gushing! ah!
the fairy! hugging! tears!

"My child!...My child!"

He embraces us...kisses us!...Ah! what a fine chap! he's
so happy to see us again!...

"Neither one of you is burned?"

Ah! he's so excited!...He's squealing with joy!...he's crying...he's yapping around us!...

"Oh! my children!...Oh! my children!"

It's such a moving scene!...

"Are you safe and sound, my children?"

The people rush up...they all want to kiss us...

It's a unanimous effusion...What can I say?...I kiss him,
too...I kiss anyone!...I kiss a fireman! a Saint John!...

But he doesn't give us time to think...

199

"Let's go home!...Let's hurry!"

"Home where?"

We don't know...

He grabs Delphine by the arm...off they go together...I'm going to follow...I'm going to follow them...I look at the house again...the flames are shooting up! whirling around! ...climbing...waltzing up above!...the yellow, the red wreaths!...Ah! some furnace!...I'm not going to stay around! ...I'd get burned again!...I get going...I force myself... I catch up with them...Ah! now, my boy, you're going to get it! When we pass the kiosk I go for him!...

"Listen, you big louse!...listen you mug!"

He doesn't answer...he's stepping on it...

Ah! that's nerve for you!

His arm in Delphine's and oops! she's got to hustle!...get a move on! She asks for a second!...she's all in!...a stitch in her side!...then her shoe!...her heel's twisting! and damn it! and damn it!...he won't let go!...Shake a leg!...Shake a leg! she's hobbling..."Come on!" he pinches her...what a shriek!...The people look at us...the whole sidewalk!...We were moving fast...to the station, the Stepham entrance... they're swallowed up...the Tube...I catch up...he gets the tickets...At last! We squat! oof! in the train...it bumps along...I ask him where we're going...

"To Cascade's, of course! You know well enough!"

I irritate him by asking...

We pass one station...two...three...

Cascade's? I don't like that...I don't want to...that's enough!...Shit! I don't want to drag around like that... disgusting!...it's awful!...I don't care if I'm sick, nuts, knocked out, limp and everything...Hell! I won't go with them!...I won't follow them!...The big filthy pig! and the other one, the old witch! Go on, strut!...I've had enough of their guts!

...and of Cascade, too!...suddenly it hits me, it sets me on fire! Ah! what a dope I am! I never in my life want to see them again! Ah! I'll have the strength, God damn it!...none of them! The little trains give you a jolting...They're jerky... They're nervous...We pass a station...we'll soon come to Clapham...

"You're not sore?" he asks me...

"Oh! no! no! I'm not sore!"

It's nice of him...

"Just wait!" I say to myself..."the next one!...Boy, am I going to beat it!....Sincerely yours!...Good sailing! my darlings!"

Clapham! That's it!...Now's the moment! A whistle!... the door! It just closes! I dash forward! squeeze it open... Zip!...That does it!...Push! on the platform!...just! on the button! Yip! Bravo, boy! The train takes off!...Oh! their mugs!...They see me! I didn't get hurt!...lucky! whisked! zip! with my leg!

"So long!...So long!" I yell to them...

There! I did it! Now some rest! Squat! first!

Wait a minute!...Got to know where I am...the stations are all right for that.

So now I'm free...I drag around like that for two...three days...I sleep here and there...I spend time in the movies... I keep out of sight pretty much...I avoid the center of town ...I watch out for meeting the wrong people! I keep track of my money...all the same, it's running out...When I've got around two or three shillings left, I say to myself that I've got to stay in the stations...It's warm, you sleep well, you wait...

I had no definite ideas...I couldn't make up my mind... I decided on Waterloo...It's got the nicest waiting-room... It's certainly the most upholstered...I knew a particular bench on the other side of the heaters that was as inconspicuous as possible...back behind the exit...from which you could see people passing...the whole crowd...all the main lines...A real torrent in those days...all the men in the services...a continuous stream of soldiers...khaki!...more khaki!...at the gate there'd be a waiting...swarms of hustlers!...they'd cross inside!...I know you!...At random...high-heeled shoes!...boas! yellow stockings!...red stockings...purple stockings!...the styles of the time...on the attack...a hot chase!...day and night!...They'd carry off Tommy Atkins with his wad! Mohamed Jouglou! Gorgovitch! whatever came along! soldiers on a spree! the dominions! the natives! the dear allies! at top speed!...tearing off a piece not a hundred yards away...in the alley to the left, first floor...Tudor Commons

202

...I shouldn't have sat down there...After all it wasn't play-ing safe! But I was pretty bored, got to admit!...That was my excuse...I didn't know anyone...I dozed awhile on the upholstered seat...I even had a rather long sleep...Suddenly ...someone's disturbing me...shaking me...

"It's you!....Ah! it's you, pretty boy!"

I jump up with a start...

"Ah! it's you, Finette?....Ah! that's nice!"

"What the hell are you doing here?"...She's questioning me..."They're all asking about you at the Leicester!"

I'd rather not talk much...I mumble something...that I'd taken a little trip...She was the one who gave me the news ...that things were fine at the "Boardinghouse"...that there were no more arguments...that everyone had made up...on the go again for a time...That Cascade had taken back all his women...that Joconde was back, cured, from the London Hospital...with her mashed-up ass...was down in the kitchen again...that Angèle was back with her bad boy...that she was breaking in the new girls...but that Cascade's sore about my breezing out on him!...Ah! he doesn't like that one bit!...

"All right, Finette! All right!" I answer..."You still haven't got me!....I can see you coming a mile off!"

Suddenly I feel anxious again...

"Who?...Who sent you?" I ask..."Spit it out!...Right now!...Cascade or Matthew?"

Ah! no monkey-business!

"Me?" she exclaims..."Ah! It's a crime! I swear to you!"

"Well?" I said, dropping my voice..."It must be about the Dingby!...say it!...or Claben? Eh?...isn't it?...Claben?"

Ah! I'm suspicious...

No beating about the bush...I come straight out with it... I insist...Ah! she looks at me...she thinks I'm queer...

"Kiss me!" she says..."Kiss me!...You're like my wounded brother...the war's been getting you too!...But he's in Athis-Mons now, home with the family...You shouldn't be going out either...Let's have a cup of coffee at the Basket...You look cold!...The treat's on me!"

Finette works the stations...or rather around them...in other words, the whole wide sidewalk up to the movie-house ...She'd make enough even for two!...She'd be satisfied with Fernande...they're pimped, naturally...but Fernande's a bitch ...she won't cheat on Big Fatso!...which causes jealousy! complications!...Big Fatso's the world-champ loafer!...He's the prize pimp!...It's all right with him if his women monkey around with each other as long as they don't hold out on his dough!...He wants to collect on both of them...on three, on ten if he could! A very demanding gentleman!...Which gets Finette sore! she'd like to hand it over only to Fernande! ...She must've had a reason for shaking me!...She wants to tell me something!...some news!...That Big Fatso's been called up again!...yes sir! That the Consulate's looking all over for him!...Seems he made a hell of a face!...Ah! no volunteering for him! Kid Gold-brick in person!...

Finette liked a good time!...She had beautiful big green eyes...like a cat...a bit slanting toward the temples...with a spark of mischief...and devilish, but on the whole a pain in the neck!...

While we drank our coffee at the Basket, she told me a couple of lousy things about the big pimp...That she couldn't take him any more...how he was too disgusting!...that they weren't clearing him out any too soon!...he could go to hell! ...She'd been waiting for that a long time!...it wasn't a luxury!...She'd burned more than one candle...He came from Montauban, the big pimp!...She didn't like people from the south!...He used to be a tenor!...so it seems...he was always yodeling!...and he hadn't sung for ten years!...He was a dope! I'm telling you, a prize dope!...Fernande didn't understand anything!...and she, Finette, was shelling out to both of them, what do you think of that!...and for years! Nice, wasn't it?...And her Fernande was a real angel!...Ah! she didn't want to play second fiddle!...Not her! Ah! she was through with that now!...She sure was glad he was going!... It was like giving her a bouquet of roses!...the two girls all by themselves!..."You'll see how I'm going to work!...What I'm doing now is nothing!...And yet I'm working like a dog! I want my little woman to be happy!...Ah! my boy!... Ah! just kid-stuff! I'm just loafing now!...Wait'll I really get going!...There'll be business! Business!...There's a whole world there!...A whole world!"

She was pointing to the station...the sidewalk!...

"You'll get a look at our clothes!...And what about you?" she reminds herself..."Say, you're not looking so good!... You've lost weight!...Why don't you go back to Cascade's? It's a good place...He's not stingy!...Since you're convalescing!...One more mouth doesn't matter!...What a family in his joint!...You should've built up your health!...You're like the rest of them! You're slipping!...You just don't know where you're at!...That's the trouble with you!"

Finette, Big Fatso and Fernande lived in an apartment not very far from the Empire Music Hall...in Wardow...They'd knock themselves silly, jealous alcohol binges, so that at times they'd lie on their backs two or three days in a row, giving each other herb tea, compresses...Passion did it! but now all that was going to change! At last Big Fatso was getting his! ...Ah! how happy she was!...really hilarious!...

"Will he be killed? You think so?"

He had a chance in the artillery!...Ah! I point out to her, he might come back! I tell her frankly...

205

"What about you? Aren't you going back?" she suddenly snaps! the bitch!

"Listen! Take it easy, you tramp!" I answer... "Listen! I've just come back!....Cool off!"

"But you're still good, darling!...You've still got some pieces left!"

She had it in for men!...

"War's a fine thing!...a fine thing!...Just look at that!"

A squad of khaki was passing in front of the windows...and behind them a whole fanfare!...The Guard Band on the way to Buckingham! The changing of the palace guard.

"Say! They're good-looking! They get me hot!...Say, does your arm still hurt?"

I'd spoken to her about my wounds...

"What about your head? You got a bullet in it, didn't you?"

"Oh! a very small one!"

"Oh! a wise guy!"...suddenly she thinks I'm funny!...She bursts out laughing, so high and so shrill, about the bullet in my head that everyone turns around...all the customers at the counter.

"Come here so I can kiss you, you poor fish!...You've got no luck! You're behind the times!"

That's what she thinks of me!

"But I'm way ahead of the times!"

She was getting me sore!...

"God! you're as big a jerk as Fatso!...You're no house afire!...Still and all you're less conceited...Why don't you go back to Cascade's?...It's a good place!"

Ah! she was dead set on that.

"He'd've given you whatever you wanted!" she continues, she's handing me a line!..."Without even asking!...just for yourself!...you'd've been in the dough!...He's got more girls than he wants!...You'd've got along!....'d've had it soft! ...He had nothing against you!...You didn't fight with him?

...Didn't you ever try to take away Angèle just for the hell of it sometimes? She's a real grandma!...Boy, she's had plenty between the legs, from the Bastille to Rio! Just imagine the racket! And the garrisons besides! with Nougat, her first guy! ...My boy!...a real hustler!...Let me tell you!...Steel-ass! ...That's what they called her at the Réole...at the Petit Soupir...almost twelve years ago!...I had my share, too!... Why talk about it!...I won't go complaining!...I'm frank! I admit! I can take it! I'm not scared of men! Though I like twats better, of course!...But the god-damned things are the injections! Boy, I'm awful about that! Boy, I'm telling you, I hate going to the doctor!...44 in a row, you realize, right in the ass!...Used to pass out after every shot!...Say, I thought I'd croak!...God, I was crapping green!...Say d'you think syph can be cured?"

The Englishwomen from the provinces who were drinking their tea screwed up their snooty noses...They suspected the sort of Frenchwoman she was...Finette started making eyes at them, they immediately turned away their heads...Just "snacks" in the station restaurants...especially Waterloo, there's an enormous number of people and of all kinds... besides, of course, the servicemen...to and from Flanders!... A stream of khaki!...Finette started thinking of her girl-friend again...

"Fernande's not loafing either!...Especially now that she's doing the Empire...We're sure going to be happy! The two of us all by ourselves!...We'll send Fatso big juicy money orders!...Ah, our man! ah! the sweet trou-trou-badour!... Life looks bright! It's coming along great!...He's got to eat over there, you know! Fatso's some eater!...I want him to croak, but not of hunger...First of all, you know she still likes him...that's a fact! I'm not kidding myself!...imagine what a dope!...She sings with him! you should hear them!... *When your big gentle eyes!*...I don't know what she sees in

him!...Whenever he touches me, I gag...Still I'm no saint!
...He just rubs me the wrong way!...It's because he's Fernande's guy! It's jealousy! That's it!...It's only natural!...
What about you, aren't you jealous?"

I admit I'm not very!...Ah! she doesn't like that. Ah! that irks her! Just what am I, after all? She looks at me...up and down...she can't stomach me any more!

"Beat it!"...she snaps at me!..."Beat it, dope!"

Doesn't want to see me any more!

"Pst! Pst!" she calls from her stool...she saw something outside...she calls through the door...a soldier on the prowl ...she runs after him...she jumps...I'm alone again...I smile around vaguely...at the countergirls...no go...an aviator's monopolizing them...they're snickering and clucking ...all right!...I'm going to sit down at a table...since I'm there...I start thinking things over again...I order a cup of coffee...another one...I just sit there...with a dazed look ...Someone signaling to me from outside through the glass ...Don't recognize who...couldn't make it out...Ah! it's the midget!...Ten-paw Lou...He's spotted me.

"You doing the stations?" he asks...He's getting a kick out of seeing me there...

His head reaches the edge of the table...To tell the truth he's almost a dwarf...he's bowlegged...

"Say, things are bad!...Don't you know what's happening? ...They're talking about you at the Leicester...Haven't you read the *Mirror?*"

No, I hadn't read it...

"Well I'll be damned!...Give me a penny!"

He goes out...he brings back the *Mirror*...The whole page, a big photo...Oh! the old guy's house!...the joint!... the rubble!...it was called the "Greenwich Tragedy" in huge letters...the smoke...the ruins...the beams...everything!

"Boy! Some hell of a sight!"

It's funny, I couldn't quite understand! I looked again...
just couldn't figure it out...It seemed strange to me.

"Do you believe it?" I ask him..."You believe it?"

"Look!...It's written down!"

"I don't know," I answer...

"Can't you read English?"

He could read English well...

"Ah! go to hell, you don't understand anything!" That's his
conclusion...We start talking about something else...He was
a cook at Barbe's in Soho Square, also an "extra" at the Royal
...that way he could fool around the unions...in good standing!...but the dwarf was especially clever with cards!...His
real racket!...his magic! Ah! gambling? nothing he couldn't
do!..."Unionized"!...Could get in anywhere...He called all
the chefs by their first names...all the London clubs...He'd
show them his terrific tricks with cards...at poker! at whist!
Backgammon! unbeatable in shuffling!...That's why they
called him Ten-paw...No one saw him go in or out...Just a
quick little game!...Let's go, gentlemen! No higher than the
table!...the midget...They'd put cushions under him so he
could play at the right height...He amused the hostesses...
and always good-natured, easygoing...and also an "extra" at
the races! ah! tipped-off like a pope! really inside stuff! Always
three to "show" at the Derby!...at least!...In London 18
years! and dough laid aside!...rejected because of his coat-
sleeve legs...never a day in the army!

"But my fingers haven't been rejected! That's what counts
in my game!"

Doesn't hide the fact that he's intelligent.

He's terrific with his fingers, he'll turn a single deck into ten
or twelve right in front of your eyes! an acrobat with cards!
...He plays only with customers, never with friends...Ah!
none of that! Out of the question!...

When he dropped in at the Leicester, right away it was

"Into the kitchen, Ten-paw!"...Ah! no monkey-business! right away! go on! Ten-paw's the boy for French fries!...no equal when it comes to soufflés...

"Get to the frying pan, Ten-paw"...they'd call from all over the house...all the girls!..."You'll get kissed!"

In fact he'd have all of them free for his potato soufflés!... They'd let him, it was all right with the men, they had a big weakness for French fries...Ah! really tasty with lard, and Saumur wine if possible!...It seems they were better than oysters when made à la Ten-Paw!...I think fried potatoes are the only real French vice!...seriously speaking...just right, to a turn, golden, salted, not too much, neither dry nor greasy, with a glass of white wine...You couldn't tear them away when the midget got to the frying pan...There'd be heaping platefuls and endless cheering...enough to bring down the whole whorehouse...Sometimes around 10 or 12 pimps crowded together at the table treating themselves to crispies... without counting the ladies, naturally!...

"Ah!" he says to me...tackling the subject..."To go on with my story...you poor mug, you sure are in the shit!"

Looking at the photographs...we read the following gibberish..."The body of Titus Jerome Van Claben, the well-known pawnbroker, was found yesterday afternoon at five o'clock"...I had no idea his name was Jerome...in addition to Titus..."badly mutilated and completely burned"...

It was easy English.

"The fire consumed the entire building and two neighboring houses as well...No fire of such violence has broken out in Wigmore Alley, the well-known promenade in our lovely Greenwich Park, since 1768. The District Officer in charge of the investigation refuses to give us his opinion as to the origin of this disaster which, according to certain experts, might be due to foul play. The private life of Titus Jerome Van Claben was not quite what it might have been...In addition to his ordinary clients, Titus Van Claben received many visits from dubious people and vagabonds...known, moreover, to the officers of Scotland Yard...Tongues have been wagging in the neighborhood of the disaster...Van Claben was known to have a certain taste for oriental dress and the smoking of hashish, long piano performances, and the easy French game of 'loto'....A middle-aged housekeeper, a former teacher named Delphine, is being actively sought..."

"But we weren't playing loto!...We never played loto!... It's a downright lie!"

I sat up!

"All right! But then you were really there?"

"How do you know?"

It's true after all, how did he know?...

I reread the lousy sheet...I started shivering...right in front of the newspaper and all...I can tell you that those nosy reporters gave me the shakes...the shivers like that morning ...in the park with Delphine...

"Listen!...Listen!...That's just my luck!...But how do you know about it, half-pint?"

"Heard about it at the Boss's place, the Leicester!...They came back two days ago! Boro and Delphine...Boy, did they eat!...Were they hungry!...You can't imagine!...They gobbled up everything!"

"What did they say?"

I had to know.

"Cascade said that he never would've thought it of you!"

"So they told everything!"

"Absolutely everything!"

"Then where did they go?"

"Go see!...Ah! they sure fixed you all right!"

"Fixed me?...Ah! wait, take it easy!"

"They gave you the works all right! Naturally!...You weren't there!...Go see Cascade!"

Ah! I could see what he was up to...Just wait awhile, wise guy!...I say nothing!...I act dumb...So I leave the restaurant with him...In other words, I'm taking a risk...all or nothing!...Outside we head for Cascade's, we're walking side by side...he's so tiny he's half-running to keep up with me ...toward Buckingham Palace...our direction...I take a look around...I'm on the lookout...Got an idea...there's nothing in front of the gate...Good!...Farther on, about two hundred yards...Suddenly I grab him by the back of the neck ...Ah! you little joker!...I carry him straight into a corner, the squirming fish!...hanging from my left fist!

"Listen, Ten-paw!"....I shake him..."Who's paying you?" I ask.

"Paying me?...Paying me?...No one!"...he's twisting and struggling...he's yelling...

"It wasn't Cascade who sent you?"

I put him down on his feet.

"Cascade doesn't send anyone!...Get that, you big dope! ...He settles things himself...But here's the way he talked ...'Ferdinand's not what I thought he was!...I took him in, in full confidence!...as a very serious young man...Ferdinand's double-crossed us!...he came to my house like a friend! ...sent by Raoul!...poor Raoul!...He's acted like a skunk! ...Especially after being sent by Raoul!'...That's what hurts him...Sent in confidence by Raoul!...'He's acted like a skunk!'"

He hadn't minced words.

"You can imagine how Boro piled it on!...You weren't there!...So go there!...'You're quite right, Cascade!'...Oh! the trimmings!...'A little criminal!'...They were talking about you!...'He bashed poor Claben on the head!...He swiped all the dough!...He set the joint on fire!...He ran away!'...Those are their very words!"

"Ah! Say listen!..."

Hearing that gives me palpitations! What a crime! Ah! they're strangling me!

"What? They dared, those fairies?...Ah, the damned lousy skunks!...Ah! just let me find them!...So that's exactly what they said?"

"In front of everyone there!"

No doubt about it.

"And what about you, you little rat?" I ask.

I grab him by the throat...

"What about you? What'd you come around for?"

We were still in the doorway...He struggles around, he's playing innocent.

"Ah! I was pimping I swear!" he gasps..."I never lie to you, Ferdinand!"

He's protesting...he's groaning...wailing...

"I know you're wounded, Ferdinand! I know you're wounded! I wouldn't want to hurt you!...Never!...I swear!...I wouldn't want anything to happen to you!...It's just for your good, believe me, pal!...They're a mean crowd at the Leicester!...Watch out!...They've got it in for you!"

"Watch out for what?"

"I don't know...I don't know."

Good, all right! I let him alone...We walk past the shops ...I keep still...all right...I'm on the watch...Ah! I'm suspicious!...the son-of-a...Just wait, you little runt!...I was thinking...You won't get away with that stuff!...I act dumb too, since that's the game!...I play along...there!...So go there!...'You're quite right, Cascade!'...Oh!

"Ten-paw, I've got confidence!" I tell him..."All things considered...all in all...you're absolutely right!...I'm going back!...I want to see them all!...It's settled!...You're sure there won't be any hard feelings?...Do you guarantee it? ...You know I'm frank and regular!...I don't like lies!... Look me straight in the eyes!"

He was too small.

I lift him up again from the ground...so he can look me straight in the eyes...He stares at me...and I talk to him.

"Ten-paw, now listen to me! I didn't steal anything! I'm telling you that now! You can believe me! I didn't touch the old guy!...Do you believe me? You believe me? I'm all clear!"

"Ah!" he says...

He doubts it...he doubts...I see it's bothering him...he'd have liked me to be guilty...

"I just swiped two sovereigns that'd fallen out of his bag! That's all I admit to and that's the size of it!...You'll tell them! It's very simple!"

I put him down again.

He takes me by the arm...He understands...I see he's glad that he's bringing me back...After all, in spite of everything ...that I'm ready to go back to the Leicester...

Ah! I'm suspicious of him!...

"Say, how'd you find me?"

I ask him the same question again.

"Just so, you know...by accident!...I was passing by!"

Sure, sure, I think to myself!...just wait, shorty! accident, my ass!

He's hanging on to my arm, he's tiny...We keep going... He gives me the latest gossip as we walk...the news at the Leicester...that two more men have left...Philippe and Julien...that they've joined up in Dunkerque...that they've left two more girls...that dough's been rolling in galore... that Angèle didn't know where to put it...that she'd already bought something like seven blue foxes and a three-quarter-length sable coat...That as for him, Ten-paw, he wasn't going to go dragging around in the kitchens of clubs!...Not by a long shot!...Even with trick cards!...The others can have it! ...Ah! no more of that!...that he was going to go into

214

business, too...into the hustling racket!...that with times as they were he'd make a pile in no time! Boy, and how! that he'd already taken up the big matter with Cascade about a little sister!...that he'd mentioned it to him...that he had more than enough to treat himself to one...That he hadn't said yes or no...Not too bad-looking a one who made out all right...

"You're going to be kind of short for a pimp!...You'll hide under the bed!"

I couldn't keep from saying it.

"Short! Short!" he exclaims..."Listen, you cluck! Can't I have a piece like anyone else? Ah! Gravy! Greetings! There's a war on!"

Ah! he was dead set on it!

"Tail, that's the business!"

Besides there were going to be widows!...That was understood, too...Cascade had spoken to him about it...He was counting on it...A widow!...maybe two!...bargains!... There'd never been such a boom...it was really the perfect business!...Whore galore!...velvet!

A nasty little stinker!

So gabbing away like that we came to the Mall, the big avenue in front of the Palace...Buckingham Palace...a fine bridle path...We sat down there on a bench...under a tree ...I feel like letting some people go by...to look at them...

"You see?" he says..."That's where the king is!"

I still remember his remark.

"It's not as nice as the Louvre!" I answer.

"That's a matter of taste, their kings liked it!...London's not Paris!"

We argue about it awhile.

"Our kings had a swell setup too...Say, I've seen the Louvre!"

But I stuck to the Louvre! he'd never convince me!

"Listen I know something about it!"
I start going into detail.
"Ah! and what paintings! millions of them in a row!"
"What was the name of our last one?"
He asks me a question. I never remember!
"Louis the Sixteenth!"
What the hell.
"You're educated, pal!" he answers back, but that imme-
diately annoys him.
"Remember, education's not everything! the thing that
counts in life, see, is natural intelligence!...And I've got it!
I can flatter myself about that! That's the main thing! I've
known women who knew five and six languages! I wouldn't
have wanted them as kitchenmaids!...stuck up! that's all!...
Swell-headed!...Just look at the suckers...They're often edu-
cated, eh?...You never saw anything so dopey!...proof!...
You ought to see the way they pass their time in the clubs!...
I can tell you about that!...They play! they lose! and I win!
...My boy, the hell with them I tell you!...What does a king
do for a good time?...'I'm a-off to war!' he announces...
'I'll be right back!...The other guys are getting killed for
me!'...He gets there around noon!...He has a swell lunch
in his tent stuck in the back of the woods...He's in the lines!
...the photographers come along! They take a photo of the
guy! on a horse! in a car! and I go home!...Nice chap!
Greetings, ladies and gentlemen! Ah! nice majesty! Badaboom!
a hundred and three canon shots! We've won! You see him in
all the magazines!...like you, pal! Hurrah! and *God Save the
King!*...You think the King worries?...I've always known
...It's natural! They got life too soft!...I'd take it easy, too!
in his place!...You, too!...If you were spoiled like them!...
You'd just fiddle around, it's only natural! if you were king!
...You just lap it up, can't help it!"
He was doing all the talking...I wasn't saying anything

216

...Suddenly he asks me, "Say, d'you know Big Fatso?...Ever heard him give out at Cascade's?...*If I Were King!*...He sure knows how to sing it!"

I'd stopped listening to him...he was wearing me out... I was feeling pooped again...especially my head...What excitement in the last two weeks!...In my state it was murderous...

"Ferdinand, you're not staying here?...You said you were coming!...Aren't you? Come along!"

That was right after all.

"Come on! Let's go!...We'll take the Tube! You're too tired, you're groggy!"

That was quite true.

"You see?"...he points to the lawns in the distance..."the sparrows are happy...for them it's the feed bag everywhere .. it's the berries everywhere!...That's the sparrow's life! ...You see the advantage!...Say, you know I like birds!... I'd have a big bird-cage if I had the dough! like at the zoo! Have you seen the one here? Cocatoos! the rainbow! all colors! ...It's beautiful! It's more beautiful than the paintings in your Louvre!...real rainbows!...hurry up!...They'll be gone!... We'll have to drop in at the Ping-Pong."

"You think so?" I ask him again..."You really think it's serious?...that I ought to go back to the Leicester?...Maybe it's better not to see them again?"

"Ah! be careful, Ferdinand!...You know Cascade, he's a decent guy!...But if he sees that you're giving him a runaround!...that you're afraid of explaining things!...Ah! he'll really think there's something fishy about you! Ah! there'll be hell to pay!...Ah! he'll get pretty mean! Boro won't have any trouble filling him with his hokum! Ah! they'll step all over you! Since you're not there!"

He was set on my making up my mind...on our taking the Tube...both of us...he insisted terrifically...Ah! he's working on me, he's making me groggy...right there in front of the station I was still hesitating...

"Oh!" I say..."Ten-paw, I'm not going!"

I changed my mind.

"You're making a mistake Ferdinand!...You're making a mistake!"

Ah! it griped him that I'd said no!...I saw his stubborn little mug...I gave in a little...I took two or three steps... I stopped...People were looking at us on the sidewalk...at the midget, the two of us arguing...I entered the station... He didn't let me catch my breath...He rushed to the ticket window...

"Come on, Ferdinand!...Let's go!...Here's your chance! ...It's better to go!...Afterwards you'll be glad!...Stop worrying!...Shake a leg!"

I follow him...I go along...I'm giving in because I'm tired, that's the truth...It was the Baker Street station...He gets the tickets...We're pushed into the elevator...smothered in the rush...suddenly I feel anxious!...My heart had been racing away since the night before...the morning...since Greenwich, in fact...now it's charging! Cooped up that way in the elevator! I'm palpitating! palpitating! an awful burst!

"Listen, midget!" I say..."Listen, are you really sure?"

It's going down...down...

"Don't be silly, Ferdinand!...Don't be silly...All you've got to do is explain!...If you don't go, they'll believe everything!...you don't realize what can happen!"

Squeezed together like that in the coop! We come right out on to the platform...he's still holding me by the arm.

"Mustn't get lost!" he says..."Mustn't get lost!"

So there we are waiting for the train...squeezed among the people. I don't know why...they're all stifling me!...I can't breathe any more!...They're all there against me! I free myself...Ah! I free myself...I take three steps forward to the edge of the track...And there opposite? who do I see? who's that there?...there facing me?...Ah! excuse me! Ah! my eyes pop!...His raglan!...His soft felt!...His mug!...It's Matthew! Matthew! there on the other platform!...Matthew looking straight at us!...My blood turns!...I stop breathing! ...I stop moving!...I stand there hypnotized...he looks at me!...I look at him! Ah! but I'm thinking!...I'm thinking fast!...It's the midget! there against me!...It's him!...It's the double-crosser!..."Good!...Good!...Good!"...It's getting ready by itself!...my scheme...I concentrate...concentrate...Not a word...calm and collected...People are talking all around us...They're waiting for the train like us...We hear the train roaring...it's coming!...there in the darkness ...in the hole...at my right...Good!...Good!...Good! ...the train's approaching. It's roaring fiercely, crashing in, swelling up...Brrr! Brrroom...Good! Good! Good!...It's near...I look at Matthew opposite...I feel the midget against me...he's got me by the arm...he doesn't want to lose me! "BRRRR!"...the locomotive emerges and "Tweet!... Tweet!" the whistle...Bop! I hit him with my ass! the midget! up in the air!...The thunder lets loose, passes below! Whistle! Whistle! Whistle!...They're all yelling! all around! the whole station!...I pull clean back! I'm magnetized! That's just the word!...positively!...I'm lifted up!...I'm light as a feather! I get going!...I'm snapped up by the exit! ...the stairway! I'm sucked up!...I'm flying off!...It's instinct! flight!...the whole corkscrew!...the four flights... I shoot up! a whirlwind! I don't feel them!...a mile a minute! ...I'm being sucked up!...I'm so light I'm not touching the stairs!...I'm a bird of fear!...I shoot from the cage into the street!...running!...running!...I'm galloping! I cross a street...two!...three!...I'm a bird of fright!...I'm off like a shot!...Another street...a square...another avenue...a park ...I turn around...I'm swooping in circles...I graze the

219

ground...just graze it...speed!...a ball of fire!...I knock
people over!...another square!...I go all around it...I slow
up...oof!...I stop...My tongue's hanging out...It's over!
...I'm going to faint!...But no!...I sit down on the curb!
...right under a tree!...They've lost me!...I look up at the
street sign! It says Berkeley Square...a swell neighborhood
...oof!...limousines and landaus are passing one another...
It must be around six o'clock...a rather busy hour...It's the
way to Regent Street. The parade of elegance...I catch my
breath a little...I'm seized by anxiety again...I start thinking
...my heart's twinging again!...It's attacking me...it's banging at my ribs...and then my head starts acting up...I can't
rest any more...I'm buzzing...tingling...overheated...it's
my common sense wobbling and wavering...I can't see anything...and then I see everything!...I'm not me any more!
...It is me!...I shook him up, the dirty midget!...up in the
air, Ten-paw!...up in the air!...Ah! say, you there!...Say!
he's bashed up right this minute! Wham! the tough guy!
Matthew there opposite! watching! staring! I still see the cop!
...umbrella and all!...Ah! popeyed!...He hadn't come
alone!...Ah! sure and certain!...Ah! Ten-paw, the rotten
little jerk! finagling little rat! Sh! Sh! Not another word!
Shit! Now Cascade!...All mine! Claben too! Ah! it's not
possible! Everything's getting mixed up!...It's all fire!...it's
flaming!...it's all growling inside my head!...like over there!
I'm in a fever!...my ass on the curb! ah! frozen like that I'm
going to cool off!...Like over there! Ah! Providence! Ah!
I'm saved! Ah! it's getting better! sitting on the stone! Hurray
for the Saint Johns! Hurray for the firemen! but it won't last
long!...I got off to a bad start!...I think of my folks!...
my mother in France in her shop mending lace...I get a
headache thinking of mamma...ruining her eyes that way
under the big gas lamp...and the customers never satisfied...
I'd let the customers have it!...I'd teach them how to behave!

...and my father at the Coccinelle transcribing addresses!...
that he'll never finish!...and my pals in the trenches, the
dumb dopes, getting it smack in the puss...it's an avalanche,
thunder, and me there like a murderer! shit!...I could see the
whole damned setup...it haunted me, set my head spinning
...I didn't dare move..."Ferdinand! Ferdinand!" I said to
myself. "You're the victim of a plot!...and no denying it,
they're out to hurt you!...Your head hurts!...That proves
it! Are you a decent guy? That's the question that staggers
me...Did Claben do you any harm?...So you robbed him
just to drink? No one has any proof!...Ten-paw either!...
He's in the Tube now!...He's even smaller!...that'll teach
him to double-cross!...It was horrible of him...Ferdinand,
you're going to pay for everything!...Matthew's got a perfect
right!...He's on duty!...No doubt about it! He's looking for
you...he has a right to!...He's got the police behind him!
...He's on the lookout!...that's his job! criminal matters!
punishment tra-la-la! Oh you riffraff! it all works out!...my
youth knocking me around again! plaguing me! sickening
me! it's all there in a heap! shaking me! the people from the
Passage du Vérododat! the nosybodies! the neighbors! and lots
more! They're accusing me! they're involving me! The nerve!
and lots more! The self-examination!...You'll see what people
are like...they won't want to look at my mother any more!
...how she's going to cry and weep!..."A deserter, Madame!
an uninteresting young man!...in fact, a monster! A bandit!
...And his poor father!...He should have boarded him
somewhere!...Not in La Roquette!...in prison with the
hoodlums! This wouldn't have happened to you, Madame!...
He deserted in London!...He was wounded!...He was
crazy!...A drunkard!...A sex-maniac!...He was a liar!...
he masturbated in every corner!...he was often caught...He
had vile instincts! He was failed three times when he came up
for his elementary-school diploma!...What rings under his

eyes!...everyone remembers it!...The way he spoke to his mother!...They were weak with him!...He stole four rolls! ...How they deprived themselves for him!...It was worth while!...He robbed his employer!...And then he enlisted! ...Then he had a little courage!...He left in September... mentioned three times in the military dispatches!...and then the military medal!...Brave at the beginning...it didn't last ...afterwards he lost everything!...Courage and everything else! all his good resolutions!...He didn't want to die·any more!...He was just a little delinquent!...I always said so! ...and the military medal!...just hotheaded!...a basically criminal nature!...They arrested him in London!...They locked him up!...They put him through torture!...He deserved it! He lost his head!...He started admitting...They plucked his eyes out!...men who knew him well! people who were sick and tired of his criminal instincts!"...I could hear the voices going in and out of the gates!...they reached my ears!...right on Berkeley Square! All I could hear was those voices...I didn't even hear the cars...They were real voices ...and even some English voices among them...with the accent...everything..."Watch your step! Watch your step! Bloody murder!...Bloody murder!"...muted...among the other voices!...with a bit of music among the street echoes ...Murder! Murder! Oh! I've got to act fast!...Things look very bad, Ferdinand!...They're going to catch you!...They're going to jump on your neck like Delphine in the tunnel...

Ah! they won't get me!...Bloody mess!...I know all about the traps! the tricks! the murderous war! the pitfalls! The hell with the dopes! So I get up very gingerly...nice and quickly ...and oop!...I make a dash!...The opposite sidewalk... I bolt!...I run!...I hug the walls!...I hit Bond Street!... Marylebone!...I know where I'm going!...My heart's racing like mad!...A drum!...A tattoo!...but in the right place! ..."With heart and soul!"...I still hear the colonel...

"Cavalry! sabers in hand!" Sir Colonel Guts!..."With heart and soul!...Gallop!...Chaaarge!" I obey his command!... I dash forward!...Ah! how I dash!...I bolt!...I fly to the charge!...Heart and soul!...All for my country!...I know the itinerary!...I don't get lost in the heart of London!...I race ahead! spurt!...Hip! Hip! Hurrah! cavalcade!...whirlwind! Heart and soul!...Valor!...Victory's my law!...Victoria!...Tottenham Court Road!...I change pace!...neck down! on the bit!...I clap spurs!...I charge the omnibus! ...the whole flock! Mastodons! they grunt! growl! quiver! big potbellies! twenty-five motors!...stopped, all red, there, alert, muzzle against croup...massed, set...all vibrating at the signal!...snuffling at the butt-ends! putt! puttl...blood buffaloes!...I confront them!...snuffle as they do!...brrrooo! brr...rr...roo...oooo!...And I charge everything! lightning! dodge!...hack the herd!...cut sideways!...arrow! escape!...right at the crossing!...in front of the Lyons, the giant tearoom, open night and day!...Ah! the stout fellow! ...Ah! the hero!...Just look at 'im! the cops are whistling at me!...Whistling!...Whistling! Futile! I step on the gas! ...Ah! every man for himself!...I tear along the walls at top speed!...Racing like mad!...Far off! at the end! it's Bedford Square! I sniff!...I get my bearings!...I dash forward!...I'm there!...I see the trees! the Y.M.C.A.!...The grounds, the fine sycamores!...the oaks!...the Consulate! ...I see it!...Go on, go, boy!...Shoot ahead!...fly!... one more dash! Hip! Hop! it's pouring! it's teeming! it's pissing! I'm soaked!...dripping! streaming in flight! I dash under the umbrellas...I stumble!...I flop!...Up! on my feet!...Faster and faster!...I don't feel myself any more! ...Bedford Square! the Consulate!...mine?...No! the Russian!...I'm a bit off!...another run!...I've got too much pep!...Got to lose it!...use it up!...I'm slowing down!... now trotting!...There're at least a dozen consulates...of all countries. . .around the trees! . . .all around the square. . .like a merry-go-round! against one another! . . .that one there! the Russian! the biggest! At least three or four buildings. . .The crowd's milling in front of the door. . .I bear down. . . I dig in! . . .I'm pushed back! . . .I succumb! . . .I collapse in the mob of Russians! . . .They're fuming! . . .they spit! . . .they call me names! . . .I'm at a standstill! . . .a stricken meteor! . . .I collapse on the spot! . . .I'm squeezed in, bundled, ground up in the crush of bodies! . . .It's an endless mob! . . .There's been a triple line around the square for days and days! for weeks! . . .They've been marking time. . .they squawk. . .they cough . . .in the sun. . .in the rain. . .the office door's closed. . .it just barely opens. . .They take only two at a time. . .They keep them for hours. .for days. . . .It's for their visas! . . .It's a teeming mob full of cooties! . . .and hard to delouse! . . .I'm scratching too! . . .It's a mixture. . .it's swarming. . .forearms . . .feet. . .They all flock to the door every time it opens. . . it's a mixed sort of mob. . .they shove one another into the railings. . .they're all scraping away at the lice. . .digging at themselves. . .tickling. . .a hodgepodge. . .and cute specimens . . .big merchants and moujiks! . . .lots of all kinds. . .show-offs in overcoats. . .professors with eyeglasses. . .peasants with kerchiefs. . .all of them milling, mashing feet, shoving, advancing a hundredth of an inch. . .Got to go through them! . . .I'll never make it! My French Consulate! there! getting farther away! I find myself deported! dragged to the left! I brace myself! tear away! I knock over some Jews in caps. . . a whole band of them! . . .sidewhiskers with big glasses. . .two popes with crosses on their bellies. . .They're squeezed tightly together. I buck right into them. . .right into the mash of meat. . .I cut through. . .push them all aside! . . .a burst! . . . Got to get to my cloister. . .to my Consulate. . .French soil! . . .It's just as compact there too! . . .They're blocking the entrance. . .a whole yowling furious mixture Franco-Belgo-Rus-

sian who-where-what!...they're all jabbering and shouting
...calling each other the lowest names...sour chambermaids
...artists...a Greek whom I recognize...a plump little
woman spouting away...a girl from Toulouse full of accent
...They're waiting for opening time...it reopens at eight
o'clock for visas for the evening train...

I'm in a much greater rush than anyone else!...I yell it to
the populace!...Got to assert myself at once! I didn't come to
wait around!...I want to see the Consul in person!...Him-
self!...and right away!...I roar it over the crowd's heads...
Monsieur le Consul Général!...That's the least of things!...
I've torn my overcoat...it's just a rag now...getting pushed
around by the crowd!...It's hanging down in tatters!...my
expensive raglan...I salute the flag over the door!...and the
coat of arms!...our three colors!..."Attention!" I order...
"Atten-shun!" in a stentorian voice over the mob...I beat my
way through...I'm trying to penetrate...The women around
me, the French teachers, call me a ruffian, a cutthroat...I
don't answer...I bang...I go at it with all I've got!...I'm
ready to smash anything!...I shove through like mad!...with
kicks!...Finally they open after all!...just a crack!...I barge
in head on!...into the usher!...the concierge!...I'm inside!
...I've made it!...But my heart can't take it! I buckle under!
...I sit down on the floor!...The effort's been too much!

"Monsieur! Monsieur!...Mister!" I exclaim..."Duty calls
me!...*Allons enfants de la Patrie!*"...I bawl it out!...I give
it all I've got!...I insult the flunky!...He answers in
English, "Go away! Go away! I'm the Commissioner!"...the
kind of uniformed lackey who hires himself out by the hour,
by the week, who defends anterooms, offices, official places...

"The French Consul!" I demand..."I want to see the
French Consul!...Monsieur le Consul Général!"

Finally a clerk comes along...A real one, with lustrine
sleeves...then three!...ten others!...all in lustrine and

spectacles, wearing celluloid collars...Ah! I stop dead! Oh, celluloid!...they flabbergast me! They're the first I've seen in London!...I sit there dumfounded! They fascinate me... They're all wearing bow ties!..."ready-made!"...I get it! ...I know where I am!...it's my whole youth!...I just sit there stunned, cockeyed...from squinting so hard at their ties! ...Ah! I can't take my eyes off them!...It's my whole childhood!...my apprenticeship!...the Passage du Vérododat!... God it's not possible? They're all wearing them, one and the same kind!...Like my poor father!...always "ready-made" ties...with chevron stripes like his! black and white...Ah! tears are welling up!

"Gentlemen!...Gentlemen!" I exclaim..."You'll forgive me!...it's weakness!...It's hunger!...Just a fainting spell!"

"You want some help, young man?...Help?...In the morning around ten o'clock...Come back tomorrow morning!"

They're clearing me out.

"Help?...Help?"

Ah! the sneaks!...Ah! my anger!

"I want to enlist, you bastards!...I want to go back to the war! To save our country!...You shitheads!...I've got my fake papers!" I scream it at them! I'm announcing it.

I can see they think I'm off my nut...They're making signs to one another.

"Follow us, young man!...Follow us!...Come up quietly ...quietly with us."

They invite me...they escort me...they close around me ...They don't want me to run away...Oh! they're smart!... I know their kind!...

We get to the first floor...two three...four offices in a row...all of them filled with typists...homely ones, pale and squint-eyed...a hunchback...

226

At the very back, the "Military Office"...written on the outer door..."Medical Officer"...We all bolt in together... we surge in...and all the typists follow!...they're clucking away, the scarecrows...They're accompanying me...They won't leave me!...

It's been some time since I've seen medics in uniform... since the hospital, as a matter of fact!...it excites me immediately!...Since Hazebrouck in Flanders...

"Atten-shun!" I yell..."Atten-shun!"

Everybody laughs...Haw! haw! haw!

"Let me see your papers, young man!...Let me see your papers!"

I tear out my inner pocket sewn up in my jacket...well preserved at the bottom of my rags!...I hand my papers to the medic...My record...my citations!...

"It's all fake!"...I warn him at the start..."It's all fake!" I'm warning him good and loud!...

"Completely fake!"...I emphasize it...

He tells me to sit down. That's perfect!...So he can examine them leisurely!...I settle down into the biggest armchair...He's going to see a thing or two...He's going to have a treat...Meanwhile I look at the mists outside...the mists floating by the window...dancing...big furbelows...the ballet of the fogs!...while he examines my papers...I hum a little tune!...It all came with the rain...the ballet of the mists...it sweeps off...flies up...toward Saint Albans... lightly!...the church, all dark!...the spire in the sky, all gold! Ah! a nice effect!...The clouds are dissolving!...Ah! I dream easily!...I just let myself go right off...Anything can get me dopey...I want him to know it...I let the medic know...I warn him very politely...

"There's something magic in the air."

A thought.

Now he knows.

"Come here, young man!" he answers, polite but firm. "Get undressed!. . . The rest of you! leave!"

Everyone leaves.

He looks at my arm. . . my scars. . .

"Atten-shun!" I roar. . . "Atten-shun!"

He feels my leg, my buttocks, my balls. . . he fiddles all over me. . . he thumps my chest, he feels me again!. . . He makes me walk. . . forward. . . backwards. . .

He nods his head. . . I can see he's turning me down. . .

"I want to go, doc!. . . I want to go!" I'm begging him. . . "Don't turn me down!. . . I've got to go!. . . They're after me!"

I'm spilling the beans. . .

"I'm the murderer, doc!. . . I killed ten of 'em!. . . I killed a hundred!. . . I killed a thousand!. . . I'll kill all of 'em next time!. . . Doc, send me back!. . . I belong at the front!. . . a-off to war!"

"We'll see!. . . We'll see!" he answers quite calmly. . . "Get dressed!"

He hadn't said three words to me. . . I thought that pretty insolent. . . I slip on my pants, my bandages, my shredded linen shirt. . . He looks me over. . . He's still nodding. . . He's a medico with a goatee, the plump potbellied kind, he's got round cheeks, he takes his glasses off, puts them back on. . . He's wearing leggings, spurs, a big revolver case. . . I wonder why?. . . He's not running any risks in his office!. . . He sends for another four-eye. . . and then for the commissioners. . . the lackeys again!. . . the ones who welcomed me at the door. . . and then they all come back. . . all the offices. . . the whole staff. . . the whole Consulate. . . all the gals with buns! it's going to be a big show! I'm surrounded!. . . They all start jabbering again!. . . whispering about my case!. . . mimicking to one another!. . .

"You may go now, my boy!. . . You may leave!"

That's his decision!

Ah! I'll be damned! what an outrage!

"Off to war!" I scream..."off to war!...I don't want to leave any other way!...I want my re-enlistment signed here! right this minute!...and without delay!...I demand it!... Take it or leave it!...Life or death!"

They don't answer.

"Off to war!" I repeat..."Off to war! Like Little-Arm Pierrot...No-Dough René...like Pretty-Kiss Jojo!...like Lucien-the-Gent!"

"But you've just come back, young man!...You've done your full duty!...You'll soon have your pension!"

Ah! a fine how-do-you-do!...He was trying to ease me out!...Ah! the flimsy windbag!...Me, conscience in person! ...He wanted to calm my scruples!...Ah! the crazy loafer! ...Repulsive!...So I hand him a line!...

"But my duty hasn't been done right!...But haven't you looked at me?...But I've still got lots of duties waiting!... And what about yours?...Tell me about them!...A pension? ...But I don't have any pension!...But I'll never have a pension!"

That's the way I argue!...

He doesn't get sore, he's still reasoning with me...He's handling me very gently...

"But you will!...You'll have it!...You're going to get it, my dear fellow!...You've been badly disabled!...One of our most valiant soldiers!...You've got 80%...Ask for an increase!...80% is all right!...2,000 francs a year!"

On the other hand, I'm getting excited!...

"But I'm a murderer, gentlemen!...A murderer!...Can't you hear straight?"

I'm talking to all of them...I bellow it out!...I roar it! ...We don't understand one another at all!...They all make sorry faces!...There're at least thirty of them in sleeve-bands standing around in a circle...stupefied...staring at me! And then they start again...jabbering!...twaddling...with lots of little sly laughs...

"I killed two of 'em!"...I start all over..."I killed ten!... and I've killed a lot more!...I'll butcher more than that!... Listen to me, doc!"

I beg him...I throw myself at his knees!

This time he's categorical again! I'm driving him wild!

"You're discharged, my boy!...Your papers! Your documents are in order!...Absolutely faultless!...Discharged!... Do you understand me?...80%!...You've been released by the Medical boards! Dunkerque! Béthune! La Rapée!...Do you remember?...Wait for your pension! The formalities are being attended to!...Are you in London with relatives?"

He seems to me too curious!...He's trying to intimidate me again! Ah! I see what he's up to! dissuading me from doing my full duty!...Ah! the wretch!...

"I killed twelve of 'em!" I raise the figure..."I killed a hundred!...It's not over!...I want to go back! I want to kill a thousand! I want to redeem my errors!...I want to go back to the line!...in the Sixteenth!...Sixteenth Cuirassiers!"

Whereupon we start talking pleasantly again...He wants me to listen to reason...He's full of concern...He starts flattering me!..."Hero!...Hero!" he calls me!...The word makes all the pen-pushers...all the office girls writhe with laughter...

"You've received the Military Medal!"

"I killed twelve of 'em, doc!...If I go back, I'll kill 'em all!...I want to get back to the platoon!...Lower my rank! ...Lower my rank! But I want to be in service!...and right away!...A private, if necessary!"

Ah! I mean business!

"Come, come, my boy!...You're nervous, that's all... You've done your duty!...Your whole duty!...Do you want

230

to go back to France?...Do you want to see the Consul?...
Are you out of funds?...We'll repatriate you!...What's your
occupation?"

I'm losing patience with the old idiot!

"That'll do!" I say..."That's enough!...Enough fooling
around!...I want to go back to the lines!...All right?...I
want to do my duty over again...That's definite!...All alone,
if necessary!...I want to kill everything!...Be careful, doc!
...you won't get away with that!...I don't want to go back
to Paris!...I want to go back to the lines!...Like Lucien-the-
Gent!...Benoît-the-Mustache!"

"But you can't, my boy! You've got 80%!"

"Then I'm going to murder you!" I snap back.

"Hand me a saber!"

And I dash to the poker that I see right near me...in the
coal bucket...I'm going to run the phony through!...him
and his goatee!...

Then four of them jump on me!...They knock me down!
...they beat me up!...I kick and struggle!...I bite them!
...They get the better of me!...they drag me...they wipe
up the floor with me! I'm polishing the corridor!...held by
my arms and legs...We pass an open bay window...the place
in the big dark salon!...Who's that I'm seeing?...there in
the back, all pale...All ghostly..."I give up! I give up!" I
yell to my murderers...to those cowards pulling at me, knocking me out of joint...

Stop! Attention! I see them!...I see them all!...Over
there! in the back!...My old friends!...standing there in the
dark!...motionless!...all together!...one...two...three
...four...five...six!...standing straight up! "Hello!" I yell
to them! "Hello! Hi, men! Hello all...Stand up, my hear-
ties!"...I absolutely saw them! Ah! that's a fact! Motionless!
just standing there! Nestor, not so tall, in the back of the room
...with his big head cut off, in his hands!...he was carrying

231

it on his belly!...a pimp from the Leicester!...he'd left the week before!...And Big Fatso next to him!...and Motorbike Fred!...and Little-Arm Pierrot!...And Pretty-Kiss Jojo!... And No-Dough René, with his belly wide open!...They were all bleeding somewhere!...That was the queer thing!...And Lucien-the-Gent and Lily-Boy!...Fly-Killer in a Marine Light Infantry uniform!...and Redheaded Lu as an artilleryman! ...all lined up perfectly at the back of the salon! in the darkness...they weren't saying anything!...all standing there!... in uniform but bareheaded...Their faces were all pale!... white...white...as if there were livid glints under their skins ...a gleam...

"Hi, men!" I call again! "Hi, men!...hi, chumps!...hi, buddies!...how's it going in there?"

They don't answer...They don't move!...

"Shit, they're frozen!"

I drag everyone along with me!...I want to go and talk to them myself! talk to them from close up!...right to their faces...Ah! no use gripping me!...I'm stronger than anything! They twist me!...I scream!...at least fourteen clerks! ...and two...three old maids!...who grab me by the balls! ...I've got the strength of ten!...the whole staff!...the ushers!...I drag them along! The whole human bundle!... toward the back!...the dark!...I want to talk to my pals! ...where they're standing all bleeding!...all pale there!... at attention...I want to touch them!...It's done!...I touch them!...They've disappeared!...Hell!...What d'you know! I yell it out loud!...A fake!...Another low-down lousy trick! ...They've fled!...evaporated!...Their tough luck, damn it!...They'll pay!...They won't find anyone in the big Hole! ...They're all cannon fodder!...I'd recognized all of them! ...All the pals from the Leicester!...They'd seen me, too! ...They simply disappeared!...With their guts around their waists...in the back of the Consulate room!...

232

"Come on! downstairs!...go on down!...Get him out of here!"

That's how I'm treated! how the ushers do their job! Ah! but it's a fight! I want to stay there on the floor, musing, thinking. I throw myself under a bench. They grab me, yank me, pull me apart. Ah! they're furious! I've driven them to the limit! Even the dear, kind doctor...No one's got any patience left!...All of them charge at me together!...All the Consul's employees!...all of them furious, men, women, girls!...I stagger! I roll! I collapse!...I go crashing down to the bottom of the stairs!..."*Vive la France!*" I yell in spite of it all... *Vive Bedford Square!...Vive l'Angleterre!*"

"Get out!...Get out!" they yell back...That's how they answer me!...And they all start viciously tearing at me again! ...pulling me apart!...ripping my jacket!...the ushers, the secretaries, the vice-consul, the Consul himself!...

"I'm the Consul!" he warns me.

Ah! the dog!...He wears glasses like the rest of them!... He comes to insult me!...

"Get the hell out of here, you bum!"

Impossible to be cruder.

"You're being coarse!" I answer..."Hurray for the French Army!"

Ah! he won't stand for that! he rears! he stamps! rage! he jumps up and down!...

"Get him out of here!...Get him out!" he says to the four "commissioners" on duty...Real huskies, Herculeses, who act then and there!...I'm lifted up!...The door wide open!... The street!...I leave in a trajectory!...A projectile!...I have a commanding view!...Hanging in the air!...A rocket!...I soar high above the sidewalk, a new weapon, over the crowd! ...and plop!...I fall smack into it!...right into the Russians ...Ah! a mess!...They gurgle awful when they get me!... I've knocked five of them clean out!...They're lying there!

233

all five!...The women start pounding me!...tearing away what's left!...I stagger into their bellies...emigrants with kerchiefs, peasants bound for America...I'm being sworn at by an entire people!...I can't free myself from the tangle of limbs and bodies. I walk on the bodies lying there...People are walking all over one another...The bodies are yelling at me horribly, in Russian, in Italian, in Czech...The meanest loudest bellyacher lying there knocked over is a little Chinaman, a little guy in a gray silk robe with a thick roll of papyrus stuck under him, a big papyrus with seals! he picks it all up in a fury, he stands up...and his umbrella and his big artist's hat...his chestnut stove...he adjusts his bow!...and he starts giving me hell!...He takes me aside!...He was a Frenchman, and no mistake!...not the slighest accent... dressed up like a Chinaman!...

At first I stood there dumfounded...then I pulled myself together...and then I let him have it!...

"You stinker!...Keep quiet!" I snap at him.

"You vandal! You hooligan!" he answers back.

"Who're you talking to?" I ask.

"To a brute!...to a murderer!"

"You're quite right, Monsieur!"...I agree with him right off! I go him one better!...Am I proud of being a murderer! ...Ah! he hit it on the head! Boy, have I killed!...Let him say it!...Ah! and how!...Ah! I'm rarin' to go!...I start reeling it off!..."I killed ten of 'em!...I killed a thousand! ...I fell from the sky!...You saw it! you saw with your own eyes, you phony Chink!"...Boy, am I laughing!...What an act!..."You stinker!" I was yelling in the middle of Bedford Square!...We were having a good time now!...not only me ...the whole crowd!...

Then I take a good look at the little hothead...I begin to get the feeling he's not so dumb as the others...I grab hold of him! Whoop! I drag him along!...by the sleeve...This

234

time it's me taking the initiative!....I had something to say to
him!...We're still being shoved and whirled around...flat-
tened...rolled...finally pushed out!...He starts adjusting
his hat...with its big brim...I had to explain things to him
...confess in detail!....I suddenly felt the urge!....it was also
a kind of excuse...to let him know how things stand!...
everything that's happened to me...and that it's out of the
ordinary!...some of the whys and wherefores of my trouble!
...so that I shouldn't keep the whole business for myself...
He reties his bow!...very carefully...We'd sat down on the
curb under the sycamore on the square...

"Hmm!...Hmm!"...he kept saying as I told my story...
pretty sceptical, I could see! He had doubts about what I was
telling him..."Listen to that big talk!" he was thinking...
"a young man showing off...wanting to dazzle an old fellow
like me!" Ah! still and all I wanted to convince him! I'm
stubborn about it! So I start all over from the beginning!...
How at the Hazebrouck Hospital they thought my leg was
done for, that they were ready to amputate it...and my arm
at the same time!...That shows what a beating I'd taken...
my head, besides...meningitis...a small splinter in my left
ear...it was so serious and feverish that they wondered from
one day to the next...on the verge of going haywire, just
about ready to kick off...I'd made a real friend in the hospital ward in Hazebrouck...Saint Eustache Ward!...exactly!
...Raoul Farcy, left hand wounded...Raoul Farcy of the 2nd
African Battalion...Like me!...same ward...two beds away!
Saint Eustache Ward...They operated on his hand. He also
yelled the same thing after his operation...He took a liking to
me...we'd made great plans...We were exactly the same
age. "We'll both go to London!"...It was settled!...He talked
about when it would be over!...He was looking forward to it
for the winter!...

"You'll get an idea at Uncle Cascade's!...about the way

235

things work!...You'll see something of life!...You'll see his place!...Uncle Cascade's been in the African Battalion too!" He was always talking about this Cascade...In short, bright prospects!...Real attractive plans!...I needed some...Life looked shitty to me!...I was even falling more and more to pieces!...Saint Eustache Ward!...Pus was coming out of me everywhere!...They'd done three eburnations of the humerus and the tibia, all of that had been attacked...I had my fun I'm telling you! and then the drains, tents and plasters...bits of bone pasted together...it hurt so much that I'd howl almost every night...Finally, little by little like that, from one good plan to another, it was Raoul who really perked me up! ...by morale, got to admit it! I needed it!

"Don't worry, pal!...Don't worry!"...that's how he used to talk to me..."We'll never come back here again!...Just wait'll you see London!...You'll get a hell of a lift!...Wait'll I'm out on convalescence!" It was really swell of him.

I was being nicely encouraged along the sores and sutures ...and I was getting my share of them!...Please believe me ...Then crash!...it all collapsed!...One morning they come asking for Raoul Farcy!...He'd been in another ward having his wound dressed and was on his way back...The military police want him and take him away!...handcuffs!...

"Where are you going?" I blurt it out!..."Down with the cops!" he yells to me..."Down with the cops!"...right in front of the whole hospital...and he reminds me from way across the room...with the cops dragging him..."Cascade! you hear!...Cascade!...Don't crap around! Down with the cops!"...Those were his words!...the last I heard...That same evening we learned the rest...Court-martialed!...They let him have it two days later!...Raoul Farcy...self-inflicted wound!...2nd African!...Maybe it was true, maybe it wasn't! ...They do as they like!...They don't worry too much...A detachment came up, convalescents from the hospital, they

236

marched in front of his body...They shot him at dawn, in the courtyard, the Barnabé courtyard, the name of the military prison. He didn't break down. "Down with the cops!" he yelled at them as they fired. That's the story.

Ah! that really made me feel bad...Not much affects me ...Me, a little chump by birth, son of my parents, working people, submissive, decent, good-natured...he'd taught me a thing or two, opened my eyes, I missed him, got to admit it... Raoul...he wasn't much when it came to writing...I wrote everything for him...with my left hand...I was the one who always wrote to London, to his Uncle Cascade...Cascade Farcy ...two letters a week...Cascade Farcy, Leicester Street...it was all settled...He was expecting both of us...absolutely, fully agreed!...We were supposed to get leave at the same time, we were married there...both of us...to English girls! all phony!...and with papers, licenses, everything!...Everything was attended to...fixed up! nice and faked! and then crash!...Raoul! some break!...With me just getting a little better...I didn't die, after all...Shit! Tough luck!...I recovered...I wrote to his uncle! Cascade Farcy, Leicester Street...

"Come!" he wrote right back..."Come, I want to talk to you!" And he knew me only from the letters!...Ah! I was scared about Raoul...I was so panicky I was pissing in my pants!...He'd disgusted me with the army!..."Don't go home!" he'd also yelled at the last moment..."They'll nab you!...Just take a look!...They're sweeping out the crumbs!" ...He meant himself...

"Go to London!...Don't forget Cascade!"...Ah! those were his very words!...They haunted me! his last words!...

That pulled me through!...I was stubborn..."Come!... Come!"...All I thought about was London!...Then the three months of convalescence...Ah! no cold feet, I shipped off. I'm invited! I take advantage! the right moment! luck!

237

I arrive!...Ah! a nice atmosphere!...Ah! real brothers...
pals to the death...those are the words for it!...Cascade asks
me for news right away...I explain to Cascade about Raoul
...Boy, it knocked him over!...He made me explain it at
least ten times in a row!...He didn't believe it!...He never
got tired of my explanation!...had to start all over!...then
again!...he really loved him like a son!...Raoul Farcy...it
staggered him!...That was my arrival in London!...provi-
dential circumstances...my luck to have known Raoul, poor
Raoul, and his Uncle Cascade...

I tell my story to the Chinaman, sitting on the curb...I
wanted him to know all about it...it did me good...

"Now you know what's happened to me!...It's your turn
now!...Tell me your story!...I'll tell you the rest later on!
...I've got lots left!...I can't tell you everything all at once!
...just falling on your head that way!...in confidence!"

Ah! it sure was funny!...Time out for a laugh!

"You realize," I add, "that he'd have liked to hand everything
over to Raoul...the whole works...all his business...the
entire Leicester...He'd have gone off to the Midi, that was
Cascade's plan...to grow daisies...that was what he had in
mind...The Leicester's no joke! overworking day and night
...needs quite a guy to keep it going!...It's like running an
army!"

My Chinaman didn't answer.

Ah! it was getting annoying...

"Say, guy! You don't talk much!" I said..."You're not
going to double-cross me maybe?"

The little stinker suddenly got me worried...Had I talked
too much?

"Oh! don't worry, young man!...I'm far too concerned
with my personal enterprises! I've got other things on my mind
than making trouble for you!...I'm no longer a child! Perhaps you've noticed it!...A plaything of passion!...A victim

238

of enthusiasms! Thank God! I'm no longer a spring chicken! Young, effervescent! not an acrobat whisking hither and yon! God no! Rubbish!...Be careful! Don't be contemptuous! Clothes make the man!"

My phony Chinaman was starting to strut.

"You were speaking of quality! well, well! a while ago!... Regarding those poor people!...You don't have the slightest idea...I understood at once!...You'll learn to know me!... Perhaps!"

And the little superior smile...

"I don't want to intimidate you!...Oh! no intention!...To dazzle you with my scientific and noble titles!...Certainly not! ...Weakness!...An old man's weakness you're thinking!"... He was meditating..."What will you do with your opportunity, young man?...You're a hero, it seems...so you claim! ...Hm! A war hero!...An easy prey!...A heroic plaything! ...A child!"

I'd annoyed him.

"At your age everything is permissible!...Valor! Valor!... As for me, and don't forget it, I've other fish to fry than to go rushing under tanks!...I've been through all the ordeals!... All!...The war is merely fireworks! Life is short!...An amusement!...What remains of it?"...He whispers into my ear..."Nothing, eh?"

He's enjoying the effect...He brushes away my whole confession with a flip of his hand...

"In short, you teach me nothing!"

The windbag.

"Listen to me! You have everything to learn! Are you initiable?"

Initiable?

"Just what am I?...Don't you know?...I attract you... You entrust me with your secrets? Is it my robe?...Are you captivated by my fluid?...so soon?"

I look idiotic.

"A Frenchman! indeed I am! Be careful!...And of good stock! I flatter myself! But without boasting! And that's how it is! a just pride!...But initiated! That's another matter! Ah! that's the heart of it! I've done much for my country!...An explorer, my young friend!...An explorer...Must I die?... Look at my costume!...Initiated, young man!...Initiated!"

He comes closer, he whispers it to me...eagerly! rattling away!...

"Tibet! Ah, Tibet! I dreamed of it...Yes!...I dreamed of it!...I admit...a grave crime...at the first calls of the horn! ...In the riflery, young man...Riflery!...Reserve officer!... to go back into service!...in my fifty-seventh year!...You'll see it on my record...to run and offer myself to Galliéni... I knew him!...At the Polytechnic!...And then...then I thought it over...I've got better things to do! with my gifts! ...my work! my labors!...to perish just at that moment when the darkness is rent asunder?...You'll know later on!... Trivial duty!...it would be suicide!...and what a suicide!... Perhaps you'll learn about it some day...Be careful!...down to business!...this is me!"

He hands me his card.

HERVÉ SOSTHÈNE DE RODIENCOURT
Certified Mining-Prospector
Explorer of Occult Hearths
Initiated Engineer

"Doesn't that name mean anything to you? Obviously!" I was nonplused...

"I suspected so...Young and ignorant!...That explains it!...One goes with the other! I, Monsieur, am Tibet!... Knowledge about Tibet? All knowledge about Tibet? Here! You understand!...it's all here!"

He taps his forehead.

"Didn't you follow the Bonvallot Mission?...No?...Don't you know anything?"

He looks me up and down.

"Bonvallot?...Strange!...Strange!"

He thinks it over.

"All in all, so much the better!"...in my ear: "What a charlatan that Bonvallot!...What a scoundrel!...That's all! ...Just between us!...A clown!...He's never seen Tibet. What a braggart...He, the Gaourisankar? Some joke!" He squeals with laughter just thinking about it! about Bonvallot! What a faker!...That damned Bonvallot!...An agent of England!...of the Trusts!...The biggest international bandit in the world! Gaourisankar! 7,022 meters!...It's all clear! Bonvallot, corrupt...What a traitor!

I take the same tone. I approve...I sneer...

"Boy oh boy! What a phony! disgusting, that Bonvallot!"

Ah! he was hipped on the Bonvallot in question, he kept at it! it gave him the evil eye, the murderous eye, just talking about him!...about that awful Bonvallot!...and I know something about looks!

"Do I interest you? Or am I boring you?...Tell me frankly! ...You probably need girls! You're not disembodied? The spell of buttocks gets you?...Voluptuousness!...Sighs!"

Ah! I make him sick! all of a sudden!...Bah! he spits!... he shoves me with Bonvallot! Ah! into the same boat!...a foul pair! and it was all his idea! there was nothing lecherous about me!

So as a result of walking and talking all around the square we were in front of the Consulate again...where we'd met... head-on!...the Consulate of the Czar...The huge flag with the black eagle was floating high above the crowds...teeming, roaring...they were all waiting for visas. A real army now, scratching themselves, spitting, cursing! an enormous din...

"You've never gone exploring?" he deigns to inquire.
"No...not much."
I admit.
"Are you really looking for work?"
"Ah! I sure am!"
"Can you ride a horse?"
What a question!
"Hah! and how! take it from me! I'll say I can! When it comes to horses I can do anything! I can saddle 'em! water 'em! make 'em trot! gallop! leap! pass! waltz!...Whatever you like!...And references, eh! Five years!...I've slept with horses! eaten with 'em! I've eaten their droppings! I've still got a mouthful! That shows you! that shows you! I'm still rearing! kicking! I'm almost a horse myself! from me to you! just between us! more than half!...I had to! Is that enough for you?"
"Fine! Fine!"
I whinny so he'll understand me, so he won't go thinking I'm lying.
Ah! a deep impression!
"I think that ought to do."
He concedes the point. And then he gets all worried again.
"Ah! but you're a commoner!"
Another shift! something else bothering him...
"You're not born! obviously!" He stressed "born"..."no noble blood?"
Commoner? I didn't get it...It was about a job...
"Your mother and father?...common people?"
The nerve!
"What about you, you big ape?"
"Sh! Sh! No insult!...You're unaware of the full implication!"
I listen to him.
"Just consider the question of ancestors...for me it's the

242

cult!...The Myth!...The cult of blood!...The Cult of the Dead!... Do you understand me?"

I'm ready to try...I try anything...

"But watch out! Don't be carried away! Beware! Beware! The Tragedy of China! Admitting everyone! Promiscuities! All the ancestors! Good Lord!...All at the same time! Anyone! ...High and low!...Discriminate! Let's discriminate!...Catastrophe!"

Wild-eyed.

"Don't you know?"

I don't know anything...

"They venerate any dead person in China! any ancestor! What a mistake! How disgusting!"

Ah! the Chinese are preposterous! what morons!

"China's washed up!...washed up! young man! and I know why!"

He knows everything.

"All the dead! They worship them all. It's very simple! All! it's a fact! I'm telling you! Their heaven? A brothel! That's the result!"

Naturally.

"A casastrophe! It's inevitable! Just imagine!...They adore their housemaids, their ancient priestesses, their queens, their goddesses, their whores, all of them, a hodgepodge! their cowards! their heroes, their bloated commoners as well as their generals! all of them jumbled up together! Their forgers with the police, their bankers along with their judges! their scholars with their rickshaw men! Nullity, my friend! nullity! That's what happens!"

Ah! the awful promiscuity drove him wild! he was making broad gestures, people were looking at us...

He didn't give a damn! Nothing stopped him! He was off!

"No, my friend! You must choose! Believe me!...the lowly die and stay dead! Such is the will of justice!...It must be so!

...Otherwise foulness triumphs!...Do you understand me?
...Your grandmother, for example! Certainly an insignificant commoner, dead! She remains dead!...quite dead!...she stops congesting! She no longer befouls the City! the High City of Memory!...whereas take my grandfather! whom I venerate and most rightly! He relives within me! An entire existence of glory! of royal services!...I give him new life with my blood!...Splendid! He survives within me...You understand me?...I cultify him!...Pious and practical!...Good blood will tell!...Worship!...All the devotions...He serves me ...I serve him!...I extend his being!...He makes mine illustrious!...I idolize him!...I carry him with me everywhere! ...The cult of the dead!...I'll show him to you very soon!... in his mystic person! He's at home with my wife!...He's been around the world with us three times! in his traveling cenotaph!"

He looks around, right and left...Ah! he's suspicious of the passers-by!

"He's flawlessly mummified! consecrated! You'll see him with your own eyes!"

That looks promising.

He's summing up...

"I take from China what's necessary!...Not everything."

That's luck!...

"Ah! let's get back to you, my child!...Here's your chance! ...You fall from the sky!"

It's working out...

"A real horseman!...A Centaur!...The two of us! Lowborn, to be sure! But what difference? You will mold yourself into nobility! That's all! No valid ancestors? We'll attend to that! You'll cultify mine! I'll transmute him toward you! a little! just what's necessary!...I'll lend you a few arms!... the coat's big enough!...Achille Norbert! 26 quarters!...A fiber of my lineage! I'll lend you a fiber!...That's it! a fiber!

...I'll dub you knight! You'll wave my standard!...but not with that face!...Oh! what a scowl!...All for the Faith! young man! the Faith!"

He yells it out loud..."All for the Faith!"

"Our motto! 'All for the Faith! Rodiencourt!' Council of Poitou! 1114!...That's not yesterday!"

I'm pleased for his sake!...

"It's up to the two of us!" he grabs me by the arm..."All for the Faith!...I want to use you! My next mission! My great work!...But listen!...I want a whole cavalry!...Pay close attention! thirty porters! A hundred fifty horses! The cost of it!...A matter of 200,000 piasters! at the very least! ...what's the difference!...We won't haggle!...the goal is worth any sacrifice!...To be sure!...When you know!... What an expedition!"

Ah! there's an idea for you!

"Oh! You can count on me!...day and night!...I've got cavalry in my blood!...I can boast about it!...Saddle horses! draft horses!...escort horses!"

I'm showing off.

"Light horses!...Bridle horses and remounts!...Mizzen horses! Parade horses!...Equal to all occasions!...They won't be able to teach me anything in China about horses, horsemanship, its ceremonies, its gear, its problems! I've got it in my bones, I've fallen off horses thousands of times!"

"Young man! I appoint you Master of the Horse! Gonfalon of my caravan! Ah! we haven't finished!...There's a God for barbarians! Your folly has most definitely thrown you into the heart of fortune! Into my arms, young man! into my arms!"

He stood back a bit to contemplate me more leisurely...

"Your head is covered!"

I didn't have a hat.

"Covered! Covered with Destiny! Perfectly! There! the aura! there! I see it!...What a fine surprise! Stop moving!"

245

He saw it on me! He described it to me in the air! a little circle around my head!

"What a destiny!...What a symbol!...Oh! you can't understand! Obviously! Opaque! Opaque but radiant!"

Ah, I disappoint him again! Ah, it made him lose all patience to see such fine gifts lost, wasted on such a silly head!...

"Splendidly endowed! That's a fact!"

He insisted...He saw it all!...I kept amazing him!...

I cut it short...time to get started!

"Well? So it's definite, Monsieur? Agreed? Decided? What day! What time!"

I was impatient...that was enough monkey-business! down to action! off to life, death! with my halo or not!

"Oh! how nervous you are, young man! Easy does it! It'll come!...Keep your head! Sh! Stop where you are! It seems to me someone's listening to us that we're being spied upon all around!...There are paid traitors everywhere!"

"Paid by who?"

"Child! Child!"

He was taking pity on me.

"Are you aware that things happen of which you haven't the slightest suspicion?"

"Oh! I believe you all right!...Oh! I believe you!"

He signals to me to keep still.

We were caught in the crowd again...the whole mob from the consulates...squashed against the railings...the raging throng around us...the waiting for visas!...holding their ground, shoved into one another!...They were trying to find some possible idiom, the better to scream at one another in their delirium, their rage at being kneaded, torn apart...But it was no go!...They came from too far away in the universe! from countries too strange, too distant...They didn't have a shit in common...a good shitty insult, nice and drippy, fat,

246

enormous, reeking. They were quibbling, jabbering, shriveled up, gasping and struggling!...They weren't getting anywhere! All the same the two of us there were approaching the door saying nothing...borne up by the surge!...our turn was really going to come...maybe we'd get knocked around a few more times...

"I wonder what your name is?"

The question occurs to him all of a sudden.

"Ferdinand! you may call me by my first name!"

"Well, Ferdinand, my friend, we'll come back another time!"

"But we're getting inside, Monsieur! We'll lose our turn!"

"Lose it? Lose it? Listen to him! A fine story!...You young scapegrace, do you have any idea what the visa may cost? our visa?"

"How do I know!"

The lunatic!

"Madrapore via Kiev? Taranrog? Kaboul? Mongolia?"

"Not at all!"

"Twenty-seven pounds! At least! Do you have that sum?"

"No, Monsieur!"

"Neither do I!"

Ah! it all collapses! About face!

We work our way out of the crowd! With a lot of trouble! What a disappointment!

Oh! but it doesn't bother him at all!...not the least bit put out!

"Young man, we've made contact! Ah! making contact! that's the main thing!"

He goes into ecstasies.

"In touch with the Waves, Ferdinand! the approach! the approach! It's the approach that counts!...Don't you feel right here the exhalations summoning from Tibet? A kind of caress? starting at the consulate railing?...from behind all these people?...They're emanating, I assure you! They're emanating! Turn away from that side!"

He makes me pivot about...he pivots, too...I didn't feel a thing!...

"You're opaque!...still opaque!...You'll get over it!"

He sighs...Still and all I do disappoint him a little.

"Can't be helped! Can't be helped!...let's leave! we'll come back in a better frame of mind! I'll initiate you a little, later on! Come over here!...off to the side!...so that you know where we are!...so that I can explain to you!...You don't know anything!...You must!"

We got away from the crowd, we were going toward Tottenham...He was mincing along in his fake Chinese costume. He opens his umbrella, he closes it a couple of minutes later...

"The sidereal shower!" he points out..."It was time! Exactly thirty-seven minutes after sunset!"

At Selfridge's there was the row of shopwindows...he turned around rather often...not very well-behaved in the street...little glances at young women...

"Nice child!...Nice child!...Smile of the earth! And of the sky!...If only I were your age!"

Kidding around all of a sudden.

He admitted being fifty-seven...He was older than that... his hair ink-black, and he wore it long like an artist...but keen-eyed and confident...His beautiful robe cramped him! he hopped along! it was a nuisance in the gutter...he had to tuck it up! We went down Oxford and Shaftesbury...all along the shopwindows...He chattering about one thing and another ...I didn't understand it all...I felt like getting rid of him, he was annoying me with his rigmarole...People were turning around to stare at us...But I held on all the same...Maybe there was a small chance that his leaving for China wasn't all hokum!...that he might take me along!...that it might happen!

My heart was in my mouth at the big crossings...Because of the newsboys...They were still hawking the same "special," the morning's...the "Tragedy" in Greenwich!...They were behind the times!...I'd done better since that! hell!...They were four days behind!...they were so excited about the "Greenwich Tragedy" that they'd stopped talking about the war...Boy, that was some mess! It was all rolling around in my head...Finally it started rolling too fast! All I could understand was the headache...More than I needed, and well! I just stopped bothering about my anxiety...

Old Foxy kept on talking!...He was attracting attention in the crowd!...Nobody asked to see his papers...That was the amazing thing!...The kids, the tarts, the soldier-boys ran after him, pulled at him, played tricks on him!...They came touching his dragon, pinching his robe, his behind...He defended himself with his umbrella, jokingly, he wasn't annoyed ...We'd taken quite a stroll...all of Regent, all Totten... almost the whole theatre district...Finally, it was inevitable, we got caught among the hustlers!...First Nini in front of the Twist whose beat was between Wardour and Marble Arch ...She sees me...she winks at me. Peg-leg Berthe, who worked the theatres, spots me in front of the Daisy...

"Ah!" she starts razzing..."Are you in the circus?... Hurray for Punch and Judy! Ferdine!...Hey! Ferdine!"

I don't answer.

She tags after us...and clop! clop! her peg-leg!...I didn't want to answer!...she yells at me...

"Hey! stinker!...stinker!"

A lunatic.

It was starting to create a scene.

"Where are you taking him?" she shouts...

She's hysterical.

I hurry along, I quicken my pace, we turn into a bystreet... we give her the slip...He wasn't bothered by such trifles... He was probably used to being pestered like that, like some

249

freak...He kept right on smiling...Besides his getup, he misbehaved in public...ogling young girls, as I've said. He was insolent, almost provocative, he talked too loudly.

"How badly people dress, Ferdinand!"...That's what struck him..."Undertakers' assistants!...a lot of undertakers' assistants!...look at the way they walk! how sinister-looking! ...Do you mean to tell me that these people are going to win the war?...ah! tell me another! You're joking! No! Crying! But they won't win anything at all! They're already burying themselves!...They're through!...They're already dressed in black! They're done for! Funerals! but they'll have to be burned!...have to be incinerated! I'm telling you!...Bombs! They stink! All of them! Fit for the charnel house!"

A look of disgust!

"Worthless people!...Clouds of cockroaches!"

And I who don't like anyone talking to me about bombs, fire, burning! Ah! take it easy! I cut him short...

"You talk too much, Monsieur Sosthène!...It seems to me you don't listen to anything! Come over here, dear Master!"

I drag him into a doorway, he's got to listen to me, by God! the damned windbag!...He's not the only one who's interesting!

"They're looking for me!...You hear me?...They're looking for me!...Monsieur Sosthène!"

I let him have it straight!

"I'm wanted, you understand?...they're after me, dear Master!...Monsieur China! You understand me now? I'm a murderer!...A murderer! I've got to get away!...They're searching for me!"

"You?...Oh! Searching for you?"

Ah! He bursts out laughing! Ah! It's just too funny! Ah! that's a good one!...a real good one! He's choking with laughter.

"But you're drunk, young man! That's the word! Raving

drunk!...A poet! a poet! You're drunk!...That's your look-out! your lookout!"

That's all he has to say.

"But I haven't drunk anything!...haven't eaten everything!" I protest! He's the one who's raving!

"All the more reason!...All the more reason!...Listen to me!"

Now he starts dragging me. He doesn't want to stay in the doorway. As soon as we get outside he speeds up...He's tearing along in his cassock...big rush!...the whole Strand...Char-ing...We race along Villiers Street down below the station... the street that goes down to the Thames...Charing Cross, the station right above it...the string of pubs...the whole slope ...full of low dives...Ginger...Three Swans...Star... Wellington...side by side, each bar an arcade...He heads for the Singapore, the saloon just in front of the tunnel...I still see the place, curlicue mosaics...festoons all over the ceiling ...luminous artificial flowers...and the big player piano, a cyclone earthquake, that never stopped day or night, booming all through the street from Regent, Strand, to the bank of the river, it jounced the drinkers, shaking them up at all the bars, making them puke like crashing cymbals, with big hiccups, spin around dancing, falling over, oop! they're gone, tearing off, wobble, crazy head to foot, from one sidewalk to the other! It's sticky all along, gooey, sooty, the whole pavement slippery black...you can't see a thing, the drunk disappears in the fog. The mists from the river choke and swallow things...You can't even see in the saloon, need brilliant lights...the bar's lit by electric...lights shining under the bottles...Have to light up everything!...Even the waitresses have bulbs, they've got little lamps in their hair...You can see Sosthène's a regu-lar customer...He waves hello to everyone...

They sit him down at a table right under the biggest Chan-delier...Ah! he starts scowling...Something's wrong...

"Be careful! the waitress!"

More suspicions.

"Two sodas, Beauty!" he orders.

"Tuppence!" she answers.

"Lend me the two pennies!"...Luckily I've got 'em!

He changes the conversation.

"I talk English like a pig!...I grant you, you may say it! I agree!...I can't manage to pronounce their *the* or *thou*."

He reminds me of Cascade when it comes to English, he was mulish about *the* too!

"And yet, young man, it's not from lack of habit! It's almost thirty-five years that I've been associating with the English!... And with all kinds, let me tell you!...The good! the awful! the best! the rich! the well-to-do! the gay! the sad! the nabobs! the bums! the whole shebang!...beneath all skies! latitudes! They all say *the*! I can guarantee you! In India! In China! in Malaya! Right here!...The hell with it! I give up! I give up!...No *thou!*...No *the*...I think in French, I pronounce in French! French is all I talk!...Got to take me as I am! That's what I'm like! Nothing to be done about it!...I'll never learn their language!...It's angry with me!...That's it!... It's angry with me!...It's not the same with Hindustani! Ah! that's different! I worship it! it's my mother tongue! That's another matter! It's an ancestor...I wish you could hear me! ...I'm Sanskrit in my heart! in my fiber!...There I'm initiated!...That's another matter! The way I talk Hindustani! Intimately!"

And then he leans over to my ear confidentially though he brays like a donkey because of the piano...You could probably have heard him from the street!...The piano was playing the Merry Widow Waltz...cymbals and storm! the whole thunder! It really was the popular tune!...It was hard to understand what he was confiding, he was trying to outyell the piano...it was a struggle...

"Water alone is propitious, young man!...You stare at me...I amaze you!...Propitious, I'll have you understand!.... Propitious to the great call of the waves!...Drink lots of water!...Do as I do!...We were both born of Amphitrite! Therefore, fish! To be sure, fish! Ah! ah that's it! Fish and horsemen alike!...Assuredly! Dolphin! Monsieur Ferdinand! Certainly dolphins!"

He was drunk.

"Dolphins of the mountains!...Dolphins of the purple clouds!...dolphins of Tibet!...I see you!...look! I see you!"

I was making him dreamy...visioning...

"Would you go? imagine! Would you go riding the dolphins of the beery sea? The elf of the sticky stout?"

He stops.

"Stout!" he orders. "Waitress, two beers! Just between us, isn't it horrible?"

He continues...

"What a heresy! an aberrant monster!"

He's taking it to heart.

"Don't let anything astonish you!...Everything bogs down, rots in this country because of the heavy stout! That's the downright truth!...Hogwash and muck!...But on the other hand, you see all the water-drinkers galloping everywhere, all around the universe! Take my word for it! I assure you! Just look at me, Sosthène! A Knight of the Waves! five and six times around the world! A water-drinker! your humble servant!"

"Waitress! another one!"

The waitress didn't bring anything at all, she knew him... she let him rant.

"No more joking!...Be careful! No blundering! Washing is another matter! I rarely wash!"

I suspected so.

"Let me explain...Achille Norbert, for example, washed

himself only twice in the course of his entire existence and he lived 102 years! You'll read about it in his letters! I've had them bound with his arms! Master of the King's Artillery! Let me explain!...Without any shame! Water? Hmph! Inside? Fine! Wonderful! Outside? No go! That's a different matter!"

Then another worry starts eating him, another bee in his bonnet! After the way it's been raining! the awful weather outside...it's fogging and raining at the same time! you can't see three yards away! He's fed up! he's going to cry out to the sky! to curse it! he opens the door wide! He addresses the sky!

"Sulphurous and mournful city! City of the wet devil! Demonic city of the weak! but I am strong! Achille! Thank you!"

The customers are yelling! He closes the door, he comes back to the table.

"All great dreams are born in London, young man! Don't forget it! you don't know London! From the mirror of its gray waters!...way down there at the mercy of its river...Ah! that's a fact! Didn't you know that?...Isn't there anything you know? The admirable Véga declares it quite expressly! Canto 14! Verse 9...The Charm!"

He leans forward to my ear.

"Are you ignorant of everything?"

"Yes."

"India?"

I admit...

"So you know nothing at all! I suspected!...Hm! Hm! You'll have trouble!"

It sounded nuts.

"Oh! of course!"

"The devil? You understand me?"

"Sure, I believe you."

"Do you follow me?"

"Of course!"

The drunks were raising hell at the bar, it was a real din plus the player piano!...So he yells in my ear...the really utterly confidential words...

"The Armadalis of Tibet? the flower of Tara-Tohé?...You know nothing about that flower?...Absolutely nothing?"

He stares at me to see if I'm hesitant...he's suspicious...

"Oh! not at all, Monsieur! I swear!"

"The Flower of the Magi?"

"No, really I don't!"

"Well, *I* know it! *I* know where it is! the way to the Sanctuary!"

Ah! I sit there flabbergasted!

"But that's nothing yet! Now listen closely! I, you hear me? I've approached the Armadalis of Tibet three consecutive times! Yes! the Tara-Tohé!...It's not where people think it is!... Ah! not at all! ah! no indeed! No!...No!"

Some joke!

"To mislead idiots! you, for example, where would you think it is? in the Convent of Arthampajar? Now I'll tell one! nonsense! phew! phew! don't hand me that!"

I was making him laugh.

"I know where they're hiding the Armadalis of Tibet!... Prospecting mercury quartz for the scoundrels in Calcutta... the Gem Proceeding Company...Ah! those bloodsuckers! What bloodsuckers! Still they've been of use to me, after all! ...I've discovered everything! Chance! exactly!...The secret of Things!"

Ah! it's superb! I admire him more. Everything's fine! My fingers go right into my nose now that I've got confidence. We'd have it easy since he'd discovered everything! I was rolling snotballs.

"I'll have you read the passages! Verses 25 and 42 of the secret Véga!...for the time being, sh!...mum's the word!

When we come to Mahé...the little monsoon port...then I'll reveal everything to you!...Mahé! Karikal! of course!"

"Miss! Miss! please two glasses of Bass! two glasses of Bass!"

He was ordering two more glasses of beer...His head must have been going round...his eyes shining...cheekbones red ...imaginarily...He was tipsy with seltzer water, the waitress didn't bring any stout or Bass! all we'd had was soda.

"So we'll put into port at Mahé, as I was saying, then Delhi! You see it, don't you?...the borders!...the little Lama Rawpidôr!...Ah! watch out! What a rascal! A shrewd little article! I interest him 50%!...Greedy!...Greedy!...I'll hook him later on!...I'll hook him!"

Things were shaping up.

"The whole Mission! Everything! You, the convoy! The porters! Off we go! Tara-Tohé's ours! My boy! At the nose of the Universe! Exactly the word for it!...At least twenty Missions at the present time!...You understand?...Dead sure! ...Very secret! Flawless! Get it straight! the most austere initiates! at this very moment exploring! stirring up! rummaging through Tibet in all directions, north and south! They're turning all the lamaseries inside out! Foiled! Not a word more! It would compromise everything! No! I won't tell you anything more!...Sh!...The Gem Proceeding Company owes me, just imagine, $25,000 at the very least!...For my quartz alone! and I'm not talking about the emeralds! or the ebonites! A fortune! my mercurous isocenes!...The mere waste products of my prospectings! What if I presented my entire bill!...In short!...A fantastic swindle!...But we'll talk about it another time!...Here are the accounts!"

He rummages around in his cassock...He takes out a big roll...He spreads it on the table...columns and columns of figures!...What additions!...staggering!...

"Credit!...My credit! Read there! in red!...25,000... right? 25,000...more! and 75,000 for something else!...

dollars! dollars! more! credit! Hindu piasters!...That tells you everything!...and pounds sterling!...And my options! ...and that's nothing!...not a tenth! Trifles!...Does that give you an inkling?...What if Gem Proceeding should learn of my return?...then it all goes wrong! Of course!...the poor victim resurrected?...The gentlemen learn of it!...the scoundrels immediately take action!"

In my ear.

"They all think I'm dead!...buried!...Some joke, young fellow!"

He beats his chest...it resounds...

"Then and there! They send their craftiest murderers out after us!...They poison our wells! all our wells!...all along our route!...I know them! capable of anything! even before approaching the places!...The Falls of Madrapore!...We'll perish murdered!...In ambush! Pfft!...It's over!...That tells everything!...Those people stop at nothing!...I know that crowd!...The Viceroy? Pfft! one of the gang! Shuts his eyes, obviously! Thick as thieves! Wait! Wait!"

He starts searching again...he hesitates...He wants to give me real proof...the utter importance of the great secret!... entirely convincing!...

"Listen, Ferdinand, at this very moment the Brahmanic Consistories would offer me all the gold in the world!...You hear me? All the gold in the world! that's something! If I turned over to them all my plans and diagrams...the sketch of the route of the summits!...Nothing doing! I'd tell them to go to hell!...No go!...mum's the word!...Ah! you see what we're in for?"

Obviously it was serious...Then he gets anxious again... he frowns...all those people around us...the coming and going at the door...Ah what a bother! the voices of the men drinking and arguing next to us...He feels in another pocket, another lining...He decides to...another roll...He unrolls

257

it...all over the table!...a big parchment...He pushes the glasses aside...It's a huge map...heights, surveys, ridges... full of mountains...a wide river...deep hollows...dark abysses...

"There!" he points with his finger..."that red cross!... there!...that blue cross!...Here! this one!...all our stopping places!"

Ah! fine...It's the beginning!

"You understand me?"

Ah! of course, I understand!...Maps, I know all about them! But watch out! I'm getting excited, I'm talking too much ...If I go shooting my mouth off, it won't look good...he won't want to any more! He fumbles around in his linings... he takes out another piece of cardboard...a colored square...

"Here's the Convent!...You hear me?...The Convent!"

"Oh yes, oh yes!"

I'm with him in everything.

"The place of Magic!"

I bend forward to get a better look.

"Oh! perfectly!"

I stare.

"There we are!"

No doubt about it.

He murmurs to me.

"The Tara-Tohé!"

He's in his stride.

"Ah! Ah!"

"The Flower of the Secret!"

I'm pleased too.

"Moscow!...Lhasa!"...He's going over it in his mind... He's muttering our whole route!...possessed by it, imbued... "Listen to me, Moscow! Lhasa!...another stage...two weeks here...the coast! We mobilize!...our transport!...our guides!...our letters of welcome!...Requisitioning of ponies! ...You attend to the foraging!...I leave these matters to you!

...I set out alone!...I go away!...I spend a few days in Swoboly, in the Province of Penwane!...The Pagoda with jade lazuli! Just a purification! I sign an agreement with Gowpur, the Lama of the Brahmans...Oh! a real bloodsucker!... I bring him my prayer rolls...perfection itself...the praying wheel I invented...37 prayers all at once!...automatic!...I grant him exclusive rights!...Oh! he's so eager!...All the customers of the Plateaus!...He wants them all!...everything for himself!...for him alone!...What a demand!...The whole Roof of the world!...Every Brahman becomes his customer!...He lets us pass!...He attends to our provisions!... fifty-fifty!...I his prayer wheels!...He our corn meal!...We barter! we can't do anything without him!...When you hear his name! Gowpur Rawpidôr...Three bows! North! South! Southeast!"

He shows me how...I execute them...I bend forward as he does...twice...three times...

He continues.

"You command our column!...Naturally!...You pick me up on the way!...I'm purified!...Rawpidôr accompanies us awhile...Three stages!...maybe two...He introduces us to his brigands...to the Chu bandits, to their chief executioner, so that they'll let us pass...Contributions, bows, gifts...there we are! twelve more days of climbing!...we're on the site!... We leave the level of moss...and then the heaths!"...

"We're coming to the mystic slope...to the steeps of the great Masvanpur!...Our trails are starting!...At the Lazuli Rocks!...Be careful!...The eyries of the Great Route...We hear the Winds of the World!...Our Convent's not very far off! We're on the very roof of the world!...Very careful now! ...You leave me for three weeks!...maybe two...You go off discreetly...very discreetly! absolutely alone!...absolutely without provisions!...The spirits sustain you!...feed you!... The Spirits of the Snows!...The heart of our trials...where blow the winds of the world! The gusts sweep you up! cast

259

you forth! plague you! tear you from the crests of the rocks!
hurl you away! You cling! to the edge of the abyss!...You
creep along on all fours!...You hang on to the slopes...It's
Strength!...Let the hurricanes crush you! don't complain! all
for the Faith! all for Strength...More strength! in the heart
of the Hurricanes of the World! You palpitate with the world!
You have to get to the Grand Convent of the Great Shroud!
The Supreme Lamasery...Do you understand me? Dead or
alive!"

Ah! that was all right with me..."All for the Faith!" I
repeated. I was talking like him...Dead or alive!

He's promising me more and still more!

"The Tara-Tohé! verse 42! you see it! At last! It's in front
of you!...What more can I say? There it is beneath your
eyes!...beneath your fingers!...You contemplate it!...
You've undergone all the trials!...Terrifying, to be sure! in-
exorable! no doubt about it!...perhaps mortal!...But what
joy!...You enter the sanctuary!...there!...no farther!...
No further doubt!...You contemplate the Great Nest!...the
goal itself...'Nest of Truth beneath the Roof of the World!
beneath the Roof of the Snows!'...I'm translating literally...
Woupagu Sanskut! 'On the Beams of the Roof of the World'!
Nest of the Snow-swallows!...'Wiwopolgi'!...and in this
nest?"

Ah! he's changing his mind! pulling back! Ah! what else
was he going to tell me? imprudent!

"Don't think I can't hold my tongue!"

He looks me up and down, mistrustful, distrustful.

I wasn't asking anything!

But immediately he's off again! A haze! even more eagerly!
sure about everything!

"The Tara-Tohé, flower of Dreams!...Seven colors!...The
rainbow!...Seven petals!...Seven colors!...exactly seven!
The figure in Véga 72...Remember that!...the magical Tara-
Tohé! The flower opens out in your hand! All the petals! with

your heat! your faith! what a proof! Is that enough, do you think?"

It was more than I'd asked for.

"The secret?...Seven petals!...Seven colors!...Be careful! The seven sins! What's the color of your soul?"

He had me there!...I had no idea....

Immediately he gets sore.

"Ah! You don't know?...Well, what then?...Which petal are you going to choose?...The green? the yellow? Blue? Indigo?"

Ah! what a jam! He's hustling me, jostling me, plaguing me, like the winds of the world!

"That's not all! Tara-Tohé! Charm of Being!...The weight escapes from your body!...You've seized the Flower!...The Waves seize you, sweep you up in turn! They carry you off!... they transpose you!...wherever you wish!"

Well! well!

"You evolve!...you travel about in the atmosphere as you please for months...months...Weight no longer exists for you! You have entered..."

Ah! he doesn't dare finish...he's seized with terror...it's too serious! I reassure him...so he whispers it to me, murmurs it...just for me alone...but I can't hear him!...I can't hear anything...on account of the player piano! He's forced to yell it to me...

"...into the fourth dimension!"

Ah! that was swell!

"Nobody can touch you any more!...Reach you!...Put you into prison!...You're free! the Free Man of the Waves! ...the darling of the strains of the world! You are, in a word, all music!...Harmony!"

Ah! that's superb!...Ah! I'm getting along fine!

"Ah! I can't ask for anything better!...But say, we're not in Tibet!" I point out...Maybe he's being carried away?

"Not yet, young man!...not yet..."

He looks at me angrily! what's wrong with me that I should doubt?...I'm with him! I get enthusiastic again!

"Ah! I'm ready to leave!"

I reassure him again! Nothing holds me back! All for the Faith!...I was thinking meanwhile of Matthew who was bound to be in a hurry...who wouldn't hesitate a second about throwing us into the jug! Ah! I wanted anything so long as we went far away and right away!...very far!...as far as possible!...without a day's delay!...So that we wouldn't run into Matthew!...for me that was the main thing!...with the magic Flower or not...to China!...to the devil!...wherever he liked!...But by God let's get the hell away!

"Well, are we going?" I ask again...I'm pretty patient, but all the same he's beginning to irritate me.

"Sh! Sh!"

He pats me on the back of my neck...he calms me like a dog.

"Easy does it!...Easy does it!...you impetuous youngster! ...Don't get delirious! you're getting worked up!"

He wasn't ready yet! More delay! more hitches! he found me impulsive...he was busy with his tie...he was tangling up his bow...he had to think about it some more...ah, listen, an idea for me!

"Here's something for you! Learn it for tomorrow!...I'm going to give you a lesson...Don't waste a minute...Prepare for your trials...We'll be seeing each other...Now learn it by heart...repeat five or six times inhaling as little as possible!...Tara-Tohé!...Madrapore!...Armantala!...Horpoli!...Horpoli!...the most common one!...And then evoke with all your might!...ah! with all your might! Evoke in green! in jade green! As hard as you can!...That's a good beginning...Do it again especially at night!...These are the rudiments!...If you see any form appearing in your dreams, don't hasten! no brusqueness...Concentrate!...That's all! Sniff at your first petal! as you close your eyes!...Armantala

262

Horpoli!...murmur this way...Horpoli! Horpoli! that's all
...murmur the name first! later on you'll shout it! Concentrate!"

Ah! he slaps his forehead! Ah! he'd forgotten!

"Ah! I've got to leave you! Ah! my visits! Ah! what a
scatterbrain! don't follow me! I'm disappearing! remain here
for a few minutes! let me go! I'm disappearing! Please be discreet!"

He smiles at me affectionately.

"Sh!"

Two fingers to his mouth!...Big mystery!...

I was about to ask him whether it was really worth while,
whether the whole thing was serious...

He cuts in!...He hands me his card, his address...everything...no discussion!

He leaves on tiptoe...Near the door, ah! he changes his
mind! about face! he comes back and whispers...

"Above all, don't talk about Achille!...to anyone!...
Achille Norbert! You hear me? Ah! to no one! the cult of
the Dead!...Oh! utterly secret!...Absolutely between us...
What jealousy!"

I reassure him.

"But tell me! where'll I see you again?"...Ah! I'm asking
questions, "What day? What time?"

In short, he's backing out.

"You'll be led by the spirits!"

I call that nerve! He doesn't wait...He turns about...
Waves good-by all round! A casual gesture!...He trots through
the bar...With the dragon on his rear...He goes out the
door...The men at the bar are laughing...They're razzing
him...I don't say a word...I don't look...I just sit...I'm
waiting for him to be far away.

All in all, I dragged around like that for two or three days
...I didn't want to go pestering him...Still, I had his address...Rotherhithe...the section just after Poplar...But I
wasn't too keen about it...I wanted to think it over some more
...whether there mightn't be another way...But I didn't
want to drag around all day long...one sidewalk to another
...to get nabbed by the cops...I find a little boardinghouse
in Beckton Lane, I lie down...fall asleep...I wake up...
Ah! feeling better!...My mind's made up!...I say to myself,
"All right, here's my chance!...I'll pull him out of bed!"
I hop into the bus...the 17... I find his place right away...
right near the bus stop...34 Rotherhithe Mansion...no different from the other houses...I look for his name on the
box...I find it! Rodiencourt 4th floor...I ring...I climb up
...Here I am!...

Someone half-opens...a head...

"What is it?"

"It's me! Ferdinand!" I call out..."Ferdinand for Monsieur
Sosthène!"

"Go away!...Go away!...Monsieur Sosthène is in bed!"
Ah! it's not easy!

And the door slams! violently!...Sorry...none of that!...
I knock...the head reappears...the person talks French but
with an accent...American...

"What do you want?"

"I want to see Sosthène...Monsieur Sosthène!"

"But I've told you..."

"I'm Monsieur Sosthène's horseman!" I insist..."He's my boss!...I'm his standard-bearer!"

Might have known about it!...

We look each other in the face...She's not so young any more...Still and all, a pretty little mug!...She must have been quite a number once upon a time...You can see the remains...but among the wreckage!...What powder! cheekbones blazing with rouge...fiery hair, a big shock full of white and yellow streaks, all unkempt, falling over her nose...

She leaves the door partly open.

"Where are you coming from?" she asks me.

She keeps her broom in her hand...She's been cleaning...I explain matters to her a little...We get into conversation...She's loosening up...all the same she's defending her door...She's wiggling her behind a little...in the doorway, while talking to me...she's getting kittenish...

Finally what with one word and another she admits he's not in...that he left very early...though that wasn't like him...

She sort of murmurs, she's boring me...she talks somewhat like Sosthène...in confidential whispers...he taught her...

"Are you American?" I ask.

"Oh yes!...from Minnesota!"

And she laughs.

I want details...I try to get her to talk about traveling...since they've traveled so much...

She puts down her broom.

"Does he really know China? and India? the way he says? I think he's bluffing me."

"Oh yes! He knows all about them!"

And then a deep sigh!...ah! enough to pierce your soul!

And bango! she leaps to my neck!...it's sudden!...I've set it off! Damn it, I didn't come for that!

I push her away...she wiggles...she grabs me...

"I'll tell you about it!...I'll tell you about it, Good-looking! I'll tell you everything!"

265

She wants me to kiss her...she insists...She'll tell me everything...

She's treacherous.

"Never believe him!"

Ah! that's interesting...

I listen.

We sit down on the folding bed...It's a big paneled apartment just under the roof...trunks...chests all over the place ...made of wicker...wood...iron fittings...huge ones, little ones, of all kinds and dimensions...Still more trunks...open ...closed...on top of one another...fabrics everywhere... Chinese robes...pottery...books all around...scrolls... parchments...lying around...a terrific disorder...almost like Claben's place...I get off the bed...I prefer the armchair... embroidered with lotus flowers and what not...more chests filled with scrolls...they're overflowing...falling all over the place...

She goes back to her housework...She rummages in a closet.

I call out to her...."So you travel a lot?"

That interests me.

"You mean he never stops!"

She sighs again, her hair falls over her face...She starts sweeping...She whips up a really big cloud...She sneezes! that's enough!...she's tired...she sits down...

"Are you from Paris?"

A question.

It makes her chuckle, she thinks it's funny that I'm from Paris...I must be lecherous...

"I think you're good-looking!" she remarks.

Ah! A hot bunny! I see what's coming, I talk about something else...

"Have you known him a long time?"

"Since we've been married!...What a joke! It'll be thirty-two years Christmas! That's not yesterday!"

"You've seen a lot of countries!"

That's the only thing that gets me excited...

"Come over here, Good-looking!"

She invites me next to her.

"I'll tell you the whole story!"

Fine, very good!...

"You're just a big bad boy, too!"

She starts pawing around!...I don't respond much...all I want is details about India, etc....

"So he'll be leaving soon?"

"Oh yes! oh yes! Darling!"

She sets the whole bed clinking...with her fidgeting... rubbing on the edge of it!...She takes off her apron...she tosses it up in the air! ah! she's pretty nervous! she dashes off to put on some powder...She comes right back...She's getting me tired...

She's certainly not pleased that I'm not responding to her cuddling. She snorts down my neck, pecks at my eyes...I manage her as best I can...she overpowers me...I'm being hugged...covered up...

"Ah! what a little lecher!" she exclaims..."Oh! he's as lecherous as Sosthène! He's come to seduce a poor little woman and then he'll drop her, won't he?...Oh! the little scoundrel! ...the rascal!"

Making a scene already!...A quarter of an hour that I've known her! I calm her down a bit...I kiss her right in her makeup! on her rouged cheekbone!

"Are you bored with me? Tell me, you little trifler!"

What could I answer?

I went back to kissing! I didn't want a scene!

"So you're going to torture me?"...she whispers passionately...

I don't feel like torturing her!...

"You've suffered too, haven't you?...I can see it in your eyes!"

She pulls me toward her, she lifts up my eyelids...to look at the blueness of my eyes...she's hurting me! she's a passionate number...that puts her into a trance! she quivers, slips out, escapes!...

"I'm going to make some tea for you, sweetheart!...Samovar tea!"

She disappears...she's busy in the back...fussing around ...in the nook behind the partition...she's rattling the pots ...I take another look at the *décor*...Chinese stuff everywhere...from India...ibises...more papers, trunkfuls... chests...and buddhas...a whole lotus tapestry... and warriors...javelins...

"Is he coming back?" I call out.

"Are you bored?" she answers.

Here she comes, balancing the samovar...She goes back to the kitchen again...a regular coming and going! She calls out over the partition..."You think I'm still pretty, don't you? ...Has he shown you my programs?...I played the Wonderful Flower!...for twenty years!...Did he tell you?"

Back again...now on my knees!...She's simpering.

"I was raped, my love!...raped!...you understand?"

"Ah? by Sosthène?" I ask.

"Yes."

Sighs.

I was going to hear it all.

I pet her...pet her...

"He and his troupe were on the Australian clipper...the giant liner *Concordia*...He was returning in triumph from the Chicago Fair!...the women passengers were all crazy about him!...If only you'd seen him!...with his big troupe of Brahmans!...You can't imagine how handsome he was!"

Suddenly she starts covering me with kisses!...she goes for my cheeks, my eyes...she laps both my eyelids!...You can't imagine how greedy she is!...she bites my nostrils!...

"Like you!...Like you!...Yes, like you!"

Good-looking as Sosthène, that's not very!...according to what I saw!...

At any rate it excites her!...

"Sweetie!...Sweetie!"...she's lapping me again...

"What were you doing on the ship?"

"I was a manicurist, my angel! Let me see your hands! Oh! what hands!...How lovely they are!"

Ecstatic right away! She gets pleasure out of everything!... she fondles them...turns them over...

"Oh! what luck!...what awful luck!"

She saw it right away!

"No heart! my! my!...No heart!"

And she snuggles up again all palpitating!...she hugs and pets me!

"Take the Flower of San Francisco!"

I can't get away from the flowers!

It's an offer.

She lies in my lap, she writhes, she convulses! What can I do?

She gets up again...she dashes to the other cupboard... She brings back a bunch of photos!...There she is in tights, it's she in 1901!...the program...the year! enthroned in a chariot of roses..."The Beautiful Fairy"! the attraction!

"The Chicago World's Fair!" she exclaims.

Ah! that's something! "The Beautiful Fairy"!

She starts necking again.

"Don't you know how to love?"

I distress her.

She pecks me, she shakes me, rolls me around.

"Not at all?"

Really I'm not interested...I'm more the curious type...I ask her why all the trunks?...All that equipment? All that dragon business?...the buddhas?

"Don't you know the magic trunk?"

I astound her!

"He's the one who discovered it all! Of course! Didn't you know?...The secret of the magic trunk?...Oh! it's prodigious, you know! You'll see!...Nothing inside!...You open it this way!...Nothing at all!...Then he invokes the Spirits! ...You see! armfuls! armfuls of roses! they come up from the bottom!...That's it!...and the fragrance!...You think you're dreaming...Marvelous!...marvelous!...and then The Beautiful Fairy! That's me!"

The memory of it sent her into ecstasies...

"It was one of his ideas! I loved him so! from the very first day! immediately! then and there! our idea!...right from the start!...I couldn't leave him...He carried me off for his troupe...He made me change ships...We were married in Brisbane!...He loved me...I loved him!...We took another ship...We had to! The *Corrigan Tweed!*...A four-master!...Oh! I regretted nothing! Because he loved me he made me flower of the trunk!...Sosthène!...what love!... What years!...For twenty years I was Queen of Magic! I appeared in the heart of the roses!...look! I popped out of the trunk! Just like that! pop!...when he uttered the word! Pop! The Rose of San Francisco! Look! just like that! it's printed there all over!"

She showed me her clippings again...always in tights... a whole album! no one else! always her! never anyone but her!...in a chariot!...without a chariot!...languid...triumphal!...in a palanquin! in a rickshaw!...Always her! with a smile!...

"How the spectators adored me! You've no idea!...They called me the loveliest of the roses!...Afterwards in Cairo!... then in Nice!...and then after that Borneo!...Sumatra! the Sunda Isles...and then India!...and then Hamburg!...two years!...Here, look, in London...the Empire!...Look, 1906! ...the Crystal! and then Paris!...the Olympia!...and then we went back to India!...again! Then Sosthène went wild!... We were welcomed everywhere with our Brahmans!...And, darling, such gifts!...it turned his head!...he saw red! If you had seen!...The lovers I refused! and the diamonds!... They all wanted me to divorce him! the Rajah of Solawkodi ...He wanted to build me, just for me, a little opal temple! ...Do you know opal, darling?...Oh! my beloved! take me! Why are you so tired?"

What could I answer?

"A little opal temple!....Can you see it?"

She was smiling blissfully!...beaming with the memory...

A kiss for the beauty! she's got to continue!...

"So Sosthène went mad! as I've told you!"

"Why?"

I wasn't listening closely...

"Jealous! my angel!...Jealous!...Imagine, he was still in love with me! What jealousy, my darling!...A madman!... He couldn't sleep because of the Rajah!...He couldn't even eat a sandwich!...or sleep!...He made love all the time!... He began to make me suffer!...On purpose!...The flowers weren't enough for him...He put me to magic death!...Do you know what magic death is?"

No, I didn't!

"He'd plunge me into a deep sleep...catalepsy!...And then all the indecencies!...All the miseries!...so I'd suffer! ...suffer more! always more! and it was never enough!... He was never satisfied...He'd lend me to his Brahmans!... A whole night long for their black magic!...then to the Davides of Bengal!...for their great orgy!...with burns and everything!...I'd come back in the morning dead...I could see he was possessed!...And I loved him more and more!... Like you! Yes, like you, sweetie!...Oh! my love, be a bit tender!...Don't you know how to caress?"

"Tell me more!"

"He dug needles into me!...During the act!...Blood flowed from the wounds! He sucked it all! Look, like that! Pff! Pff! He walked over my feet! And me so sensitive!...

271

And then when it was time for the trunk he really locked me in!...I really stifled!...He even thought up something better! ...That was his prize act!...He sawed off my head every evening...and two matinees besides...Then I really used to die of fright!...He'd carry me off to his dressing-room... He'd take me in that state! in Rangoon I was really dead! Ah! the sound of the saw!...listen! rrr!...rrr!...rrr!...the blood flowed down to the orchestra!...The spectators would faint! ...His eyes looked like this!"

She imitated Sosthène's eyes...how frightful they were... extraordinary! you couldn't look at them! you'd die of fright!

"He'd have me brought back to the stage!...They'd carry me on a stretcher with his Brahmans! What a triumph! Imagine!...And then when we got back to the hotel he'd make love to me! you don't know what it was like! He'd strangle me again very gently!...I'd get scared again...The temple was driving him crazy! Here, you do it to me too!"

Her neck was soft and full of folds...I squeezed a little.

"Squeeze, my pet!...Squeeze!...Your tongue!...Your tongue!"

I had to stick my tongue out at the same time!...It was complicated!...

I did my best.

"Then what happened?"

I wanted to know the details!...

"Around the world again twice!...Two months in Berlin! ...Six months in New York!...I didn't recognize him any more, he had changed so!...He was mean and insulting with almost everyone...He who had always been so pleasant, who spoke with such refinement...He slapped a lady in Copenhagen...our orchestra leader in Hamburg...and then the manager...Those scandals did us a lot of damage!...the impresarios canceled us...they black-listed us...Nobody wanted us any more!...and our magic trunk...we were stuck

in Singapore...I'd got so thin that I was impossible in tights!
...it even made a horrible noise every time he beat me!...
the skeleton!...it was awful for the neighbors!...We were
put out of hotels!...We went back to India...Then came
the final catastrophe!...he who had never gambled...I mean
baccarat! He started gambling! he plunged recklessly...he
played everything...The fiend!...He played the races! heads
or tails! whist! roulette! anything!...He'd win!...He'd lose!
...He'd spend nights at it!...He stopped making love to me!
He forgot about me!...And then he went at it again!...even
more furiously! ferociously! the tiger!...He tore off one of
my nipples! Here! Look!"

She shows me her breast...It's a fact, the tip was off!

"He bit me, look, like that!...He didn't want me on the
stage any more!...He clawed all our orchestra leaders! He
couldn't stand them!...The result was we were living in poverty."

Ah! she stops...Ah! it's too sad...she didn't want to tell
any more...she wanted me to undress...a sudden whim!...
She was dead set on it!...She wanted to see my nipple!

I take off my jacket only...I want her to continue.

"He put all the money we had left into a company! listen,
a mining company!...Since they weren't moving fast enough!
at least according to him!...then he was afraid they'd rob
us!...twenty years of savings from the theatre!...he decided
that we'd go prospecting ourselves...that we'd make an enormous fortune in emeralds...in lapis lazuli...God knows what!
...it was called the Gem Proceeding Company."

Ah! he'd spoken to me about that! I couldn't deny it!...

"Ah! my darling! how I've suffered!...I was so cold in
those mountains...We were looking for veins!...All our
savings went into it!...He made scenes, even up there! on
the plateaus of Tibet!...Still jealous!...always the Rajah!...
'You'll have your opal temple!' He'd beat me in front of the

porters! He treated me worse than a dog in his jealous fits!...
I didn't want to leave him!...Would you like me to make a
little fire?"

"No!" I thanked her.

"Me, accustomed to luxury, sleeping among those savage
Mongolians! caked with lice!...When I complained a bit!...
immediately insults!...blows!...atrocities!...He'd throw his
fit...the Temple! the Temple! his bugbear!...The Rajah! he
couldn't shake it off! He'd go crazy again!...To go back to
Delhi we borrowed money, twelve piasters, from, now hold
tight, the Catholic Mission!...That shows you how we stood!
...Fine!...He thinks up something else!...A new idea!...
'Pépé! Pépé! I see what's lacking!'...It lights him up!...
'We'll never succeed!'...'What's lacking?' I ask...'An ancestor!'...I didn't see why an ancestor?...why that idea?...
he'd got it into his head going from convent to convent talking with the monks...talking Baluchi with them, the language
they speak there. 'This is going to be something!' I said to
myself...ah! it was something! we had an ancestor!...we
went back to France to get him!...we trotted him around...
we brought him back...again! then here! back there! everywhere!...he's here now! They removed him from his vault
...it was very expensive! very very expensive!"

She pointed to the end of the garret...next to the wardrobe
...just under the roof...the ancestor's wicker chest...a long
flat one...

Sosthène was the one who interested me.

"Will he be leaving again soon?"

I was fishing.

"Where's the money coming from, darling? Luckily we don't
have any left!"

Ah! that was a relief! a comfort! for her! they'd be forced
to stay in London! She couldn't see herself back in Tibet!

"Kiss me!...Kiss me!...Ah! You're not ready to leave

either! Go on! You're not ready!...Look, here it is!...Here it is, do you feel it?"

I had to give her another taste of it!...on the neck, the torture spot where there was still a scar...a circle all around...

I was waiting but he hadn't come back.

I wondered what the hell he was doing outside, that Chinese guy...What if he stayed out a week? a month?...would I have to sleep there? She kept trying to get a rise out of me...

"You see, darling, I'm putting some powder on for you!... There! it's on!...But I can do without it, you know!...Touch my skin...Feel how soft it is...He used to want me to powder myself!...white!...white!...always paler!...He preferred me that way!...'Pépé, my little dead darling!' he called me...since the day I almost stayed there because of the saw! ...If you had seen that act!...I'm still pretty, you see! But in Melbourne!...if you had seen!...I'd never been so lovely! ...All the Brahmans in the act, even though they were used to me, couldn't believe their eyes!...It was they who unnailed the cover...I was supposedly dead!...I appeared in a flood of roses!...What applause!...it lasted twenty minutes... Once three-quarters of an hour in Sydney!...all the people were standing and shouting, I looked so magnificent!...Tell me! Do I kiss well?...Wouldn't you like to take me in the flowers?...You see that trunk?...under the transom...it's still full of roses!...artificial ones...but they're perfect! You've never seen anything like them!...so lovely!...you'll take me in them!...Wait'll you see!...They come from Bongsor Malaya...You can't imagine what they can do with petals...bits of velvet! real flowers dried in the monsoons!... I'll show you!"

She leaves me...she hops over...she plunges into the trunk! ...she sends all the roses flying!...a cloud of petals! they scatter all over! all around!...another armful and another! ...a rain of petals...in a big cloud of dust!...Both of us sneeze...what laughing! Ah! we're having a great time!...

Ding! Ding!...someone's knocking! banging at the door...

She readjusts her petticoat...she runs in her slippers...It's a chubby little boy with a bottle of milk...

"Thank you!...Thank you!"

And a big kiss for the little boy!...Another one! another big kiss! dear little chappy!...and she makes a grab for the little devil! he's wheedled, pawed, licked, smothered in the twinkling of an eye! caresses! right on the doormat! just standing there!...the baby errand-boy!...Ah! the little rascal!... He squirms and clucks just like her!...It's probably not the first time!...He's probably delighted to bring up the lady's milk!... No one's worrying about me!...I'm left in the lurch, sitting there on the bed...All the same I think it's a bit thick!...Suppose someone comes up?...I don't think she's in her right mind!...The old hag's on fire!...That'll cause another row!...what a mess if someone comes up!...I'd better shut the door...As if, damn it, I'm not in enough trouble! ...Now another jam!...with cops all around! this time a sex-maniac! Ah! nothing doing! I get up! no! down again! hell! I can't move! my legs are like lead!...let 'em play! fedup! good-by! I'm too dazed by the sidewalks...I've done too much walking since last night...I'm pooped!...she's getting livelier! It's her nerves! A case of nerves! She's all steamed up, fiddling around with the kid!...Kitchy-kitchy! Maybe that's my fault, too! Everything's my fault these days!...I'm going to kick 'em out! both of 'em! They're making me boil! down the stairs!... I'll let 'em have it! head first!...I'll make 'em cluck! Just wait!

I stand up! I start going! just then a yelling...from downstairs.

"You bitch! you bitch!" from the street..."Get inside, hide yourself, you filthy slut!"...from all the way downstairs... from the corridor.

I don't know what the hell to do with myself!

"Will you let that child alone!"

The kid makes a dash!...Boom! his hobnailed boots! He's running!...She spins around! throws herself on me! into my arms!...sobbing in wild fright!...Sosthène's standing in the doorway...on the mat...He's looking at us...

"Listen!...Listen!..." I begin...

He breaks in on me.

"I understand!"

He moves forward...he's offended! He refuses to shake hands...Then he breaks down, trembles, plops on the edge of the bed...he's all in...he's grunting...choking...spitting...

"*Oh! là là!*" he mumbles..."*Oh! là là!*"

He's still wearing a Chinese robe but not the same flowered one...this one's yellow and red...with ibises all over...He doesn't take off his big hat...he just sits there dreamily...

"*Oh! là là!*" he mumbles..."*Oh! là là!*" And then he gets sore again...he stands up in a fury...he goes for the bitch! Boy, oh boy! he shakes his umbrella over the slut's head! she throws herself at his feet...she writhes...she crawls...

"Pépé! Get up!...I'm ashamed of you!"

"I know, my beloved!...I know!"

She kisses his robe, his shoes...she's overwhelmed...convulsing with remorse!

"My darling!...my darling!...my life!"

That's what she calls him.

"Stand up!...Stand up!...you wretch!"

"Yes, I am a wretch! Oh! Yes! I'm damned!" she answers. "That's what I am!" Shaky! sobbing...

It's agonizing...it's horrible...

"Go on, turn around!...beg my pardon!"

She obeys.

She bends down on the other side...

277

He tucks up her rags.

"Look at that behind! that abomination, young man!"

He calls me to witness...The kid's come back, too.

She seesaws...she undulates her fanny...she wiggles her can...

"Oh! what an ugly ass!...Isn't it ugly, Monsieur?"

He's saying it to me.

And whack! and whack!...with his umbrella!...and bang! a big kick in the rear end!...She goes bouncing into the roses! ...She's still bawling, but not so loud, just little sobs now...

He rushes off, runs, rummages around on the other side... behind the partition...the faucet...he turns it on...

"Coming!...Coming!" he yells...And he's back again!... full of pep! He tucks her up again!...oop! and the whole bucket of water! Splash! right in the can!...He runs out again ...he comes back, he's starting all over...she's lying there all stretched out on the floor...her ass all bare...

"Deary! Deary!" she's imploring him.

"Ass on fire!...Ass on fire!...There!...Another one!"

He heaves! he splashes everything!...the floor's a pool!... slushy!...She's floundering around...wriggling in it...he slips...he stumbles...Boom!...he goes flying!...the bucket ...everything!...his hat!...he tumbles on her!...He throws a fit!...She busts out laughing!...Ah! the slut!...He tries to get up!...ah! a fit! he flops again!...he gets tangled in his robe!...She screams with laughter! All right then!...he's wild with rage!...He rips off everything!...his robe!...his jacket...his coat...he jumps around all naked!...right on the spot! in a frenzy!

"She'll drive me crazy!...She'll drive me crazy!"

He's screaming it out.

"Get out of here!...Get out of here!"...he's chasing her out..."Get out of here!...Never come back!"

She stands up again laughing away...she grabs the kid...

278

she goes to the door, all perked up, wiggling!...The tramp!
she leaves with the cherub!

"Good day!" she yells..."Good day!"

He sits down, he's whimpering, he's puffing...

"Ah! young man, did you see that?...You call that a life?
Did you see that lunatic?"

He goes to slip on a pair of pants...He comes back...
He's still sighing...I want some information...Scenes aren't
everything!...It would be a good thing to know what's
what...

"So China's over?"

I repeat the question.

"China! China! what a notion! more than ever!"

Ah! full confidence! all sure of himself!

He looks me over.

"Do you think I've been wasting my time? Don't be silly?"

Really I'm stupid.

"Let's get down to figures!...There are my calculations!"
...He points to one of the trunks beneath the transom...
"Now let's see!...25,000 pounds at least!...We'll know
definitely in Calcutta!...Well, let's say 30,000 or so! not
counting surprises!"

He interrupts himself.

"Pépé! Pépé!"...he's calling her again.

He whispers to me very low, "She listens at doors!...Be-
ware!...Beware of women and especially foreign ones!"...
He's giving me advice..."Sh! Sh!...Never marry an American!"

He rummages around again in his rags...in all his linings
...his beautiful robe, all torn up...he pulls out a pack of
newspapers...I see the *Mirror* among them...the *Sketch*...
I was already sure...I glance at the photos...the headlines
...I take a look...nothing in this one...or that one! or the
other one either!...just war photos...the Battle of the Somme

279

...the prisoners, the barbed wire, Wilhelm II, burning planes, etc. Not a word about us! That's amazing!...they've dropped it...all of a sudden!...They've stopped bothering about us! ...completely! by magic! Sosthène's not looking at the photos but at the classified ads...he's looking with a pencil...he's hunting for a heading...not this one...not that one...never the right one! he's getting fidgety...I can see he's irritated ...he's floundering around...he can't read the ads...

"It's not Chinese!" I kid him. "I'll help you!"

We've got to read the *Times!* the *Times!* he digs down again and pulls out the *Times* from another robe lying on the sofa...Ah! here we are!...Always at least ten pages of ads in the *Times!* squeezed together! and very small! Ah! something to work on! but what's he looking for? He doesn't tell me...Columns and columns...Marriages...Vacations... Help Wanted...Situations...What variety!

"Are you looking for a job? What do you want?"

Investments...It's investments he's looking for...Capital ...Ah! he's checking...he checks every line...he's getting excited...crosses everywhere...he's writing down the sums, he's getting worked up! He tries to read line by line...He's botching it all up!...I was better at it...I figure it out as I go along...He's looking for a certain ad under Partnerships ...He knows! someone told him...he's informing me...Oh! in great demand!...a certain ad..."You've got to scan the columns."...and very closely...minutely! Partnerships! for babies' bottles...for de luxe automobiles, elastic mattresses... light garden furniture...children's toys...exporting of layettes...fountain pens...movie houses, at least a hundred!... sport goods! twelve breweries...Ah! that's it! here it is! a whole series! Gas masks!...That's what he's looking for! *Gas Mask Engineers. Wanted promptly young engineers...* That's it! that's for us!...He's quivering...something for us! ...*For trial perfect gas masks. Very large profits expected.*

280

Immediate premium 1,500 pounds. Partnership granted. War Department Order...That's for us all right!...Colonel J.F.C. O'Collogham, 22 Willesden Mansions, W.1.

"Ah! the stars are with us!"

I think so! I think so! His confidence is getting me! I'm excited! Ah! right then and there! I'm getting worked up! Something at last!

I've never yet seen him so gay! all of a sudden with such go! blazing! the ads do him good! me, too! Ah! we're sure happy!

"We're approaching Gemini!"

That's what he comes up with!

Jaunty whistling!

"But be careful!...Let's act!...Certain solstices last only two seconds! We must act!"

I want nothing better!

"Sh! Sh!"

Another mystery!

"Watch out for women! They mess up everything! They muddle up our slightest emanations. They perturb our destiny! I'm going to lock mine up! As soon as she gets back!...What a slut!"

I was being warned!...That was one thing!...But what about Colonel O'Collogham and the gas masks?...What the hell were we going to do at that guy's place?...take his dough away? Partners? Where else were we going to kick around!

Sosthène was thinking...He'd settled into the armchair... He was looking at me as if I were miles away...

"Monsieur," I venture, "so Tibet is finished?"

"On the contrary, it's the very beginning."

He jumps up.

"You little fool! Ah! don't say anything in front of my wife! You talk too much!"...He gives me another order... "Go bring me my tea!...serve it to me here!"

Now I was the maid!

"It's cold, Master!...It's cold!"

I go to the stove...I putter about...I prepare...I was beginning to feel at home in the garret!...Only it had a stale stink since he'd come in...His shoes had an awful smell... I'd already noticed that...It's the humidity of the streets... Shoes are awful in London!...I probably smelled, too...it's much worse even than the army...They get spongy in no time...There was some ham in the buffet, a low little buffet ...I make myself a sandwich...I serve myself...first! Knock! Knock! Knock!...Someone at the door...

I go to open it.

It's Pépé back! Cuckoo!

"Ah! my ducky! My love!...My angel!"...two bounces and she's on top of Sosthène! the caresses start all over! Ah! it's love again!...More kisses!...and still more!...They go play together on the sofa...She's brought some food back, more ham! some brains! fresh sardines! just when I'm ready! ...In the nick of time! I see the snack! I'm going to brown it all in butter!...I look around while it's cooking...the décor, the room, the trunks...those trunks again...gilt chests ...black chests...So the ancestor's in that corner?...The cult of the dead!...I don't waste time!...the two of them are having fun there! ah! it's all made up! It's full of junk all around...Chinese curios all over the place...masks...grimaces, blue ones, red ones...banners with signs...still more trunks...split...crammed...scrolls hanging out...books... all over the floor...It was smaller than Claben's place but just as jammed with bric-a-brac, and that's saying a lot!...

All right! things are coming along!...tea, a little snack! I carry it in! it gives a man a lift! I'm going to serve Monsieur and Madame!

Ah! I'm perfect in my line! I know how to manage things in families! All smooth sailing now! They're just as sweet as pie! The way they go for my sardines! Ah! I'm quite a hand

when it comes to broiling them! It's a real lover's snack! Ah!
I join right in! I enjoy the whole thing! Every time he squeezes
her she winks at me, wiggles and gives me the eye! at every
kiss! she's got the devil in her belly, the old buzzard!

"Come on!"...I'm needling him..."Let's get going!"

It's true, it's time!

"You're right!...Get started, young man! I'll be right with
you!"

Ah! he's got to make up his mind! They're not going to
neck around forever!

"Pépé! my green robe!" he orders.

And make it snappy! She goes to get the beautiful robe...
it's in still another trunk...a shot silk with little mimosa
seedlings...she rummages about, digs it out, she dresses him,
powders him, primps him...now his hat!...the umbrella!...

We're all set!

"Say, take down the address!"

Already forgotten! I look for the *Times* clipping. I copy...
he repeats slowly..."O'Collogham! Colonel!...41 Willesden
Green...Willesden Mansions."

That does it! He tries hard to remember it!

"All right! All right!"

And then he looks me over.

"Your shoes are disgusting!"

That's true...He sighs...

"Your grooming! after all!"

I distress him.

He throws me some cloth...to brighten me up...a piece of
kimono...

"Your appearance, young man!"

That does it.

"Ah!"...he's thinking things over..."You'll let me speak,
won't you?...You won't interrupt me?"

Oh no! by no means...that I promise!

Pépé wants to kiss him again...a last embrace!

"Come on! Let's get going!"

He pushes her off...No more time...He dashes down the stairs...I'm at his heels...I'm following!

We hurry along! But Pépé won't have it! Ah! she hangs on! bawls! miaows! she doesn't want to stay there all alone! she wants us to take her along!

"Ah! I should have locked her in!"

It's too late.

Outside, people immediately form a crowd...that makes another scene...we never can escape it! we argue with Pépé! she's doing it on purpose so that people'll look at us! she just won't understand anything! we reason with her, Sosthène kisses her!...She just won't understand...that it's about the mask business!...finally it penetrates a little...she gives in but we've got to pamper her!...that's the condition...she wants to be coddled!...Sosthène knows her...she walks part of the way with us...just to the corner...Aldersgate...the end of the tramline...Ah! that's where...to the tobacco and candy shop!...we have to buy her whatever she wants!...goodies, all her whims...in the showcase, then at the counter...first a big box of candy, then two Havana cigars...then three bags of marshmallows, then a bottle of eau de Cologne...Ah! that just about does it...No! she still wants some toffee...she's a bloodsucker!...In order to pay we have to take out all we've got! all our coins! Sosthène and I! There's just enough! just! She's taking my last pennies! Ah! finally she's ready to go home ...but it doesn't satisfy her...she leaves in a sulk...she doesn't even say good-by...

Bus 29! ours! that's us! Shake a leg! He tucks up his robe! ...we jump on!

THE END